THE
CONGRUENT
KING

Book Five of the Congruent Mage Series

The Congruent Mage Series

www.CongruentMage.com

The Xenotech Support Series

www.XenotechSupport.com

Dedication

To the Atlanta Radio Theatre Company
and all its talented members who devote
their time and energy to proving
There Is Adventure in Sound!

Cover and Map designs by Dan Paulson

ISBN-13: 978-0-9978319-6-2

Spiral Arm Press
1725 Carlington Court
Grayson, GA 30017

www.SpiralArmPress.com

Prologue

"I don't know if I can do this," said Nûd.

"Do what?" asked Bonnie who was cuddled up in the dark beside him, resting on a straw mattress and tucked under a heavy quilt. She had just arrived that afternoon through a newly made fixed gate joining a cavern in Tamloch with this one.

It had been more than a month since Sírénae's forces had landed and the wizards of Dâron, Tamloch, Occidens Province, and Bifurland were only now connecting their underground refuges with fixed gates. Nûd and Bonnie's private pallet was in a secluded passage of the cave-complex beneath the mountains of Dâron's southern provinces where many people from that kingdom had hidden from the invaders.

"Be king," Nûd replied. "I only know how to be a servant, not wear a crown."

"Kings *are* servants," said Bonnie. "They serve their kingdoms."

"Yes, but they also lead armies into battle, wear armor, and swing swords," Nûd answered. "I can't do any of that."

"Is sword-swinging an essential part of the job description?" asked Bonnie.

"It is for Dârio and Bjarni," said Nûd.

"King Bjarni swings an axe," said Bonnie.

"Same difference, at least for the Bifurlanders," said Nûd. "It takes a lot of time and practice to be good with either weapon."

"You're good with a crossbow," Bonnie noted.

"That's different. With a crossbow, you just point and shoot."

"I think you're underestimating the part about aiming," teased Bonnie.

"Maybe," said Nûd. "It did take a lot of practice to hit what I wanted."

"See," said Bonnie. "If you put in the time, you can learn how to swing a sword with skill, too." She squeezed his upper arm and kissed Nûd's cheek. "You already have strong biceps. That should make learning swordplay easier."

"Have you seen King Bjarni's arms?" asked Nûd.

"The ones that would be legs on most people?" Bonnie answered. "I think you should look to Dârio for comparisons. His build isn't that different from yours."

"Maybe," said Nûd. "It's just that Dârio has known he'd be a king all his life. I'm new to the idea."

"Why don't you ask your cousin for help, then?" asked Bonnie. "I'm sure he'd be glad to teach you king things."

"Dârio is busy with his own challenges," said Nûd. "I don't want to bother him. Tamloch needs a lot of help to recover from the late King Túathal's mad mischief."

"His delusions of grandeur, you mean," said Bonnie. "At least Dâron didn't have to endure more than a few years of Princess Gwýnnett."

"True enough," said Nûd. "Is this where you tell me to stop feeling inadequate and *do* something?"

Bonnie spoke a soft pair of magical syllables and the tip of her index finger began to glow. She moved it close to Nûd's face.

"What's that for?" Nûd asked.

"I wanted to see your eyes," she said. Bonnie stared into Nûd's for a moment. "As I thought," she continued. "I didn't need to tell you. You told yourself."

Nûd smiled and so did Bonnie.

"I still appreciate your wise counsel, dear scholar-mage," he said. "What should I do next?"

"Why don't you tell me?"

Nûd's smile turned into a grin. "Answering a question with a question must have been the first thing you learned at the Institute in Bhaile Pónaire."

"That was the second thing," said Bonnie. "The first was where to find the refectory."

"Of course," said Nûd. "Even scholars care where their next meal is coming from."

"Scholars *especially* care where their next meal is coming from," said Bonnie. "Thinking is hard work."

"I *think* I should find another skilled instructor to teach me the art of the sword," said Nûd.

"Do you have anyone particular in mind?" asked Bonnie.

"The person who taught Dârio?" Nûd suggested.

"I expect Duke Háiddon would be pleased to instruct you," said Bonnie.

"We'd have to find somewhere private for my lessons," said Nûd. "I don't want people watching me make mistakes."

"Could you use Fercha's tower?"

"No, it's too tempting for Sírénae's wizards," said Nûd. "She's removed all her property and has changed the trigger words on the gates there, but it still radiates so much magic Umbrose's spies will seek it out the minute they get that far west."

"What about somewhere in that hamlet Eynon is from? Haystack or something like that?" asked Bonnie.

"Haywall," said Nûd. "There's an empty milking barn there that could work, but I don't relish falling into old cow manure. I expect to do a lot of falling as I'm learning."

"There's that quarry where Viridáxés was sleeping," Bonnie suggested.

"That's too open—and I'd rather fall on cowpats than jagged stones."

"Understandable," Bonnie replied. "You sound like you may have somewhere in mind?"

"I have some friends who live south of Melyncárreg," said Nûd. "They have a nice broad lawn that should be covered with soft green grass by now."

"Wonderful," said Bonnie. "How can I help you get out there for training?"

"A gate between the two locations would be ideal," said Nûd. "Eynon's been there. He can construct one end."

"And I can handle the other," said Bonnie. "I'll get started in the morning."

"Eynon will need more magestone dust for the gate," said Nûd. "We're running low with all the gates we've built to interconnect our various caverns."

"I'm sure a mage as powerful as Eynon will have no trouble finding more magestone dust," said Bonnie. "He can get plenty from Viridáxés' quarry."

"Agreed," said Nûd. "I feel so much better now." He took a deep breath and felt his muscles relax.

"You know," said Bonnie as she canceled the spell causing her finger to glow. "Kings have other duties beyond swinging swords."

"They do?" asked Nûd. "Such as?"

"Fathering heirs," said Bonnie, whispering into his ear.

"Isn't that just sword-swinging of a different sort?" teased Nûd.

"I hope not," said Bonnie. "I expect you'll be more of a considerate lover than a cocksman."

"I'm not very experienced," said Nûd.

"Neither am I, as you know quite well," said Bonnie. "Neither one of us has had much opportunity."

"We'll have to learn together then," said Nûd. "Are you sure you want to do this before we're formally married?"

"I don't care about the formalities, though I expect we'll have to have a big ceremony, with you being the king and all," said Bonnie.

"I don't either," said Nûd. "I feel like we've made a commitment to each other and I'm *very* glad you're willing to endure the burdens of being a queen."

"I wouldn't do it for any other man," said Bonnie. "But you make me want to try."

"Shall we start by seeing what this heir-making *burden* is all about?" asked Nûd.

"That's one royal duty I'm excited to take on," said Bonnie.

"So am I," said Nûd. "I understand it's an acquired skill."

"Practice makes perfect," said Bonnie. "Is that one of Ealdamon's epigrams?"

"I think it's far older," said Nûd. "And I've heard that lovemaking doesn't have to be perfect to be good."

"For a first time, I'll settle for not-too-painful," said Bonnie.

She slid off her nightgown and pressed herself against Nûd, then helped him remove his nightshirt.

"This feels wonderful," said Nûd when they were finally skin-to-skin.

"Your Majesty," said Bonnie tentatively.

"Uh, yes?" said Nûd.

"Kiss me."

Chapter 1

At the Green Magestone Quarry

"Look out!" shouted Merry from the other side of the ring-gate.

Eynon turned and took a step back. His feet slipped on the wet floor of the green magestone quarry and he nearly landed on his backside before catching himself and throwing up a shield of solidified sound. With a whistling shriek of displaced air and an impressive crunch, a jagged rock the size of a cow smashed into the space he'd just occupied. The rock shattered into hundreds of shards and Merry activated her own shields to intercept the sharp slivers of stone coming through the ring-gate toward her.

Chee, Eynon's raconette familiar who'd been exploring nearby, sought shelter behind a boulder that protected him from the lethal barrage. Merry had to hold back *her* familiar, Ace the rockhound, to prevent him from jumping across the ring-gate and into the fray.

Through the haze of pulverized stone dust surrounding Eynon, Merry saw five wizards in motley brown and gray robes descending into the quarry on flying disks. Two were preparing fireballs, two were charging up for lightning blasts, and one held a crossbow armed with a quarrel big enough to take down a charging wisent.

"Step through," she urged Eynon, encouraging him to cross the open ring-gate interface so she could close it and they could both escape the attackers.

"Not yet," Eynon replied. He modified his shield to make it a lens with an inner and an outer layer. The new shield absorbed the pairs of fireballs and lightning bolts, storing his opponents' magical energies between the layers. The wizard with the crossbow fired at Eynon's lenticular shield and the outer layer of the shield vanished like a popped soap bubble, releasing all the accumulated energy back at the motley wizards in one massive burst of power.

All five wizards were blown off their flying disks and began to fall toward the quarry's floor. Eynon intercepted them three feet above the ground with hemispheres of solidified sound. He then merged the half-globes together, so the quintet of wizards was packed tightly and held in place with new bands of red-tinted force Eynon created on the spot.

Mary watched Eynon carefully from the other side of the ring-gate.

"That wasn't very nice," said Eynon to the wizards. "You could have killed me."

The five captive mages looked sullen and stayed silent. Eynon tightened the magical bonds that held them until one of them decided to speak.

"I wish we had," said a sour-faced woman in brown robes with red-ochre trim and black feathers around its neckline.

Eynon wasn't prepared to hear such a blunt response. He saw the woman's eyes grow wider when she saw his red magestone hanging from a gold chain around his neck.

"You're *him!*" spat the woman. "The thrice-blasted wizard who brought down the side of the mountain! You killed six of my cousins."

"I'm sorry for their deaths," said Eynon. "It wasn't my intent to kill anyone, but we *were* at war."

"We're always at war," said the woman. "Three of those cousins were better off dead, anyway, but that doesn't mean *you* deserve to live."

"Brave words from someone I've captured," said Eynon matter-of-factly.

"You don't need to be brave to speak the truth," said the woman. "Just stubborn. We Southern Clan Landers know how to hold grudges."

"So I've heard," said Eynon. "Wouldn't it be better if we could forget old hurts and learn to get along?"

Merry almost laughed at Eynon's optimistic naïveté but she maintained a serious expression on the outside, at least.

"Hah!" said the woman. "My family still holds grudges back ten generations."

"I'm sorry for you," said Eynon. "In the Coombe, we only manage one or two generations."

The Southern Clan Lander wizard smiled.

Eynon saw the glint of an agate magestone affixed to a leather bracer on her forearm. "May I have the honor of knowing who I'm feuding with?" he asked.

"Brùtha of Bald Peak, a wizard of the Falcon Clan," said the woman. "And you're Eynon of Haywall. We know about you."

Eynon nodded in acknowledgment. "Why are you here?" he asked.

"That's no business of yours, Dâroner dolt."

"Now, now," said Eynon. "I didn't call *you* names." He squeezed and slightly relaxed the bands of force around Brùtha and her companions to remind them he had them in his power. "What possible reason could you have to be in this quarry?"

"Magestone dust," said a man trapped next to Brùtha. He wore a small brown jasper magestone on a leather headband.

"Quiet!" Brùtha commanded.

"It won't matter what I say," said the man. "We need magestone dust to build wide gates so we can move to the Coombe and the Rhuthro Valley."

"I *knew* we shouldn't have taught Merrillōn's friends how to make wide gates," Eynon muttered softly.

"What?" asked Brùtha.

"It doesn't matter," said Eynon. "We didn't have a choice."

"You could *choose* to let us go," said the wizard with the jasper magestone.

"And have you occupy the Coombe? I don't think so," said Eynon.

"You're not using it," said Brùtha.

"Because the Siren Hawk's forces would kill or enslave us if we stayed," said Eynon. "We plan to starve them out, so they'll leave."

"That's not our problem," said Brùtha. "Your lands lie empty, and they're far better than ours. If you choose to hide like frightened rabbits, the Southern Clans will take your land."

"And the Roma invaders will make you their slaves and steal whatever crops you manage to grow," shouted Merry from the other side of the ring-gate. "We should work together to fight the invaders and drive them from Orluin."

"It will be years before Sírénae's legions march this far west," said Brùtha.

"But days or weeks before her scout-wizards fly over this region," said Eynon. "If I led the Southern Clan Lands, I'd much rather fight the kingdom of Dâron's small army than the emperor's forty legions."

"He has a point," said the wizard with the jasper magestone.

"Hush! Let me think," said Brùtha. "One thing's for certain, this young fool *doesn't* lead the Southern Clan Lands."

"Maybe it would be better if..." began the jasper-magestone wizard.

"Hush, I said," barked Brùtha. "There are other ways to get what we want."

Eynon and Merry saw a sly smile flash across Brùtha's face, then Eynon screamed when something heavy struck the back of his head and sharp needles seemed to dig into his skull. More needles from a second avian attacker pierced the skin above his collarbone while black feathers blocked his vision and beating wings battered his face.

Merry saw the bands of solidified sound holding the Southern Clan Landers vanish and watched the wizards fall three feet to the quarry's rocky floor.

Chee reacted faster than Merry and bounded up to Eynon's shoulder where his small, raccoon-like hands tried to tug away the falcon that had landed on top of Eynon's head.

Ace was only seconds behind Chee. He launched himself through the ring-gate and slammed into the falcon attacking Eynon from the front, dislodging the bird and sending it to the ground. The raptor quickly righted itself and rose, swiftly beating away from Ace faster than the rockhound could follow.

Brùtha sent a blast of wind at Eynon, knocking him on his back where he balanced like an awkward turtle on his flying disk.

Chee twisted agilely to avoid being crushed when Eynon fell as the falcon who'd attacked Eynon's head flapped its way to Brùtha and perched on her shoulder. The bird seemed to smirk, regarding Eynon, Ace, and Chee with disdain.

Merry was torn between rushing through to defend Eynon and maintaining the ring-gate to provide a quick escape. She decided she could do both and stuck her head and one hand through the

interface, keeping her other hand in control of the ring. With a sly
smile rivaling Brùtha's, she generated an illusion of a dozen soldiers
in sky-blue Dâron surcoats holding crossbows on top of the cliff at
the north end of the quarry. As she simulated the crossbows firing, she
shot out narrow beams of tight light from one hand that smacked
into several of the Southern Clan Lands' wizards with the force of
speeding quarrels.

"Let's get out of here!" shouted the mage with the jasper magestone.

"If we must," said Brùtha. She retrieved her flying disk and boarded it,
then sent a powerful blast of wind at Merry's exposed head to drive her
back. "Everyone grab some rocks!"

Merry watched with frustration as the five wizards picked up
chunks of green rock from the floor of the quarry then sped off to
the southwest.

Ace landed next to Eynon in his flying-carpet form, then
switched to dog-form and began lapping blood off Eynon's upper
chest and face.

Chee turned to chatter noisily at Merry.

"Oh blast!" said Merry. "Eynon can always *ad hoc* gate us back to the
caverns." She stepped mostly through the ring-gate, shrank it behind
her, and collapsed the gate, pulling the ring itself through at the last
second. She confirmed the five invading wizards were truly gone, then
crossed to Eynon's side and knelt beside him.

Eynon tried to sit up, but Ace's weight on his chest made that a challenge.

Merry patted the ground next to her. Ace hopped off Eynon and
sat where she'd indicated.

With a wince and a shake of his head, Eynon sat up. He put his
hand to his scalp and pulled it back to see a sticky red mess. "I'm
bleeding," he said. "What hit me?"

"A falcon," said Merry. "Two falcons, really. You should have paid
attention when Brùtha said she was part of the Falcon Clan."

"I should have kept my shields up," said Eynon weakly.

"Yes," said Merry. "You should have." She rummaged in her belt-
pouch and removed a small, stoppered bottle. "I'm glad I brought
a healing potion with me."

"One of yours?" asked Eynon.

"No, one of yours," Merry replied.

"I'd better drink the whole thing, then," said Eynon.

Merry helped steady his arm as he drank. Ace shifted to a position behind Eynon and began licking his bleeding scalp.

"Does he have to do that?" asked Eynon.

"Let him," said Merry. "There's something in his saliva that deadens pain and stops blood from flowing."

"If you say so," Eynon replied.

Chee moved to sit on Eynon's lap and made soft, reassuring *cheeee* sounds that Eynon found soothing. He reached down to stroke the raconette's velvety fur.

Merry added a few strokes of her own. "Chee attacked the falcon on your head," she said. "Ace went for the one on your chest."

"I'm grateful to them both," said Eynon. "And to you."

"How are you feeling?" asked Merry.

"A bit better."

"Good enough to gate us back to the caverns?"

"Or maybe to Farnham's cabin on the Rhuthro?"

"You *are* feeling better," said Merry. "Even *your* healing potions work sometimes." She smiled at Eynon. "Maybe we'd better go to the cabin first," said Merry. "I can clean you up, since we don't want you to come back looking like you've just been through a battle. It wouldn't be good for morale."

"That makes sense," said Eynon. He slowly got to his feet and was amused by Ace's ability to hover behind him and continue to lick his scalp. "After you clean me up you can help *my* morale."

"Yes," said Merry. "The potion is definitely working."

They pulled their flying disks from their backs, climbed aboard, held hands, and gated out.

Chapter 2

On a Bearskin Rug

"If I'd known bearskin rugs were so comfortable, I would have found one of my own years ago," said Dârio.

"Don't tell your aunt—*or* your uncle we've been using their rug," said Jenet. She was lying beside Dârio on the bearskin with her elbow down and her chin on the back of her hand as she regarded her fiancé.

Dârio was staring up and counting tiny glow lights in the ceiling. He noticed Jenet looking at him and turned to face her. "What?" he asked.

"I'm watching your lips move as you count," said Jenet. "It's charmingly immature."

"We can't *all* be mathematical savants," said Dârio. "And I don't always silently mouth numbers," he added.

"I've watched your lips move one word ahead of the heralds when they're reading pronouncements in court," said Jenet.

"It keeps me from being bored," said Dârio.

"It distracts everyone else in the room," teased Jenet.

"Maybe it just distracts *you*, dear lady," said Dârio. He pushed at Jenet's elbow and her head fell forward against his chest. "I think my lips entrance you."

"I think your ego is boundless," she said. "You don't have to play the part of being a vain and brainless crowned head any longer."

"Sometimes I forget," said Dârio.

"For the record, I do like your lips," said Jenet. She leaned in and kissed him to support her statement. When they broke the kiss, Dârio was smiling.

"I like yours, too," said Dârio.

"Better than my little sister's?" asked Jenet.

"Marginally," said Dârio.

Jenet used three fingers on Dârio's unprotected ribs, tickling him. Dârio squirmed and grimace-laughed until she stopped.

"I guess I deserved that," he said.

Jenet frowned at him and stuck her tongue out in mock anger.

"You know very well I haven't kissed your sister since you caught us cuddling in your father's hayloft five years ago," Dârio protested.

"I offered to join you, but Linette didn't want to share," said Jenet.

"At least now that I've sampled both, I can truthfully say I prefer kissing *your* lips, my love," said Dârio.

"What's wrong with my sister's lips?" asked Jenet, her mock-frown returning.

"Nothing is wrong with your sister's lips," said Dârio. "They were quite delicious, but I much prefer yours."

"Nice recovery," said Jenet. She kissed Dârio again—longer this time.

"Thank you," said Dârio when they broke the kiss.

"For what?" said Jenet.

"For the distraction," Dârio answered. "It's been a slog trying to show Tamloch's nobility that a person can be a decent human being and still a king. They only have experience toadying to Túathal's capricious whims. It's hard work getting them to tell me the truth instead of what they think I want to hear."

"I'm enjoying the distraction, too, my love," said Jenet. "Trying to find food and shelter for hundreds of thousands of people on short notice hasn't been easy. Everyone insists on having more than their share of rations or a better place to sleep. My deputies are constantly having to break up fights that are largely caused by cramming too many people into too small a space for too long a time. We'll have to do something about that soon."

"Absolutely," said Dârio. "And you also need space for the army to muster and drill. We have to maintain our ability to defend ourselves."

"Much as I don't relish the thought of facing a dozen legions in the field, we still need to train as if that might happen," said Jenet. "Maybe you could..."

"Talk to Verro?" asked Dârio.

"I was thinking about calling a general meeting of our senior wizards and leaders to find a solution to the problem that would work for all of us," said Jenet. "I'm confident we're all dealing with similar issues."

"I expect Nûd is having an easier time of it with the Dâron nobles," said Dârio. "They're kittens compared to the Tamlocher wildcats I have to deal with."

"Like the Duchess of Whitrose?" asked Jenet. "And Baron Nobblig?"

"Maybe I shouldn't be envying Nûd after all," said Dârio. He rubbed the stubble on his shaved head.

"At least your cousin has my father to help him," said Jenet. "You have to put up with me and my inexperience."

"You're doing fine," said Dârio. "No one has been killed in any of the Tamloch refuges yet, and you've managed to have archery practice and weapon's training continue on a small scale."

"It's not enough," said Jenet. "Thank goodness so many people keep busy making love. It gives them something to do, even if I worry about the birthrate jumping in eight or nine months. We don't have enough hedge wizards and midwives."

"At least it keeps people from fighting," said Dârio. "Are you trying to tell me something? Are you going to be adding to the list of future births?"

"No," said Jenet. "At least not yet. I've been too busy herding cats and fighting fires, and you're up late beating leadership lessons into hard Tamloch skulls. We've both hardly had time to do more than fall asleep at bedtime. Thank goodness Princess Rúth and Doethan are here to help keep the peace when trouble starts," said Jenet. "Without them, everything would be a lot harder—and we wouldn't have been able to make time for each other."

"My people really love Princess Rúth, don't they?" said Dârio.

Jenet kissed Dârio again.

"What was that for?" he asked.

"You said *my* people," Jenet replied. "That means you're finally starting to feel like the king of Tamloch, not Dâron."

"It's going to take me more than a few months to really start thinking of myself as a Tamlocher," said Dârio.

"But you look so good wearing green and gold," teased Jenet.

"You look good wearing anything—and nothing," said Dârio.

"Will you like how I look after I've had three or four children?"

"Count on it," said Dârio. "Watch my lips." Dârio mouthed *I love you* to Jenet without speaking and won another kiss for his sentiment.

"Still better lips than Linette's?" asked Jenet.

"I'm not going there," said Dârio. "You're fishing for more compliments and you'll tickle me again no matter what I say."

"Probably," said Jenet. She smiled. "Speaking of fishing, I'm so glad we've been able to supplement our stores with fish from the river above the Great Falls thanks to Inthíra's help hiding the nets and fisher-folk."

"I don't want to talk about Inthíra or fishing right now," said Dârio. "I'd prefer to be distracted some other way."

"Should I ask Linette to come up from the lower caverns and distract you?" teased Jenet.

"That won't be necessary," said Dârio. "You're all the distraction I need—for now."

"You'll pay for that qualifier," said Jenet. "Let me get a quilt and lose this dress."

Chapter 3

Queen Carys Consulted

Dowager Queen Carys, widow of the Old King, Dâroth XXIV, woke when a plain gold ring on her right hand began to vibrate. Her quarters were at the end of a long side passage in a large cavern, part of Dâron's complex of subterranean refuges. The queen's servant, sleeping twenty feet away up the passage, didn't stir when Carys woke and accepted the communications ring's connection and the three soft chimes that accompanied it.

"Hello?" said the queen, sounding a bit sleepy.

"Oh!" said the person on the other side of the interface when the ring expanded to its usual two-foot diameter. "I didn't mean to wake you. It's earlier here, and I forgot it would be later back in Dâron."

"I forgive you," said Carys. "You know I always love to hear from you. I miss having you nearby."

"And *I* miss *you*," came the reply. "I wanted to let you know I expect to be out of touch for a lot longer and didn't want you to worry."

"I'll always worry about *you*," said Queen Carys. "You're a mother yourself and should know such things."

"You're right, as always," said the other person's mellow alto. "The fact of the matter is that you probably *should* be worried about me."

"Is *he* getting you into trouble again?" asked Carys.

"Don't start *that* again, Mother. I'm worried enough about what we're going to do as it is without you opening old wounds."

"I never understood what you saw in..."

"And you didn't need to," said the alto voice. "I'm the one who married him, not you."

"What has he talked you into now?" asked the queen.

"Nothing," said the voice. "We decided together to travel to Nova Eboracum and offer to serve Sírénae."

"You're not turning traitor, I assume?"

"Far from it. We want to be on the inside so we can keep an eye on Sírénae and report back to you and the Alliance."

"Interesting," said Queen Carys. "And probably foolhardy, but when has that ever stopped him—or you?"

"Never comes to mind," teased the person on the other side of the interface.

"Do you plan to go in openly, as yourselves?" asked the queen.

"Goodness, no. He will probably offer to muck out stables…"

"That sounds about right for him," said Carys. "So long as they keep him away from the kitchens."

"For once, I agree with you. I'm the one who will probably apply for a job peeling turnips, though I hope I can rise to be one of the emperor's ladies in waiting."

"Does Sírénae *have* ladies in waiting?" asked the queen. "She doesn't strike me as the sort to sit around doing embroidery and discussing who's with whom around the palace."

"Very true. But she does like having retainers nearby she can browbeat and bully."

"And you hope to present her with a challenge," said the queen.

"Precisely. The more I resist her attempts to beat me down, the more she'll want to keep me close."

"That sounds dangerous," said Carys.

"I told you it would be."

"What's *his* end game? Serving wine in a taverna to get legionnaires' gossip while you listen in on Sírénae?" asked the queen.

"Something like that," said the person with the mellow alto voice. "That will depend on how the invaders' stores of wine are holding out. You can't sell what you don't have."

"Clearly you've never been a merchant," said the queen.

"Don't change the subject," said the woman across the interface. "From what we can tell, the Alliance's starvation strategy is working. The invaders are on very tight rations. Sírénae is going to be pushing Umbrose and Callidus hard for information that will let her capture supplies from our caverns—along with slaves to plant and tend crops."

"My sources tell me the same thing," said Queen Carys. "I expect they'll have to start slaughtering elephants soon, since Viridáxés and Zûrafiérix have been doing such a good job destroying the nets of their fishing vessels."

"Without being seen, I hope?"

"So far," said the queen. "Sailors are reporting sea monsters, not giant dragons."

"Good. The less Sírénae knows about them, the better."

"What about your magestones?" asked Carys.

"Changing the subject again?"

"No," said the queen. "Returning to an old one. How do the two of you expect to work for the invading Roma if you still wear your magestones? Umbrose and Callidus would spot them in minutes."

"Callidus might keep silent, but you're right. Umbrose and his spy-wizards *would* be a problem."

"How to you plan to get around it?" asked the queen.

"By hiding them somewhere in the city. If we're not wearing them, they can't be detected."

"And you won't be able to work magic," said the queen. "I don't like it. Why can't you recruit non-wizards for the job?"

"We're doing that, too." The woman on the other side of the ring's interface smiled. "Salder is driving a wagon with the supply train for the five legions headed up the Abbenoth Valley to fight the Northern Clan Landers. He looks just like a Roma from Lugdunensis and has a terrible accent to match. There are so many Roma who came over in the invasion fleet to support the legions that they'd never suspect he's from Dâron."

"Good," said the queen. "He's a reliable young man who can keep his head in a crisis."

"Agreed. He did a great job for us in Tamloch."

"Uirsé won't thank you for putting her fiancé in harm's way again," said the queen.

"Uirsé understands the threat posed by Sírénae's legions. She knows Salder has a job to do. The better a job he does of gathering information, the less work she'll have healing the wounded."

"Will you be contacting Laetícia for advice about Nova Eboracum and how best to approach the invading Roma to ask for work?" asked the queen.

"I've done that already. I saved calling you for last to make it harder for you to talk me out of it."

"Should I be pleased about that?" asked Carys.

"Probably." The woman shrugged her shoulders. "I wanted to tell you about our plans and get your advice *without* being told how risky they are. We know they're dangerous."

"Very well," said Queen Carys. "I hope everything goes well and you're both not enslaved by the Roma within an hour of appearing. I love you. I even love *him* because you do."

"Thank you. I love you, too."

"I do have one piece of advice," said the queen.

"What's that?"

"Talk to Doethan before you head for the city," said Carys. "He may have some advice to offer about where to hide your magestones."

"You mean with Távi?"

"Go," said Queen Carys with a wry smile. "You're already two steps ahead of me. Just do whatever it takes to throw these invaders back into the sea. I don't want to live out my last years in a hole in the ground, even if it's clean and dry, not nasty, dirty, and wet. I'd much prefer to die in my own comfortable feather bed back in the palace in Brendinas."

"We'll do what we can to hurry things up," said the woman. "And don't talk about dying. You're going to live forever."

Queen Carys shook her head. "One thing I *don't* want to do is outlive my only remaining child. Be careful—both of you."

"We will, Mother. We will."

The ring's connection broke and three soft chimes echoed against the cave's stone walls.

Chapter 4

Placing Blame

Sírénae paced back and forth in an outer room of the apartments in the governor-general's palace in Nova Eboracum that had formerly been used by Quintillius and Laetícia. Thraxa, her snow-gryffon, sat on her haunches beside Sírénae's elaborate chair and followed the emperor's movements by turning her head. Umbrose, Magister Callidus, General Machaera, Lieutenant General Belisaria, and Admiral Pixo were perched on uncomfortably hard chairs around the edge of the room, tracking the emperor with wary eyes.

"Why haven't you been able to *find* any provincials?" Sírénae spat at Umbrose. "You should have found where they've gone by now!"

"I'm sorry, Your Imperial Majesty, but..." Umbrose began.

"I don't want excuses," said the emperor. "I want results." She stopped pacing in front of Callidus. "And you," she said. "What do you have to show for a month of research trying to duplicate their wide gates?"

"We're hard at work puzzling it out, but none of the wizards assigned to me are strong on theory," said Magister Callidus. "They're battle mages, not scholar mages. We have to work it out by trial and error."

"More excuses," said Sírénae. "If you keep making errors, we'll skip trials and go straight to executions. That should speed things up."

"Three of my wizards have already been killed going through unstable gates," Callidus protested. "It's going to take time."

"We don't *have* time, you fool," said Sírénae. She marched over a few feet to confront the least-senior person in the room. "Belisaria, you're my new quartermaster. Tell them where we stand."

"We're on half-rations now," said the lieutenant general. "Even with cutting that back further, we've got another month, at most, before our food is gone."

"What about the elephants?" Callidus heard his own voice say.

"That's *with* eating the elephants, starting in two weeks," said Belisaria. "A quarter of a million people can make short work of even a hundred elephants."

"I wonder what elephant soup tastes like?" General Machaera asked Admiral Pixo with a grin.

"Who cares, so long as the cooks don't add a rabbit to it?" Pixo replied.

"Because nobody likes a..." began Machaera.

"Complete that sentence and I'll throw *you* in the soup," said Sírénae. "This is no time for levity. We've got to get more food."

"Sorry," said Machaera.

"Pixo," said Sírénae, picking a new target. "Why aren't your sailors catching more fish?"

"Something keeps stealing their nets, Sírénae," said the admiral.

Sírénae glared at him for daring to use her first name in front of the others. Pixo quickly backtracked.

"We think it's deliberate sabotage but aren't sure how it's happening. The sailors are claiming some nonsense about sea monsters."

"Send Callidus out to sea with the fishing fleet," said the emperor. "It might require a wizard to deal with a monster."

"But Your Imperial Majesty, the wide gate investigations require my continual attention," said Magister Callidus.

"Your strongest sub-magisters can guide the investigations," Sírénae pronounced. "They can hardly do worse than you have."

"As you will, my emperor," said Callidus. "May I ask Xaxidiánus to join me?"

"Set a monster to stop a monster, you mean?" asked Sírénae. "Why not. You won't be far from land in case I need you both."

"Thank you, Your Imperial Majesty," said Callidus. He lowered his chin and bent his tall frame to bow to the emperor.

"I'd planned to send the fishing fleet to the northern cod banks again," said Pixo.

"Keep them closer to Nova Eboracum this trip," said Sírénae. "We'll see if your sea monsters follow the cod or some other species."

"If I must," muttered Pixo. He shook his head in frustration when Sírénae's attention shifted.

"Machaera!" Sírénae nearly shouted. "When will you have five legions ready to march against the Northern Clan Landers? Their insults are hard to bear."

"We're ready to march north as soon as tomorrow morning, Your Imperial Majesty," said Machaera. "I've been waiting for word from scout-wizards on the size and disposition of the Northern Clan Landers' forces before departing. It wouldn't be wise to attack them without knowing what we're getting into."

"Umbrose! Why haven't your spy-scouts given Machaera the information she needs?"

"I send them, but they don't come back, Majesty," said Umbrose.

"Just like the nets on the fishing boats," said Sírénae. "Are there sea monsters up the Abbenoth, too?"

"Not to my knowledge," said Umbrose. "Though my spies have heard reports about a giant green dragon that destroyed a castle upriver."

"A *giant* dragon?" asked the emperor.

"One five times the size of Xaxidiánus," said Umbrose. "My people discounted such stories as the exaggerations of people drinking too much ale or eating bad rye."

"Why are you just telling me this now?" asked Sírénae.

"Because you would have told me not to report foolish peasant stories?" offered Umbrose.

Sírénae shook her fist toward Umbrose. "Let me be the judge of the truth of such stories," she said. "Weren't there tales of giant dragons at Riyas as well?"

"Those were proven to be illusions," said Umbrose. "The reports my spies collected before everyone went into hiding said as much."

"Speaking of that, Spymaster," said Sírénae. "Why haven't your embedded spies identified the locations of the provincials' hiding places?"

"They have, Majesty," said Umbrose.

"What?" said Sírénae. "Where are they?"

"They're in caves," said Umbrose.

Sírénae glared at him.

"No, really," said Umbrose. "That's all we can tell. They went through gates and now they're in caves. Underground."

"That's where caves are usually found," said Machaera.

"Except for sea caves," said Pixo.

Sírénae's expression suggested a thundercloud was gathering over her head. Thraxa snapped in the direction of Machaera and Pixo.

"Keep such childish observations to yourselves in the future," the emperor ordered the two senior officers. She swung back on Umbrose. "Are you saying they can't tell you where they are because they don't *know* where they are?" asked Sírénae.

"Precisely," said Umbrose. "It's been quite vexing for my agents."

"I'm pretty blasted vexed about it too, Umbrose," said Sírénae. "Can't any of them escape?"

"Passageways to the surface are well-guarded," said Umbrose.

"In every cavern?" asked Sírénae.

"When they check in, I'll ask all my agents to redouble their efforts to get out," said Umbrose. "I don't think they've tried poisoning guards yet."

"Offer them incentives," said Sírénae. "I'll give a barony to the first spy to provide the location of extensive stores."

"That should encourage them," said Umbrose. "Though I expect I'll lose quite a few in the process and never know it until they fail to report at all."

"I'm fine with that," said Sírénae. "They're not much use to me now."

"I understand, Majesty, and will present them with your offer," said Umbrose. "It may make a difference."

"It blasted well *better* make a difference," said the emperor. Sírénae clenched and unclenched her hands. "Machaera, send those five legions marching north in the morning. They can stretch their supplies with venison and other wild game. That should help Belisaria make our rations last down here."

"Gladly," said General Machaera. "We'll teach those Northern Clan Landers the folly of mocking Roma and retrieve the eagles they stole in years past." She smacked her fist against her decorated breastplate, making it clang.

"Take three dragons with you," said the emperor. "Xaxidiánus will tell you which ones will be best for scouting terrain *and* scorching irregulars."

"Thank you, Your Imperial Majesty," said General Machaera. Her fist clanged again.

"Have the dragons on guard for ballistae," said Umbrose. "Northern Clan Landers are reportedly fond of them."

Callidus looked away so Sírénae couldn't see him roll his eyes. Xaxidiánus had told him long ago that dragons hated the big bolt-throwers.

"Callidus," said Sírénae.

The magister turned back quickly and hoped his face didn't reveal his thoughts.

"Increase your surveys to the west in Dâron. That realm has highly productive farmland and should have lots of crops stored up to get them through the summer. See if your wizards can find stores of food that may not have been taken underground and have them retrieve anything they find."

"Yes, Your Imperial Majesty," said Callidus, repeating his bow. "I will see that started before I leave with the fishing fleet."

"Good," said Sírénae. "Have them particularly be on the lookout for hives and honey," said Sírénae. "I'd like at least something to be sweet about this conquest."

Everyone nodded at their emperor and rose to leave. They knew from her tone of voice that her last comment was a dismissal.

Thraxa opened her mouth and licked the edge of her sharp beak with her rough tongue as she regarded the departing staff members. She knew it would soon be time for her to be fed and she wondered if any of the men and women leaving the chamber would be on her upcoming menu.

Chapter 5

On the Side of a Mountain

Northern Clan Lands High Chief Arminta climbed the last hundred feet up the mountainside to inspect the trap set for any force entering the mountains from the south. It was still cool under the trees, so she wasn't sweating, but her legs could feel the effort it took to ascend the steep slope.

I wonder if I could have one of our wizards tame a flathorn for me to ride, she thought. Then she reconsidered. *It would probably be more trouble than it's worth and many of the younger would-be high chiefs would use her mount to say she was too old for her position.*

From below, the collection of loose rocks and tree trunks looked like a natural formation, an organic component of the mountain. Once Arminta was above the trap, its true nature was revealed. Shoving a few key tree trunks would send the whole mass of rocks and wood rushing down the slope to crush any force unlucky enough to be on the road at the bottom of the valley.

Arminta walked another dozen paces to stand beside Nèàch, the man responsible for building the trap. He was of medium height with a wiry build, thinning red hair, a red beard, and freckles so thick from exposure to the sun that they almost joined together in one continuous pattern.

"It's looking good," said Arminta. "You should be able to take out a quarter of a legion with this one."

"There are three more traps farther along the road," said Nèàch. "They should leave us with one less legion to fight."

"I hope the next three don't look just like this one," said Arminta, knowing it would provoke a protest from Nèàch.

"Do you take me for a novice, then?" Nèàch responded. "The traps are as different as children from four different mothers."

"Good," said Arminta.

"The next one is completely screened by two rows of pines," said Nèach. "I'm particularly proud of the one after that. It's quite devious. We dammed a stream and..."

Arminta broke in, knowing well how long Nèach could talk about his engineering creations. "Excellent," she said. A good leader always started with praise. "I do have a few small suggestions, however."

Nèach looked at Arminta and waited. He knew the High Chief didn't offer her suggestions idly.

"You may not have heard that the invaders have dragons," said Arminta. "We got that much out of the Roma spy-wizards we captured. I know you've camouflaged your traps so they can't be identified from above, but please make sure they can be triggered without help from *our* wizards. Dragons might be able to sense wizards and either trigger your traps prematurely or incinerate them before they can fall."

"Ah, and I'm a step ahead of you in that, Chief," said Nèach. "Not that I can often say so." He grinned at Arminta. "All my traps can be triggered by two or three strong lads or lasses and I've taken care to make sure they're hard to spot from the air. We've had to deal with wizards on flying disks for generations, after all."

"That's good to hear," said Arminta. "Just be extra-careful. We're not dealing with Tamlochers and their foolish nobility. These invaders are Roma who've been fighting for most of their lives. They've never lost. Even now, coming to Orluin, they didn't stay to fight against high odds and lose. They sailed across the Ocean determined to win *our* lands."

"I'll take care, and tell my levies to do likewise," said Nèach. "You can be assured of that. We'll do fine against them so long as we can avoid stand-up battles on level ground."

"I'm pleased to hear it," said Arminta. "Our sources say five legions are moving north from Nova Eboracum in the morning."

"We'll be ready for them," said Nèach.

Both Northern Clan Landers were surprised when a shadow blocked the late afternoon sun. They looked up to see a golden figure descending toward them on a flying disk. Arminta couldn't be sure if it was one of her wizards, so she only loosened one of the throwing knives on her belt. Néàch reached for the sword strapped to his back, but Arminta motioned him to wait. A few seconds later, an amber-robed figure landed gracefully a few paces away. The wizard's arms were held wide in a gesture of peace.

"Are you High Clan Chief Arminta?" asked the wizard.

"I am," Arminta answered. "Who are you?"

"An emissary offering you aid from King Bjarni and Queen Signý of Bifurland," said the wizard. "I seldom speak, but my queen said I must until our foes are defeated. You may call me Amber."

"Well, Amber," said Arminta. "What could we possibly want from Bifurland?"

"Something to counter the two hundred elephants coming north with Sírénae's legions," said Amber.

"What's an elephant?" asked Néàch.

"A huge animal with legs like tree trunks, a nose like a snake, ears like tent walls, and a tail like a rope—with teeth bigger than a sabercat," said Arminta. "I saw a picture of one in Robin Goodfellow's *Peregrinations.*"

"Are they good for hauling?" asked the ever-practical Néàch.

"Yes, but that's not what's important," said the Bifurland wizard. "We can offer you three hundred mammoths to counter the elephants."

"What's a mammoth?" asked Néàch.

"A bigger, hairy elephant," said Arminta and Amber simultaneously. They smiled at each other.

"Why would we need mammoths?" asked Arminta, her expression turning serious. "It's not like these centuries of Roma elephants can climb mountains."

"You'd be surprised," said Amber. "These are Afarikan forest elephants. They love mountains and trees."

"I wouldn't like having a beast ten times the size of a flathorn tromping around near *my* home," said Néàch.

"Neither would I," said Arminta. "We need to stop them before they get to our settlements."

"That will mean stopping the elephants on the plains of the Abbenoth Valley," said Amber. "We can gate in our three hundred mammoths on level ground, bash the Roma elephants, and—

with luck—gate them out with the mammoths back to northern Bifurland so you won't have to worry about them attacking your homes."

"I like the sound of that," said Néàch. "Except for the part about fighting on level ground. We *never* do that. The invading Roma will kick our —"

"As much as I agree with your opinion in general," said Arminta. "I think we need to hear Amber out about how best to use mammoths against elephants in battle." She turned to the wizard. "Bifurland will be providing troops as well, correct? We'd be glad to accept a few thousand of your warriors with axes and round shields to help put the invading legions in their place."

"My king and queen are glad to offer such aid," said Amber. "Have you heard of the Orluin Alliance?"

"Bifurland, Tamloch, Dâron, and the Roma of Occidens Province coming together against these newly arrived Roma?" asked Arminta. "I heard about it, but don't expect it to last more than a few months."

"It will last until we starve out Sírénae's forces and remove them from our lands," said Amber.

"I'd drink to that," said Néàch. "And if we get to pick our ground, I can think of quite a few traps that would work on a plain, not a mountainside."

"You have my attention, wizard," said Arminta. "Tell me more..."

Chapter 6

Underground Roma

"Mater, when can I go out and play?" asked Tertia.

"You can play any time you want," said her mother Laetícia. "There are lots of children your age in this cave-complex, that's one of the reasons we're here, not some other cave."

"I don't want to play underground," Laetícia's younger daughter protested. "I want to play in the sun. I *miss* it."

"We all miss it," said Laetícia. "But we all have to make sacrifices to defeat Sírénae."

"She's not a nice person, is she?" asked Tertia.

"That's an understatement," said Laetícia.

Tertia looked at the stone walls and tooth-like stalactites and stalagmites around her. "It's an underground understatement," she said, proud of the new phrase she'd created. "I want to put Sírénae underground, but not in a cave." The little girl slashed the air with an imaginary sword.

"I keep wondering if you're going to be a wizard, like me, or a warrior like your father when you grow up," said Laetícia.

"Why can't I be both?" asked Tertia.

"It's seldom done," her mother replied.

"Felix is both," said Tertia. "He has the claws and spikes on his cat armor, *and* he's a wizard."

"He's a better wizard than a warrior," said Laetícia.

"Didn't he rescue you on the evil emperor's flagship?" asked Tertia. "I overheard you telling Pater."

"That's right, he did," said Laetícia. "Maybe you can be a wizard *and* a warrior. You don't have to decide a path now. You're only three."

"Almost four," said Tertia. "How will I know when it's my birthday if I can't see the sun to count days?"

"The grownups are keeping track," said Laetícia. "We'll be sure to tell you when it's your birthday."

"Good," said Tertia. "Pater promised I could have a real knife on my fourth birthday."

"Let's hope that's still an option now that we're in hiding," said Laetícia. "A great many things are different now."

"I have complete confidence in the governor-general," said Tertia, repeating a phrase she'd heard Laetícia say hundreds of times.

Laetícia laughed and hugged her daughter. "So do I, dear one. Your father will find a way to keep his promise, I'm sure."

"He'd better," said Tertia. She pouted and stamped her foot, just to make her mother laugh again, then she smiled. "When will Pater be back?" Tertia asked.

"Soon," said Laetícia. "He's gone through a gate to a cave-complex west of here with Felix. They're looking for a cavern large enough to drill legionnaires."

"It would take a really big cavern to hold a legion," said Tertia.

"That's very true, daughter," said Laetícia. She held back a smile thinking about how precocious Tertia was. The little girl had grown up on her parents' discussions of logistics, drinking it in as if it were mothers' milk. "The cavern wouldn't have to hold all five thousand legionnaires. A tenth of that would be good enough for practice drills. The commanders can rotate their forces through to keep everyone sharp."

"And every gladius sharp, too," teased Tertia.

"You're too sharp for your own good, little one," said Laetícia.

"Thank you, Mater," said her daughter. "Will we be fighting Sírénae's invaders soon? It feels so strange to think of Roma fighting Roma."

"That's one of the reasons we're *not* confronting Sírénae directly," said Laetícia. "I don't like the idea of Roma fighting Roma, either. That's why we're hiding instead of fighting. When the invaders run out of food, they'll have to leave."

"And we can go back in the sun?"

"That's right," said Laetícia.

"I want to go outside sooner than that," declared Tertia.

"A meeting has been called for all the leaders of the Orluin Alliance," said Laetícia. "We've reached everyone except Eynon and Merry and hope to have it two days from now in a big cavern in the mountains of southwestern Dâron."

"Can I come?" asked Tertia. "I'm tired of *this* cave-complex."

"We'll see," said Laetícia.

"That means *no*," said Tertia.

"It means *we'll see*," her mother replied. Laetícia knew how the game was played. "Where are your brother and sister?"

"I don't know."

"Tertia, I can believe lots of things, but you not knowing where Primus and Seconda are isn't one of them."

"They're exploring," said the girl.

"Exploring where?" asked Laetícia.

"Side tunnels," said Tertia.

"Which side tunnels?"

"The ones they're not supposed to explore."

"Of course," said Laetícia. "Why would they be anywhere else?" She raised both eyebrows and changed her line of questioning. "Where's Noskóma?"

"Nurse is drinking sweetened wine in her chamber."

Laetícia knew Noskóma's chamber—a small alcove carved into the rock on the passage where Laetícia's children slept—was a favorite spot for the children's nursemaid and governess to enjoy bottles and jugs of wine, rather than glasses of it. "Did Primus give her a jug?" Laetícia asked.

"I don't know," Tertia replied.

"That means he did," said Laetícia.

"It wasn't a jug, it was a bottle," said the little girl.

"Thank you, Tertia," said Laetícia. "Is that why you're playing out here instead of farther down the passageway?"

"I'm here to be a diversion," said Tertia. "I'm supposed to tell you Primus and Seconda are visiting the legionnaires and practicing their archery."

"Instead of exploring places where they shouldn't be," said Laetícia.

"I don't know," Tertia repeated in a sing-song voice. She smiled at her mother.

"I'm a spymaster, so I can't tell you to always be honest, little one," said Laetícia. "But I do have a lot on my mind and don't want to worry about Primus and Seconda falling into a pit or running into a sleeping cave bear. I have a sizable investment in parenting those two rascals and don't want to waste it."

"You could always have more children, Mater," said Tertia. "Then I would be the oldest."

"Now you're sounding like Sírénae, child," said Laetícia. "She only thinks about herself, not other people."

"I'm sorry," said Tertia. "We could go for a walk that just might go past the side tunnel that my brother and sister may or may not be exploring."

"And you could stop to tighten the laces on your sandals outside the tunnel in question?" asked Laetícia.

"Uh huh," said Tertia, looking innocent.

"You're not going to be a wizard or a warrior," said Laetícia. "I think you're on your way to being a lawyer."

"Oh no, Mater. Anything but that!" said Tertia using a tone of voice she'd learned from Primus.

"Come along, daughter," said Laetícia. "Let's find your siblings before they run into too much trouble."

Chapter 7

At Farnam's Cabin

Eynon and Merry popped into the air above Farnam's cabin, a way-stop for travelers on the Rhuthro. A gentle wind kept things cool in the river valley, and the hardwood trees in the surrounding forest were a hundred shades of green with new spring growth. Ace jumped from Merry's flying disk, spread the thin membranes between his front and back legs, and soared, reveling in the clean, fresh air.

Chee let out a single sad *cheee,* and Ace circled around to allow Chee to jump on his back and enjoy his flight.

"That's odd," said Merry when she finally had a chance to look around after observing the two familiars' playful antics.

"What?" asked Eynon. He was still a bit disoriented from the falcons' attack.

"That," said Merry, pointing toward the cabin.

"It looks the same to me," said Eynon. "Log walls. Shingled roof. Chimney with white smoke drifting east in the breeze."

"Think about that last part," said Merry.

"Oh!" said Eynon. "Someone's in the cabin."

"Exactly," said Merry. "But are they friend or foe?"

"I guess they could be more Southern Clan Land raiders," said Eynon.

"Maybe," said Merry. "It seemed like the ones in the quarry were the vanguard, though. I don't think they've made it as far as the river yet."

"Agreed," said Eynon. "Maybe they're stragglers who didn't make it into the caverns?"

"The two dukes did a good job of rounding up strays," said Merry. "My father said everyone from the valley had gone to caves in the mountains north of the earl's castle at Rhuthro Keep."

"How do you propose figuring out who's inside?" asked Eynon.

"I was thinking we could try going up to the door and knocking," said Merry.

"That works," said Eynon. "We'll keep our shields up. Do you want to use your magic to disguise us as old women offering apples or something?"

"What, do you expect to find a fair maiden and seven short miners inside, like in the children's tale?"

"Wouldn't it be fun if we did?" asked Eynon.

Merry laughed. "I think we should just be ourselves. It's simpler. Let's land."

The two of them brought their flying disks down on an open space near the entrance to the cabin. They stowed their disks across their shoulders and stepped to the heavy oak door. Eynon looked at Merry for guidance on next steps. She rolled her eyes, raised her hand, made a fist, and rapped the door three times. The sound echoed and moments later the door opened.

"What are *you* doing here?" asked Gruffyd, Merry's childhood friend.

"We might ask the same of you," Merry replied.

"Show some courtesy and invite them in, Gruffy," came a pleasant soprano from inside the cabin. A few seconds later, Nyssia, Gruffyd's new wife, appeared in the entryway beside her husband. Her long blonde hair was in a single tight braid and she carried a thin sword with a polished hilt on her belt. Nyssia was of medium height, about the same size as Merry, but beside Gruffyd's height and bulk she seemed tiny.

"Yes, *Gruffy,* invite us in," teased Merry. "It's good to see you, Nyssia. You, too, Gruffyd."

"Hello," said Eynon from two paces back. Of all the people he considered might be in Farnam's cabin, Merry's old friend and his new wife weren't on the list. After standing quiet for a few seconds, looking like an owl in bright sunlight, he said, "Weren't you both in Brendinas?"

Nyssia tugged Gruffyd back out of the doorway and into the cabin to make room for Merry and Eynon to enter. She hugged Merry as she entered and smiled up at Eynon, sensing that he wasn't himself as yet.

"Sit down," said Nyssia, pointing at two of the rough-hewn wooden chairs by the cabin's table. "I'll get you some strong cider. You look like you could use it."

"I could, certainly," said Merry. "But none for Eynon. He was just injured and is processing a healing potion."

"One I made myself, Merry tells me," said Eynon. "I'm not that good at making them."

"The cuts on your face seem to be getting better from minute to minute," said Gruffyd. "That means you can't be that *bad* at making them."

"You'd be surprised," said Merry. "He tested the first one he made on himself and it made his face turn green."

"Because it tasted like moldy skunk cabbage leaves, not because it didn't work," said Eynon.

"How would you know if it worked or not?" asked Merry. "There was nothing wrong with you when you took it."

"True enough," said Eynon. "Though I felt sick to my stomach immediately afterward. Thank goodness the unpleasant sensation didn't last."

Nyssia jumped in. "I'm just glad you're on the mend. What brings the two of you all the way to this cabin? I thought you'd be in the southern caverns with King Nûd, working on ways to drive out the invaders."

Eynon was about to answer, but Merry spoke first. "We were at the quarry west of the Coombe, near Wherrel. Have you told Nyssia about that yet, Gruffyd?"

Her childhood friend shook his head from side to side.

"I guess that's not important," said Merry. "I didn't know about it until I met Eynon. It's not far from where he grew up and it turns out to be where Viridáxés had been sleeping since the time of the First Ships two thousand years ago."

"The great green dragon?" asked Nyssia.

"That's him," said Merry. "Anyway, the quarry turned out to be full of magestones, or magic-infused rocks at least. Viridáxés soaked up magic for all those years and grew bigger and bigger. When he broke free the floor of the quarry ended up covered in fragments of stone just waiting to be ground up into powered magestones."

"What's that good for?" asked Gruffyd. He put a mug of hard cider in front of Merry and another filled with cool river water beside Eynon. Both drank, then sighed.

"We use powered magestones to make wide gates," said Eynon. "Like the ones we sent the wisents through to defeat the Tamloch forces south of Brendinas."

"It's important, then," said Nyssia.

"Correct," said Merry. "But what's really important is that we ran into five wizards from the Southern Clan Lands at the quarry. They were checking it out to get their own powdered magestone dust and to reconnoiter the Coombe and the Rhuthro Valley before *they* invade it."

Gruffyd smacked his hand into his fist. "That's not good," he said. "We're in real trouble if the valley is being attacked from the east *and* the west."

"I imagine the Southern Clan Landers are putting themselves in line to be attacked by the invading Roma, too," said Nyssia.

"They're just too dumb to realize it," added Merry. She shifted her gaze from Gruffyd to Nyssia and back. "We've told you why we're here, now tell us why you're here."

"No you haven't," said Gruffyd.

"Haven't what?" said Merry.

"Told us why you're here," said Gruffyd. "You told us why you were at the quarry, but not why you're here."

"She sort of did, Gruff," said Nyssia. "You had to read between the lines."

"I hate to read," said Gruffyd. "Explain it to me."

Merry was used to dealing with Gruffyd's obtuseness from their time together as children, so she added more details. "Eynon was attacked by the Southern Clan Lands wizards. He was holding them immobile with bands of solidified sound, but they attacked him with falcons—their familiars—and left deep puncture wounds in his face and scalp. I gave him a healing potion as soon as I could, but we thought this cabin would be a good place to come to give Eynon time to recuperate before going back to the caverns to report."

"How did you drive off the wizards?" asked Gruffyd.

"With beams of tight light"—Merry used strands of force to press Gruffyd against one wall of the cabin—"and illusion magic"—she cast a simulation of an angry bear ready to attack because it was more impressive than simulated soldiers with crossbows. After three breaths she released Gruffyd and canceled her illusion.

"That was impressive!" said Gruffyd when he was released, and his eyes had returned to their normal size. "I'm glad you're on our side."

Nyssia began to clap. "Well done," she said. "I'll bet they ran back home as fast as they could travel."

"Flew back," said Eynon. "They were on flying disks."

"Right," said Nyssia. "You sound like you're starting to feel better. I'll fetch more water from the river and get you some clean cloths so you can get the blood off your head and face and chest."

"Thank you," said Eynon.

"I'll go with you," said Gruffyd. "You'll need someone to protect you from hungry bears." He looked at Merry and smiled.

"While you're there, please bring me back a smooth, flat rock the size of a dinner plate," said Eynon. "I'll use the last of the water in the bucket to put out the fire."

"We don't want smoke attracting attention from invaders from either direction," said Merry.

"But how will we cook dinner?" asked Nyssia. "I was just about to get our evening meal started."

"That's what the flat rock is for," said Eynon.

Nyssia was about to speak but closed her mouth. After Merry's display of power, she was willing to give them both the benefit of the doubt.

Merry sloshed the last few cups of water in the bottom of a wooden bucket on the fire in the hearth. The flames went out with a hiss and clouds of steam started up the chimney.

Eynon intercepted them with a sphere of solidified sound, which he compressed and cooled until it was coated with drops of water he allowed to drip into the ashes. "I should have put the fire out by absorbing its heat," he said. "At least I stopped even more smoke from rising."

"We're both still learning to be wizards," said Merry. She held out the empty bucket.

"Thank you," said Nyssia. "We won't be long." She left the cabin with Gruffyd close behind her.

Eynon and Merry chuckled when they overheard Gruffyd muttering, "What is it about wizards and rocks, anyway?" as he departed.

"Alone at last," said Eynon.

"I'm sorry we won't be by ourselves tonight," said Merry, "but it will be nice to catch up with Gruffyd and Nyssia."

"I don't know what she sees in him," said Eynon. "She's probably good enough with that blade of hers to slice up a bear before it could lay a paw on her."

"Of course," said Merry. "But she's wise enough to know that Gruffyd needs to be needed—and he also feels a bit jealous with you around."

"Me?" asked Eynon.

"You stole the heart of his childhood sweetheart," said Merry.

"I thought we gave our hearts to each other?" Eynon replied.

"We did, but Gruffyd is still learning that being a good man is more than being a strong warrior," said Merry. "Watch him and Nyssia together and you'll see. At first I thought the only reason she was interested in him was for his father's title."

"But not anymore?" asked Eynon.

"No," said Merry. "She's as much of a warrior as he is—they have that in common—but his love for her, his *joy* about them being together—is shifting her perspective. I think she loves him, too. He's not just a way for her to become a noble."

"I'm glad I didn't know you were a baron's daughter when I fell in love with you," said Eynon.

"So am I," said Merry. "It's good to know you don't want me just for my cider."

Eynon glanced up at the rafters. "Look!" he said.

Merry did and Eynon deftly switched their mugs and swallowed a long draught of cider while her attention was diverted. "You *do* want me for my cider!" she declared.

"My cider," said Eynon, holding the mug protectively.

Merry hugged him, gave him a tender kiss, and tried to switch the mugs back.

"Get your own cider," he said when she saw her maneuver had failed.

"I will," said Merry. "And it *is* my cider. You can see the Applegarth mark on the jug." She drank the water in the other mug—Eynon had finished most of it—and filled it halfway with the contents of the jug. "It's not Applegarth's Finest, but it's good. We had an excellent harvest two years ago."

"You're welcome to come back and try to distract me again," said Eynon.

"And you clearly *are* feeling better," said Merry. "I'm glad. Once we clean you up, you'll be fit as a fiddler."

"Why are fiddlers fit?"

"All that bowing keeps their hearts strong," Merry replied.

"So why don't we say *fit as an archer?*" asked Eynon. "They do a lot of *bow*-ing."

"Maybe you're not feeling that much better after all," said Merry.

"I'll be feeling a lot better if you distract me more."

Merry was about to sit on Eynon's lap when the door opened. Nyssia and Gruffyd bustled in. Gruffyd slammed a large, smooth, flat stone down on the table while Nyssia put the bucket of water by the hearth and moistened a length of white linen that she gave to Merry.

"Here's the stone you asked for," declared Gruffyd to Eynon. "How is it going to help us get our dinner?"

"Watch," said Eynon. He stood up and carried the stone to fireplace, setting it gently into the warm ashes. Putting one hand on his red magestone, Eynon willed heat to enter the stone. He recited three phrases, then a binding that tied his spell to the stone.

"Where did you learn that?" asked Merry.

"From one of Rōlin and Peregrína's books," said Eynon.

"It's a lot like what Doethan did enchanting a coin with cold," said Merry. "How does it work?"

Nyssia and Gruffyd were leaning in, watching the stone.

"I've taught it three commands," said Eynon. "Stone Hotter, Stone Cooler, and Stone Stop. Try the first one, Nyssia."

"Stone Hotter," she said, addressing the stone like a mother patiently instructing a child.

The stone began to glow red.

"Say it again," said Eynon.

"Stone Hotter!" Nyssia commanded in a louder voice.

"That should work for boiling," said Eynon. "One more would be good for frying and the first one will work for simmering."

"I assume Stone Stop is to make it stop heating completely, so we can transport it?" asked Nyssia.

"Yes," said Eynon. "And it cools instantaneous. You won't need to wait to pack it up. An extra Stone Cooler will even chill your drinks."

"Wonderful," Nyssia replied. "It will help us a lot on our mission."

"What *is* your mission?" asked Merry.

"Gruffyd can tell you while you help Eynon clean up," said Nyssia. "I'll get dinner started."

"Sounds like a plan," said Merry. She started to daub the wet linen cloth on Eynon's face and scalp.

Before Gruffyd could start explaining, something heavy slammed into the cabin door.

CHEEEE! came a high-pitched voice from the other side.

"What was *that?*" asked Gruffyd.

"Just a couple of *familiar* troublemakers," said Merry. "You'll need to clean the rest of the blood off your face and chest on your own, Eynon. I'll let them in."

Chapter 8

A King's Concerns

Nûd sat at a makeshift desk contrived by putting a wide board on top of a couple of rocks a dozen feet inside a side tunnel. He flicked beads on the frame of a calculator, making them clack together in a hypnotic pattern. From time to time he would say things that weren't quite words but gave the impression he wasn't pleased with the way the numbers were coming out.

Bonnie stood a few paces away and watched as Nûd's brows narrowed. She saw the tip of his tongue extend past his lips as he leaned forward and concentrated. "What the problem?" Bonnie asked when Nûd stopped moving beads for a moment.

"Everything," said Nûd. "We didn't think this through. We're going to run out of food for the cattle soon and will need to start slaughtering them, but if we do that, we'll go hungry later."

"Uh huh," said Bonnie encouragingly. He was clearly just beginning his list of challenges.

"Then there's the children," Nûd continued. "They need places in the sun to play, and the rest of us would do well with more light for that matter. It's not healthy for people to live underground too long." He took a breath that turned into a sigh and went on. "Our soldiers need space to drill, and we should really find somewhere to plant crops to get us through *next* year. On top of that, some people are taking more than their fair share of our stores. There's a lot of grumbling over certain people taking what's not theirs. If it weren't for so many people finding dark side passageways to make love, I'm sure we'd have fights breaking out every day. As it is, the fights we do have are over who's sleeping with whom."

"We're part of the finding dark side passageways group," teased Bonnie.

"Yes, and that's helped keep *my* disposition sunny, despite the lack of light down here," said Nûd. "I just wish I had answers for all these problems."

"The mages in our cave complex could make even more wizard lights," Bonnie suggested.

"Wizard light isn't the same as sunlight," said Nûd. "It illuminates but doesn't warm your face."

"I could make a fireball if you want your face warm," said Bonnie with a smile.

"I'd prefer you to make my face warm in other ways, dear lady," said Nûd.

Bonnie blushed, then laughed at herself for doing so. "Could we help you extend access to more parts of the complex?" she asked. "Maybe there are larger caverns to give us all more space?"

"I could use more space for drilling soldiers, but that's only a stopgap," said Nûd. "What we really need is a chance to get outside, but we can't because Sírénae's scouts might find us."

"We could let some people out at night, but that doesn't solve anything, does it?" asked Bonnie.

"No, and we can't risk it," said Nûd. "The emperor's wizards could be using night-sight lenses. We know they've made it this far south and west searching for us." He shook the calculator's frame, rattling the beads on thin rods inside it.

"Didn't you grow up a long way from here?" asked Bonnie. "Is it far enough away Sírénae's spies aren't likely to get there?"

"You mean Melyncárreg?" asked Nûd. "It's two thousand miles away. I doubt her spies would get there in less than a decade."

"Why can't we go there?" asked Bonnie.

"Because there are only a few small gates between Dâron and Melyncárreg," said Nûd. "Fercha has one from her tower, but I don't know the new code to open it. My grandparents have gates to the royal palace in Brendinas. Neither one of them has been seen for more than a month and I never knew their pass-phrases." Nûd rested his chin on the back of his left hand, looking like a child overdue for a nap."

"Aren't you forgetting something?" asked Bonnie. She pointed at the plain gold band on Nûd's right hand. "You have a way to contact Fercha whenever you need her."

"I do, don't I," said Nûd. He lifted his hand and contemplated the communications ring with a link to his mother. "We've spoken so infrequently over the years I'd forgotten I can contact her whenever I want."

"Why didn't you and your mother speak for so many years?" asked Bonnie.

"It was just a matter of trivialities, really," said Nûd. He took Bonnie's hand and stared at the cave's rough stone floor. "Fercha never told me about my father."

"Verro?" Bonnie confirmed.

"Correct," said Nûd. "She also forgot to mention the insignificant fact that I was heir to the throne of Dâron."

"I can see how such a thing might be disconcerting," said Bonnie. She kept her face a perfect mask for a few seconds before beginning to laugh.

"It's not funny," said Nûd. He tried to frown at her while the corners of his mouth kept turning up.

"Yes," said Bonnie. "It is." She tried to hold back more laughter and the laughs came out as giggles. "I'm glad you and your mother are back on good terms now," said Bonnie after she'd regained some measure of control.

"I wouldn't go that far," said Nûd. "Still, you're right. I should contact her and get her advice on the best way to return to Melyncárreg. We'll need her help to open a wide gate there anyway."

"Good," said Bonnie. "One thing though…" She put her hand on Nûd's shoulder.

"Yes?" asked Nûd.

"I thought you'd told me the air smells bad back where you grew up," she said. "You said something you breathed in made your voice sound funny. We don't want to send our people—especially our children—somewhere malodorous."

"There's plenty of better land for farming south of Melyncárreg," said Nûd. "South of Rôlin and Peregrína's *Travelers' Rest,* too. It's a good place for cattle if the wisent herds are grazing to the north and the soil is fine for raising wheat."

"That sounds ideal," said Bonnie. "Call Fercha right now and we can explore the territory and determine a good spot for the people in this cave-complex to go. They need to be back in the sun soon."

"Agreed," said Nûd. "Just give me a little time to work up my nerve."

"You're the king of Dâron," said Bonnie. "She's a Dâron wizard. You can pretend it's an official call."

"But she's my mother," Nûd protested.

"Hah," said Bonnie. "You haven't met *my* mother yet. If you think you need to worry about Fercha..."

"Very well," said Nûd. "You win." He pulled a specific ring from the second finger of his right hand and spoke a few syllables. Three chimes sounded and the ring expanded, revealing Fercha and Verro on the other side of the interface.

"Nûd," said Fercha. "What a surprise! And Bonnie. How nice to see you. Verro and I were just about to call you. We want to build wide gates to the lands south of Melyncárreg and move most of our people there."

Bonnie and Nûd began grinning. They tried not to look at each other because that made it worse.

"What did *you* want to talk about?" asked Fercha.

"I believe they'd reached the same conclusion," said Verro. He winked at Nûd.

"Oh," said Fercha. "That makes sense. It's obvious once you think of it. You'll go with him to scope out the best spots, won't you, Bonnie?"

"Of course," Bonnie replied.

"Excellent," said Fercha. "You can use the gate from my tower. Verro will *ad hoc* gate you there and I'll come along to give you the new code phrase for the gate, since I've locked it. We'll gate to your cavern and can take the two of you tomorrow morning, so you'll have plenty of time to be back for the council meeting."

"Can you transport Rocky, too?" Nûd asked Verro.

"I can, but it will take a separate trip," Verro replied. "He's a big fellow and it will be better if I'm riding him to do it. Will he accept me as a rider?"

"I'm sure he will if I ask politely," said Nûd.

"Thanks for all your help, you two," said Bonnie. She was still a little nervous when talking to Nûd's parents and squeezed Nûd's hand for reassurance. "We really appreciate it."

Fercha winked at Verro then spoke to Bonnie and Nûd. "By the way," she said. "Have the two of you set a date yet? The banquet hall at the castle in Melyncárreg would be a perfect spot for a wedding."

"What was that, mother?" asked Nûd, cupping his hand to his ear. "We can't hear you. The communications spell seems to be fading. We'll see you tomorrow." With another word of command, he severed the connection.

Chapter 9

The Great Purple Dragon

"Are you sure this is a good idea?" asked Kennig, the master illusionist. "It feels far too much like walking into a lion's den."

"A snow-leopard's den, more like it," answered his first cousin Hibblig, also a powerful mage. "We're not going underground with the rest of the scared mice in Tamloch or Dâron, and the empress is sure to be pleased to accept offers of service from two such strong wizards as ourselves."

Each of the two cousins had a non-wizard passenger standing behind them on their flying disks as they skimmed above the trees heading southwest from Riyas to Nova Eboracum.

"You don't think she'll have us killed?" Kennig replied.

"Not if we can also tell her the locations of some of the caverns where the scared rabbits are hiding," said Hibblig.

"First mice, now rabbits," teased Kennig. "Can't you be consistent in your choice of small mammal?"

"I can consistently blast you out of the sky," said Hibblig. "That's good enough for me."

"Only if you can see me," said Kennig. He disappeared and Hibblig laughed.

"You have me there," said Hibblig. "That was quite a nice job of illusion-casting back on the battlefield, too."

Kennig reappeared in the same position he'd previously occupied and the woman standing behind Hibblig with her arms around his waist decided to comment.

"It was my idea," said Princess Gwýnnett, her raven hair hidden under the hood of a black cloak. "I could tell Dârio and his allies wouldn't stop attacking us until they thought Túathal was dead."

"You looked quite foxy when you killed him, my dear," said Hibblig.

"Kennig disguised me as a rural baron's son with a vulpine face," said Gwýnnett. "Túathal's death was a complete illusion."

"I was surprised when Eynon managed to put a protective sphere around your fireball, Hibblig," said Kennig.

"Not that I actually threw it," said his cousin. "That was another one of your illusions. Thank goodness you have good reflexes and could adjust your simulation to fit *inside* the young wizard's sphere of solidified sound.

"It was quite convincing," said Gwýnnett. "Everyone is sure Túathal was vaporized."

"The reports of my death are greatly exaggerated," said the tall, thin older man behind Kennig. His normal speaking voice sounded like his face held a perpetual sneer. "Once we arrive, I'm confident Emperor Sírénae will be pleased to welcome us and provide sanctuary, as a courtesy from one ruling monarch to another."

Kennig and Hibblig exchanged a quick glance and half a smile. They knew Túathal was quite mad and only kept tractable by drugs from Gwýnnett's extensive pharmacopeia.

"I'm planning to get a job working for Umbrose," said Gwýnnett. "I'm sure he's one who can appreciate my many talents."

"Just not *those* talents," said Hibblig with a flash of jealousy.

"With Umbrose, I will focus on my expansive knowledge of poisons and medications to control minds," said Gwýnnett. "For the amorous arts, I will stick to what *you* can teach me."

"I'll certainly stick you well, my princess," said Hibblig.

Kennig stifled a laugh. His cousin was wrapped so tightly around Gwýnnett's finger he'd lost all perspective. It was clear that Gwýnnett was using Hibblig, though to be fair, he was using her as well. *I'll let them sort it out themselves,* thought Kennig. *They're enough alike in their manipulative personalities to deserve to be together. For myself, I hope I can get a job as a wizard for the emperor and avoid dying. Once that's accomplished, perhaps I'll find a wife who's worth having and settle down.*

Kennig imagined Gwýnnett rolling her eyes. "How do the two of you recommend we approach the city without being blasted out of the sky?" he asked Hibblig and Gwýnnett.

"I'm not really sure," said Hibblig. "Perhaps we could land to the north and approach on foot?"

"Don't be foolish," said Gwýnnett. "We're trying to impress Sírénae with our power. Kennig should generate some grand illusion to guarantee their attention."

"Like what?" asked Kennig.

"A huge golden ship sailing into the harbor?" Gwýnnett suggested.

"A phoenix immolating above the governor-general's palace?" offered Hibblig.

"A great, green dragon breathing fire," said Túathal, his lips drawn in a tight smile.

"I like it," said Kennig. "That reminds me. We can also tell the invading Roma about the two gigantic dragons who appeared outside Riyas. That could be important news for Sírénae if her people don't know much about them already."

"Good," said Gwýnnett, "since we're mostly guessing about which caves people are using to hide themselves."

"Sírénae doesn't need to know that," said Hibblig.

"Soon, with the Emperor's help, I will be returned to my throne," said Túathal.

"Yes, Your Majesty," said Gwýnnett. "Of course you will. By the way, it's time for your next pill."

"Oh good," said Túathal. "I like your pills. They make me happy."

Hibblig and Kennig brought their flying disks close together so Gwýnnett could pass a large white pill with flecks of green in it to Túathal. He popped it into his mouth, removed the cork from a wineskin, and washed the pill down with a stream of red liquid.

"Your pills make me feel invincible," said Túathal. He stretched his arms out as if accepting a crowd's adulation, then turned to face Gwýnnett. "I'm glad you're my queen," he said.

"So am I, Your Majesty," said Gwýnnett.

Túathal looked away and soon a vacuous smile crossed his face as the drugs took hold. The two wizards moved their flying disks apart and flew on towards Nova Eboracum.

Kennig looked to his right and confirmed Gwýnnett was rolling her eyes at Túathal's behavior. For all that Túathal wasn't right in the head, he was much happier with the former ruler of Tamloch standing behind him on his flying disk than he would be with transporting Gwýnnett. The woman made his skin feel like an army of ants was marching over it.

"What's it going to be, cousin?" asked Hibblig.

"The dragon, I think," said Kennig. "They're always impressive. What color would be best, do you think?"

"Green!" said Túathal, shouting into Kennig's ear.

"Blue," suggested Hibblig in a normal tone.

"Black would be mistaken for one of Sírénae's own fire drakes," said Gwýnnett. "That wouldn't be as novel. Red would get her attention but would clearly mark us as not being Roma."

"You're suggesting purple, then?" asked Kennig. "Or gold?"

"Definitely purple," said Gwýnnett. "It's the Roma imperial color and Sírénae should consider choosing it as a salute in her honor."

"Hmmm..." said Kennig. "I can do that. It will have iridescent, deep purple scales that shimmer in the light of the sun and wings that change hue from almost indigo near its body to lavender at their tips. "I'll use the big green dragon's head as my model for that part and will recolor the blue one's body for the rest."

"That should get their attention, cousin," said Hibblig. "With such a monster in the air above Nova Eboracum, we *could* walk up to the front gate of the governor-general's palace and stroll inside without anyone noticing."

"Take Túathal," said Kennig, moving his flying disk close enough to touch Hibblig's. "Then move off a quarter-mile or so. You can tell me if my illusion is working."

Gwýnnett helped Túathal shift flying disks, though she made sure to keep Hibblig's body between herself and the deposed king.

Kennig didn't blame her. Túathal made his skin feel like marching ants almost as much as Gwýnnett did. When Kennig saw that Hibblig and his passengers had moved far enough away, he began to shape the gigantic illusion in his mind. Bit by bit, piece by piece, he created a purple dragon that was even larger than the two he'd seen outside the walls of Riyas. When the construct was complete, he triggered his illusion.

Hibblig, Gwýnnett, and Túathal reacted in a way that convinced Kennig he'd succeeded in creating a truly impressive simulation of a dragon. Despite knowing better, his cousin reflexively threw up a shield of solidified sound. Gwýnnett gasped involuntarily and squeezed Hibblig tight enough to make him wince. Túathal, following the dictates of his own twisted mind, waved to the illusion then clapped his hands. Satisfied by their responses, Kennig fixed his illusion in place and kept his dragon flying while drifting his disk over to join the rest.

"Is it effective?" he asked.

"You know blasted well it is," grumbled Hibblig. His skill with illusion-magic was limited to changing his face, and he wasn't particularly adept at that.

Gwýnnett seemed to regain control of herself in the seconds it took for Kennig to return. She relaxed her grip on Hibblig. "That dragon simulation will do nicely," she said. "If Sírénae's not impressed, I'll be quite surprised."

"When she sees what I can do, she'll be impressed with me as well," said Hibblig.

"Of course she will," said Gwýnnett.

Kennig smiled without letting it show. Gwýnnett was using the same tone of voice on Hibblig as she had been on Túathal. He looked over at Túathal and dispelled his illusion. The dragon disappeared like a dream on waking.

"Help me get him shifted back onto your disk," Gwýnnett ordered Kennig.

The master illusionist moved his disk directly beside Túathal and extended a hand to help the former king across.

Gwýnnett leaned over and inserted another pill in Túathal's mouth. It was smaller than the last one. She squirted more wine past Túathal's lips and watched him swallow reflexively. "That should keep him some-what lucid for a few hours," she said. "He needs to be at his best when we meet the emperor." Gwýnnett spoke in Hibblig's ear. "Can you prevent him from speaking?" she asked.

"I can put a band of transparent solidified sound over his mouth, but others will still see his lips trying to move," said Hibblig.

"If you handle that, I can mask his face with a small illusion," offered Kennig.

"While still energizing your dragon?" asked Hibblig.

"Now that I've saved the dragon's design in my magestone, I can summon it back when I need it," said Kennig. "Taking care of a simple mask won't be a problem."

"If you say so," said Hibblig. "Just don't mess it up."

"You can count on me," Kennig replied.

Gwýnnett caught Kennig's eye and held his gaze for a moment. Kennig felt like he was being weighed and Gwýnnett was trying to decide to shift the object of her manipulation from Hibblig to himself. He was thankful she looked away and put both her arms around Hibblig again. Kennig resolved to be extra careful about checking everything he ate in the future.

They continued flying southwest and soon reached Isla Longa Sound. Kennig spotted Roma ships loaded with nets sailing east and spun a cloud illusion around his party to keep them hidden from Roma scout-wizards.

"Time to turn west to the city," said Gwýnnett.

The two mages shifted course and soon the wizard-lamp torch of the copper-clad New Colossus statue could be seen in the distance.

"It's time," said Gwýnnett.

Kennig regenerated his gigantic purple dragon a thousand feet ahead of them. He was still quite pleased with how well his design had turned out.

Gwýnnett inspected Túathal where he stood on the neighboring flying disk behind Kennig and brushed off the deposed king's robes with a few brisk strokes of her hands. "It's time to meet the emperor, Your Majesty," she said. She kept him facing away from the dragon illusion.

"Thank you, my queen," said Túathal.

A short interval later, the purple dragon flew over the city of Nova Eboracum. Kennig could hear screams and angry shouts coming from the streets below as the four of them skimmed along close to the ground and approached the gates of the palace.

As expected, no one paid attention to them. Their eyes were on the purple monster in the skies above.

When they were inside the front courtyard of the palace, seven black dragons descended to surround the great purple dragon. The one in the lead blasted Kennig's illusion with its fire. Kennig was ready for that, however. As soon as his illusion was dispelled, he regenerated it, so it seemed like the purple dragon only briefly blinked out, then reappeared.

Kennig had been in the governor-general's palace in Nova Eboracum once before when he provided the backdrops and scenery for a troop of traveling players. After landing and strapping his flying disk on his back, he guided his party through the corridors of the palace. As they'd hoped, all the imperial guards had abandoned their posts. Finally, they arrived at the room where Kennig expected to find Sírénae. Unbeknown to him, it was the same room where Doethan and Princess Rúth had been married a month before. Everyone there was staring out the window, including someone who must be the emperor.

A snow-gryffon hissed at the new arrivals, but she was chained, so Kennig wasn't worried about her attacking. He grinned, dispelled his purple dragon illusion overhead, and regenerated it right outside the room's windows where the emperor and her entourage were gazing. In an attempt to add verisimilitude, Kennig made the purple dragon roar. The sound was loud enough to shake the room's walls. His purpose accomplished, he snapped his fingers and the dragon disappeared.

Sírénae was the first to turn around. Kennig bowed. So did Hibblig, Gwýnnett, and Túathal.

"Your Imperial Majesty, I am Kennig, Master Illusionist, and these are my friends," he said. "I created the purple dragon illusion."

"Welcome to my court," said Sírénae as she stroked the feathers on her snow-gryffon's head to calm it. "I could use someone like you."

"Thank you, Your Imperial Majesty," Kennig responded.

"I'll say this," Sírénae continued. "You certainly know how to make an entrance."

Chapter 10

The Sweet Mission

Chee and Ace were sleeping under the table where Eynon, Merry, Nyssia, and Gruffyd were enjoying fresh berries from pricklebushes near the cabin. The sweet berries were an excellent complement to the venison stew and dumplings they'd just enjoyed for dinner. Merry and Eynon's familiars' bellies were full of a bat Ace had caught in the rafters and an apple from Merry's backpack, respectively. The rockhound and the raconette made comedic complementary low and high snuffling, snoring sounds as they slept.

"So why are you here?" Merry asked Gruffyd and Nyssia when she'd popped the last berry into her mouth, savored, and swallowed.

"You'll like the answer," said Nyssia. "It's sweet."

"So are you," said Gruffyd, smiling as his wife.

Nyssia smiled back. "Tell them," she instructed.

"We're here to fetch honey from my father's hives," said Gruffyd. "It will be a treat for our people stuck living underground..."

"...and prevent the invaders from getting it," added Nyssia.

"Wouldn't it have been easier to send a wizard with you to help transport the honey?" asked Eynon.

"Umm..." said Gruffyd.

"We wanted time alone together and volunteered to do it ourselves," said Nyssia quickly.

Merry smiled on the inside but didn't let it show. She imagined Gruffyd would be embarrassed about making love in a crowded cave system. "Maybe we can help you," she suggested. "Better yet, come to Applegarth and help *us*. We have more hives and there will be plenty of honey to share."

"That would be great," said Gruffyd. "You family's honey is delicious."

"Excellent," said Merry. "Where's your boat?"

"It's a canoe," said Gruffyd. "We pulled it up under the tree line so it couldn't be seen easily."

"And made a smoky fire?" asked Eynon.

"Told you," teased Nyssia.

"I wanted a hot dinner," Gruffyd protested.

"Now you can cook all you want without smoke," said Merry, nodding at Eynon to acknowledge his magical gift.

"Like I said," noted Nyssia. "The cookstone will help us a lot on our mission."

"We can start upriver in the morning," said Gruffyd.

"Tell you what," said Merry. "You can do that and Eynon and I will fly to Applegarth tonight to check on my family's orchards and our own hives. There should be enough light. We'll meet you at Applegarth when you get there." She turned to Eynon. "If you're feeling up to flying, of course."

"I'm much better," said Eynon. "I could fly to Brendinas tonight if I had to."

"Straight into one of the Emperor's new strongholds?" asked Nyssia with a hint of a laugh in her voice.

"Which is why I'll go with Merry to Applegarth instead," Eynon replied. "One battle is enough for a day."

Merry gave Eynon a quick kiss on his cheek and spoke to Gruffyd. "Do you have your family's pullstone?" she asked.

"Uh huh," said her friend. "But we won't have to force our way through the rapids by Rhuthro Keep. Our canoe is light enough to portage around them."

"Good, since there won't be anyone available to work the locks if you didn't want to run the rapids," said Merry. "Given time to portage, that means you should get to your estates by late afternoon tomorrow. Your pullstone was always faster than mine."

"I knew you were jealous," teased Gruffyd.

Merry shrugged to acknowledge the truth of Gruffyd's statement, then nudged Eynon gently with her elbow. "Ready to go?" she asked.

"Of course," said Eynon. "I'm as fit as a thieving archer."

"What?" asked Nyssia.

"It's a private joke," said Merry. "He wants to *take a bow* for his bad pun."

"If you say so," said Nyssia. "Safe travels and smooth flying." She caught Gruffyd's eye and raised her eyebrow conspiratorially.

Merry knew how to read that expression. Nyssia and Gruffyd would be glad to be alone in the cabin again, and Merry had plans for Eynon in her own feather bed once they reached Applegarth. "Come along you two," she said, gently nudging the sleeping familiars under the table. "We have things to do and places to be."

"Cheeee?" asked the raconette.

"Chee indeed," said Merry.

Ten minutes later Eynon, Merry, Chee, and Ace were flying up the Rhuthro Valley as the sun was setting behind the low mountains to the west. Chee was on Eynon's shoulder and Ace was curled around Merry's feet. Eynon nodded and the four of them instantaneously *ad hoc* gated to a spot a hundred feet above Applegarth's dock. Across the river, the wetlands were dotted with tall cattail stalks and colorful wildflowers.

"Here we are," said Eynon. He scanned the dock and its vicinity, searching in vain for the small, round coracle he and Merry's father had ridden in on the first day of his wander year. An extended investigation located a larger four-person coracle a dozen feet up in the ample foliage of a massive maple tree twenty yards from the bank.

"I still wish *I* could *ad hoc* gate," said Merry. "It would have taken me an hour to get here using line-of-sight gates."

"You may learn how eventually," said Eynon. He put an arm around Merry's shoulders and hugged her. She leaned into his embrace, causing Chee to switch to Eynon's other shoulder. The raconette was too wise to protest.

"Let's go to the back door," said Merry. "It's closer to my room."

Eynon followed Merry as she flew in a descending arc until they landed on a small courtyard paved with smooth river rocks behind her preferred home. Merry's parents, Derry and Mabli, were the baron and baroness of the Upper Rhuthro and had a stone castle farther upriver, but they preferred spending time at Applegarth, a one-story log manor house near their extensive orchards. Eynon thought Applegarth must be much more comfortable to live in than any cold, drafty castle.

"Before we go in, let me check the storage shed," said Merry. She put her flying disk on her back and walked to a large outbuilding, also constructed from whole logs, on the other side of the courtyard. Ace followed at her heels and Eynon and Chee trailed a few steps behind them. Merry lifted the heavy timber holding a pair of large wooden doors closed and opened the right-hand door just enough for her to enter.

Merry and Eynon walked into the shed single file, accompanied by their familiars. "Llachar!" Merry commanded and a brightly glowing ball of magical light appeared above her head, illuminating the dark interior.

Ace shifted form and flew into the rafters in search of bats and Chee scampered down from Eynon's shoulder and went off exploring the shed's interior. It smelled strongly of apples inside and Eynon assumed Chee would be searching in corners for any stray fruit that might have been overlooked by Derry or Mabli when they departed for the caves.

"Helloooo!" said Eynon, enjoying the way his voice echoed inside the shed. His eyes were still adjusting to Merry's wizard light, but he didn't see anything inside the shed—certainly not any of the barrels of cider, large and small, that had been inside it when he'd first come to Applegarth and helped Derry and Merry roll huge tuns of hard cider onto a boat to take to Tyford.

Merry tugged at Eynon's arm and led him toward the back wall. He saw that vertical wooden planks separated part of the shed from the rest.

"Here we are," said Merry, opening a door in the back wall.

Inside Eynon saw beekeeping implements, like the smokers Eynon always thought resembled watering cans, plus heavy gloves, netted hats, and a dozen wooden honeycomb frames hanging from pegs. In the corner was a honey spinner—a barrel lined with fired clay mounted on a mechanism that allowed it to be spun, forcing honey from combs. "All this equipment will make collecting your honey easier," he said.

"Yes, but the honey spinner is broken, and I doubt my father had a chance to fix it before the evacuation," said Merry.

"I don't think that will be a problem," said Eynon.

Merry could see him grinning and knew he had a few ideas on how to separate out honey using wizardry. "You can show me what you have in mind in the morning," she said.

"I could show you other things I have in mind tonight," he teased.

"You *are* feeling better," she replied.

"That was kind of you, leaving the cabin to give Gruffyd and Nyssia time alone together."

"I had an ulterior motive," said Merry. She took Eynon's hand and led him out of the shed, keeping the door open so Ace and Chee could get out when they were ready.

Eynon nodded. "That's what I thought," he said. He tilted his head and looked back at the shed. "I guess your father left the beekeeping supplies because there wouldn't be much need for them underground?"

"I expect so," said Merry. "There aren't many flowers in caves." She had a moment's concern that Eynon's thoughts were focused on practical matters, not amorous ones.

"Whereas here above ground, we have birds *and* bees?" asked Eynon. He was trying to keep his expression innocent but failing.

Merry grinned. "Very true," she said. "Would you like to study them both with me?"

"Absolutely," said Eynon, squeezing her hand. "I think you said something about a feather bed?"

Chapter 11

With the Fishing Fleet

Callidus stood next to Admiral Pixo near the prow of the admiral's flagship, the *Menodorus Maximus*. Overhead, Xaxidiánus soared, searching for threats in the waters of the Ocean nearby. Around the flagship bobbed three dozen transports recently repurposed to catch fish. This wasn't as much of a challenge as it might seem, since the ships had originally been built as fishing vessels and later commandeered by the emperor to transport legionnaires to Orluin.

"What do you think?" Callidus asked Pixo.

"I think we're in for quite a bit of rough weather," the admiral responded after confirming there were no crew members close enough to hear him.

Callidus looked up the sky, which was clear. He glanced behind him, to the west, and saw no clouds, then nodded at Pixo.

"Rough weather, then," said the magister. "That's as good a name to give it as anything."

"The weather has always been—challenging," the admiral continued. "But it's becoming more and more capricious as time goes by."

Callidus nodded. "Do you ever wish you'd stayed back on the other side of the Ocean?" he asked.

"Every day," said Pixo. "I'd even bought a villa on one of those Athican islands—the one with the circular harbor. It would have made a great place to retire."

"I was looking at a spot in the mountains of Éberria," said Callidus, thinking of the tower he'd once hoped to build in a high meadow with flocks of sheep for company.

"We're a pair of fools, aren't we?" said Pixo.

"That remains to be seen, my friend," said Callidus. "I hope neither one of us falls victim to *the weather*."

"Or her pet," said the admiral, breaking their previous pattern of coded speech.

The two men stood in companionable silence for a dozen breaths, enjoying the fresh salt air in their faces.

Callidus was the first to speak again. "There may really be a great dragon," he said. "Maybe even two of them."

Pixo's glance contained an unspoken, "How?"

"On our way to Nova Eboracum I was caught up in an Alliance raid to reclaim Valentius," said the magister.

"I heard about that, though I was with Second Fleet up the Moravon when it happened," the admiral replied.

"Your people must have told you about the great kraken that attacked the ships of the main fleet?" asked Callidus.

"They did," said Pixo. "It was puzzling because kraken never..."

"It wasn't a kraken," said Callidus. "It was a dragon—a *blue* dragon four times the size of Xaxidiánus or maybe even larger. I saw it underwater when I was pulled down with the *Cloud Dancer*. Alliance mages had strapped the ship to the back of the dragon with bands of solidified sound."

"I... see..." said Admiral Pixo slowly. He rubbed his chin then shook his head slowly from left to right. "You think this monstrously large blue dragon is attacking our fishing fleet?"

"Not the fleet itself," said Callidus. "The dragon has been remarkably careful not to kill any of our sailors."

"But the creature has done quite a bit to prevent us from returning home with any fish," added Pixo. "It's odd to think of a dragon that doesn't revel in death and destruction."

Callidus looked up at Xaxidiánus circling overhead. Pixo followed his eyes.

"Even *our* dragons mellow with age," said Callidus. "My friend Xaxidiánus now tries to rein in the worst tendencies of the junior dragons."

"While *bouts of bad weather* encourage them to bad behavior?" asked Pixo.

"Precisely," said Callidus.

"It sounds like you don't think this gigantic blue dragon will try to sink the fleet, just foul our nets," said Pixo.

"Or do whatever else is necessary to prevent us from bringing back any fish," Callidus added.

"What if I split up the fleet?" Pixo suggested. "The dragon can't be everywhere at once."

"That may work," said Callidus. "Though I expect this dragon can travel very quickly underwater. You'd have to keep your ships widely separated."

"And then I'd have to worry about the dragon deciding to sink individual ships if it couldn't foul their nets," the admiral mused. "I really don't want to lose any sailors if I can help it."

"Perhaps Xaxidiánus can fly a net-full of fish back to the emperor," Callidus suggested. "That would mollify her and be at least *somewhat* productive."

"Let's wait a few hours and see what happens after we cast our nets closer to Nova Eboracum," said Pixo. "The water isn't as deep here as it is by the northern cod banks. Maybe your huge dragon needs more room beneath it and won't bother us here."

"I wouldn't count on that," said Callidus. "I think the dragon is as smart as we are and possibly smarter."

"That's a sobering thought," said Pixo. "At least it isn't bent on destroying us." He narrowed his eyes. "I wonder why?"

"I blame Laetícia," said Callidus. "She never wants to take lives unnecessarily."

"Quintillius would be glad to slaughter us all?" asked Pixo.

"I never said that," said Callidus. "He's never avoided casualties in battle, but never sought them either. I remember him saying it's easier to rule a conquered province if you haven't killed too many future subjects in the process."

"That sounds like something Emperor Valens in Alexandria would say," noted Pixo.

"Laetícia and Valens are related, after all," said Callidus.

"On a completely different topic," said Pixo, "why did you decide to send my grand-niece to western Dâron? Not that I'm against indulging Sírénae's sweet tooth. When the emperor's temper is sweeter, it's smoother sailing for us all."

"She's a competent wizard," said Callidus. "I wanted to give her more responsibility and a chance for independent action to see how she handles it."

"That makes sense," said Pixo. "But she's so *young.*"

"Sixteen isn't young when you're sixteen," Callidus responded.

Pixo shrugged. "It's been a long time since *we* were that age, my friend."

"True enough," said Callidus. "We made our share of mistakes in our youth and she needs a chance to do likewise."

"I'm just a concerned great-uncle," said Pixo.

"Then you'll appreciate my ulterior motive for sending your niece west," said Callidus. "Umbrose has been trying to recruit her and I wanted to get her away from his far-from-benign influence for a week or two."

"Thank you," said Pixo. "I'm much happier with her working for you than for Umbrose."

"Let's see how happy you are if a giant Alliance dragon cuts your nets," said Callidus.

"Then we'd be in for a hurricane, I'm sure," said Pixo. "I never did like hurricanes."

Chapter 12

The King's Justice

"It's not fair," complained Duke Láidre to King Dârio in the spacious cavern that served as a throne room. "The people from Duke Néillen's former duchy have the caves on the right-hand fork while my people were assigned the left. I have more people and the caves on the right are twice as large as the ones on the left. We need more room."

King Dârio tried to look regal, or at least as regal as possible given that he was sitting on a rock, not a throne and his crown was boxed up in a storeroom for safekeeping. "I understand your dissatisfaction, Your Grace, but please understand that we are keeping the majority of our supplies in the caves on the right-hand fork. If anything, Duke Néillen's people have less room per person than yours do."

"That's another thing," said Duke Láidre, his voice growing louder. "My people are convinced Néillen's people are taking more than their fair share from our consolidated stores. I won't stand for that!"

"My marshals inventory our stores every week," said Jenet. She was standing behind Dârio holding the sheathed sword of state, point down, representing the King's Justice. "I can assure you; no one is stealing from our stores."

"That's not what my people say," Duke Láidre grumbled. "You can see that *their* faces are gaunt, while the people of Duke Néillen's former duchy are still well fleshed."

"Everyone gets the same share of food," said King Dârio.

"If your people are getting thin, I would look to those overseeing distribution of rations to your people, not the folk on the right-hand fork," added Jenet. She knew from Tibbo, one of the two proprietors of the *Blue Whale* inn, that the duke's people were expert raiders themselves, frequently stealing cattle from neighboring duchies and baronies.

"Are you questioning my word, *Earl Marshal?*" asked Duke Láidre. He was a tall man with dark, angry eyes, massive shoulders, and wrists that didn't narrow from years of swordplay. His hand went to the hilt of his sword.

"Not your word," said Jenet quietly. "Just your judgment in choosing quartermasters." Her hands shifted on the sword of state—not as a threat, but to indicate her readiness to counter Duke Láidre if he tried to attack.

The situation appeared ready to escalate swiftly when Dârio stood.

"Your Grace," said the king. "It's clear that enforced inactivity has made us all on edge. Let's get some exercise to help clear our minds. This chamber should be large enough for sword practice if everyone clears back against the walls. I know I would enjoy a practice bout against a swordsman of your prowess."

"Yes," said the duke, wheels turning behind his eyes. "I'd welcome a chance to *practice* with you," he said, his voice still tinged with the angry tone he'd used earlier.

Dârio turned to take his smaller and lighter personal sword from where he'd left it on top of a nearby rock. The finely crafted weapon had a bell-shaped guard and a long, thin blade quite unlike Tamloch's massive sword of state. Jenet smiled at him when his body blocked her face from Duke Láidre's view and held the sheath of his personal sword as he pulled the blade with a pleasant chime of metal against metal. She continued to support the sword of state.

Duke Láidre unsheathed his own blade with a less harmonious rasp and removed his sword belt, handing it to one of his retainers. The two men found spots to stand around thirty feet apart at the two foci of the oval chamber. The three dozen or so spectators sought safety behind spikes of rock coming up from the cave floor or down from the ceiling.

Jenet stood behind the rock Dârio had used as a makeshift throne. She admired Dârio in his gold tunic embroidered with green trefoils. It provided quite a contrast to the duke's black surcoat bearing a silver appliqué of an armored arm, bent at the elbow, holding a sword. Jenet's upper teeth pressed against her lower lip. Dârio was an excellent swordsman, but Duke Láidre was reputed to be the best with a blade of all Tamloch's nobles.

The duke was bending his knees and stretching his arms at the far end of the cavern. His sword was massive. It would have been a two-handed blade for anyone whose arms weren't as large and muscled as most people's legs. Láidre seemed to handle his weapon like it was half its weight. The duke was smiling at Dârio like an adult about to teach a child a lesson. "Are you sure you don't want to spar with practice blades?" Láidre asked Dârio, his voice echoing from the cavern's ceiling.

"Steel blades should do nicely," Dârio replied. "I'm sure you'll only hit me with the flat of yours and I doubt I'll be able to get through your guard at all."

A few of the people observing from the edges of the cavern laughed. They were all dressed in the black and silver livery of Duke Láidre's Duchy of Strongarm.

"Very well," said the duke. "We will see if Dâron's teaching swordmasters measure up to Tamloch's."

Jenet frowned. That comment was more than just its bare words. The duke's tone implied it was a critique of Dârio's right to be Tamloch's king. The two men, one in gold, the other in black, prepared to begin, but before they could start, Princess Rúth and Doethan entered the cavern from a passageway near Jenet.

"What's going on?" asked the princess.

"It should be obvious," said the duke from ten yards away.

"Duke Láidre and I are going to practice together, Aunt Rúth," said Dârio. "It will be an interesting learning experience."

Rúth nodded and faced the duke. She spoke softly, but her voice carried easily across the cavern. "Just keep the edge of your blade away from my nephew," she said. "We don't want to waste a healing potion because of your error."

"There's no need to worry about that," said Duke Láidre. "I always know precisely where my blade will go, though I have to hold it back since it always wants to cut off my opponents' heads."

"I know your sword's reputation," said Princess Rúth. "And yours."

"Healing potions don't work on decapitations," said Doethan, making his phrase seem light, not serious.

"He knows," Rúth replied.

Láidre smiled a feral smile and bowed at the princess.

Doethan glanced at Jenet. His expression told her he'd be glad to assist Dârio with magic, if necessary. Jenet moved her head slightly from side to side, telling Doethan not to interfere.

Dârio broke the tension. "Don't worry, this is just friendly sparring to stretch our muscles and test our skills," he said. Dârio looked down the cavern at Duke Láidre. "Ready, Your Grace?"

Láidre nodded.

Dârio looked over his shoulder at Jenet. "Give the word, Earl Marshal."

"Lay on!" said Jenet with the voice she used to shout orders on a battlefield.

Duke Láidre took ten paces forward, swinging his sword in front of him in wide, easy strokes like he was reaping a field.

King Dârio walked toward the duke with his right hand in his sword's bell guard positioned behind his head and his sword's long, flexible blade extending down his back, out of the duke's sight.

"Where's your sword?" asked the duke. "Are you afraid my wide blade will cut your narrow one in half if they cross?"

"No, Your Grace," said Dârio, stepping closer to the duke until they were only a few inches more than a sword's length apart.

Duke Láidre held his heavy blade in front of him with his elbow slightly bent, mimicking the pose of the arm and sword on the duke's surcoat. A small steel roundshield, no more than a foot across, was suddenly on the duke's left hand.

Where did that come from? Jenet mused. *Maybe Duke Láidre had been prepared and intentionally provoked this confrontation?"*

"Adding more protection?" asked Dârio. "From me?"

"It's another alternative to striking with my edge," said the duke. "And any advantage that can be gained in a fight, be it for practice or to the death, is worth taking. The important thing is to win, whatever it takes."

"I see," said Dârio. "I'll keep that in mind."

The duke extended his sword, testing Dârio and forcing the king to back away from its point. Dârio quickly approached inside the duke's reach and attempted to thwack Láidre's sword arm with the flat of his blade, but the duke retreated fast enough so Dârio's strike hit only empty air. Láidre pivoted on the balls of his feet and sent the flat of his sword arcing toward Dârio's ribs with substantial force.

The king started to dance away, but some of the power of the blow landed.

Dârio let out a gasp as air left his lungs involuntarily. He retreated and nodded at the duke, acknowledging a good blow. Dârio increased the distance between them and circled to Láidre's left, away from the duke's sword, with his own blade still hidden behind his back. The duke turned with him.

Suddenly, the sound of steel on steel rang through the cavern. Duke Láidre seemed puzzled. He hadn't struck a blow and he hadn't seen Dârio's sword except, perhaps, as a blur of metal that struck his roundshield. Láidre held his left arm and the round-shield out toward Dârio. "Is this what you want to hit?" he asked Dârio. "You should be aiming for me, not my buckler."

"My apologies, Your Grace," said Dârio. "I'll try to do better."

The king took two steps closer, inside the guard of the duke's sword, and Duke Láidre pulled his blade back and to the side so he could smack Dârio in the ribs again and bring a quick end to this contest. Instead, he felt the leather strap on his roundshield fail and heard the metal disk fall to the cavern's rocky floor with a clang.

"What?" said the duke. He backpedaled swiftly, sweeping his sword as he went to encourage Dârio to keep his distance. "Is that the game you're playing?" Láidre asked. "Try getting that close again and I won't use my sword, I'll just squeeze you until you lose your breath." The duke backed up until the far wall of the cavern was less than ten feet away.

"Forgive me if the only one I want to be that close to is Jenet," said Dario. He stepped to where Duke Láidre's roundshield had fallen and flipped it up with his foot, catching it in his left hand

and holding it by its edge. "You seem to have lost this, Your Grace," said the king, waving the small shield back and forth.

"I don't need it to spar with you," said Duke Láidre. He charged forward, angry as a taunted bull, and swung the edge of his blade toward Dârio's neck.

Jenet wanted to cry out but kept silent as she saw Dârio duck beneath the duke's blow. He hit the duke's left kneecap with the edge of the roundshield and the duke stopped his attack, allowing Dârio to step out of reach.

"You'll pay for that!" Duke Láidre shouted. "It's not fair using a shield to attack." He rubbed his left knee, keeping his sword extended to ensure Dario didn't come at him again.

"You seem to have an unusual concept of fairness for a noble who advocates winning, whatever it takes," said Dario. "Perhaps you don't understand fairness in distributing space and stores as well."

"I'll make you *eat* that roundshield," said the duke. "I won't stand for being lectured by a boy half my age."

"What about being instructed by your king?" asked Dario. "As you said earlier, any advantage in a fight is worth taking."

Duke Láidre's expression was puzzled again. He was used to fighting other nobles with broadswords, not striplings with toad-stickers. He had enough time to see Dario throw the roundshield toward him, but he saw the throw was poorly aimed and could tell it would miss. The last thing the duke heard before being struck in the back of the head and collapsing unconscious to the cavern's floor was the sound of his roundshield chiming as it bounced off the wall of the cavern behind him.

"Well fought!" exclaimed Princess Rúth, clapping her hands.

A few cheers—and gasps from retainers in silver and black—circled around the cavern.

Dario made a small bow, returned his sword to Jenet after giving her a hug, and walked over to where Rúth and Doethan were standing.

"I'm sorry, Aunt Ruth," he said, gesturing toward Duke Láidre. "It looks like we'll need a healing potion after all."

Chapter 13

New Servants

"Magister, an old man and woman are at the palace gate," said a servant standing in front of an imposing dark-stained wooden desk.

"Why is that any business of mine?" grumbled Umbrose from his seat behind the desk. He was displeased to be interrupted, having been about to take a ring from a series of steel spikes inserted into a black marble slab on his right. Umbrose planned to use the ring to contact an agent embedded with a group of Tamloch citizens hidden somewhere underground. "Tell them to see their legate if they have a problem."

"That's just it," said the servant. "They don't have a legate. They're not Roma."

"They're locals?" asked Umbrose. "Above ground?"

"It seems so to me," said the servant who couldn't be more than eighteen. "Shall I bring them in?"

"Please do," said Umbrose. "A chance for a thorough interrogation will be a welcome diversion."

"Shall I bring some food as well?" asked the servant. "They seem very thin and said they were hungry."

"No," said Umbrose. "At least not until we know if they have any value. We need to keep all *our* food to feed ourselves."

"As you say, Magister," said the servant.

A few moments later, the servant escorted an old man and an old woman into Umbrose's office. The man was as shriveled as a plum dried overlong in the hot sun. His head was as bald and speckled like a turkey's egg and he wore a faded blue workman's tunic that was more patches than original fabric. The old woman's face and hands were the only part of her that showed. She wore a motley gown and a once-white wimple that was now closer to gray in color. Her face was shadowed under a broad, blue, weather-stained felt hat with a wide brim.

From what Umbrose could see, the servant was correct. This pair of old crows were starving. Their cheekbones stood out like ship's prows from the sunken skin around them.

"What do you two want?" asked the magister.

"Food," said the man in an ancient, creaky voice

"And work," said the woman. "We're hungry, but we want to earn our way."

Umbrose scowled. He knew it was best to keep petitioners off balance. "Where are you from?" he asked.

"The palace," said the old man.

"Not *this* palace," said Umbrose, his tone turning the statement into a question.

"No, your mageness, sir," said the woman. "We worked at the king's palace in Brendinas. My husband was a groom and I helped in the kitchens."

"Why aren't you off hiding somewhere with all the other Dâroners?" asked Umbrose.

"We didn't go," said the old man.

"We hid in a closet," said the old woman. "We didn't want to live our last days underground, *umm,* or wherever the others went."

"We walked to my wife's sister's house near the Valley of Towers," said the man.

"But it was empty, and they had left," said the woman.

"Then we ran out of food," said the man.

"We ate some berries and wild onions," said the woman.

"But thought we might get work at the only palace we know of that has people in it," said the man.

"Seeing that we have experience in service and all," said the woman.

"We've had legions in Brendinas for nearly a month," said Umbrose, caught up in their tale despite himself.

"They must have arrived after we left, Your Mage-estry," said the man.

"We couldn't stay for long without food," said the woman.

"What are your names?" Umbrose asked. He'd learned that knowing a person's name made them easier to question.

"I'm Côbb and my wife is Réah, Your Wizardness," said the man.

Umbrose shook his head slightly at the man's mangled use of his title. It was easy to see why he'd been assigned to work with horses, not nobles. "Why should I hire the two of *you?*" he asked. "We have plenty of servants already."

"Because we know things," said the old woman. "We know where to find caves near Brendinas."

"You do?" said Umbrose. If he'd had less self-control the corners of his mouth would have turned up.

"I hauled manure to them," said Côbb.

"Why would you take manure to caves?" asked Umbrose.

"For the mushrooms," said Réah. "You know how to get the best mushrooms, don't you?"

"Actually, no," said Umbrose, realizing that hole in his knowledge with surprise. "Tell me."

"Keep the spores in the dark and cover 'em in horse manure," said Côbb.

"Interesting," said Umbrose, not sure if he'd really wanted more details about applied mycology beyond what he needed to prepare poisons. "I hope you wash them before you serve them."

"There's no need," said Réah. "We cut off the bottom of the stems before we serve them.

"Good to know," said Umbrose. He resolved to avoid eating fresh mushrooms in the future and glared at the pair of old birds. "Can you take my people to these caves?"

"I'd like to, Your Magic-ness," said Côbb. "But I don't know if I can manage the trip. I'm *so* hungry I can barely stand."

"That's easily addressed," said Umbrose. He clapped his hands and the same servant who'd brought in the old man and woman appeared at the door. "Get this man something to eat," Umbrose commanded.

"And my wife," said Côbb.

"If I must," said Umbrose. "Get them both something, then."

"Immediately, magister," said the servant who disappeared and reentered with a tray of food and a pitcher so promptly that Umbrose knew it had been prepared in advance.

Behind his impassive expression Umbrose's mind was not displeased. He appreciated servants who took initiative, up to a point.

Côbb and Réah ate dark bread and hard cheese like bears emerging from their dens in the spring. Umbrose turned away and spoke to the servant, conveying instructions to have two of his spy-wizards report here promptly.

"You'll be flying back to Brendinas in a few minutes so you can show us these mushroom caves," said Umbrose.

"Very good, Mage-ister," said Réah. "I'll bring back some baskets of fresh mushrooms to prepare for dinner."

Umbrose was about to say, "That won't be necessary," but remembered Sírénae was particularly fond of them. "Very well," he said.

"We will start our new jobs when we return," Réah continued.

"Since we have to earn our keep," said Côbb. He touched his hand to the center of his forehead and bowed to Umbrose.

The spymaster was impressed by the way the old couple had played him. He'd keep them around as long as they continued to be useful. They might know the locations of more caves, after all, and what were two more mouths when they needed to find enough food—long term—for two hundred thousand.

Two wizards in the black and gray livery of Umbrose's corps of spies entered his office and Umbrose sent them south with the old couple. As Côbb stepped out into the corridor, Umbrose heard him talk to one of his wizards.

"We're flying?" said the old man. "In that case, I know a shortcut to mushrooms."

While the servant cleared up the mugs and dishes that had held the drinks and food Côbb and Réah had voraciously consumed, Umbrose pondered the wisdom of offering the old man and woman the same generous bonus Sírénae had told him to extend to his spies embedded in the locals' caverns.

Maybe a big reward would lead to more progress finding hidden enemies and obtaining more substantial stores than a few baskets of mushrooms?

Chapter 14

Stranger Things

"What's that marvelous smell?" asked Merry as she entered Applegarth's kitchen.

"Breakfast," said Eynon. "I thought I'd make something unusual—and green—to start the day."

Merry stepped close to Eynon by the hearth, hugged him, and stared into the round, long-handled cast-iron pan where her lover was stirring the source of the mouthwatering smell. "Unusual?" she said. "Cattail sprouts aren't unusual. We eat them all the time in the spring."

"They're unusual to me," said Eynon. "There aren't a lot of them in the Coombe, but you have thousands of them growing along the river. I added some wild onions, too. Unfortunately, it's too soon for leeks."

"I expect my mother saw to it that all the early leeks were harvested and taken underground," said Merry. "They won't grow much without sun, though." She smiled at Eynon. "And it's not thousands, it's millions."

"Millions of what?" asked Eynon.

"Cattails," Merry replied. "There are hundreds of thousands of them on this side of the river, but more like millions on the east bank where it's swampy. There are millions of wildflowers blooming over there, too."

"And millions of bees as well?" asked Eynon.

"Sixteen dozen hives worth at last count," said Merry. "And that's just the ones in our boxes, not counting wild hives."

"Which means plenty of honey to harvest?"

"I expect so," said Merry. "I worry about what we'll collect it in, since my father seems to have taken all the jugs we used to store it."

"I have an idea about how to solve that problem," said Eynon. "For now, let's focus on breakfast. I want to build my strength up."

"After I wore you out last night?" teased Merry.

"I *am* recovering from an injury," Eynon protested. He shifted position and Merry noticed flatbread cooking on a soapstone griddle on the embers in the back of the hearth.

"Where did you find our old griddle?" she asked.

"Off to one side of the fireplace," said Eynon. "Its black bottom was out, and it blended in with the other stones."

"Our good fortune, then," said Merry. "What about the frying pan?"

"I brought that with me in case I had a chance to do some cooking," said Eynon.

"That's definitely your style," said Merry. "You'll make some lucky person an excellent husband someday." She tried to keep from smiling but only partly succeeded.

"Thank you," said Eynon. "Do you have any particular person in mind?"

"I might," said Merry. She hugged Eynon again and gave him a peck on his cheek. "How soon until the cattail shoots and wild onions are done?"

"They're done now," said Eynon. "I made lots. I'm just waiting for the second batch of flatbread to finish browning."

"I'd set the table, but my parents took all the plates and cups," said Merry.

"We have our own mugs," said Eynon. "You can fill them from our water skins, then we can refill our skins from the river after breakfast."

"Sounds like an excellent plan," Merry replied. "I'll add a few squirts of cider for flavor."

"Great," said Eynon, who was focused on the griddle. "Do Roma eat cattails?" he mused.

"I expect so," said Merry, "though I'm not sure if they grow across the Ocean."

"They do, and I'm quite fond of them," came a pleasant alto voice from the doorway leading to the back porch. "May I join you for breakfast? I've got jerky."

Eynon and Merry turned to see a young woman of medium height with short, coal-black hair wearing wizards' robes dyed a deep purple and covered in intricate embroidery. Her obsidian magestone glinted in a silver setting on a choker around her neck and she was holding out a small canvas bag.

"Is that the jerky?" asked Eynon. His good manners seemed to circumvent his sense of caution. "What kind?"

"Beef," said the woman. She seemed to be fifteen or sixteen, about the same age as Eynon and Merry.

"Who are you?" asked Merry. Her sense of caution was a good deal stronger than Eynon's as she interrogated the new arrival. "Where did you come from? What are you doing here? What do you want?"

The young woman smiled at Eynon and Merry, then tossed her canvas bag to Eynon, who caught it, opened it, and confirmed its contents.

"The jerky is from across the Ocean," the young woman told Eynon. "I think it's from a ranch in north Afarika." She turned her head to respond to Merry. "My name is Celéri. I'm based in Nova Eboracum now, though I'd been happily living in Nárbo for the past three years. My uncle Pixo is high admiral of the emperor's fleets. I'm here to spy on the allied kingdoms—and I want some breakfast. It smells wonderful."

"Thank you, I'm Eynon and she's Merry," said Eynon. "We're from Dâron."

"I figured that out from your sky-blue wizards' robes," said Celéri.

Eynon noticed Celéri had an aquiline nose and dark brown eyes accented with some sort of purple paint.

"Don't be *nice* to her," said Merry. "She just told us she's a spy."

"Spies have to eat, too," Eynon replied. He deftly floated a piece of flatbread off the soapstone griddle with a plane of solidified sound and filled it with fried cattail shoots and spring onions before handing it to Celéri. Merry's mouth was hanging open, so Eynon filled another piece of flatbread, rolled it up, and pretended to insert it in Merry's mouth. She intercepted it, caught the savory item with her fingers and bit off an inch with an audible snap of her teeth that Eynon knew meant to send him a message.

"This is quite good," said Celéri. She hadn't quite finished chewing her most-recent bite and the distortion of her continued mastication reinforced her words. "I'd be glad to have you as a future husband."

"How long have you been listening to us?" asked Merry.

"Only a few minutes," Celéri responded. "If you were trying to hide your presence, you shouldn't have a started a fire in your hearth."

"Eynon!" Merry exclaimed. "We just made a cookstone for Gruffyd and Nyssia. Why didn't you make one for *us* and use it?"

Celéri tried not to smile and covered her mouth to hide one that escaped. Merry's head swiveled as she tried to decide whether she wanted to glare more at Eynon or at Celéri for her *future husband* comment. Eynon just shifted the weight of his tall, thin frame from foot to foot, looking like he'd rather be up in the rafters with Ace and Chee.

"I'm sorry," he said. "I forgot."

"You're not in the Coombe anymore and this isn't peacetime," Merry continued. "You have to be more cautious."

"Of course," said Eynon. "I'm really, really sorry. Breakfast is cooked now anyway." He extinguished the fire in the hearth—it was mostly coals now—using a hemisphere of solidified sound. "Who wants jerky?" he said, facing the women again and holding out the bag Celéri had given him.

They both smiled this time since Eynon was so obviously trying to change the subject. Merry rolled her eyes and took a piece of jerky from the bag. She didn't eat any until she watched Celéri take a piece of her own, then bite, chew, and swallow. Eynon noticed what Merry was doing and copied her.

"I wouldn't poison you," said Celéri. "You're too valuable as sources of information—and that jerky and some travel bread is all I was given to eat on my scouting expedition."

"Your *spying* expedition, don't you mean?" said Merry.

"Scouting, spying, they're much the same," said Celéri. "It's just a matter of perspective."

"She's right, you know," said Eynon. He closed his mouth as soon as he saw Merry's expression and turned back to assemble more cattail-shoot-and-flatbread roll ups.

"All I know is that you're a representative of the Siren Hawk," said Merry. "That's enough for me to be sure you're bad news."

"I can understand that perspective," said Celéri, grinning at the chance to use the word a second time. "There are some of us who aren't that fond of our emperor, either. And I'll share some *good* news with *you*. Your plan to starve us is working. We'll have to start butchering elephants in a few more days."

"Really," said Eynon. "I don't know what to think about that. I'm happy and sad at the same time. I've never seen an elephant."

"I've seen mastodons," said Merry. "There's a small herd of them in the mountains north of Rhuthro Keep and sometimes they come down to the river to drink."

"I've only seen pictures of mastodons in books," said Celéri. "They're hairy and their proportions aren't the same as elephants."

"I've seen pictures of elephants, mastodons and mammoths in..." Eynon began.

"Robin Goodfellow's *Peregrinations*," said Merry and Celéri in unison.

Merry gave Eynon a warning glance that he correctly interpreted meant not to say anything about Rōlin and Peregrína. All three of them laughed.

"I was sent to scout, or *spy out* three things," said Celéri. "First, where people from the kingdoms and Occidens Province were hiding. Second, where additional sources of food could be found, like all the cattails in the marshland across the river." She waved a hand toward the east. "And third, where we could get honey for the emperor."

"The emperor has a sweet tooth?" asked Eynon.

"The emperor has whims," said Celéri. "Magister Callidus says Sírénae's whims are more important than her orders, because they keep her in a good mood."

"Magister Callidus?" asked Merry. "I met him in Nova Eboracum. I like his dragon."

"Xaxidiánus is impressive," said Celéri, "and he and Magister Callidus have worked together for many years, but Xax doesn't belong to the magister. All our dragons belong to the emperor."

"Our dragons belong to themselves," said Eynon. When he realized what he'd said, he slapped his hand across his mouth and tried to avoid looking at Merry.

"Don't worry, you're not giving away too much of a secret that you have dragons," said Celéri. "Magister Callidus told me about the rumors of huge green and blue dragons as big as castles."

Eynon was embarrassed when he felt a square of transparent solidified sound against his lips, projected by Merry. He wasn't going to tell Celéri that Viridáxés and Zûrafiérix weren't quite *that* big, though they were probably the size of a long castle wall. He passed out more roll ups and ate one himself, after signaling to Merry the shield across his lips was no longer necessary.

"I suppose you're going to return to Nova Eboracum and tell Magister Umbrose all about us—and the cattails," said Merry.

"Not at all," said Celéri. "I work for Magister Callidus, not Magister Umbrose, and the two of them have different aims. Callidus and my great-uncle Pixo want what's best for the Roma. Umbrose and the emperor want what's best for themselves."

"Like King Túathal," said Eynon.

"The king of Tamloch?" asked Celéri.

"The former king," said Eynon. He pressed his lips together so he wouldn't say anything about Dârio—or Nûd.

"That's right," said Celéri. "They told us something about that, but I had a book in my lap during that briefing and might have missed it."

"What will you tell Magister Callidus?" asked Merry. "Assuming we allow you to leave."

"Allow me to leave?" said Celéri. She flexed her shoulders and seemed a few inches taller. "You *don't* want to fight me. I'm a highly trained Roma battle mage." She summoned a blazing fireball as large as a flying disk inside her outstretched arms, then dispelled it with a *pop* as if it hadn't existed.

Merry watched Celéri take a deep breath and consciously calm down. She stared at Celéri until the other woman answered Merry's question.

"I'll tell Magister Callidus everything," said Celéri, "but I doubt if he will tell Umbrose more than a tenth of what I tell him."

Merry and Eynon didn't react to Celéri's fireball, not even to smile. Celéri didn't know who they were and Merry promised herself she wouldn't let Eynon reveal their identities.

"You must know *lots* of battle magic," said Eynon. "I'm just an apprentice wizard, and my master hasn't started teaching me offensive spells yet."

Now it was Merry's turn to hide a smile. Eynon was finally understanding their situation and feeding misinformation to Celéri.

The Roma mage looked at Merry, then at Eynon, then back to Merry. "He's handsome, don't you think? Does he do more than cook?" She winked at Eynon.

"Excuse me?" said Eynon. His face turned red, though it could have been a reflection from the firebricks lining the hearth's interior.

"He does what he wishes," said Merry, her voice suddenly turned as cold as a snow-fed stream.

"I thought so," said Celéri. "You're mates. I won't get in the way, unless I'm invited. You're quite handsome, too, you know," she told Merry. "I'd even say beautiful."

Now Merry's face went red. "Uh, thank you. You, too," she said.

"You're both so nice," said Celéri. "Each of you deserves a gift." She removed two small pins from the collar of her robes and attached one to Eynon and Merry's robes in turn. They were silver, with green cloisonné stalks and dozens of tiny amethysts forming blossoms for sprigs of lavender. Each pin was no longer than a little finger.

"They're beautiful," said Merry. "Thank you."

"Something beautiful for some*one* beautiful," said Celéri with a smile.

Merry looked away, then stepped close to Eynon and took his hand. "I assume you'll be heading back to Nova Eboracum now," she told Celéri.

"Not quite yet," Celéri replied. "With all the marsh flowers on the other side of the river there are bound to be bees and I need to find honey for Sírénae. My spying expedition will be a sweet success if I can satisfy the emperor's iron whim and return with some."

"We were just about to harvest honey from hives on the east bank," said Eynon. He paused as he felt Merry's fingernail dig into his palm. "The faster you get what you need, the quicker you can be on your way," he continued.

Merry nodded. "You can help us with the harvest and have a share of what we collect. With luck, you'll have enough in a few hours and won't have to spend the night."

"That sounds like fun," said Celéri. "Though with luck of a different sort perhaps I *will* need to spend the night." She rubbed her chin. "I've never robbed the bees before. That's what we called collecting honey back in Nárbo. Our honey was made from lavender flowers and had the most delicious aroma." Celéri licked her lips and stared at Eynon and Merry. They didn't meet her gaze.

"The sooner started, the sooner done," said Eynon.

"That's from Ealdamon's *Epigrams*," said Celéri. "I read a copy when I crossed the Ocean."

"It's full of good advice," said Merry. *"Honey and maple syrup are both sweet, but trees don't sting,"* she recited.

Celéri laughed. "I understand," she said. "The queen bee will defend her hive."

"That's not how bees work," began Eynon. Merry stabbed his palm again and he stopped and thought. "Oh," he said.

"Come on, then," said Merry. "Let's get started. I used to work for this household and know where the beekeeping equipment is kept." She pulled Eynon toward the door to the back porch.

Celéri followed. She caught up with Merry and Eynon before they left the kitchen, tugged on Eynon's sleeve, and planted a quick peck of a kiss on his cheek. "That's because I like you," she said. "And I wouldn't want to distract you once we were collecting honey."

Eynon didn't say anything. Quick strides of his long legs took him out onto the back porch and then across the yard toward the storage shed well ahead of the two women.

Merry hadn't seen the kiss but deduced what must have happened from Eynon's reaction. She didn't say anything to the other woman, but smiled to herself, hoping Celéri wasn't skilled in manipulating solidified sound, since there weren't any thick protective tunics in the storeroom and the bees on the east bank were famed for aggressively defending their hives. She wondered if Celéri would still be interested in Eynon—or in her—with her face, arms, legs, and torso swelled up in a dozen places. *I can only hope she doesn't have a healing potion with her,* thought Merry.

Eynon walked on, oblivious to Merry's thoughts. He did his best to forget the feeling of Celéri's lips on his cheek and walked even faster. His mind was spinning as he distracted himself by coming up with ways to use magic to make collecting golden honey along the Rhuthro as easy as separating gold dust from the gravel in the river near Melyncárreg.

Chapter 15

The King's Wisdom

Thwack!

Wooden swords crossed and Nûd's blade didn't snap back into position fast enough.

"Keep your guard up," said Duke Háiddon.

"Sorry," said Nûd.

"Less talking, more sparring," the Duke continued as he threw a combination of blows at Nûd and forced him half a dozen paces back along an isolated underground passage lit only by a pair of portable wizard lamps.

Wap! Thwack! Smack!

"Ouch!" said Nûd. "You caught my ribs that time."

"All the more reason to keep your guard up," said Duke Háiddon. "Let's take a break." He let his sword fall back against his shoulder and it made a *clack* as it landed.

The practice blade and its mate in Nûd's hands were made from *boo*-wood, a strong, light reed that grew locally in the southern provinces of Dâron and had originally been imported across the Ocean from Indja, on the far edge of Roma's Eastern Empire. Splitting the staves of *boo*-wood into quarters and binding back them together with heavy thread helped the blades make a sound like an axe hitting a tree when they struck. You knew you'd been hit more by sound than by impact—unless you were hit by someone with the strength and skill of Duke Háiddon. He'd pulled his blow at the last second so the shot to Nûd's ribs had merely stung, not ached.

"Thank you for agreeing to a preliminary training session here in the caves," said Nûd. "I'll arrange for somewhere more private with more room soon, but I wanted to get started with your evaluation of my skills right away. I've got a *lot* to learn before I'm any good with a sword."

"You're doing better than I expected, really," Duke Háiddon replied. "Your defense is sound, and your offense shows promise, though you seem to have forgotten swords have edges and points."

"I think I'm treating my sword as a quarterstaff," said Nûd. "That helps with blocking, but it feels odd to have my hands out of position."

"If you hold a real sword like a quarterstaff, you'll lose fingers," said the duke. "I'm glad you didn't forget and try to hold your *boo*-wood blade that way. I don't want you learning bad habits."

"And I'd prefer to keep my fingers," said Nûd. "I guess my experience with a quarterstaff explains why I'm not taking advantage of my blade's edge, anyway. It doesn't matter which side of a quarterstaff I used to disarm or bash my opponent."

"Quarterstaffs don't have points, either," said Duke Háiddon, "unless you've used one with a spike at the bottom."

"I *have* used ones with spikes," said Nûd. "I used them to kill basilisks back in Melyncárreg. I'd fit them with two-foot round shields a few feet up the shaft from the spike and would stare at the shield, not the basilisk, when it was time to stick 'em."

"I'm glad we don't have basilisks in Dâron," said the duke. "They seem like thoroughly nasty creatures."

"They are," said Nûd. "And they're especially dangerous in large numbers when you don't know where to look. Remind me to tell you a story about Eynon and basilisks someday."

"I doubt if you could surprise me with *any* story about Eynon," said Duke Háiddon. "That young man could fall into a castle privy and come out clean holding the lost crown of King Dâroth the First in his hands."

"It seems that way, doesn't it," said Nûd. He grinned at the older man.

"And Baron Derwen's daughter is the same way," the duke noted. "She goes down the Rhuthro with Eynon and turns into one of the best illusionists in the kingdom."

"My mother had something to do with that," said Nûd. "Along with Doethan and Inthíra."

"You're right, they did," said Duke Háiddon. "Getting back to your training, I'm glad you've had some experience sticking basilisks.

Fighting from horseback is much more lance and spear work than sword and shield—and a quarterstaff with a spike is more than halfway to a spear."

"I have no intention of ever fighting on horseback," said Nûd.

"But it's expected—even required—for a nobleman, especially a king," said Duke Háiddon. "Kings must be mounted."

"I'll be mounted," said Nûd with a smile. "But I'll be riding Rocky, not a horse."

Duke Háiddon rubbed his chin. "I can see how being astride a black wyvern would be even more impressive than riding a warhorse," said the duke. "You and Rocky will have to train with the king's guard, so *their* mounts don't shy fighting next to a wyvern."

"I don't think that will be much of a problem, Your Grace," said Nûd. "I plan to fight from the air, not on the ground, if I can manage it. I'll have my crossbow with me so I can make myself useful."

"Hah!" said the duke. "I can see you surprising more than one enemy wizard that way." He narrowed his eyes for a moment and looked thoughtful. "Hmm…" said Háiddon. "Do you think Rocky might consent to being painted blue so it would seem like you're riding the kingdom's symbol."

"I doubt that Rocky would put up with being painted," said Nûd. "But maybe Merry or Inthíra or Eynon could make Rocky *seem* to be dark blue."

"Maybe you could ask one of them after the council meeting?" Duke Háiddon suggested.

"I will," said Nûd. "Just remember, Rocky is a wyvern, not a dragon."

"I doubt your subjects will be counting Rocky's legs, Your Majesty," said Háiddon.

"True enough," said Nûd. "It matters more out west where we have wild dragons *and* wyverns to worry about. In Melyncárreg, dragons hunt in wings or packs while wyverns hunt alone. And wyverns can't speak, while dragons can."

"Wyverns aren't intelligent, then?" asked Duke Háiddon.

"Don't let Rocky hear you say that," teased Nûd. "Let's just say that wyverns can't speak. I'm convinced Rocky understands quite a bit."

"I expect you're right," said the duke. "Are all the preparations in place for the meeting?"

"Bonnie says they are, and I trust her," said Nûd. "It's not until the day after tomorrow and I'm eager to go through the gate at Fercha's tower with Bonnie first and identify places south of Melyncárreg where our people can settle temporarily. We *really* need to get them out in the sunlight, especially the children. Our supplies of fish liver oil are running low."

"Our stock would be glad to be somewhere other than caves as well," said Duke Háiddon. "And I'd feel a lot better if we could get some crops in the ground *somewhere,* so we don't risk starvation ourselves. It would be ironic if our people *and* the emperor's forces all starved at the same time."

"I wish we could have just gated everyone to Melyncárreg and Three Mountains Valley initially, but it was much faster building gates to local caverns," said Nûd. "We couldn't be sure how far west the emperor would send scout-wizards, either."

"I understand," said Duke Háiddon. "You did what was necessary to ensure the safety of our people and we *do* have enough stored supplies to last us quite a while. I just don't want us stuck with only our emergency barrels of beans and twice-baked biscuits to sustain us months from now."

"I won't let that happen," said Nûd. "The growing season is shorter near Melyncárreg anyway, so we can get seeds for fast-growing plants in the ground and still harvest crops. Game is plentiful, too, so we'll have lots of meat."

"More wisents?" asked Duke Háiddon.

Nûd nodded. "A *lot* more wisents—and flathorns and deer and mountain goats—plus rabbits for a less challenging sort of game to capture."

"Excellent," said the duke. "Now let's get back to testing your skill with a sword." He looked at Nûd who was standing with his knees slightly bent but faced Duke Háiddon directly, instead of from the side. "Stance, Nûd, stance! What did I tell you about presenting the smallest target for your opponent?"

"Sorry," said Nûd.

Thwack!

The *boo*-wood blade clacked against Nûd's ribs again.

"Stop saying you're sorry," Duke Háiddon commanded. "You're a king. It's not king-like to apologize."

"We will have to agree to disagree on that, Your Grace," said Nûd. "Kings must *serve* their people, and that means offering apologies when we fail."

"Kings also have to *inspire* their people, and it's hard to do that if you're saying *sorry* all the time."

"Sorry," said Nûd. Then he laughed and Duke Háiddon did, too. "I understand," said Nûd. "I'll try not to use that word so often."

"Good," said Háiddon. "Because I plan to thwack your ribs every time you do—with a sword, if I have one, with a stern glance if not."

"I don't know which one would hurt more," said Nûd, feigning a pained expression.

"You're as bad as Jenet," said Duke Háiddon, reflecting the look on Nûd's face back at him.

"I'll take that as a compliment," said Nûd. "Shall we continue?"

"We might as well," said the duke. "See if you can do a better job of guarding your ribs."

"Yes, Your Grace," said Nûd.

Your Grace seemed to echo off the walls and both men could hear someone calling, "Your Grace, Your Grace," in the distance.

Nûd and Duke Háiddon had time to stow their *boo*-wood swords behind a boulder before a royal retainer arrived with a man who seemed to be a prosperous farmer striding along beside him.

"There you are!" said the farmer, as if the king and duke were his personal servants. "You've *got* to do something about my cows!"

"What's wrong with your cows?" asked Duke Háiddon.

"For one thing, there are a lot fewer of them," said the farmer. His face, burned by years in the sun, grew redder as he spoke. "Why are *my* cows always the ones being chosen for slaughter? And what are you going to do about getting them green grass? Half my herd is wasting away from insufficient fodder and their milk is drying up. I'll lose most of my cheese production for the year at this rate. You've got to *do* something about it."

Duke Háiddon glanced at the boulder where his practice sword was hidden as if he wanted to retrieve it and smack the farmer with several firm blows to the ribs or the skull. He was about to speak when he felt Nûd's hand on his arm.

"I'm sorry to hear of your troubles," said Nûd. He saw the hint of a smile flash across Duke Háiddon's face at his use of that particular word. "You are, of course, welcome to leave the caves and make your way back to your home on the surface with your herds."

The farmer faced Nûd and put his fists on his hips. "If I do that, I'll be captured by the emperor's troops and enslaved. They'll take all my cattle and leave me less than nothing."

Nûd nodded. "I can see you're a wise man—and a practical one. We appreciate your sacrifice to help everyone by allowing your cows to be slaughtered. You can see we're in a challenging situation and I hope my quartermasters told you that you'll be paid for the cows we're appropriating."

"Paid?" said the wealthy farmer. He moved one fist under his chin and looked thoughtful. "That changes things," he said. "A little." He looked at the rocky floor of the passage for a moment before returning his gaze to meet Nûd's.

"We're very concerned about getting everyone in the caves out into the sunlight as well—without them being captured by the emperor's legions," Nûd continued. "In fact, in two days I'm attending a meeting with the leaders of the allied kingdoms and all our best wizards to find a solution."

"Oh," said the farmer. "I didn't know. Thank you for telling me."

"You're welcome," said Nûd. "I'm sorry I wasn't able to tell anyone sooner, but you know how it is. Do you have children?"

"What?" the farmer responded, caught off guard by the change in subject. "Yes," he said after a breath. "A girl and a boy, eight and six."

"Do you tell them about a special surprise before you know for sure it will really happen?" asked Nûd.

"No," said the farmer. "Of course not. I wouldn't want to disappoint them."

"Rightly so," said Nûd. "You're a good father."

"Thank you, Your Majesty," said the farmer. He rubbed his chin again and tilted his head as if trying to make things fall into place inside his head.

Nûd nodded to the royal retainer and the woman escorted the farmer back down the passage.

Everything was quiet for a few seconds except for the regular rhythm of water dripping from the ceiling into a small pool on a side passage.

"I'm glad you asked me to teach you swordplay," said Duke Háiddon at last.

Nûd arched one eyebrow in an unspoken question.

"Because you seem to be doing a pretty good job of being a king already."

Chapter 16

A Net Win with Dragons

"May I come, *please,* Zûra?" pleaded Viridáxés. "I'm *so* tired of this island I could flame its stones to slag and its beaches to glass!"

"That's why you *can't* join me, Dáx," said Zûrafiérix. "This mission takes finesse and I don't think you can control your temper—especially against the Roma."

"I *can,* I *can,*" wheedled the great green dragon. "I promise I won't destroy any ships or drown any sailors."

"You say that now," Zûrafiérix replied. "But what if one of those sailors pierces your scaly hide with a harpoon? I doubt you'd keep your temper *then.*"

"I will stay underwater, out of harpoon range," said Viridáxés. "They'll never even *see* me."

"Hah!" snorted Zûrafiérix. Paired clouds of steam puffed from her nostrils. "You're more likely to surface in the middle of the emperor's fishing fleet and crash down to crush as many ships as you can manage."

"I *wouldn't!*" Viridáxés protested. His rapidly whirling green eyes slowed their spin as he considered various options. "Unless they hurt *you,* my treasured mate. Then I'd sink them all and eat every crew member."

"You're not helping your case, Dáx."

"But I *want* to help!"

"I suppose it would be unfair not to give you a chance to see if you can control your temper," said Zûrafiérix. Her own blue eyes spun slower as she contemplated the risks associated with allowing Viridáxés to join her. "Would you promise to *only* cut nets and not butt your snout into hulls or try to pull fishing boats below the surface?"

"I would," said Viridáxés. "I will. I *do!*" The dragon's massive head bobbed up and down on the end of his sinuous neck. "When do we leave?"

"Soon," said Zûrafiérix. She'd received word from Laetícia that the emperor's fishing fleet had recently left Nova Eboracum. The vessels would pass near Bucket Island, where the dragons were living, on their way to the Grand Cod Banks, but Zûrafiérix thought it would be wise to intercept the fleet earlier in case they decided to start fishing closer to their home port.

"Now soon, or in-a-little-while soon?" asked Viridáxés. The tip of his barbed tail was wagging in excitement.

"Now soon," Zûrafiérix replied. "We will have to stay underwater for most of the trip."

"I can do that," said Viridáxés. "Do I have to just *cut* the Roma's nets?" he asked. "Couldn't I take nets full of fish to Nûd and Dârio in their caves? They must be ready for something fresh to eat?"

"Laetícia and the people of Occidens Province, too," said Zûrafiérix. "They're staying underground with people from Tamloch and Dâron—but we can't risk it. We're not exactly inconspicuous. If we flew nets full of fish directly to the caverns, Sírénae's wizards would track us and find our friends."

"I didn't mean fly the fish directly to the caverns," said Viridáxés. "I thought we could take them back to Bucket Island and dump them through the gates used by Dârio, Nûd, and Laetícia when they visit us."

"Well," said Zûrafiérix, considering her partner's suggestion. "That might actually work—though having thousands of pounds of fish arriving through these gates might be disconcerting."

"It would, wouldn't it," said Viridáxés. His tail lashed from side to side even faster. "Let's not tell them. It can be a surprise!"

"Hmmm..." said Zûrafiérix. "That's true. And since we're not sure we'll be able to capture any nets full of fish, we can't exactly promise in advance to deliver them."

"Oh, good!" said Viridáxés. "This will be *fun!*"

"Just focus on staying inconspicuous," said Zûrafiérix. "We can't show ourselves above the surface or close enough to it to be identified."

"Right," said Viridáxés. "Mischief, not destruction."

"It seems you *do* understand," said Zûrafiérix. She rubbed her jaw with a foreclaw. "Dáx?"

"Yes, Zûra?"

"If any Roma dragons dive down after us, you can't engage. You'll have to go deeper or swim away."

"I can do that," said Viridáxés. "Unless a Roma dragon attacks you—then I make no promises."

"I can take care of..." Zûrafiérix began but stopped. "Thank you, Dáx."

Viridáxés nodded, the up and down movement of his head providing a counterpoint to the back and forth motion of his tail. He rubbed his head along Zûra's neck and twined his neck with hers. "When do you think you'll be laying eggs?" he asked.

"I don't know," said Zûrafiérix. "I'm new at this, and there's nothing in the old books I read before I was buried in the quarry about patterns of reproduction for dragons our size."

"We could mate again before we leave," Viridáxés suggested.

"Or after," said Zûrafiérix. "Mating makes me sleepy."

"Mating makes *me* want to mate again."

"Everything except eating a whale in one session makes you want to mate again," teased Zûrafiérix.

"I'm sorry I didn't share my whale," said Viridáxés.

"I forgive you," said Zûrafiérix. "Let's get on with our plan, then. I'll nudge them—you cut their nets."

"I'll race you to the fishing fleet," said Viridáxés. He launched himself from the top of a rock formation and began to fly southwest.

"Dáx!" bellowed Zûrafiérix as she leapt to follow him. Then, softer, so only she could hear, she spoke. "I will have to remind Viridáxés of the meaning of the word *inconspicuous*."

* * * * *

"This looks promising," said Admiral Pixo as he and Magister Callidus stared down at thick schools of fish off the port bow of the *Menodorus Maximus*. "Cast nets!" the admiral shouted. The two older men heard the order echoed from ship to ship as sailors—aloft and on-deck—passed it along.

Callidus watched the crew of a nearby ship release heavy nets from their sterns and tow them along behind, collecting flitting finned creatures from the hundreds of thousands of fish all around them. "Would you like me to fly up and watch for trouble?" asked the magister.

"Hold off for now," said Pixo. "Let's see if we can haul in any of our catch first."

"As you wish," said Callidus. He suspected the huge blue dragon he'd seen underwater when Valentius and his ship, the *Cloud Dancer,* disappeared, was responsible for disrupting the fleet's earlier fishing expeditions. Most of the ships nearby had released their nets and had slowed their forward progress as fish accumulated in their nets. Then Callidus saw a ship a hundred yards away jump forward as if it was shoved through the water. Net lines floated to the surface and trailed behind it. Something had cut its nets and the ship surged ahead of the others like an eager hound after a rabbit.

"Thunder and lightning!" shouted Admiral Pixo. "The *Province of Aquitaine* has lost its nets."

Callidus heard curses and commands from the *Aquitaine's* officers across the water and watched them lower a course of sail so the vessel didn't get too far ahead of the rest of the fleet. He admired their colorful vocabularies and forthright insults, which were so different from the cuts of Sírénae's subtle and scalpel-like tongue. Not for the first time, he wished he wasn't the senior mage on this expedition. It was tiring to worry more about rivals like Umbrose than their true enemies.

Who are my true enemies? Callidus mused. *The allied kingdoms and Occidens Province? Or Sírénae herself? She certainly threatens to feed me to Thraxa often enough.*

"Callidus!" said a voice that the magister finally realized was Admiral Pixo's. "Callidus! I think I *would* like you to fly up and reconnoiter for me," said the admiral. "And look—there's a dragon!"

The magister looked up to see the shadow of a dragon above him. "Xaxidiánus!" said Callidus. "Why are *you* here?"

"To watch over *you,* my friend," said the dragon, bellowing down from above. "What seems to be the problem?"

"Something is cutting our nets—that's the problem," said Admiral Pixo. "Can you see anything?"

"I cannot," said Xaxidiánus. "But the water is dark and there are schools of fish obscuring my vision. I don't know if I would be able to see anything short of a giant albino ray in these seas.

"Dive down, then," said Pixo. "Find out who or what is cutting our nets!"

"I'll join you," said Callidus. He pulled his flying disk from his shoulders and shot up to join Xaxidiánus.

Below them, another ship, the *City of Lugdunum,* was jumping ahead.

"There!" shouted Callidus, pointing directly behind the *Lugdunum.* He created a protective sphere of solidified sound around himself and followed Xaxidiánus into the water. The dragon fell like a stone, or more realistically, like a great boulder, displacing so much liquid all the ships around his point of entry were spun away by powerful waves. Callidus generated goggles of solidified sound to help correct for the distortion of the water and looked for Xaxidiánus below him.

It was still quite dark, so the magister shouted *Llachar!* inside his bubble. His command triggered a powerful light spell that made the sea around them as bright as midday in the deserts of the Southern Empire. Now Callidus could clearly see Xaxidiánus and two other shapes—immense dragons that made Xaxidiánus seem like a new hatchling—swimming nearby. One was holding a net full of fish in its jaws. The other was shooting up on a collision course with Xaxidiánus.

For all that sound would carry inside his bubble, Callidus could not warn his scaly friend about the impending attack. Instead, he built a yielding barrier of solidified sound that blunted the force of the giant dragon's blow when it struck Xaxidiánus. The black Roma dragon was not knocked unconscious, but *was* flipped end over end, spinning like a plebe after drinking too many glasses of spiced wine.

The attacking dragon—it was blue, Callidus realized—was now approaching the magister. He reinforced his shields, expecting a blow, but the dragon merely placed its great head near his and *winked* before turning away and diving far below where the bright rays from his light spell couldn't penetrate. Callidus was disoriented. He sat suspended for a few moments, unsure of what to do next, sensing ships hulls passing far over his head. They prompted Callidus to look up. With a start, he saw Xaxidiánus above him, tossed by the waves and apparently stunned. His friend's mouth and nostrils were in the water.

Like a bolt from a powerful crossbow, Callidus shot up to join his much larger, scaly friend. Manipulating shapes of solidified sound, he lifted the black dragon's head out of the water with one construct and compressed his chest with another. Streams of liquid sprayed from the Roma dragon's mouth and a hogshead's worth of water gushed from his mouth. Xaxidiánus spluttered and coughed, spreading his wings to steady himself against the small waves on the surface.

"Are you damaged?" asked the magister once the dragon's eyes resumed their usual steady rotation.

"Only my pride," said Xaxidiánus. He shifted his body, so he rode like a ship on the sea and extended his wing membranes to dry them. "What hit me?" said the dragon.

Callidus paused for a moment, hovering in the air near Xaxidiánus and debating what to say. If he revealed the existence of the gigantic dragons, Sírénae would be forewarned, and he wasn't sure he wanted her to emerge victorious in the coming conflict.

"I couldn't tell," he said at last. "It may have been some sort of great kraken."

"Like the one that attacked our ships as we approached Nova Eboracum harbor?" asked Xaxidiánus.

"I suppose," said Callidus, realizing his mind had selected a believable alternative to what he'd actually seen. "Are you strong enough to fly to shore where you can rest?"

"If I float a bit longer and eat some of the larger fish in these waters, I should be able to make it all the way back to Nova Eboracum," Xaxidiánus replied. He inspected Callidus with one eye. "Were you attacked, too?"

"No, old friend, I was lucky," said Callidus. "Whatever it was ignored me. I must have been too small for it to bother with."

"As you say," the dragon replied.

From his tone, Callidus wondered if Xaxidiánus had seen more than Callidus realized and was also keeping quiet about what he knew. "I'm going to talk to Pixo," said the magister. "Let me know if I can be of service to you before you leave and wait for my return before you speak to the emperor."

"Of course," said Xaxidiánus. "I will be too weary to talk by the time I fly back, anyway."

"Understood," said Callidus. They didn't need to exchange winks to understand the subtext of their conversation. Callidus flew back to join Pixo on the foredeck of the admiral's flagship.

"Is Xaxidiánus all right?" asked Pixo.

"Not at present, but he will be," said Callidus. "He was struck by something—perhaps a massive tentacle."

"The Great Kraken!" exclaimed Pixo. "It's following the fleet."

"I couldn't tell," said Callidus. "I was knocked about as well—and hit from behind."

"It must be the same kraken that attacked us when we first arrived," said Pixo. "There can't be two of them." He shook his head and scowled. "The monster stole all our nets as well. Sírénae will have our heads if we don't return with fish."

"She may have mercy on us when she sees Xaxidiánus," said Callidus. "It takes a formidable monster to batter a battle dragon of his experience."

"We can hope," said Admiral Pixo. "Though it's unlikely. Mercy is not one of our emperor's most often demonstrated qualities."

"True," said Callidus. "Maybe Celéri will return with good news about where to find Dâron's underground sanctuaries and food supplies."

"She might at that," said Pixo. "My grand-niece is a resourceful young woman."

"Better yet," said Callidus, "she might return with honey."

The two men exchanged glances that spoke volumes about the emperor, but wisely left their words unspoken.

"Can you?" asked the admiral after a few moments of silence.

"Retrieve your nets?" asked Callidus. "I can try. It depends on how far they've fallen."

* * * * *

Viridáxés and Zûrafiérix flew the last few miles to their home on Bucket Island. Viridáxés didn't speak, but not because he didn't have a lot he wanted to say. His mouth was full of net ropes and the net he carried was full of fish. He landed in front of the rock formations that held the narrow gates used by Dârio, Nûd, and Laetícia for their visits. The huge green dragon scratched the stones in front of the gates with one long claw.

"Just a moment, I'll open the gates," said Zûrafiérix. In quick succession she recited the phrases that triggered the gates and watched the shimmering interfaces appear.

Viridáxés released one end of the net from his jaws and lifted his head. Tens of thousands of squirming iridescent fish spilled out and most of them disappeared through at least one of the three gates.

Zûrafiérix shoveled fish still on the ground through the nearest gate with the tip of her snout. "There," she said. "That should do it."

"So much for being inconspicuous," teased Viridáxés. "You got to have all the fun—doing what you told me not to do!"

"I *had* to do *something*," said Zûrafiérix. "And you were busy holding a net full of fish. As it was, I hit that black dragon hard enough that it might have knocked his most-recent memories out of him."

"So maybe we didn't give away our presence after all?" asked Viridáxés hopefully.

"There's a chance," said Zûrafiérix. Her eyes locked with Viridáxés rapidly spinning orbs.

"Want to mate?" he asked, but he never got to hear Zûrafiérix's reply.

"Hey!" came a human woman's voice from one of the gates. It was Laetícia and she didn't look happy. "Which one of you overgrown lizards just dumped ten thousand fish into my sleeping cavern!"

Chapter 17

Invasion Preparations

"You did a good job as the emperor's quartermaster, so I'm giving you primary responsibility for the expeditionary force against the Northern Clan Landers," said General Machaera. "You'll have my best legate, Giérra, to keep you out of trouble. Be sure to listen to her advice and don't step on your gladius. I'm counting on you."

"I appreciate your faith in me and won't let you down, general," said Lieutenant General Belisaria as she stood beside General Machaera along the river, reviewing the force now assembling to subdue the Northern Clan Landers. "I am puzzled about something, though," Belisaria continued.

"What?" asked Machaera. "Ask your question. I won't bite—unless you should really know the answer already."

Belisaria swallowed and adjusted the neckline of the wool tunic she wore beneath her *lorica segmentata*. It was feeling tight now, though it hadn't a moment earlier. "I just wanted to know—where are the fodder barges for the elephants?" she asked.

"I wondered if you'd notice they were missing," said Machaera. "Unfortunately, you don't get them. The elephants will have to forage as you go."

"But I'd planned to take the fodder barges north."

"Sírénae overruled you," said Machaera. "She wants to keep all the hay in the city for the horses."

"Blast and double blast," said Belisaria. "That's really going to slow our rate of march. We'll be lucky to travel at half speed."

"It can't be helped," said Machaera. "The legionnaires will be foraging as well, so it won't be just the elephants."

"I don't see how the emperor expects our troops to fight effectively on short rations," said Belisaria. "Let's just hope they can find deer in the forests farther up the Abbenoth. There's not a whitetail alive within twenty miles of Nova Eboracum."

"True enough," said Machaera. "There aren't any squirrels or rabbits or pheasants left either."

"Thank goodness for fish in the river," said Belisaria.

"I'm tired of fish," said Machaera.

"Agreed," said Belisaria. "I hope the Northern Clan Landers are well supplied," she continued. "I'd like to capture some flour and enjoy fresh bread instead of chewing on ship's biscuit hard enough to break teeth."

"You're supposed to soak it first," said Machaera. She grinned at Belisaria, since they both were well aware of all the tricks camp cooks used to soften the twice-baked rations. Machaera shook her head slowly. "Don't get your hopes up about recovering stores of bread flour on this expedition. Did you read the reports I sent you about the Northern Clan Landers?"

"I skimmed them," said Belisaria. "They're just more barbarians for our legions to smash."

"You need to read the reports," said Machaera. "Especially since I'll be staying back in the capital to protect you from the emperor's whims. Remember, those barbarians have taken five eagle standards."

"That was hundreds of years ago," Belisaria replied. "They weren't fighting well-trained modern legions."

"But our legionnaires are hungry," said Machaera. "Unless wild game is plentiful on the way north, they won't be at peak strength."

"That should just make them *mean*," said Belisaria. "They'll fight harder knowing they can claim their enemy's wine as the spoils of victory."

"The Northern Clan Landers drink beer," said Machaera.

"Beer, then," said Belisaria. "And bread. They must bake with *some* kind of flour."

"Probably not wheat," said Machaera. "More likely oats, rye, or barley."

"If it's barley, the legionnaires are more likely to brew it themselves than bake it."

"I don't doubt it," said Machaera. "All I'm saying is that these Northern Clan Landers have managed to stay independent for centuries. They're reputed to be masters of unconventional tactics, like the slaves in the Servile Wars."

"We'll smash them anyway," said Belisaria. "Or perhaps, given our elephants, I should say *trample* them."

"Hannibal had elephants, and *he* was defeated," said Machaera. "Though only *after* dealing us a crushing defeat at Cannae."

"Point taken," said Belisaria. "I will guard against my own hubris, along with being alert for barbarian traps."

"There's the wise woman I promoted," said Machaera. "Wisdom isn't just not making the same mistake twice; it's learning from history, so you don't repeat other people's mistakes."

Belisaria nodded. "Since I made the mistake of only skimming your report on the Northern Clan Landers, what makes them such effective opponents?"

"Terrain is a large part of it," said Machaera. "The Northern Clan Landers live in the mountains north and west of the upper Abbenoth. They know their land well and are reputed to have traps set on their borders to discourage visitors. They avoid direct confrontations and are said to prefer attacking from ambush instead of frontal assaults whenever possible."

"We've fought and defeated similar foes in northern Éberria years ago," said Belisaria. "Our dragons ate their sheep and blasted them out of their refuges with dragonfire."

"Northern Éberria wasn't covered in thick forests," said Machaera. "It's hard to catch barbarians you can't even *see*."

"Our elephants will help flush them out," replied Belisaria. "I was told they're forest elephants. They won't be daunted by a few trees."

"More than a *few* trees," said Machaera. "I don't know about elephants, but it's a lot easier for dragons to find, kill and eat sheep grazing in high meadows than deer hiding in woodlands."

"We'll manage," said Belisaria. "Two of our legions were recruited from the Black Forest. I'm sure they won't be fooled by these Clan Landers."

"I noticed that, and highly approve," said Machaera. "But it's still going to be a challenge to fight these forest-dwelling adversaries, since they won't stand and meet us in the field."

"Don't forget," said Belisaria. "*We* will have dragons."

"Not enough dragons," said Machaera. "Sírénae's only giving us three for this campaign. She's keeping three with her in Nova Eboracum and sent Xaxidiánus off to follow Magister Callidus and Admiral Pixo with the fishing fleet."

"Three dragons—and two hundred elephants—should be more than enough to support five legions against the Northern Clan Landers," said Belisaria.

"We can hope," said Machaera.

"Why are you so concerned?" asked the younger woman. "What's so special about *these* barbarians?"

Machaera's voice grew soft. "I've fought them before," she said.

"I never knew you served in Occidens Province?" said Belisaria. The lieutenant general's face looked as surprised as it had when she'd realized the fodder barges wouldn't be coming upriver.

"I didn't," said Machaera. "But I fought people from the same barbarian tribes in the north of the White Isle. That was when I was just a junior legate with the Sixth Legion, and we were assigned to invade Caledonia and integrate the people there into the Western Empire."

"How did it go?" asked Belisaria.

"It didn't," said Machaera. "It was years ago, and you were still a centurion serving in Persia when it happened. Sírénae's predecessor as emperor of the West kept it quiet, but the *Caledonii* held off eight legions for a year before we pulled back south after taking heavy casualties."

"What happened?"

"What *didn't* happen?" Machaera replied. "The ground opened up in front of us, dropping legionnaires into pits. Ballista bolts killed our dragons. Rocks fell out of the sky at random intervals, crushing tents and wagons. We nearly froze to death at midsummer— and it never stopped raining."

"I... see..." said Belisaria. "They used weather magic?"

"I don't think so," said Machaera. "I think the climate is just that miserable in Caledonia all year 'round. Our commanders set us to doubling the height of the wall separating Caledonia from the rest of the White Isle and building it twice as thick as well. We were told to say there was nothing north of the wall except manticores and capricairns."

"What are capricairns?" asked Belisaria.

"Carnivorous goats the size of war horses with a single spiral horn growing from the center of their foreheads," said Machaera. "They're harder to kill than wild boars and have as good a chance of killing you with that spike of theirs as you have of killing them."

"Sounds unpleasant," said Belisaria. "Don't tell me—the Caledonii ride capricairns into battle?"

"No, thank goodness," said Machaera. "I don't think *anyone* could ride a capricairn. The Caledonii ride tough-looking ponies as shaggy as sheepdogs and dismount to fight."

"I'm glad to hear *that,*" said Belisaria. "A capricairn cavalry charge would be terrifying."

"Ten thousand screaming, naked, blue-painted Caledonii armed with swords, spears, and bull-hide shields charging your position is even more of a challenge," said Machaera.

"I can only imagine," said Belisaria. The sun was getting higher in the sky and she wiped sweat from her forehead. She looked at her superior. "Blue-painted?" she asked.

"Yes," said Machaera. "The paint may have some sort of stimulant effect." The general tilted her head and regarded Belisaria for a moment before continuing. "Do you remember the excellent maps drawn by artists in northwestern Éberria?" she asked. "The people there share ancestors with the Caledonii."

"I remember the dark blue ink they used," said Belisaria. "They were beautifully drawn."

"The woad maps of Éberria are famed across all four empires," said Machaera. "The Caledonii use the same blue pigment from the ink to dye their bodies before battle."

"I can see how that would be disconcerting," said Belisaria. She smiled at Machaera, but the older woman didn't smile back.

"You have no idea," Machaera replied. "Can you see why I don't want to underplay the threat posed by the Northern Clan Landers?"

"Yes," said Belisaria. "I can now. I'll read your report thoroughly tonight."

"I just wish Sírénae could have bothered to read it," said Machaera. "She's too much of a political animal and was more pleased by the fact of her predecessor's failure than the reasons behind it."

"You think she would have sent more legions if she had?" asked Belisaria.

"I think she would have sent more dragons, at least. And more advance scout wizards."

"I thought she *did* send scout wizards, and none came back," said Belisaria.

"Which should have told her something about our foe," said Machaera. "I have a bad feeling about this."

"That's understandable, given the circumstances," said Belisaria. "What's your plan to avoid what happened to the Sixth?"

"We need to draw them out and make them fight on a battlefield of our choosing," said Machaera. "Somewhere on level ground between the Abbenoth and the mountains."

"How will you force such a change in tactics on their part?" asked Belisaria.

"With *that*," said Machaera. She pointed to a gilded barge that was just now floating up from the south to join the rest of the collection of supply barges. It was loaded high with strongboxes and heavy canvas sacks.

"A treasure boat?" said Belisaria. "Do you think they'll fall for it?"

"We can hope," said Machaera. "The Caledonii have as much or more appreciation for gold and precious gems as any other people. Perhaps their relatives, the Northern Clan Landers, do as well."

"Such a boat would surely capture *my* attention if I were a barbarian," said Belisaria. "But putting treasure on a gilded barge is far from subtle. Won't they suspect it's a trap?"

"Of course they will," said Machaera. "But what choice do they have if they want to claim the treasure? The Northern Clan Landers are used to coming down to the west bank of the Abbenoth to capture Tamloch merchants' barges. If you review my report, you'll see that the Whale River—the one that empties the Inland Seas—is linked to the Abbenoth by way of canals and a pair of large lakes. There's a spot twenty-five miles south of the southern lake that would be ideal for our legions and elephants to meet the Clan Landers."

"It sounds like at least a few scout wizards returned to give you topographical details," said Belisaria. She rubbed her palms together, thinking about crushing Clan Landers.

"The ones that didn't try to fly over the mountains," said Machaera. The general interlaced her fingers and rested her chin atop them as she gazed at the assembled barges. She smiled after turning her head to take in the wagons and soldiers ready to be ferried to the west bank as well.

"One question," said Belisaria.

Machaera gave her subordinate a slight nod.

"What do we do if they don't take the bait?"

"Well," said Machaera, drawing out the word. "We do have dragons..." She spread her arms wide. "...and forests burn."

Chapter 18

Robbing the Bees

"Hello!" shouted Gruffyd from the courtyard behind the main house at Applegarth.

"Hello!" Nyssia repeated with her hands cupped around her mouth. She took a deep breath and projected even louder. "Eynon? Merry? Anybody? We're here to help collect honey."

"Maybe they're *busy*?" Gruffyd suggested.

Nyssia understood his unsaid meaning and her cheeks turned a shade redder. She was saved from further embarrassment when Merry stuck her head around the door to the equipment shed and smiled.

"You're *here!*" said Merry. She rushed to greet them and gave Nyssia a long hug and Gruffyd a short one.

Eynon followed Merry and repeated the process in the opposite order. He was taller than Gruffyd but not nearly as wide across the shoulders. Nyssia stood on her tiptoes and Eynon leaned down when they hugged. As he had at previous meetings, Eynon admired the strength and suppleness of Nyssia's arms. The fair-haired young woman reminded him of the slim blade she carried, while Gruffyd was more of a heavy, not-too-sharp broadsword.

Ace barked and Chee chittered at the new arrivals from the lower branch of a mature chestnut tree on one side of the courtyard. The rockhound was staring down an aggressive gray squirrel clutching the branch closer to the trunk and Chee was looking for bugs under a loose section of bark. Gruffyd waved to acknowledge Merry and Eynon's familiars. The pair seemed quite content in their current location and showed little interest in Gruffyd or Nyssia.

"You made great time," said Merry. "We didn't expect you until this afternoon at the earliest."

"After you left, we dallied for a bit, then decided to spend the night in his family's castle," said Nyssia.

Merry saw how Nyssia's cheeks were glowing and decided she knew what sort of dalliance Nyssia was obliquely referring to.

"That sounds like fun," said Merry. "How did you see on the river at night?"

"My father loaned me a wizard lamp along with the family's pull-stone," said Gruffyd. "Doethan made it for him years ago in return for three barrels of flour and a haunch of venison every month for a year."

"I'll bet the venison was for Rowsch," said Eynon, referring to Doethan's canine familiar.

"No, it was for Doethan," Gruffyd replied. "I was there when the old wizard told my father Rowsch preferred to catch and kill his own meals."

"He *does* like to run with wolf packs," said Merry. "Though he's never turned down anything I've offered him."

"Wait a minute," said Eynon. "Where's Gruffyd's family castle? I don't remember seeing it."

"You had your head down watching for rocks when we went past it," said Merry. "I remember how nervous you were in the boat."

"And you didn't make it any easier, teasing me about not liking me," said Eynon.

"I wasn't teasing," said Merry. "Middle Rhuthro Castle is built into the side of a mountain, well back from the river. We used to have more trouble with Southern Clan Lands' raids years ago and it's highly defensible."

"How did I miss it?" Eynon wondered.

"There are lots of tall pines near the dock at Gruffyd's steading," said Nyssia. "We had to hike for a mile to get to the castle. It's impressive."

"My parents asked me to check on the castle and our manor house by the river, assuming the Roma weren't here already," said Gruffyd. "I'm pleased to report everything was in good shape, including the secret passageways."

"Gruffyd and I used to play in the secret passageways at Upper and Middle Rhuthro Castles when we were young," noted Merry. "We heard a lot of things we shouldn't."

"Upper Rhuthro?" asked Nyssia and Eynon simultaneously.

"That's Merry's family's castle," said Gruffyd. "It's five miles south on the west bank. We grew up as neighbors."

"I thought you said you *worked* for this household, not that you were a baron's daughter," came a voice from the shadows inside the shed.

"I did a *lot* of work for the household, my mother and father saw to that," said Merry.

"Who's that?" asked Gruffyd.

Celéri stepped out into the sunlight and Eynon introduced her to the new arrivals. "This is Celéri. She's a Roma spy-wizard."

"Then why are we talking to her?" asked Nyssia.

Gruffyd moved his hand toward his heavy blade but Nyssia stopped him.

"You won't stop her with a sword, my love. Can't you see she's a wizard? Let Eynon and Merry deal with her."

"But she's an enemy spy and they're *not* dealing with her," Gruffyd protested.

"I don't need to be dealt with," said Celéri. She flashed Gruffyd an overly wide smile. "I'm harmless, really. Just a girl in purple robes with a flying disk. I'm only here for some honey for the emperor."

Gruffyd grumbled to himself and frowned.

"Have you heard the old saying, 'Keep your friends close and your enemies closer?'" asked Eynon.

"No," said Gruffyd. "And it's my job as a member of the royal guard to keep Dâron's enemies far away from us or die trying." He rotated his shoulders to show off his swordsman's muscles, reinforcing his statement.

"I'm sure *one* of those options could be arranged," said Celéri in an extra-sweet voice. She repeated her smile.

Merry pressed her lips together to keep from laughing. Gruffyd and Celéri reminded her of a big dog being tormented by a small cat using sharp claws to bat at the dog's nose. "Come on, you two," she said. "Let's get on with collecting honey. There's not much a pair of apprentices can do against a trained Roma battle wizard anyway. The sooner Celéri has her honey, the sooner she'll be gone."

Now Celéri directed her overly wide smile at Merry. "Unless things run long and I have to stay the night," she said.

It was Nyssia's turn to stop herself from laughing when she saw the confusion on Eynon's face. She'd grown up in Dâron's capital city, Brendinas, but knew Eynon was from the hinterlands and—if that was possible—even more naïve than Gruffyd.

"But you and Eynon aren't..." Gruffyd began.

Nyssia put her hand on Gruffyd's forearm. "Of course they are," she said. "Eynon and Merry are apprenticed to Doethan the hedge wizard, don't you remember?"

"Oh," said Gruffyd. "That's right. I forgot. Thinking about Doethan always confuses me. I keep remembering how Rowsch threatened to eat me when I was little."

"He was doing his job as a guard dog and you were trying to get inside Doethan's tower without an invitation," said Merry. "The answer is for you not to think so much." Merry waved the others forward. "Come into the shed, everyone. You can help us carry the honey-harvesting equipment."

"I'll trigger a light spell so we can see what we're doing," said Celéri.

"Finally, you're doing something useful," said Merry as they entered the shed.

"Has anyone ever told you that you're cute when you're angry?" Celéri asked Merry.

"No," replied Eynon, thinking Celéri's question was directed at him. "At least I don't think so."

* * * * *

The five of them soon stood on Applegarth's dock. Gruffyd and Nyssia's narrow boat was pulled well up on shore nearby, securely located twenty feet above the bank. They were contemplating the tall pile of wooden frames and the odd collection of metal equipment spread out before them and nearly covering half the dock's surface.

"We've got a problem," said Merry. "We don't have enough smokers."

"What's a smoker?" asked city raised Nyssia.

"That metal cylinder with a wide, conical pour spout on top," said Gruffyd.

"The one that looks like a watering can?" asked Nyssia, nudging the nearest likely item with the toe of her boot.

"Exactly," said Gruffyd. "You put something that will burn and make lots of smoke inside the can, then use the spout to direct the smoke into the hive to calm the bees."

"Doesn't the smoke make them mad?" asked Nyssia.

"No," said Gruffyd. "I don't know why, but it seems to calm them down."

"Doethan told me bees talk with smells," said Merry. "The smoke interrupts their conversations."

"Be that as it may," said Nyssia—she paused when she realized her inadvertent pun—"what's the problem? We've got two smokers."

"We've also got almost two hundred hives to harvest," said Merry. "With only two smokers and figuring a minimum of an hour to work on each hive, it would take us eight twelve-hour days to do them all."

"There's another problem," said Gruffyd. "Where are we going to store the honey once we harvest it? Your family took every bowl, jar, jug, and barrel at Applegarth with them."

"Blast," said Merry. "I'd forgotten about that. Maybe we could hollow out some logs?"

"I'm good at working with solidified sound," offered Celéri. "I could create a sphere to hold the honey for transport."

"Sorry, there's no way we're letting you transport honey to the Dâron, Tamloch, and Occidens Province refuge caves," said Merry. "Try again."

Celéri shrugged and turned up her hands in a *you-can't-blame-me-for-trying* motion.

Eynon was staring at the trees just up from the riverbank along the path that led to Merry's family's steading. "I may have an idea," he said.

"What is it, handsome?" asked Celéri.

Eynon ignored Celéri and pointed at the lowest branches of a hundred-year-old oak tree close to the dock. "Do you think we could transport honey in a coracle?" he asked.

Merry's eyes followed Eynon's outstretched hand and saw a familiar circular shape wedged into a fork formed by three large branches. She pulled Eynon's arm down and levered his upper torso over enough so she could kiss him. "You're a genius!" she said.

"Everybody knows that," said Gruffyd.

Nyssia turned her back on Celéri and wagged her finger at Gruffyd before pinching her lips together.

Sorry, Gruffyd mouthed without speaking.

Celéri's attention was on whatever it was wedged into the tree limbs, so she missed their exchange. "Is that a boat?" she asked.

"It's a coracle," said Merry. "That's a round boat made from woven reeds and lined with pitch to be waterproof. It should do a fine job of holding lots of honey."

"Good," said Eynon. "I'm not very good manipulating solidified sound myself, but if Celéri is skilled working with it, I may have more good ideas on how to speed up collecting honey."

"Just tell me what you need," said Celéri, managing to make the innocent phrase sound suggestive. "I can form almost any shape or combination of shapes."

"Wonderful," said Eynon. "We use ceramic hives in the Coombe, but Merry told me her family uses wood-frame hives, which should make things easier."

"That's right," said Merry. "And we won't have to harvest *all* the hives, just enough to fill the big coracle."

"Plus honey for me to take to the emperor," said Celéri.

"You may not need to make a sphere," said Gruffyd. He shifted his body until he was flat against the wooden dock, peering through a gap between two boards. "I thought so," he said when he stood up. "The two-person coracle is tied up under the dock. Your father only put the four-person coracle in the tree, since it wouldn't fit underneath."

"Good for you," said Nyssia.

"I'd forgotten about the little one," said Merry.

"I'll never forget it," said Gruffyd. "It dumped me in the water more than a dozen times when I was learning how to get into it."

"You needed to hold on to one of the posts and ease yourself..." Merry began.

Eynon smiled, remembering his own challenges with the little craft.

"Could we start collecting honey instead of spending time sharing childhood memories?" asked Nyssia. "Once you get Gruff started, he can tell stories about when he was growing up for hours."

"Sorry," said Merry. "I'll show you how to harvest honey from one wooden framed hive and we can see if Eynon has any ideas about how to speed the process." She handed strange implements with blades and polished maple handles that looked more like scrapers than knives, then passed smokers to Nyssia and Gruffyd. "They're filled with scrap burlap sacks," said Merry. "They'll give off lots of smoke."

Eynon rescued the large coracle from the tree with a quick flight and Gruffyd pulled the smaller one out from under the dock using his broadsword to extend his reach. Both coracles ended up on a flat stretch of ground covered in pebbles close to the dock.

"These are frames," said Merry, pointing to the wooden squares on the dock. "The bees fill them with honeycombs."

"And honey!" said Gruffyd with a bit too much enthusiasm.

Merry smiled at her childhood friend. "They work like drawers. You can slide them in and out of the hive boxes."

"That sounds a lot easier than the ceramic rings we use in the Coombe," said Eynon.

"It doesn't disturb the bees as much, and we only take off the top few frames, so the bees have plenty of honey to feed themselves."

"What does it matter?" asked Celéri. "They'll all be dead before winter, except the queens, anyway?"

"If we take good care of the bees through spring, summer, and fall, we can harvest a lot more honey," said Merry.

"That's right," said Gruffyd. He glared at Celéri. "Good beekeepers protect their hives."

"I understand," said the spy-wizard. "Show us what to do."

"Nyssia can ride with me, and Gruffyd can ride with Eynon to fly across the river," said Merry. "You can carry the frames, the smokers, and the hive tools."

"Whatever you say," Celéri responded. She helped stack equipment on her flying disk and joined the others as they flew to a smaller dock on the opposite bank.

Merry surreptitiously created thin, form-fitting shields of solidified sound around Nyssia and herself and was confident Eynon had done the same thing for Gruffyd. It was too bad Celéri could work with solidified sound and protect her own skin from bee stings, but it was worth it if Celéri could do the hard work so Eynon and Merry didn't have to reveal their own talents.

"There's a hive twenty yards up the hill," said Merry. "We can start there. Smokers first."

Eynon lit the burlap rag inside the smoker with a tiny fire spell that any apprentice would know and handed the device to Gruffyd. The royal guard waited until a dark cloud poured out and held the smoker near the entrance to the hive.

"You can pull the top frame out now," said Merry.

Nyssia stepped close and pulled on the frame. "It's stuck," said Gruffyd. "Use the hive tool to loosen the bee glue."

"Bee glue?" asked Nyssia.

"It holds various parts of the hive in place," said Gruffyd. "Slide the edge of the tool between the frames and lever the top one out."

Nyssia wielded the tool with the same attention to detail she applied to her sword. The top frame popped loose and came free. Eynon took the frame full of honey and honeycomb from Nyssia and put the frame on his flying disk. Most of the cells were capped, so it didn't leak—at least not much. Merry handed Nyssia an empty replacement frame and the slender swordswoman slid it carefully into place. Two more frames were removed and exchanged for empty ones.

"We have enough empty frames for four more hives before we have to go back for more," said Merry. They repeated the process until Eynon's flying disk held a tall stack of twelve full frames. Merry hovered on her flying disk and kissed Eynon on the forehead. "Now, my love, we get to see if you have any good ideas."

The five of them flew back across the river to the Applegarth dock with Nyssia riding with Celéri this time. Merry considered ferrying Nyssia and Gruffyd back across the river to collect more honey once they restocked on empty frames, but she wanted to see how Eynon planned to replace the function of the broken honey spinner with magic.

If I'm being honest with myself, thought Merry, *I don't want to leave Eynon alone with Celéri. I trust him, but I don't trust her. It's like that old puzzle about getting a fox, a chicken, and a sack of grain across a river without any of the three being eaten in the process.* Merry's mind followed a path it shouldn't have. *Celéri is the fox, that's clear,* she thought. *But is Eynon the chicken or the sack of grain? He's more a cock than a chicken,* she mused. That notion took her brain in still other directions.

"Can you make a plane of solidified sound inside a sphere?" Eynon asked Celéri.

"Of course," the Roma wizard replied.

"Try this," said Eynon. "Lock the twelve frames together inside a sphere of solidified sound, then use a sharp plane of force to cut the wax off one side of the combs."

"That sounds simple enough," said Celéri. She proceeded to do as Eynon recommended. "That was easy," she said. "What do I do with the extra wax?"

"Can you squeeze it out one side of your sphere?" asked Eynon.

"Certainly." The wax Celéri had cut from one side of the frames was compressed into a sticky ball and presented to Eynon, who took it and licked his fingers.

"Delicious," he said.

Merry, Gruffyd, and Nyssia were avidly watching Eynon and Celéri. Even Ace and Chee came over to observe.

"Here you go, friends," said Eynon. He broke the ball of wax in half and tossed the pieces to the familiars. Ace began to chew on his wax hemisphere and seemed happy at its sweet taste. Chee squeezed his piece into a ball, then licked his fingers and chittered.

"Now what?" asked Celéri, still maintaining the sphere holding the dripping frames.

"Now we go for a spin," said Eynon.

"Do we now," said Celéri, giving Eynon a look that Merry considered particularly vulpine.

Stop that, she told her brain.

Eynon began to rotate his arm in a large circle, like a waterwheel turning.

Celéri understood his intent. She rose a dozen feet on her flying disk and started spinning the sphere of solidified sound like a child playing with a rock on the end of a string.

"Faster," said Eynon.

Celéri complied until the frames were only a blur as they spun.

Merry noted that Celéri didn't move her body as the frames went around. The Roma wizard was doing it all with her magic.

"That's enough," said Eynon. "Please hover over the small coracle now. You deserve to get your share of the honey first."

"I think not," said Celéri. She shifted her flying disk until she was above the large coracle and opened a hole in the bottom of her sphere for the amber liquid to escape. When all the honey had been transferred, she gently lowered the frames to the dock. Merry and Gruffyd showed Nyssia how to help open the frames and extract the empty combs.

"We can put these on the kitchen table later," said Merry. "The wax will be good for candles."

"Or Eynon and *I* can," teased Celéri.

None of the others replied. They all looked away.

A few inches of honey were in the bottom of the large coracle.

"We need a system," said Eynon. "Nyssia and Gruffyd, you extract the frames from the hives. I'll ferry full and empty frames across the river. Celéri will extract the honey and Merry will remove the combs from the frames so they can be recycled. If we're quick about it, we can fill both coracles before sundown."

"Not too far before," said Celéri.

Eynon laughed. "You just want to enjoy another one of my meals," he said.

"Right," said Celéri.

"Ri-i-i-ight," said Merry, stretching out the word.

Nyssia exchanged a knowing glance with Gruffyd. They were both glad they'd be on the other side of the river the next several hours.

They followed Eynon's plan for the rest of the day and had filled both coracles nearly to the top as the sun was setting. The combs were stacked neatly on a spare trestle table Merry had discovered and decided to use instead of the kitchen table. They should be fine if they weren't totally consumed by hungry ants before Eynon and Merry could return.

"Sweet," said Celéri after she licked the finger she'd just dipped into the amber liquid in the small coracle. The Roma mage had also been assigned the additional duty of making sure Ace and Chee didn't steal too much honey. "What's for supper?"

"Griddle cakes," said Eynon. "Nyssia and Gruffyd brought some flour."

"With honey?" asked Celéri.

"Of course!" everyone replied.

Merry and Celéri floated the coracles inside Applegarth's main building and found spots for them in the great room. That task completed, Merry assigned one spare bedroom to Nyssia and Gruffyd and another to Celéri.

"Can't I sleep with the two of you?" asked the Roma wizard.

"I'll see if Eynon is interested," said Merry. "Wait for several hours to make sure Gruffyd and Nyssia are asleep, please. Then knock on our door and we'll see."

"You won't be disappointed," said Celéri.

Merry smiled and left to help Eynon cook supper. The griddle cakes with honey were excellent, and if Celéri was distracted by good conversation and ended up eating two cakes for every one the others consumed that didn't seem out of the ordinary, especially after all the magical energy she'd expended. She was so tired even her magestone was dimmed. A diligent host, Merry ensured Celéri's mug was full of the special tea Mabli had always made when Merry couldn't sleep. The young Roma wizard could barely keep her eyes open to walk to her room before falling into her bed.

* * * * *

In the morning, Celéri used her chamberpot, put her robes back on, and stumbled to the kitchen, only to find a note waiting for her on the table near the hearth. The large coracle full of honey was gone, but the small one remained.

Celéri, the note began. *You were sleeping so peacefully we hated to wake you. Thank you for all your help collecting honey yesterday. I hope the emperor enjoys it. We left early this morning since we didn't want problems if you tried to follow us.*

Blast! thought Celéri. *They drugged me!*

The note continued. *It was a pleasure to meet you, though you really didn't need to try to seduce us to learn where our caves are located. We wouldn't have told you even if we had taken you to bed with us. That sort of thing only works in stories, and not the best ones.*

I guess I deserve that, Celéri considered. *Maybe I am a better battle mage than a spy mage? Still, this is only my first assignment.* She looked back at the scrap of paper.

Please tell your superiors that there's plenty of room on this side of the Ocean for everyone without you invading Roma taking lands that are already populated. There are beautiful islands to the south where you can harvest crops three times a year. We would much rather be your friends than your enemies.

That's intriguing, thought Celéri. *Open lands to the south without having to fight? I'll have to find a map and see what they're talking about.*

P.S. — There are leftover griddle cakes for you next to the pile of honeycombs. Safe travels — Merry and Eynon

Celéri frowned and took three deep breaths to prevent her anger from rising. *I hope Uncle Pixo and Magister Callidus are back from their fishing trip by the time I return,* she thought. *I'm going to need their advice.* Celéri absentmindedly walked over to the table where the honeycombs were stacked and found a griddlecake to munch on while she considered her situation.

Wait, she realized. *We spent ten hours robbing the bees yesterday without a single one of us being stung. That means Eynon and Merry must know how to manipulate solidified sound—and do it well enough for me not to notice. Interesting. What else? Gruffyd and Nyssia. He can't possibly be as dense as he seems, can he? And the two of them have a boat.*

"That's it," said Celéri, just to hear her own voice. "I can make better time flying than they can on the river, even with the current. I'll shadow Gruffyd and Nyssia and follow them to their caverns. I still have a chance to redeem myself."

She reclaimed her pack and her flying disk and stepped outside, pausing briefly by the dock to throw cold water on her face. Celéri only remembered she'd left the small coracle full of honey back at Applegarth when she was five miles down the river.

Chapter 19

Côbb and Távi

Côbb sat on a low bench on one side of the stable yard next to a wide opening in the curb that led to a storm sewer. It often rained hard in Nova Eboracum, and Roma engineering had built a vast network of sewers to handle the water. The old servant had a lumpy cloth bag and a brown crockery jug beside him on the bench. He had a small knife in one hand and a piece of wood he was whittling into a dragon in the other.

It was nearly dusk, and the stable yard was deserted. Most servants were still inside enjoying their dinners. None of them—except his wife Réah—missed Côbb.

"Doethan sent me," said the old man softly.

"What's the password?" came a high voice from the storm sewer.

"There isn't one," said Côbb.

"Good," said the voice. "At least you didn't try to bluff your way through the question."

Côbb laughed, turning it into a single syllable. "Heh," he said. "You sound like my grandson."

"Is that meant to be a compliment?" asked the voice.

"That depends," Côbb replied.

"On what?" asked the voice.

"On whether or not my grandson is intentionally annoying me or only doing so unintentionally."

"If I decide to annoy you, old man, be assured you'll know," said the voice.

"Understood," said Côbb. "Do you have a name?"

"You can call me Távi."

"Is that a boy's name or a girl's name?" asked Côbb.

"Yes," said Távi.

"Intentionally, then?" said Côbb.

He didn't receive a reply.

"Are you nodding?" asked Côbb.

"Yes, sorry about that," said Távi. "Do you want to hear my news?" Côbb was silent.

"Now *you're* nodding," said Távi.

"Took you long enough," said Côbb. "What have you heard?"

"Belisaria and Giérra are heading up the Abbenoth to fight the Northern Clan Landers in the morning."

"Tell me something I *don't* know," said Côbb. "It's hard to mobilize five legions, three dragons, and two hundred elephants without people noticing."

Now it was Távi turn to laugh. High-pitched giggles echoed up from the opening to the storm sewer. "You don't know that Belisaria hasn't spent enough time studying her enemy," said Távi. "She's expecting an easy victory over undisciplined barbarians."

"That's good to hear," said Côbb. "I'll pass the word. What about Machaera?"

"She's less arrogant, but she's also worried about maintaining the emperor's favor," said Távi. "I don't know how far she'll stray from Nova Eboracum."

"Understood," said Côbb. "Confusion to the enemy." He moved the blade of his knife to carve a detail into the wooden dragon's wing. "Here's a tidbit for you," he said. "Nova Eboracum will soon be Sírénaeopolis Magna."

More giggles came from the storm sewer. "Really?" asked Távi.

"Really," said Côbb. "My wife heard it from one of the emperor's personal servants. Everyone was talking about it in the kitchens."

"She'll make that snow gryffon of hers a consul next," said Távi.

"Sírénae is more likely to appoint Thraxa her Chief Executioner," said Côbb. "The beast already has the job on a limited basis."

"Not limited enough," said Távi. "That does fit in with other rumors I've heard, though."

"What do you mean?" asked Côbb.

"The emperor was talking to Magister Umbrose while walking in the governor-general's gardens and didn't think anyone could hear her," said Távi.

"But one of your little—um—*squirrels* was close by below them?" asked Côbb.

"Go ahead, call them rats. We don't mind. Rats thrive in the sewers and are quite a bit smarter than squirrels," said Távi. "From what was overheard, Pixo and Callidus should both be worried about their job security."

"Sírénae's ready to move and get rid of them?" asked Côbb. "There are several naval commanders who could move up into Pixo's role, but I thought she needed to keep Callidus in place, since he's one of the few powerful mages willing to stand up to Umbrose."

"And the biggest Roma dragon likes him," added Távi.

"Xaxidiánus would be unhappy if anything happened to Callidus," said Côbb. "But there isn't much he could do about it if Sírénae decided to purge the magister." Côbb put his knife on his lap and rubbed his chin. "Why would she want to get rid of a senior mage who can *ad hoc* gate?"

"From what I'd heard, she's hoping to replace him with a powerful wizard from one of the Orluin kingdoms."

"Fascinating," said Côbb. "I wonder where she got *that* notion?"

"From the three men and a woman who appeared just after the purple dragon," said Távi.

"I thought that was just an illusion?" said Côbb.

"Illusion or not, they're the emperor's new advisers," said Távi. "And two of *them* are wizards."

"Are they?" said Côbb.

"I said they were," complained Távi.

"Don't get your tunic in a twist," said Côbb. "It was a rhetorical question. What's the woman like?"

"Unpleasant," said Távi. "Nothing's ever good enough for her. She behaves like a spoiled princess."

"A princess," Côbb repeated. "I wonder..."

"The man who isn't a wizard is unpleasant, too," Távi continued. "But he seems more befuddled than willful. He acts like he's eaten bread made from spoiled rye."

"Describe him, please," said Côbb.

"I can't," said Távi. "My mates and I haven't *seen* any of the emperor's new advisers. We've just heard them."

"From the storm sewers?" asked Côbb.

"And echoes through the channels for the hypocausts," said Távi. "From the sound of things, I think the woman is sleeping with one of the wizards—and I mean *sleeping* as a euphemism."

"I understood what you meant," said Côbb. "From what you've said, I think I know who Sírénae's new *advisers* might be, and I'm not happy about it."

"My mates and I aren't happy about anything related to the emperor's arrival," said Távi. "We have to hide from the legionnaires and it's four times as hard to find food. We can't beg for it, either. We have to steal it."

"About that," said Côbb. He began to reach for the lumpy cloth bag and brown crockery jug when he heard heavy footsteps approaching nearby and did his best to cover the bag and jug behind folds of his patched tunic.

Távi retreated deeper into the shadows of the storm sewer's opening in the curb.

The newcomers turned out to be five legionnaires—three men and two women—who were wearing clanking *loricas* and decidedly unhappy expressions. It was easy to see why they were unhappy. They were covered in smelly brown muck from the soles of their hobnailed sandals to their knees.

"That's the last time I'll ever muck out the elephant dung pit," said one, a grizzled veteran with gray hair just over her ears and an old scar on her cheek.

"We all know we'll muck it out again and keep mucking it out if our centurion orders it," grumbled a man about the same age with a broken nose that hadn't been reset properly.

"Don't remind me," said the first speaker. She noted Côbb's presence on the bench and held up her hand, so her little group of soldiers stopped. "Who are you, grandpa?" she asked.

"Côbb. I work in the stables."

"What are you carving, old man?" asked broken nose.

"A dragon," Côbb replied.

"Let me see," said the man. He reached out a calloused hand to take the carving, but Côbb pulled it out of reach, revealing the cloth bag and jug by his movements.

"He's got a jug," said the gray-haired woman. "What's in the jug old man?"

"Give me the carving," said broken nose. "I want to see it. I have a grandchild who might like it." He lifted his knee and put his dung-covered sandal on top of the bench, catching the edge of Côbb's tunic and holding Côbb in place while he reached for the wooden figure. Côbb tried to hold on to the dragon, but another legionnaire—a younger one with a missing front tooth—snatched it from Côbb's hand.

"Here you go," said missing tooth. She tossed the wood carving to broken nose.

While Côbb had been distracted, the gray-haired veteran had picked up the crockery jug and removed the cork stopper. She sniffed at the contents. "It smells like vinegar," she said, wrinkling her face. "And some sort of unpleasant herb."

"Teaberry mint," said Côbb. "It's medicine for my wife's muscle aches. She works in the kitchens."

"You can have it then," said the veteran. "Why are you here instead of in the mess?"

"It's too noisy there," said Côbb. "And I finished my dinner. I just wanted peace and quiet to sit and whittle."

"Finished your dinner, did you?" said missing tooth. "What's in the bag, then?"

"Dead rats," Côbb replied. "I catch 'em in the stables trying to get into the horses' grain. My wife feeds 'em to the kitchen cat."

"You can keep them, then," said missing tooth. "Though if we have to go much longer on half rations, I may stop by the kitchens to find that cat."

"We'd have more of a feast if the emperor would give us one of the elephants," said the veteran. "An elephant steak would compensate us well for all our work in the dung pit."

"As if any of us would ever get a steak," said broken nose. "We'd be lucky to get a bit of entrails."

"There are a *lot* of entrails in an elephant, I'd bet," said the youngest legionnaire. "Quite a bit more than a sheep, I suppose," he added, trailing off when everyone turned to stare at him. The lad had orange-red hair and freckles and looked like he'd just enlisted from the Green Isle before the emperor was deposed and sailed west.

"I suppose you know quite a bit about *sheep*," teased missing tooth. She tilted her hips suggestively and smiled when the youngest legionnaire's cheeks turned the color of his hair.

"I'm going to keep this carving, old man," said broken nose. He turned the dragon back and forth, admiring the details on the wings.

"Let me have it a few more days and I'll finish it and give it to you," said Côbb. "You don't want to give your grandchild an unfinished carving, do you?"

"I think I'll keep it and finish it myself," said broken nose. He lifted his foot down from the bench, releasing Côbb's tunic. "Machaera is sending two more legions north along with the five picked already. We're leaving in the morning."

"Have the dragon, then, with my compliments," said Côbb. "It's too bad, though. I was going to stain it purple with berry juice, like the purple dragon that appeared above the palace."

"That was just an illusion," said the gray-haired veteran. "But if you know where to find berries, you'd best inform the cooks. The emperor has been asking for fresh berries to be served with her fish, but there are none to be found."

"She wouldn't like *these* purple berries," said Côbb. "If she ate them, they'd be her last meal."

"That's different," said the veteran. "Berries for dying wood—and dying of a different sort."

"Warn your troops to avoid purple berries on evergreen shrubs," said Côbb. "The red ones aren't recommended either, though you'll die a lot slower if you eat them."

"I'll keep that in mind," said the veteran. "There are a lot of strange plants here." She waved her arm at the other four legionnaires.

"Come along, you dung flowers. We need a dunk in the river to get the worst of the stink off, then a long soak in the baths before we're fit for human company."

"What about our dinner?" asked missing tooth.

"You think you'll get dinner?" said the veteran. "We can get some jerky and biscuits from one of the cooks and chew on it while we wash off. Hurry it up, now. I want to talk to our centurion and find out if the elephants will be behind us or ahead of us in the order of march tomorrow."

"Behind us, please," said the young redhead. He fell in step behind the others as they quickly marched across the stable yard and disappeared around a far corner.

Even the echoes of the legionnaires' footsteps had disappeared when Côbb spoke. "They're gone," he said.

"I know that," Távi answered. "Two more legions heading north?"

"That's what she said. Machaera must really be worried about the Northern Clan Landers."

"She is," said Távi. "And I expect the emperor is pleased to have fewer mouths to feed in... *Sírénaeopolis Magna*."

"Undoubtedly," said Côbb.

"What's in the bag?" asked Távi.

"Rats, like I told the legionnaires."

"What's *really* in the bag?"

"Jerky, dried apples, and ship's biscuit," said Côbb.

"They would have beaten you if they'd opened the bag," said Távi.

"I know," said Côbb.

"Thank you," said Távi. The stable yard was quiet for three breaths. "What's in the jug?"

"Mint drink," said Côbb. "It's refreshing."

"We'll see," said Távi.

Côbb put the cloth bag and the jug by the opening for the storm sewer. Both disappeared. "I need to know more about the emperor's new advisers," he said.

"I'd already figured that out," said Távi with a grin. "You're a wizard, aren't you?"

"I don't have a magestone on my person," said Côbb. "I can't work wizardry without it."

"The mage makes the magestone, not the other way around, or something along those lines," Távi replied.

"Where did you hear that?" asked Côbb.

"A friend read it in a book," said Távi.

"I'll bet I know which one," said Côbb.

Távi didn't answer.

Côbb took a deep breath and slowly got to his feet. *It's too bad I lost that carved dragon,* he thought. *I wonder how long it will take Nûd and Bonnie to give me a great-grandchild?*

Chapter 20

Three Mountains Valley

"Wheee!" shouted Bonnie with a volume loud enough to trigger an avalanche. Her mouth was quite close to Nûd's left ear and he reached up to rub away the pain from Bonnie's expression of glee.

"Am I to assume you like flying on wyvern-back?" he asked.

"Like it?" she said. "I *love* it!" She squeezed Nûd's waist with both arms. "It's *almost* as good as..."

"You don't have to complete that sentence," said Nûd. "And thanks for saying *almost.*"

Bonnie moved her lips close to Nûd's ear, kissed it, and whispered, "Maybe we could try combining the two sometime."

"We don't want to shock Rocky with our amorous behavior," Nûd teased.

"You wouldn't be shocked, would you, Rocky?" asked Bonnie.

Rocky bobbed his scaly black head and showed more of his sharp white teeth in reply.

"See," said Bonnie. "He's smiling."

"Or laughing at us," said Nûd.

"Could be both," Bonnie replied.

Rocky snorted and puffs of dark smoke emerged from his nostrils. Bonnie nibbled on Nûd's earlobe and could feel him shiver.

"Stop that," he said. "You should be appreciating the scenery. I decided to fly instead of gate so we could keep Rocky with us, and I could show you the beautiful countryside."

Verro had transported Fercha, Nûd, Bonnie, and Rocky to Fercha's tower and Fercha had sent them through her gate to Melyncárreg. Now Nûd, Bonnie, and Rocky were flying south to Three Mountains Valley and Travelers' Rest, the home of Nûd's friends, Rōlin and Peregrína. The craggy, heavily forested land near the castle where Nûd had grown up had changed to more open country between purple, snow-capped peaks. The broad valley below was covered in tall grass.

"What are those?" asked Bonnie, pointing over Nûd's shoulder at a large herd of some sort of antlered animal.

Nûd looked where she was pointing. "Those are elk," he replied. "There are lots of them out here. They make good eating and are a welcome change from wisent meat."

"I don't think I've tasted either," said Bonnie.

"One's a lot like venison, the other is like lean beef," said Nûd. "That's only to be expected, since elk are big deer and wisents are big cows."

"Wisents don't look much like cows," said Bonnie.

"They are, though," said Nûd. "They don't shed their horns like deer shed their antlers."

"I think I've spent too many years stuck in classrooms at the Institute at Bhaile Pónaire, scratching on slates with pieces of chalk," said Bonnie. "I'm glad to be exploring the wider world—with you."

"I'm glad to have you with me," said Nûd. "Look there!"

"Oooo!" Bonnie exclaimed. "It's so blue!"

"That's Big Beaver Lake," said Nûd. "According to Rōlin and Peregrína, giant beavers dammed the river farther south three hundred years ago and made the lake. Before then, it was just a slightly wider spot on the river."

"There have been people out here for three hundred years?" asked Bonnie.

"No, less than a hundred," said Nûd. "Rōlin's grandfather..."

"Robin Goodfellow!" noted Bonnie.

"Correct," said Nûd. "Robin Goodfellow built the castle at Melyncárreg—except for three of the towers—then moved south to Three Mountains Valley to get away from the sulphurous stink."

"Then how did Rōlin and Peregrína know the dam was built three hundred years ago?" asked Bonnie.

"Peregrína said it had something to do with counting rings on the logs the giant beavers used to build their dam," said Nûd.

"I know about that," said Bonnie. "Scholars at the Institute used that trick to confirm the timbers holding up the roof of the refectory are over a thousand years old." She laughed close enough to Nûd's ear that it tickled.

"What?" he asked.

"We used to joke that some of the faculty members at the Institute remembered it being built," she said.

"Did you consider slicing one of them in half to count their rings and confirm it?" asked Nûd.

"Hah!" said Bonnie. "You would have fit in well as a student at the Institute. I suggested the same thing and ended up washing dishes for a month."

"Actions have consequences," said Nûd.

"Are there fish in the lake?" asked Bonnie.

"Lots," said Nûd. "Rōlin used to take me fishing there when Damon was talking to Peregrína about..."

Nûd never finished his sentence. He couldn't see what had happened, but suddenly Bonnie arms weren't around his waist. He turned around and saw the leather strap holding her to the saddle on Rocky's back had been sliced through as if by a knife—or sharp talons. A scream of triumph came from above. Nûd looked up to see a mother gryffon holding Bonnie by the flying disk slung over her back. She was carrying Bonnie north and west toward one of the higher peaks and accompanied by three smaller gryffons who must be her offspring.

A fifth winged creature too far away for Nûd to recognize appeared to be pursuing the gryffons. He could see it was nearly as large as the mama gryffon and a much faster flier.

Does the newcomer want Bonnie, too? Nûd wondered. He put that question aside, having more pressing items to worry about—like rescuing Bonnie.

Rocky was a step ahead of Nûd, relying on instinct rather than deliberation. He tilted his wings and adjusted his course to follow the gryffons, beating his wings faster than a skilled cook whipping egg whites into a froth. Nûd leaned close against Rocky's neck so his body didn't reduce the wyvern's aerodynamic efficiency.

When they saw Rocky was gaining on their mother and her struggling prize, the three smaller gryffons turned to discourage the wyvern's pursuit. Two approached Rocky's shoulders from either side, staying well back from his head, while the third planned to attack from behind.

Gryffons' claws and beaks could do a lot of damage, even to a wyvern's hard scales, Nûd realized. He drew his sword—the one Duke Háiddon had been helping him learn to use—and turned in his saddle to help deal with the third gryffon. Hovering over Rocky's hindquarters, that crafty beast was ready to pounce and bring its sharp beak down on the base of the wyvern's spine.

Not if I can help it, thought Nûd. He extended his body as far as he could, but it still wasn't close enough to let him reach the soon-to-be-attacking gryffon. Nûd grabbed the severed strap that had been holding Bonnie on Rocky's back. One end was still connected to the saddle, so he adjusted the buckle to make the strap as long as possible and grabbed its far end, giving himself a few feet to maneuver. *How much harder could this be than walking along the top of the narrow battlements back at the castle in Melyncárreg?* he considered.

Nûd took a deep breath, focused on his balance, and stepped out along Rocky's back with one hand on the strap and the other on his outstretched blade.

The third gryffon swooped in and Nûd was just about to stab it when Rocky gyrated and shifted his massive body first left, then right. Nûd heard the sound of fire jetting from Rocky's mouth just before he lost his footing and found himself flat on Rocky's back, still clutching the strap in one hand and his sword in the other. A moment later he smelled charred feathers and heard squawking, roaring protests from the two gryffons attacking from the front.

Two huge eagle's legs with sharp talons appeared in front of Nûd's eyes. They were ready to dig into Rocky's back, but Nûd was quicker. He rolled on his back, let go of the strap, grabbed his sword in both hands, and stabbed upward, aiming for the part of the gryffon where its eagle front met its lion back. More squawking, roaring protests came from the third gryffon, who retreated to join its siblings several hundred yards away from Rocky.

Nûd fumbled behind him until he found the strap, made his way back to the saddle, and secured himself. He looked up in time to see the mama gryffon flying away from Rocky like she had been shot from a ballista. The strange new creature pursuing the mama gryffon had taken Bonnie and claimed her as a prize. *Blast!* thought Nûd. He hefted his sword and tried to figure out its precise balance in case he had to throw it at the flying beast—*definitely not a gryffon*—who was almost on top of them. *Why isn't Rocky flaming?* he wondered. *Because he doesn't want to hurt Bonnie, of course,* came the answer from the still functioning part of his brain.

Bonnie's voice came from back of the odd-looking new creature. "Nûd, are you hurt?" she said. He didn't answer, so she cast a quick listening spell on both of them to improve their communications. "Are you hurt?" Bonnie repeated.

"I'm fine," Nûd replied. "How are *you?*" He looked at the creature again and saw that Bonnie was riding comfortably on a beast that seemed half bear and half owl. It was gryffon-like, but not an eagle-lion, and the bear part was lithe and muscular, not hulking like a cave bear. The owl part had prominent *horns* like the great horned owls in the forests of Dâron and powerful wings clearly strong enough to propel it through the sky at great speed. "How did you escape the gryffon?" Nûd asked.

"Nûd, meet Béryl," said Bonnie. "She's an *owlberron*—and my new familiar."

"An owlberron?" asked Nûd. "I've never heard of them."

"There are illustrations of one in an old bestiary back at the Institute," said Bonnie. "I know they used to live in the mountains of Athica, but I had no idea there were any here."

"Béryl," said Nûd. "I like the name. She's like you, always wise and fierce when necessary."

Bonnie beamed and stroked the feathers on the owlberron's head. "That fits," she said. "I never thought I'd have a familiar, let alone an owlberron."

Rocky curved his head back on his long neck to catch Nûd's eye. Both wyvern and man shrugged.

"Welcome to the family, Béryl," said Nûd, waving to Bonnie and her mount hovering close by.

"Should we still head for Travelers' Rest?" asked Bonnie.

"Of course," said Nûd. "I expect even a Tamloch scholar-wizard showing up on the back of an owlberron won't surprise our hosts."

"They *do* know we're coming, don't they?" asked Bonnie.

"Of course," said Nûd. "Fercha let them know before she unlocked the gate from her tower to Melyncárreg."

"Good," said Bonnie. "Three Mountains Valley *does* look beautiful from the air; you were right about that."

"I used to love coming down here to visit," said Nûd. He waved his hands to take in the entire valley. "There's plenty of land nearby for growing hay and raising cattle." Nûd tilted his head and Bonnie could almost hear wheels inside his brain turning as he thought. "I'll need to talk to Rōlin and Peregrína about places for planting wheat," Nûd said a few seconds later. "And the best location for the dairy farmers from the Coombe."

"I want to see the vast herds of wisents you told me about," said Bonnie, interrupting.

"That may have to wait for another trip," said Nûd. "Here's Travelers' Rest."

* * * * *

Rōlin and Peregrína took Béryl's arrival in stride.

"We've seen far stranger things in our travels," said Peregrína.

"Like the people with eyes, noses, and mouths in the middle of their chests," said Rōlin.

"And the strange folk in Afarika with one giant foot," added Peregrína.

"Stop teasing Bonnie," said Nûd. "I've read *The Histories*. Herodotus made that up."

"Or shared other writers' imaginings," said Bonnie. "I've read Herodotus, too. We like to laugh at the illustrations."

"We can't fool them," said Peregrína, adding a quick grin. She turned her head to look out the window. "It was kind of Rocky to bring back an elk for Béryl."

"He brought back a flathorn for himself," said Rōlin.

"I'm glad they're getting along," said Bonnie. "Given the traditional antagonism between birds and snakes."

"Don't let Rocky hear you call him a snake," said Nûd.

"That's wise," said Bonnie. "And I'm not sure how Béryl would feel about being referred to as a bird."

"I'm sure she'll bear it," said Nûd.

Bonnie groaned softly, shook her head, and wagged a finger at Nûd.

"He was like that even as a child," said Peregrína. "You'd best learn to live with it."

"Are you sure the two of *you* can get used to having more people around?" asked Nûd. "There will be tens of thousands, even hundreds of thousands coming."

"It will be nice to have company after being mostly alone here for so long," said Rōlin. "Maybe there will be wizards and artists willing to help us carry on our work among the new arrivals, too?"

"That would be nice," said Peregrína. "Do you have any interest in cartography, Bonnie?"

"No, I'm sorry," the younger wizard replied. "My academic focus is on congruencies and non-Euclidean geometry. I'm going to work with Fercha on building wide gates from all our refuge caverns to here."

"We all have different talents," said Peregrína. "Rōlin, where is the best place for the wheat farmers to relocate?"

"There's good land for growing wheat due east of here," Rōlin replied. "And fields ready to be cleared that should work well for barley farther north. They're covered in wildflowers right now."

"Sounds like good land for honeybees," said Bonnie. "I used to help harvest honey from hives near the Institute."

"Maybe you should bring some bees out here along with the people and livestock," said Peregrína. "Sweet-root juice just isn't the same."

"Sweet-root?" asked Bonnie.

"It's one of Rōlin's projects," said Nûd. "There's a root that grows wild in the valley that's something like a turnip, but a little sweet. Rōlin has been selectively breeding them to make them sweeter."

"We squeeze out the juice and boil it, like maple syrup," said Rōlin. "You can try it on the wheatcakes I'll make you for breakfast."

"I'm afraid we can't stay the night," said Bonnie. "Though I'd really like to. Your home and the land around it are quite beautiful."

"There's a council meeting for the leaders of the Orluin Alliance tomorrow morning," said Nûd. "We need to get back. Everyone will be glad to learn they're welcome here."

"Of course," said Peregrína. "Just ring us if we can provide any information that might be helpful." She tilted her head in thought.

Bonnie watched Peregrína and realized where Nûd had learned the gesture.

"If you can give me an hour," Peregrína continued. "I'll make a copy of my map of Three Mountains Valley and Rōlin can mark in what areas are best for which crops or livestock."

"That would be a big help," said Nûd."

"And waiting won't be a problem," said Bonnie. "Béryl isn't finished eating her elk."

"While Rocky is still roasting and consuming his flathorn," added Nûd. "It's getting messy in that part of your yard."

"Don't worry. The coyotes will clean up anything remaining," said Rōlin. "I'll just have to set our wards a little closer to the cabin tonight."

"What's a coyote?" asked Bonnie.

"A wild dog—bigger than a fox, smaller than a wolf, and smarter than a raccoon," said Nûd. He paused and rubbed his chin. "That gives me an idea. Coyotes are *very* good at finding food. I wonder how the emperor's invaders would deal with a few hundred coyotes in Nova Eboracum?"

"I could build a wide gate to transport them," Bonnie offered.

"I hope you know what you're doing," said Peregrína.

"So do I," said Nûd.

"Don't worry," said Bonnie. "He'll be too busy doing more immediately important king things to worry about gating coyotes."

"That's probably for the best," said Peregrína.

Chapter 21

Imperial Advisers

"Have more stuffed dormice, Your Majesty," said the emperor as she extended a large golden platter holding eight *somethings* to Túathal. The rolled-up items arrayed on the platter looked like giant sausages. The former king of Tamloch transferred one of the dormice to his plate, nodded at Sírénae in thanks, and began to eat, ignoring everyone else at the breakfast table.

"What are they really?" Gwýnnett asked the emperor quietly. "Stuffed rats?"

"Of course not," said Sírénae. She bisected a dormouse with her knife and claimed one of the halves. "Supplies are short, but not *that* short—at least not for me." Sírénae frowned, then smiled to hide her frustration. "They're squirrels," she told her guests. "And squirrels aren't that different from the dormice we have back across the Ocean." Sírénae used the tip of her knife to point to the interior. "The cooks tell me they're stuffed with meat from other squirrels, plus pine nuts and the stems of wild onions, all flavored with garum."

Gwýnnett took the platter from Sírénae, claimed the other half dormouse, and passed the platter to Hibblig on her right. "You Roma do love your fish sauce," she said. "You seem to put it on everything."

"Nearly everything," confirmed Sírénae. "I have quite a sweet tooth, you know, and love the version of this dish that's made with honey, not garum, but we've used up all the honey we brought with us. Magister Umbrose and Magister Callidus have their wizards out searching for more."

"We'll have honey for you soon, Your Imperial Majesty," said Umbrose, who was seated on the Túathal's left. "My scout-wizards are out looking for some now."

"I hope your spies are successful," said Hibblig. "I can tell them which estates near Brendinas have the most hives."

"I have reports on those estates already," said Umbrose. "The hives that *should* be there are missing."

"That's strange," said Kennig, who took a dormouse for himself after poking Hibblig to pass the platter. "I can't see bees living happily underground."

"Don't be foolish," said Hibblig. "Of course they're not underground."

"Fool, fool, gold means rule," said Túathal. He waved his hands as if he was conducting musicians, then crossed his hands on his chest, leaned back in his chair, and wiped excess garum off his lips with the linen napkin tied around his neck.

"You liked the dish, good subject king?" asked Sírénae. She adjusted the vellum crown covered with gold leaf and faux-painted gemstones she'd had made for Túathal, so it sat straighter on his head.

"Subject, predicate, yes I liked it quite a bit," Túathal answered. He smiled at Sírénae as if waiting for her to praise him. She responded with a smile and a pat on his shoulder. His own madness and the drugs Gwýnnett gave him made Túathal well suited to be Sírénae's court jester.

"Excellent," said the emperor. She looked up to acknowledge the arrival of a servant carrying a bowl of something that smelled far worse than fish sauce. Sírénae took the bowl, glanced at its contents, and dismissed the servant with a nod. "Your Majesty," said Sírénae, capturing Túathal's attention. "It would please me if you would feed Thraxa."

"I need to feed, indeed, agreed," said Túathal. He stood up, revealing his impressive height, and extended a long arm to take the bowl offered by the emperor. Túathal sniffed and turned up his nose, then recited more nonsense. "Awful offal, as you wish. Guts from squirrels, not sauce from fish!" He walked down to the corner of the room where Thraxa was chained and held a squirrel's heart, liver, and lungs between his fingers.

"Careful," said Sírénae. "You can lose a hand that way."

"Thraxa won't harm me," said Túathal. "She'd much rather charm me."

Kennig couldn't stop watching Túathal and Thraxa. It was clear the former king of Tamloch had no idea how dangerous it was to hand feed the snow-gryffon. Still, the ill-tempered beast did not attack Túathal. *Maybe Thraxa senses that Sírénae is fond of Túathal so she's decided to accept him as well?* Kennig considered. *Or maybe there's something to the old stories about mortal threats passing madmen by?* He took another bite of his stuffed dormouse and reminded himself to ask Gwýnnett which drug she'd recently added to Túathal's collection that caused the former king to speak so oddly.

"You promised us information about caves where the people of this so-called alliance could be hiding," said Umbrose. He had a stuffed dormouse on his plate but hadn't yet taken a bite of it. "When can I get the details?"

"Today, if you'd like," said Princess Gwýnnett. "There's a large cavern complex in the mountains of Dâron's southern provinces. I was impressed by the size of them."

"Southern Dâron has a lot of mountains," said Magister Umbrose. "Can you be more specific?"

"I was quite young when I visited," said Gwýnnett. "My father hired six wizards to fly us to see a natural bridge made of stone. It took us two days to fly to the caverns from our estates north of Brendinas and another day after that to reach the natural bridge. You can't expect a child to remember more than that. Just ask the locals, they'll tell you how to find the caverns."

"There *aren't* any locals, they're all underground," Umbrose complained. He held a piece of dormouse near his mouth on the end of his knife and Kennig thought the spymaster seemed ready to use his knife on Gwýnnett without additional provocation.

"That's not *my* problem, is it?" said the princess.

Kennig spoke up to head off potential bloodshed. "I'm sure the natural bridge would be easy to spot from the air," he said. "I remember seeing a picture of it in the royal palace in Brendinas." Kennig used his illusion magic to generate a small model of the curved stone bridge in the air above the table. Everyone, including Thraxa and Túathal, looked up to stare at Kennig's illusion.

"Pretty. Far from the city," said Túathal.

"What do you know about it?" snapped Sírénae.

"Chiming sounds, underground," said Tamloch's former king.

"What's he talking about?" asked Umbrose.

"I remember," said Gwýnnett. "Our guide tapped several of the stone icicles with a hammer and they made a musical sound like handbells."

"Not sure where, but I was there," said Túathal.

Thraxa nudged Túathal with her beak. He held the bowl of squirrel innards close enough so she could retrieve them with her tongue.

Sírénae turned to Gwýnnett. "Can you make him less confused?" the emperor asked. "If Túathal has been to the caverns in southern Dâron you spoke of, we'll need his mind clear to help find them."

"I have just the thing for that in my suite," said Gwýnnett. "When do you want him coherent?"

"Now," said Umbrose. "Today. As fast as you can. I'll fly south with a scouting party and we'll find the place where the alliance fools are cowering."

"Towering, overpowering," said Túathal. He put the bowl on the floor in front of Thraxa so the snow-gryffon could lap up the blood it still held.

The emperor shook her head. "How would Túathal ever have visited caves in southern Dâron?" she asked.

"There was a time when Dâron and Tamloch were at peace," announced Hibblig. He used a voice more appropriate for a challenge during a wizards' duel than a conversation at the breakfast table. "Túathal could have toured Dâron then, as a guest of the Old King."

Umbrose swallowed the piece of dormouse he'd been chewing. "What about other caverns?" he asked. "There must be more places of refuge to hold everyone."

"I can tell you about the caves near Brendinas," said Hibblig. "Plus a few north and west of Tyford."

"Good," said Sírénae. "We won't need to worry about Gwýnnett adjusting *your* medications."

Kennig brought his napkin to his lips to hide his smile. *I wouldn't be so sure about that,* he thought. "There are caves behind the Great Falls connecting two of the Inland Seas," Kennig offered. "Maybe some sought refuge there?"

"Do you know about these falls?" Sírénae asked Umbrose.

"They're far to the west," said emperor's spymaster. "I can show you on a map."

"Has anyone confirmed that caves aren't marked on the maps of Orluin in our possession?" asked Sírénae, realizing that possibility after Umbrose's statement.

"I'm not sure, Your Imperial Majesty," said the unctuous spymaster.

"That would be very. Legendary," said Túathal.

"I think he means check the maps' legends to see if caves or mines are marked," said Kennig.

"I knew what he meant," barked Sírénae. "Do any of you know of more caverns?"

Gwýnnett cleared her throat and wiped fish sauce from her lips. "When Túathal was less mad, he had mentioned places where he may have hidden treasure. I assume most of them would be in Tamloch. I have ways of making him more suggestible and willing to talk about his hiding places. We could interrogate him before he heads south."

"That's an excellent idea," said the emperor. "Umbrose, you'll want to take notes. The princess seems like she might be a welcome addition to your staff."

"That is my fervent hope, Your Imperial Majesty," said Gwýnnett. She fixed her gaze on Umbrose and shifted to a sensuous throaty whisper. "I'm sure there are many ways I could prove my usefulness to *you*, Magister Umbrose."

Kennig watched Hibblig's face while Gwýnnett was speaking. He worried that his cousin might overreact to Gwýnnett's attempts to flirt with the spymaster. Hibblig was watching Umbrose, however, and noted that Umbrose didn't rise to Gwýnnett's bait. *I suppose he's had quite a few women try to gain his favor one way or another,* Kennig considered. *His face doesn't give away his thoughts, at least. That must be a survival trait if you work for Sírénae.*

"We'll see," said the emperor. "The more caves we can identify, the more likely we'll be able to find the cowards cowering below ground and commandeer their stores. I miss fine manchet bread—and honey."

"It won't be long now until we find them," declared Umbrose.

"It had best not be," said Sírénae. She looked over her shoulder at Thraxa and the spots of blood on her beak and feathers. "Magister Kennig," she said. "You'd mentioned something about the Alliance having dragons earlier?"

"That's right," said Kennig. "A green one and a blue one. They're quite large."

"As big as our blacks?" asked the emperor.

"Far larger," said Hibblig, who decided to insert himself into the conversation. He took a deep breath to emphasize his own broad frame. "Each one is bigger than five or six of your black dragons."

"That's ridiculous," said Sírénae. "Xaxidiánus is the largest dragon in the world."

"I assure you, these Orluin dragons *are* much larger than yours," said Kennig. "Let me show you."

Two heartbeats later, the breakfast table held small copies of Viridáxés and Zûrafiérix. They were stretched out on a simulation of the battlefield outside the walls of Riyas so that the emperor could appreciate their vast size. Then Kennig added one of the black dragons he'd seen flying above Nova Eboracum when they'd approached the palace. The black dragon was shorter than Viridáxés' tail and much less massive.

"I. See," said the emperor. "That changes things. Umbrose, why didn't you find this out for me earlier?"

"Like Your Imperial Majesty, I didn't believe it, and therefore discounted any reports as mere rumors," said the spymaster.

"Rumor, tumor, leave us in bad humor," said Túathal. He took the last dormouse from the platter, stuffed half of it into his mouth, and tossed the other half to Thraxa who caught it in the air.

"We're going to need to rethink our strategy if the Alliance can send such dragons against us," said Sírénae.

"At least they don't seem to be in a hurry to attack us," said Umbrose.

"So far," said Sírénae. "Though I expect those dragons are behind the problems we've been having with the fishing fleet."

"As you say, my emperor," Umbrose intoned.

"Pull the three dragons back from the expeditionary force attacking the Northern Clan Landers," said Sírénae. "And get Xaxidiánus and Magister Callidus here immediately. We'll need potent magic to fight dragons of that size."

"I'll see to it," said Umbrose. He rose, nodded to Sírénae, and left the room.

"My powerful wizardry is at your service," said Hibblig. He stood and walked to stand behind Gwýnnett, then put his hand on her shoulder. "The princess stands with you as well."

Gwýnnett leaned away from Hibblig so his hand slipped down and he had to regain his balance. "I can speak for myself," she said. "And I'm still sitting, for now. I'll stand when it's time to adjust Túathal's medications and interrogate him."

Sírénae directed a feral smile at Gwýnnett. Both women nodded. "It's time," said the emperor.

"Time, slime, rhyme," said Túathal.

When Gwýnnett stood, Sírénae beckoned her close so the emperor could whisper in Gwýnnett's ear. "When you adjust what you're giving him, see if you can make him stop talking that way," said Sírénae. "It's annoying."

"I'll try," said Gwýnnett.

"Sigh. Fly. Die," said Túathal in a sing-song voice.

Kennig rose to leave and sincerely hoped Tamloch's former king didn't have a gift for predicting the future.

Chapter 22

Celéri the Spy

"Blast!" Celéri protested to the sky around her. "Where *are* they?"

She'd been flying north along the Rhuthro looking for Gruffyd and Nyssia and their boat for over an hour and had just flown past a short tower on the east bank without catching sight of them. Celéri had considered stopping at the tower to see if it held any treasures—or food—but decided against it when a large hound began barking at her from the tower's dock.

Who do you *belong to?* she wondered. *And how could the big guardsman and the slender swordswoman have gotten so far ahead of me?* She shook her head in frustration. *I wonder when they left Merry's steading? Why did I have to oversleep? And what did Merry put in that tea?*

Celéri resolved to stop crying over spilled cider. *There's not much I can do about it now except find them,* she told herself. With an unspoken command to her magestone, she rose a hundred feet higher and increased the resolving power on the distance-viewing lenses she'd created from solidified sound. Unfortunately, neither greater altitude nor enhanced eyesight was much help, because the banks of the Rhuthro were heavily forested. A small boat propelled by a pull-stone would be quite hard to spot and it wasn't like she could ask anyone along the way if they'd seen a broad-shouldered man and a woman with long blonde hair float by recently. Celéri hadn't seen another human being since she'd gone to bed last night. Reluctantly, she descended until she was only a dozen feet above the water.

There are plenty of animals, though, she noted, appreciating her new vantage point. Deer, squirrels, and rabbits were everywhere along the Rhuthro. A family of beavers had built a dam on a tributary stream that had once fed directly into the river, creating a small lake behind it. A red fox looked up at her flying disk from the top of a boulder farther downstream and she saw a curious raccoon-like creature hanging from a tree branch only a few feet overhead. *I have to remember that this isn't Nárbo,* she thought. *I'm used to cities, not wild countryside.*

A mile further north Celéri overtook a snake undulating along the river with the current. It was tan with dark hourglass markings and a copper-colored head and seemed oblivious to her passage. *I'm not going to forget about you, however,* she considered, determining to be especially careful if she ever stopped to hunt for food. *I'm probably too squeamish to kill a rabbit or a squirrel,* Celéri determined. *And killing a deer would waste too much meat, but I could probably snag a fish with a bubble of solidified sound if I got hungry, so long as I do it from high enough up to avoid swimming snakes.*

Celéri laughed, realizing that growing up in the capital of the Western Empire meant she was more used to getting her meals from the special dining rooms established for military wizards or occasionally from a local *taverna*. The last meal she'd actually *cooked* for herself was a sausage on the end of a stick held over an open fire when she'd dropped in to update some legionnaires with a scouting report while on campaign in northern Éberria. "Can I put a fish on the end of a stick?" she asked a passing cloud.

For the moment, she wasn't hungry, thank goodness. It was mid-morning and the griddlecakes with honey she'd had earlier would be enough to tide her over until noon, at least. *How long do I keep following the river?* she asked herself. *Two more hours should do it,* Celéri concluded. *If I don't spot them by the time the sun is at its zenith, I'll have lunch and fly back to reclaim the small coracle full of honey. The emperor will appreciate that, I'm sure, even if she'd be a lot happier to learn the location of one of the caves where the locals were hiding.*

After another hour of flying, Celéri saw something to break the monotony of her trip. A structure appeared in the distance. It was a large stone castle that seemed to be on the west bank, though she wasn't completely sure because the river wandered back and forth like a swimming snake. The castle seemed to be made of gray

stone and had four massive square towers—one at each corner,
as if designed by someone lacking architectural talent who could
only draw straight lines. When Celéri flew closer she could see a
beautiful circular keep in the center. It rose higher than the four
corner towers and was made from a lighter-colored gray stone that
reflected as white where the sunlight caught it.

It's probably a later addition, thought Celéri. *This is probably the
home of a Count or Duke, if I'm remembering the martial hierarchies
used by these western kingdoms.* She thought about her lessons on
Orluin history. *Maybe it's Jarl, not Count,* she considered. *No, Jarl
is what that Nordland-descended kingdom uses for its nobles. Earl!
Is that the usage in Dâron?* Celéri was pleased with herself for
remembering, but soon forgot anything to do with local titles. She
had just come around a bend in the river and could appreciate the
castle's impressive presence properly.

The castle's walls rose somewhere between sixty and eighty feet
high and seemed to be anchored in bedrock. A corner of the
giant fortress stuck out into the Rhuthro and vast stone docks
along one wall seemed ready to support the trade of a rich and
sizable territory. No vessels of any kind were in evidence, however.
Where are all the boats? Celéri wondered. *I can see individual
barbarians, I mean members of the Orluin Alliance, going into hiding,
but what sort of place could they hide where they could take their boats
with them?*

Celéri flew above the castle's walls and looked down at the
courtyard inside. It was deserted, except for a pair of doves cooing in
a nest wedged into an architectural detail on the circular tower.
Celéri flew closer and saw the doves were tending to a pair of
eggs inside the nest. *I can always boil an egg and might be able to
bring myself to pluck a dove,* she thought. She enclosed the birds,
nest, and eggs in a bubble of semi-permeable solidified sound and
proceeded down the river. The doves' soft coos grew louder but
didn't bother Celéri. In fact, she enjoyed their company.

I hope I don't get a small bird as my familiar, she thought. *I want
something more impressive!*

"Coo-coo..." said the doves, unsure what to make of their new spherical home.

"No, I'm not crazy," said Celéri to the doves. "I'm just trying to find Gruffyd and Nyssia."

She purposely flew along the narrow gap in the rocks the Rhuthro cut just downstream from the castle. Below her, the water frothed like milk warmed by a hot poker. "I'm glad I'm not trying to take a boat through that passage," Celéri announced. This time, the doves were silent.

It was nearly noon, Celéri's self-imposed deadline for finding her quarries, when the young Roma wizard spotted another tower. This one was built of white stone, accented by a spiral of blue-colored rocks forming a stairway around the outside leading from the ground to its crenelated top. *It must belong to a wizard,* thought Celéri. *And one with a sense of style,* she noted as she admired the design of the blue spiral.

Celéri warned herself to be careful approaching the tower, since many wizards set traps to prevent anyone from entering their magical sanctums. After thorough scans of the roof revealed nothing dangerous, Celéri decided to land there and see if she could get inside from the top. Unfortunately, the trapdoor she discovered was locked by some sort of wizardry. Celéri tried a few of the most common door-opening spells, without success.

She contemplated, then rejected eating the doves or boiling their eggs for lunch. It was too much trouble. Instead, she pulled more jerky and ship's biscuit from her pouch and started the laborious process of changing both into something edible. Soaking the biscuit in an ounce of wine from her wineskin would help, so she put the biscuit and the wine in another sphere of solidified sound to soften while she chewed on the dried, spiced strips of beef.

The doves—unaware of their close escape—decided to sleep, since Celéri had put their sphere of solidified sound down on a well-trimmed flat stone between two crenellations. Following several more attempts at opening the trapdoor, Celéri gave up and sat beside the doves, dangling her legs out over the southern edge of the tower while her teeth worked on somewhat softened biscuit. She wisely kept her flying disk strapped to her back in case she slipped. *I don't want the emperor to be deprived of the illustrious career I plan to have as a wizard,* thought Celéri, smiling.

She was peering down between her boot-shod toes when a large hidden door in the base of the tower slammed open, making a tremendous noise and waking the doves.

"Coo?" they cried.

"Quiet," Celéri whispered, continuing to stare below.

A black wyvern and an odd flying creature something like a gryffon built from an owl and a bear, not an eagle and a lion, shot out through the door heading south at high speed. Celéri watched the door close behind them and noticed a tall man was riding the wyvern and a woman with a flying disk strapped to her back was atop the strange beast.

Well now, Celéri thought. *They look like a far more interesting group to follow.*

She cast a simple illusion around her body to make it invisible, released the doves, climbed aboard her flying disk, and set off in stealthy pursuit of the new arrivals.

Chapter 23

Reporting In

"I'm *so* glad you were able to join us, Callidus," said Sírénae. Her face, however, looked far from happy and her tone confirmed her displeasure.

"I came as fast as I could," said Callidus. "Admiral Pixo came, too." *And Thraxa isn't here,* he noted, thankful for the beast's absence.

"The only reason you arrived as quickly as you did was because you called Xaxidiánus back to transport you," said Sírénae. "Without," she sniffed, "authorization from *me.*"

"We assumed your summons was an urgent one," said the admiral.

"Of course it was," said the emperor. "I can't *wait* to hear more bad news." She looked around the table and raised an eyebrow. "Am I wrong? Do any of you have *good* news to share?"

Machaera, Pixo, and Callidus, seated around a small conference table near Sírénae's suite in the imperial palace, were silent.

"No, Your Imperial Majesty," said Callidus at last. "At least I don't."

"Neither do I," said Admiral Pixo. "Except for a single net full of fish to add to the imperial larder."

"That's something," said Sírénae. "What kind of fish?"

"It's very large, Your Imperial Majesty, and its flesh is pink and tasty," said Pixo. "I think it's almost as good as beefsteak."

"I'll be the judge of that," said Sírénae. "I hope for your sake you're right. See that the fish are delivered to the imperial kitchens."

"As you command, My Emperor," said the admiral, not risking Sírénae's further ire by letting her know the fish had already been delivered as specified.

"I take it the pescatarian expedition was a failure?" said the emperor, making her question seem more of a statement.

"Sadly, you're correct," said Magister Callidus. "Something cut our nets before we could haul them in."

"Something?" asked Sírénae, turning her head from Callidus to Pixo.

"It was very large," said the admiral. "But it stayed underwater, and we couldn't see it."

"Large enough to be a dragon?" asked the emperor.

"Larger," said Pixo. "It might have been the same kraken that attacked our ships near Nova Eboracum harbor."

"You mean Sírénaeopolis Magna harbor," said Sírénae.

Machaera caught Pixo's eye and nodded her head a fraction.

"Why yes, that's indeed what I meant," said the admiral. "Sírénaeopolis Magna harbor."

"I don't think you encountered a kraken," said Sírénae.

"Oh?" asked Pixo.

"I think you had a run-in with a giant dragon," the emperor continued. "Possibly more than one of them. New arrivals—turncoats from Dâron and Tamloch and the Southern Clan Lands—have confirmed that two almost impossibly large dragons *do* exist and are supporting the locals against us."

"Impossibly large?" asked Magister Callidus, trying to judge just how much Sírénae knew.

"More than a hundred feet long, each one," said Sírénae. "They say there's a green one *and* a blue one."

"For Tamloch and Dâron," muttered Callidus quietly.

"What did you say?" demanded Sírénae.

"I was thinking that green is the color of Tamloch, while blue is the color of Dâron," said the magister. "I was wondering if each petty kingdom has its own dragon."

"If they do, defeating the local kingdoms won't be as easy as we expected," said Machaera. "We'll need more big spear-throwers, more mages..."

"And more dragons," said the emperor. "I'm going to call back the dragons I sent with you to fight against the Northern Clan Landers and keep all seven of our dragons together, so they'll be more effective if the giant Orluin dragons try to attack *me.*"

Cut off the beast's head and it will die, thought Callidus. *Unless Umbrose decides to support someone else in Sírénae's place.* He rubbed his chin, unable to decide whether the spymaster's potential new choice—given the likely candidates—would be better or worse. *Worse,* he considered. *Definitely worse.*

"Where's Magister Umbrose?" Callidus asked.

"He's off with those new arrivals I'd mentioned—two wizards, a Dâron princess, and the mad former king of Tamloch—tracking down a major lead on the location of one of the local cowards' cavern hideaways," said Sírénae. "He, at least, seems to be producing results for me."

"No one would be happier if Umbrose found an Alliance refuge— and associated supplies," Magister Callidus affirmed.

"My own niece is out scouting for honey for Your Imperial Majesty," said Admiral Pixo.

"She's a capable mage, if a bit young," said Callidus.

"I hope she can work quickly," said Sírénae. "That pink-fleshed fish Pixo mentioned would be even better basted with honey, I'm sure."

"No doubt," Pixo confirmed.

"What do *you* have to say for yourself, general?" Sírénae asked Machaera. "Are you going to report more failures before your legions are two days out of the city?"

"No, Your Imperial Majesty," said Machaera. "I want to let you know that we should be able to handle the Northern Clan Landers with the five, now seven legions you've allocated, along with the two hundred elephants you've assigned."

"At least I don't have to tell *you* to be wary of the Northern Clan Landers," said Sírénae.

"True," said General Machaera. "I've encouraged Belisaria to share my respect for them as well, but you've given us an over-whelming force we can use to crush them and crush them we will."

"Even without three dragons?" probed the emperor.

"Even so," said Machaera. "We'll use the Clan Landers' own siege engines against the giant dragons if they decide to fight us as well."

"Take care not to hit any of *our* dragons with ballista bolts," said Sírénae. "Any siege engineer damaging one of *my* dragons will be fed to Thraxa."

"Understood, Your Imperial Majesty," said Machaera. "The legions are marching up the Abbenoth and so far, the supply barges, legionnaires, and elephants have been unmolested. The countryside is deserted. We don't expect to fight until we get to the Clan Landers' mountains."

"Excellent," said Sírénae. "It sounds like you're making good time. How soon do you expect to get there?"

"Not for several days," said the general. "The soldiers have to stop to find their dinners by catching wild game and the elephants have to forage. We're marching at half the rate we would if we had enough supplies."

"That can't be helped," said Sírénae. "I need to hold food in reserve for the imperial household."

She means herself, thought Callidus.

"And we need to keep oats and hay for our horses," the emperor continued. "Cavalry isn't of much value if you can count the ribs on the *equites'* mounts."

"I'm sure your Imperial Majesty's knights and their horses will do their usual superb job of taking the battle to your enemies," said General Machaera.

Callidus admired the way Machaera played to Sírénae's vanity. He could play that game as well but had grown tired of it ever since Sírénae and her fleet went west. He suspected Sírénae's desire to keep her cavalry close by and well fed had more to do with paranoia than planning. As if sensing Callidus was distracted, Sírénae addressed him next.

"Senior Magister," Sírénae began. "How is the research into creating wide gates proceeding?"

Callidus let out a breath, slowly. "We haven't made much more progress since our last report," he said. "Though we haven't lost any more mages to test-gate problems."

Sírénae huffed. "I told you to accelerate that research. What do I care about sacrificing junior battle wizards when we *know* wide gates are possible? Every day that goes by without us having that capability puts us more at risk."

"I understand," said Callidus, "but we're not losing junior battle wizards, we're losing some of my most experienced mages—the closest thing I have to scholars of magic—in all this accelerated testing."

"What sorts of things are going wrong?" asked Machaera, trying to divert Sírénae's anger.

"It's mostly stability issues," said Callidus. "The gates will seem stable for a few seconds, then start to implode. The wizards anchoring the corners get pulled in and end up who knows where. I think it has to do with relative motions of the two points since the odds of problems go up based on the square of the distance between..."

"Enough of that," said Sírénae. "Just keep at it and bring me good news—*soon!*"

"Yes, Your Imperial Majesty," said Callidus.

"One more thing," said the emperor.

Callidus was instantly wary. *One more thing* was one of Sírénae's favorite ploys to catch her subordinates off guard. "My emperor?" he said.

"Have any of your wizards recently mastered *ad hoc* gating?" she asked. "It would be quite valuable to have another mage or two with that talent."

"As you know, it's very rare," Callidus replied. "Magister Umbrose and I remain the only two mages with that ability."

"That's unfortunate," said Sírénae. She turned to Admiral Pixo and discussed options for using ships from the fleet to catch fish in the larger rivers of Orluin, the Abbenoth, the Brenavon, and the Moravon.

Callidus pretended to listen, but spent his time thinking instead. *She wants to replace me, that's clear,* he concluded. *Sírénae would have done it before the fleet landed if she had a better alternative—she threatened to often enough. Maybe one of these new turncoat Orluin mages is a good candidate?*

He nodded when part of his mind saw Pixo nod. *Equally clearly, her new potential Senior Magister candidate can't* ad hoc *gate and she can't eliminate me until she finds someone with that skill, too.*

Pixo shook his head, so Callidus mirrored the admiral's motion. *I'm not in danger of being fed to Thraxa immediately then. Good.*

"What sort of catch do you expect on the rivers?" Callidus heard Sírénae ask when his focus on the actions around him returned.

"No more than a tenth of what we'd catch in the Ocean," said Admiral Pixo.

"Then use ten times as many ships," said the emperor.

"I don't have enough ships with shallow drafts to *do* that," said Pixo.

"Then build more," Sírénae ordered. "There's plenty of timber here."

"Yes, Your Imperial Majesty," Pixo replied. Building ships would take months they didn't have. They'd be out of food far sooner.

Callidus recognized the signs in Sírénae's face. The meeting was over. Before he could rise, the doors to the chamber swung open with enough force to slam against the plaster-covered walls. Two people strode in—a man and a woman. Callidus recognized them both—Umbrose and Celéri.

"Emperor! Uncle Pixo! Magister Callidus!" shouted Celéri. "We found them!"

Sírénae waved away the agitated guards who stood at the entrance to the chamber behind the new arrivals. "Who did you find?" she asked.

"Not who, what!" the young mage continued, still shouting. "We found caverns where the locals are hiding."

"You found them?" asked Sírénae.

"I thought I sent you off to scout for honey," said Magister Callidus.

"You did," said Celéri, "and I found that too, but I also found the entrance to a cave complex in the mountains of southern Dâron."

"To be fair, so did we," said Magister Umbrose. "Kennig, Hibblig, Gwýnnett and I transported Túathal south to the natural stone bridge, then flew north along the mountains until he recognized the mouth of the cave complex."

"Teams of battle wizards and legionnaires are assembling to fly there and assault the caverns," said Umbrose. "We're certain to capture them now."

"Good," said Sírénae. It was the only word she got out before she was interrupted.

"I intercepted Umbrose and the others in flight so the man on the wyvern and the woman on the gryffon didn't see them," said Celéri. "Then we saw the man and woman fly into the side of a mountain and disappear. The mountainside is an illusion—it's really a cave entrance. I used my best listening spell and could tell from the echoes there were lots of interconnected caves below, and lots of people, too. Kennig kept *us* hidden while we explored. He's a powerful illusionist and handsome and..."

"Who *are* you, young wizard?" asked Sírénae. "I don't think we've met?"

"We *did* meet, in Nárbo," said Celéri, speaking very fast. "I was my uncle's guest for a dinner party you held after your victory over the Pyrénéans in Éberria."

"Sírénae, this is my grand-niece Celéri," said Admiral Pixo with a smile.

"She's a promising young wizard on my staff," added Magister Callidus. "We were just talking about her."

"I find it very hard to believe you were at one of my dinner parties and I didn't notice you," said Sírénae.

"Uncle Pixo made me promise not to say anything more than three words at a time all evening," said Celéri. "And it was a long time ago—four years back when I was only twelve."

"I see," said Sírénae, suppressing a grin. "It's a pleasure to meet you again as an adult." She nodded to Celéri and turned to Umbrose. "Where are the others now?"

"Túathal is sleeping," said Umbrose. "The trip took a lot out of him and so did whatever Gwýnnett gave him to keep him coherent. He's much better company when he's speaking in rhymes. The man takes arrogance to new heights."

"Hah," said Sírénae. "I suppose Gwýnnett dosed him with a sleeping potion now that he's back."

"Correct," said Umbrose. "I left Gwýnnett, Hibblig, and Kennig in the kitchens getting a late lunch. They're eating some sort of pink fish."

Sírénae stared at Pixo, but the admiral just shrugged. "Did I hear you say you'd found some honey?" she asked Celéri.

"Uh huh," said Celéri. "I know right where I left it, too."

She closed her eyes, stood up straight, took a deep breath, and disappeared. Moments later, she returned to the same spot, but this time she was floating a foot off the floor on her flying disk and holding some sort of giant wicker basket over her head. When she lowered the basket to the floor it was the emperor's turn to shout.

"It's full of honey!" said Sírénae.

Blast! thought Magister Callidus. *Celéri just made an* ad hoc *gate.*

"Congratulations, grand-niece," said Pixo. He stepped around the wicker basket and gave the joyful young wizard a hug. "That was impressive. Finding alliance caverns *and* honey."

"Sweet!" said Celéri. She was so excited she stuck out her arms and began to spin.

"Send the honey down to the kitchens," said the emperor, "and tell the cooks to hold my dinner. I'm coming with the troops attacking the caverns." She turned to the admiral. "You're in charge of the city while I'm gone," Sírénae commanded.

"Yes, Your Imperial Majesty," Pixo replied.

"We can have a feast afterward to celebrate your victory!" said Celéri.

"An excellent idea!" said Sírénae, echoing Celéri's youthful enthusiasm.

Callidus smiled on the outside, but somehow, on the inside, he didn't feel like celebrating.

Chapter 24

The Council Meeting

"I'm glad everyone could make it," said Princess Rúth. "We've got a lot to talk about."

The princess presided over the meeting because everyone admired and respected her. It helped that she wasn't a ruler or a provincial governor-general herself. Rúth's work helping refugees from Dâron, Tamloch, and Occidens Province turn dark caverns into safe homes was recognized as an important service by every part the Orluin Alliance—even Bifurland, which had not yet been occupied by the emperor's legions.

The council members sat in a diverse collection of chairs around a large oval table of polished stone Verro and Fercha had fashioned from rocks conjoined by magic into a single, smooth surface. The table occupied the center of a spacious chamber in the cave-complex where a large part of Dâron's population—and some from Occidens Province and Tamloch—had temporarily relocated. Inthíra had brightened up the space with a collection of wizard lamps and banners in the colors of the various kingdoms.

Dârio, Jenet, Duke Néillen, Grand Admiral Sónnel, and Verro sat below yellow and green hangings, while Nûd, Bonnie, Duke Háiddon, Eynon, Merry, and Fercha—sitting next to Verro—had banners in dark blue and sky-blue above them. Sable and purple fabric—or the illusion of it—was draped over the heads of Quintillius, Laetícia, Mafuta, Valentius, and Aleña, while King Bjarni, Queen Signý, and Amber, their master mage, sat beneath sparkling gold banners fringed in black.

Queen Carys did not attend. Living underground had aggravated longstanding problems with her breathing, so she remained in the caverns near Brendinas where she had been taken for safety.

Princess Rúth chaired the meeting from one end of the table, with her new husband Doethan beside her. Rocky and Béryl, Bonnie's owlberron, occupied the opposite end. Rocky was prepared to follow the discussion to come, as much as he was able, while Béryl—her ursine aspect ascendant—napped. Merry used one of Eynon's ring-based portable gates to connect with Viridáxés and Zûrafiérix, so the big dragons could listen in from their island.

Ace and Chee, along with a pair of small, gold dragons, were being entertained elsewhere by a pair of Bifurland girls, Sigrun, King Bjarni and Queen Signý's daughter, and her cousin Rannveigr.

"First," said Princess Rúth, "We should thank Eynon and Merry for bringing back a literal boatload of honey on their recent expedition. Our cooks promise some sweet treats to boost our spirits soon."

"Well done, young wizards," said King Bjarni, whose own hives were famous across Bifurland.

"And even better, you've denied Sírénae and her minions your golden treasure," added Queen Signý.

"About the honey..." Eynon began, but Duke Háiddon cut him off.

"You can tell us about your dalliances with the birds and bees after the meeting," said the duke. "We have more important things to discuss at present."

"That's right," Princess Rúth announced. "I've been told King Nûd and Bonnie have great news to share."

"You're pregnant?" asked Jenet, catching Bonnie's eye.

"After you," said Bonnie, recognizing Jenet's teasing for what it was, but blushing, nonetheless. "I don't have *that* sort of great news. Nûd has found us an above-ground refuge from the invaders."

"Where?" asked Dârio.

"South of Melyncárreg, in Three Mountains Valley," Nûd replied. "Two of my friends have a steading there. It's wide-open country, with a lake for fishing, fields of good pasture for herding, and well-drained land for planting crops."

"Your friends won't mind hundreds of thousands of people appearing all at once and occupying their territory?" asked Jenet.

"We won't send *everyone* to their valley," said Nûd. "There's plenty of fine land to the south and east as well."

"Melyncárreg?" asked Laetícia. "That mysterious academy for wizards in the far west Ealdamon started?"

"Correct," said Nûd.

"I look forward to seeing it," said Laetícia. "I want to know how accurate my sources were in describing it."

"Sources?" asked Eynon.

"She means her spies," said Merry.

Viridáxés snorted on the other side of the mobile gate. A puff of smoke entered the chamber through the interface and slowly rose to the ceiling.

"What about shelter?" asked Duke Háiddon. "I hear it gets cold in the western mountains."

"It's finally spring in the west," said Nûd. "That means we're only likely to get a *few* more inches of snow."

Several people laughed until they realized Nûd wasn't joking.

"Some people can stay in the castle in Melyncárreg initially," Nûd continued, "but there are vast pine forests nearby and we should be able to build cabins for everyone quickly."

"And military tents can tide us over while the cabins are constructed," said Quintillius. "I'm glad I didn't let my supply officers grind our old tents into paper stock when the new tents arrived from Alexandria last summer."

"A wise commander is prepared for emergencies," said Mafuta. "Even if bureaucratic inertia is the true reason the tents are still available."

"What about getting crops planted?" asked Duke Háiddon. "It's late for wheat, isn't it."

"No," said Nûd. "The growing season starts later in Three Mountains Valley. We'll have to plant oats and rye and barley, too."

"What about sorghum?" asked Quintillius. "My troops will want their beer."

"You'll have to make do with beer from barley," said Nûd. "The valley is too cold for sorghum."

"I'll settle for it being far enough west that we won't be found," said Quin.

"Are you sure it will be safe?" asked Duke Néillen. "What about Sírénae's spies?" His work expediting the evacuation of Tyford had returned him to Dârio and Jenet's good graces—provisionally. Now, the professional paranoia he'd cultivated while serving Túathal was surfacing.

"They're still sticking close to Nova Eboracum, Brendinas, and Riyas," said Duke Háiddon. "Sírénae is reluctant to split her forces more than that. I don't think her scouts or soldiers have pressed farther west than Tyford and the Moravon."

"But..." Eynon began. He stopped when King Bjarni interrupted him.

"She's just sent five legions north..." said Bifurland's king.

"Seven legions," said Laetícia, interrupting.

"Seven legions, then," said Bjarni. "They're marching up the Abbenoth to attack the Northern Clan Landers."

"Hah," said Duke Néillen. "That should be interesting. I wouldn't command Sírénae's legions against the Northern Clan Landers if you promised to make me emperor."

Amber ignored the duke's hyperbole. "General Machaera and Lieutenant General Belisaria will have two hundred elephants as well," added Bifurland's Master Mage.

"Those elephants may not be as great an asset as the emperor hopes," said Laetícia. Her eyes danced as she squeezed Quin's hand and smiled.

"Tell me more—later," said Amber, exchanging nods with Laetícia.

"Bifurland has a long history with the leaders of the Northern Clan Lands," said Bjarni.

"Yes," said Duke Néillen. "You'd coordinate attacks with them to hit us from two directions."

"That's water over the falls," said King Bjarni.

"We're on the same side now," said Queen Signý.

"I believe you were about to make a point," said Princess Rúth, encouraging Bjarni.

"I was indeed," said Bifurland's king. "We're going to *help* the Northern Clan Landers fight the seven legions Sírénae is sending against them."

"Can I join you?" asked Duke Néillen. "I'd love to see the tricks the Northern Clan Landers used on Tamloch's army—but directed against our enemies."

"You'd be welcome," said Bjarni. "With King Dârio's permission, of course."

Duke Néillen turned to his sovereign.

"Go ahead," said Dârio. "We can discuss force dispositions later. We will need a lot of strong backs to get cabins built out west, so I can't spare many people."

"You *can* spare quite a few," said Jenet. "We're not fully understanding the implications of wide gates for mobility. When Bjarni and Signý and Néillen are ready for our troops, we can gate them through close to the battlefield, without losing time for building cabins and planting crops in Three Mountains Valley."

"You're right," said Dârio. "Though we will probably want to move our soldiers in at least two stages so our opponents can't easily slip through one of our wide gates and immediately find where we've gone."

"That's just a detail," said Jenet. "You can work out the specifics later."

"Remember," said Quintillius. "We don't want to fight open-field battles with the invaders. We want to annoy them, not kill them."

"The Northern Clan Landers will certainly annoy them," said Duke Néillen. "There's no end to their trickery."

"I'll second that," said Quintillius. "My solution for dealing with the Northern Clan Landers was largely *not to*. If they stuck to their mountains and didn't interfere with trade from the Whale River down the long lakes to the Abbenoth my legions wouldn't bother them."

"Sometimes we'd pay them to annoy you," said King Bjarni.

"I know," said Laetícia. "They often told us so they could get paid twice—once by you, once by Occidens Province."

"Make that three times," said Duke Néillen, laughing.

"Four," said Duke Háiddon, prompting more laughter around the table.

"Now that we've established the Northern Clan Landers are skilled at diplomatic as well as military trickery, can we work out a schedule for moving our people from the caverns to the west?" asked Princess Rúth.

"If we're going to do it, we'll need to do it quickly," said Laetícia. "My sources in Nova Eboracum tell me that traitors have contacted Sírénae and may be feeding her details about where our caverns are located."

"My, umm, sources confirm that as well," said Doethan. He looked at Dârio. "From what they've said about the description of the traitors, I think your father may be alive."

"My father?" asked Dârio. "That's impossible. I saw him die."

"One of the wizards with them is reputed to be a powerful illusionist," said Doethan. "It might not have been wise of us to trust our own eyes."

"I wondered about that," said Inthíra. "It was too convenient. The illusionist must have been the wizard who escaped with Hibblig."

"That makes sense," said Doethan.

"My father's not dead?" said Dârio slowly, chewing on his words as if trying to digest something toxic.

"I can hardly believe it," said Verro. "Your father. My brother. I should be pleased, but I can't find it inside myself to be anything but worried. If Túathal is alive, who knows *what* trouble he could cause for us by working for Sírénae?"

Fercha put her hand on Verro's arm to offer comfort.

"There's more," said Doethan. "I think Princess Gwýnnett is with him."

"My mother?" said Dârio. "That's great news."

"I'm surprised," said Fercha. "I thought Gwýnnett was far from one of your favorite people."

Dârio shook his head. "You misunderstand," he said. "It shames me that Gwýnnett is my mother—but I'm thrilled she's working for the emperor. Unless Sírénae is particularly careful to have mages analyze her meals and tasters sample her food before she eats anything, Gwýnnett may eliminate her for us."

"We can hope," said Laetícia. "Sírénae's lasted this long without being poisoned."

"I hope they poison each other," said Dârio. "That would solve quite a few of our problems."

"Agreed," said Laetícia, "but we can't count on it. Let's get back to my question. Does everyone agree we have to evacuate quickly?"

"YES!" said Eynon, loud enough for his voice to echo around the chamber. "We have to get everyone out *right now!*"

At the foot of the table, Béryl opened one eye, flicked a wingtip, and went back to sleep.

"Eynon's right," said Merry. "You didn't let him explain about the Roma spy at my family's steading on the Rhuthro."

Quintillius looked at Laetícia.

"Not one of mine, husband," she said. "She means one of Umbrose's spies."

"Boiling oil!" said Quintillius. "They're searching west of the Moravon."

"That's not the worst of it," said Merry. "Tell them, Eynon."

"Celéri wasn't a very good spy," said Eynon. "She was young— about my age—and nice, actually. She helped us harvest honey. Her mission was to find honey, not caves. She said Sírénae has a sweet tooth."

"She does," said Quintillius. "But I'm afraid you were duped, Eynon. She tricked you into thinking she was nice so you would open up to her."

"In a manner of speaking, that's correct," said Merry. "But I think Eynon is right about her not being a good spy. We drugged her and left her asleep in a feather bed when we left. She couldn't have followed us."

"Are you sure?" asked Princess Rúth.

"I can't see how she could have followed us," Merry replied. "Eynon and I used a set of mobile-gate rings to help our friends Gruffyd and Nyssia get back to their refuge in caves north of the Coombe."

"It was easy since part of that cave system is flooded," said Eynon. "They just slid their boat into the river by Applegarth and paddled through."

"Well done," said Doethan.

"We'll have to remember to get their share of the honey to our friends, too," said Merry. "We didn't really have anywhere to put their portion."

"Have I met Nyssia and Gruffyd?" Princess Rúth asked.

"I don't think so," said Doethan. "Gruffyd is the son of a baron with estates on the Rhuthro. Nyssia is the daughter of a sword master from Brendinas."

"Her father is a former captain in my royal guard," said Dârio. "He's an excellent teacher and I learned a lot from him."

Nûd looked at Bonnie and she nodded. Bonnie could tell Nûd planned to find the sword master when they all got to Three Mountains Valley, since Duke Háiddon would likely find it hard to put in all the hours it would take to teach Nûd how to use a blade. An alternative and highly skilled instructor would make scheduling secret lessons easier.

"Where did you leave this imperial spy when you left?" asked Doethan.

"Asleep in my brother's bed," said Merry. "She drank enough sleepy-tea to be out for at least a few more hours after we departed."

"I'm sure Salder didn't mind, since I expect he's back in Uirsé's favor," said Doethan.

"He is," said Princess Rúth. "They're such a well-matched couple."

"Yes, my love," Doethan continued, receiving a smile from Rúth.

"Wait," said Laetícia. "What was the spy's name again? Keleri?"

"Celéri," said Eynon. He pronounced the name slowly. "Sell-AIR-ree."

"I think I know her," said Laetícia. "She's Admiral Pixo's niece."

"The one who talked constantly?" asked Quintillius.

"That's her," said Laetícia. "It was when we stopped in Nárbo on our way to Alexandria years ago. I think she was nervous. She was just a child, though quite a bit of what she said made sense even then."

"Now that you've established Celéri's identity," said Doethan to Quin and Laetícia, "can we get back to what I was saying?"

"Of course," said Laetícia.

Doethan returned his attention to Merry. "What would you do if *you* woke up and found the steading deserted?"

Merry didn't answer immediately, so Eynon jumped in.

"I think Celéri would have gone upriver, looking for Gruffyd and Nyssia and their boat," he said. "She knew we could fly and would be hard to track, but if our friends were sailing north along the river, towing the coracle full of honey behind them, she'd probably be able to catch up to them."

Merry looked at Nûd and Bonnie, then at Rocky at the far end of the table. The wyvern nodded his head and prodded Béryl with a front claw until the owlberron woke from her nap, stretched, let out a yawn that was more than half a screech, and stood beside Rocky looking back at Merry.

"When did the two of you return from Melyncárreg and emerge from Fercha's tower?" Merry asked Nûd and Bonnie.

"About noon yesterday," said Bonnie. "We flew south as fast as we could to return for the council meeting."

"Are you sure *you* weren't followed?" Merry asked.

"No," said Nûd. "We can't say one way or another." He looked down the table. "Rocky?"

The wyvern flexed his wings in a motion that was close to a human shrug. Béryl screeched again and those sitting nearby covered their ears.

"I agree with your new familiar," Princess Rúth told Bonnie. "I react the same way when I hear unpleasant news." The princess stood and rapped her knuckles on the stone table. "This changes everything, my friends. We *must* gate everyone west immediately. We also need to get word to leaders in the other cavern refuges so that *they* can move quickly as well. Fercha and Eynon, the two of you can take the lead on putting gates in place."

Eynon and Fercha nodded and stood.

"Verro," said Rúth. "You inform the Tamloch refuges. Amber, take Merry to alert the Dâron caverns. Laetícia, you can update the caves used by people from Occidens Province. There are a lot of refuges with mixed populations, so put your heads together to figure out who's going where and get moving. You can all *ad hoc* gate so it should go fast."

Verro, Amber, Merry, and Laetícia rose.

"We have communications ring links to a number of the caverns," said Doethan. "I can ensure we use them, so there are fewer places for the others to gate to."

"Good," said Rúth. "Jenet, you know the caverns that are already connected by permanent gates. Send runners out to all of them."

"Right away," Jenet replied.

"I will help Fercha and Eynon with building gates," said Bonnie.

"So will I," said Mafuta. "I'll get Felix to help me."

"What do *we* do?" asked Dârio.

"We help Princess Rúth with everything needed to get people— and their supplies and food—ready to leave," said Nûd.

Dârio looked at his cousin respectfully, with *I should have thought of that* clearly written on his face.

"How can we help?" asked Valentius, waving his hand to indicate himself and his new wife Aleña. As a newcomer used to such deliberations in the Southern Empire, he had wisely decided to listen rather than speak, until now.

"I need Duke Háiddon and Duke Néillen to help their respective kings with wrangling our people," said Rúth, "but you have extensive military experience. I'd be pleased to have you to coordinate our defense in case Sírénae attacks before the evacuation is complete."

"I am at your service," said Valentius. He stood and bowed.

"Quintillius can take the lead and Inthíra can assist you," said Princess Rúth. "She's our best illusionist and I expect stealth will be more effective than swords in that regard."

"It would be my pleasure to fight beside you, cousin," said Valentius, slapping his fist against his chest to salute Quintillius.

"I will assist with the preparations to leave," said Aleña. "I'll be more useful there."

"So will I," said Grand Admiral Sónnel. "An admiral isn't much good on land," he said, "but we do know how to move people and stores efficiently."

"Excellent," said Princess Rúth.

"With all due respect to Bifurland's Master Mage, I'm not riding along with Amber to help find Dâron's cavern refuges," said Merry. "Let me help Inthíra with our defense."

"I can assign one of my staff to accompany Amber," said Duke Háiddon.

"Fine," said Princess Rúth before turning her attention back to Merry. "I'd forgotten you're a powerful illusionist as well, which I should have remembered from your convincing projections at the battle at Riyas." She looked around the table again. "I'm glad we all have our assignments," said Rúth. "Let's get on with them."

"Aren't you forgetting something?" asked King Bjarni.

"Or are we just pickled herring to this alliance?" added Queen Signý.

"Not at all," said Rúth. "You have the best part of all."

"Really?" asked King Bjarni.

"Of course," said Rúth. "Didn't I say? You get to provide a diversion by attacking Nova Eboracum."

"What fun!" said Queen Signý, clapping her hands.

"I think the emperor is calling it Sírénaeopolis Magna now," said Doethan.

Princess Rúth turned her head toward Doethan and gave him a *did you have to bring that detail up now* look.

"We'll be able to find the place no matter what she calls it," said King Bjarni. "You can be sure of that."

"What about us?" asked Zûrafiérix through the interface of the mobile gate. "Are we still trying to avoid revealing our existence?"

"I want to kill invaders," said Viridáxés. "Or at least discourage them. May I attack Sírénaeopolis Magna, too?"

"Quintillius and I would be happier if you didn't," said Laetícia. "We want Sírénae's forces to leave, not have our city in flames."

"We are trying to keep you under wraps," Princess Rúth told the dragons. "I don't expect that situation to continue for much longer, though, since Gwýnnett, Túathal, and the other two wizards will be sure to tell the emperor about you."

"If they're willing, Zûrafiérix and Viridáxés can work with us," said Queen Sign. "We have quite a few illusionists among Bifurland's wizards and they can adjust the dragons' appearance, so their true natures remain hidden."

"I like it," said Princess Rúth. "You'll keep Sírénae off balance."

"Please don't destroy too much of my capital," said Quintillius. "My people will need a home to return to."

"There will still be a few stones standing," teased Zûrafiérix. "But I can't promise how many."

"Now *you're* sounding like Viridáxés," said Laetícia.

"We can't have *that*," said Zûrafiérix.

"Why not?" asked Viridáxés indignantly.

The chamber filled with laughter as everyone departed.

Chapter 25

Rapid Deployment

Magister Callidus and Emperor Sírénae sat across from each other on well-padded chairs in the emperor's private study. Between them was a circular table, just over a yard in diameter, made of ebony. Its surface was an inlaid mosaic of semi-precious gems, including a few squares that Callidus could sense were imbued with magical energy. Unbeknownst to either of them, the table had been a gift from Laetícia to Quintillius. It came from West Afarika and had been one of the governor-general's favorite possessions. The sun had set hours ago, but the study was brightly illuminated by three wizard lamps and a glowing log in an ornately carved marble fireplace.

"The legionnaire shuttles are working effectively," said Magister Callidus, beginning his report. "One of my best mages came up with the idea based on how giant obelisks are transported in the Southern Empire. Four wizards can transport sixty-four legionnaires if one of them generates a plane of solidified sound for the soldiers to stand on."

"Won't that many be too heavy for the wizards to lift?" asked the emperor.

"Four wizards can manage it if the legionnaires aren't in armor and we transport their equipment and supplies separately," said Callidus. "It's just over a hundred leagues to the locals' caverns in the southern mountains, and this way we can get a sizable force there quickly. It's not instantaneous, like our opponents' wide gates, but it should help us deploy our troops rapidly."

"Aren't the legionnaires vulnerable to attack when they're in the air?" asked Sírénae.

"That's why we'll need dragons to protect them," replied Callidus.

"I suppose it is acceptable to deploy my dragons for this mission, since I'll be joining you," said the emperor. "There are still twenty legions in the capital, after all."

"With three legions in Tyford and five each occupying Riyas and Brendinas," added General Machaera. "Orluin is strongly held."

"When will the deployment begin?" asked Sírénae.

"It already has," said Callidus. "We started sending batches of legionnaires a few hours ago, after we confirmed the location of the caves. We're staging them an hour's march north of the main cavern's entrance so we can attack in force with a few thousand troops instead of a few hundred."

"Good," said Sírénae. "See if you can deploy a full legion, though. Five thousand legionnaires would be more effective than two thousand."

"I don't know if we have enough wizards to get that many soldiers to the southern mountains by morning," said Magister Callidus.

"Just make it happen," said the emperor. "I don't care how. You're a resourceful man."

Callidus pressed his lips together to prevent himself from saying what he wanted. "I'll do what I can," he said, after a slow breath.

"Find a way," said Sírénae. "You can gate me through to the staging area just before we're ready to attack." Sírénae paused and tilted her head for a moment before resuming her normal posture. "Better yet," she said, "send Pixo's niece to get me. What was her name, Carrôt?"

"*Celéri*, Your Imperial Majesty," Callidus replied. He was sure Sírénae knew Celéri's name but was enjoying tormenting him by intentionally misremembering. *Having a third wizard who can make* ad hoc *gates pushes everything off balance,* thought Callidus. *Before, only Umbrose and I had that ability. Will a three-legged stool be more or less stable than one with only two? And will Celéri's new abilities make it more or less likely Sírénae will eliminate me?* He debated the point in his mind. *More,* he decided.

"Umbrose will remain in Sírénaeopolis Magna," said the emperor. "He can alert us if the locals stage a raid."

"I don't think that's a good idea," said Callidus.

"He shouldn't alert us?" asked Sírénae.

"He shouldn't be left alone in the capital."

"Why Callidus, are you warning me against Umbrose?" asked Sírénae. "I didn't think that was your style—though it's undoubtedly his."

"Umbrose is an ambitious man," said Callidus. "He models himself on you."

"And you think I would betray my sovereign if left unsupervised?"

"In the beat of a hummingbird's wings," said Callidus with a smile.

"I suppose I deserve that," said Sírénae. "I'm proud of it, really, though I only did it twice."

"Three times, Your Imperial Majesty. Don't forget the time when we..."

"I'll forget that incident if I choose to," said Sírénae, stopping Callidus with a raised palm. She stretched her arms wide and brought them back together, rubbing her hands together beneath her chin as if she was about to savor a favorite meal. She smiled at Callidus. "Though perhaps I *should* make an effort to remember it. I think fondly of the day I seized Nova Cartago when the province's Imperial governor was away visiting his mistress on Mallórca."

"That was the beginning of your long rise to the purple," said Callidus, shaking his head slowly. "You seized his ship when he returned—and there wasn't much the governor could do about it."

"I *was* clever, wasn't I?"

Callidus nodded. "I'll never forget the look on his face when you informed him the Western Emperor had approved you as his replacement," he said, hiding his distaste. "The governor killed himself with his own *gladius* rather than accept the disgrace."

"It's too bad I was lying," said Sírénae. She chuckled quietly for a few seconds, then caught Callidus in her hawk-like gaze. "You don't have to worry about Umbrose trying to replace me," said the emperor. "We have an understanding."

"What *sort* of understanding?" asked Callidus.

"He would rather work from the shadows and considers himself the true power behind the throne," said Sírénae. "I allow him to continue in that delusion—so long as he is of use to me—just like *you,* Callidus.

"I live to serve," said the Magister.

"You live because I haven't yet decided to serve you to Thraxa," said Sírénae.

"I'm too old and stringy for even Thraxa to take much pleasure in consuming me."

"Perhaps, but don't think that protects you."

"Trust me, I don't," said Callidus. "I know my life is in your hands." He leaned in toward her and spoke his next words softly. "Tell me, my emperor, why do you treat your senior advisers so poorly?"

"You know why," said Sírénae. "An emperor must wield a granite fist in an iron glove."

"Some say the glove should be made of velvet."

"Those who say so are fools," Sírénae answered. "It is better for a ruler to be feared than loved."

I once loved you, thought Callidus as his mind went back to a time when the two of them were decades younger. *And I thought you loved me, but you only loved power.*

Callidus lowered his head. "You *are* feared, Your Imperial Majesty," he said quietly.

"Let us ensure that the people of the Orluin Alliance fear me as well, Senior Magister," said Sírénae. "Leave me and get on with ensuring my legionnaires are ready to capture the cravens in the caves—and their supplies."

"Yes, Your Imperial Majesty," said Callidus.

* * * * *

His mind spinning, Callidus left the room and strode off down the marble-tiled palace corridor, his rapid footsteps sending quick staccato echoes off the stone ceiling. He needed to find Celéri so she could *ad hoc* gate him to the staging area, since he obviously needed to shift between the capital and the mountains frequently to oversee the deployment. *I'll have to get Celéri a communications ring,* he thought. *I want to help build her loyalty to me, not Umbrose.*

Callidus stopped by his suite, collected a pair of matched rings, and considered where he'd most likely find Pixo's niece. *I'll start with her quarters,* he decided. *She's probably tired after a long day of flying.*

After consulting a servant, Callidus followed a complicated set of directions until he located the door to Celéri's room. He knocked on it, none too gently. "Hello?" he said. "Are you awake?" No one answered, so he repeated the process.

The adjacent door down the hall opened and a young woman with tousled hair wearing only a sleeping gown and an unhappy expression stuck her head out. "Pipe down," she said. "Some of us are trying to sleep. Celéri's not here." Callidus turned to face the woman and her expression changed. "Oh! Senior Magister Callidus, I'm so sorry. I didn't know it was you. Can I help you with anything?"

Callidus smiled. "You can tell me where I'd be most likely to find Celéri," he said. "I'm sure you'd know better than I would."

"Of course, Senior Magister," said the woman. "She said she was going to have a drink with the emperor's newest advisers. I expect she's with them."

"Very good," said Callidus. "You've been quite helpful. Thank you."

"I'm glad to be of assistance, Senior Magister," said the woman. "I'm sorry I yelled at you. I'd been practicing making gates all day and was trying to get some sleep before I have to fly to the caverns later tonight."

"I understand," said Callidus. "Were you on the team working on wide gates?"

"No, Senior Magister. I'm still a junior wizard. I'm just trying to make a gate I can walk through."

"We all have to begin somewhere," said Callidus. "Traditional narrow gates *do* have their uses. Thank you again and rest well."

The young woman gave Callidus an awkward smile and closed her door.

Callidus thought about narrow gates all the way to the large suite Sírénae had assigned to her new advisers. Unlike Celéri's single room, a pair of imperial guards stood outside *this* door. They came to attention as Callidus approached.

"Is there a young wizard—a woman with short black hair—inside?" asked Callidus.

"Aye, Magister, y'have the right of it," said the guard on the right. She was obviously a Caledonian from her accent, and her freckles.

"How long has the young wizard been here?"

"Nigh onto an hour, yer magisterial excellence," said the guard. "The lassie sure knows how to talk."

The guard on the left was a stocky man with a broken nose. He gave the guard on the right a look that said *and so do you.*

"I'm going inside," said Callidus. "No need to announce me."

"That's fine, seein' as yer the emperor's top wizard and all, savin' fer Magister Um-brose," said the guard on the right. She stepped back and opened the door.

Callidus didn't take the guard's words as a particularly good omen. What he saw inside the suite's main room emphasized the point. Celéri was there, sitting next to one of the Orluin wizards— Kennig, if Callidus remembered correctly—on a high-backed divan. Well, she wasn't sitting, actually. She was leaning into Kennig with her head on his chest. She held a large, richly enameled goblet in both hands and seemed to be snuggled up against him. Kennig had his arm around her shoulders with his fingertips positioned indecorously.

Celéri wore only a thin undergown. Her elaborately embroidered purple wizard robes were folded over a straight-backed chair by a small table. From her expression, Callidus supposed the goblet did not hold Celéri's first cup of wine.

Gwýnnett and Hibblig sat on a second divan that faced the first, though they occupied opposite ends instead of sitting in close proximity. Túathal was asleep atop a braided rug on the floor, snoring softly.

"Hello, Magister Callidus," said Celéri. "Have you met my new friends? We found the locals' caves today."

"I know who they are," said Callidus. "Their reputations precede them."

"As does *your* reputation, Magister," said Gwýnnett. "Though no one said you were so handsome, in a distinguished sort of way."

"Skip the flattery, I made peace with my graying hair years ago," said Callidus.

"Don't worry, there's nothing special about *you*," said Kennig. "She's like that with every man she meets, young or old."

"At least I know what category I belong to," Callidus replied.

"You'd best be in the category of keeping your hands off," said Hibblig. "The woman is mine."

"You have the most amusing delusions, Hibblig," said Gwýnnett. "But I'll keep you around as long as you're useful to me."

Where have I heard that *before?* thought Callidus, keeping his amusement to himself. "You're the mother of the king of Dâron?"

"I was," said Gwýnnett. "Now I'm the mother of the king of Tamloch."

"Intriguing," said Callidus. "You'll have to tell me the story of how that happened a bit later when I have more time."

"Gladly," said Gwýnnett. "Would you like some refreshment before you go?"

"Not if you're serving," said Callidus. "In that, too, your reputation precedes you."

"I understand your caution, all things considered," said Gwýnnett. "What brings you to our quarters?"

"Your guest," said the magister.

"Don't tell me you're here to take away my new friend," said Kennig. "We were just starting to get better acquainted, weren't we, dear?"

"We were," said Celéri, "but we'll have plenty of time to widen and deepen our friendship in the future." She hugged Kennig and pecked his cheek before standing and facing Callidus, who could only detect a slight unsteadiness to her posture. "How can I serve you, Senior Magister?" she asked, after she had slipped into her wizards' robe.

"Are you sober enough to gate me to the staging area in the southern mountains?" he asked.

"No, but I will be after a piece of ship's biscuit and a cup of mint tea," said Celéri.

"Then follow me," said Callidus. "You can get both at the senior officers' mess. They have cooks available until quite late." He nodded to the other three people in the room. "Until another day," he said.

Gwýnnett smiled and Hibblig frowned.

"Hurry back," said Kennig.

Celéri didn't answer before Callidus gated the two of them away.

* * * * *

Magister Callidus watched Celéri as she dipped ship's biscuit into her tea. Her motions were slow and deliberate. The warm water helped make the biscuit at least somewhat more digestible and Callidus supposed the pleasant scent of the mint helped sober Celéri up as much as the mechanics of eating. He had his own mug of mint tea and held it below his nose for a few seconds, gently inhaling before he took a sip. There were quite a few things he wanted to say to the young wizard, but he was wise enough not to say them.

Something he'd said to that other young wizard in the hall near Celéri's quarters earlier stuck in his mind. *Traditional narrow gates* do *have their uses.* "I wonder..." he said.

"What?" asked Celéri, looking up from her mug.

"We don't know how to build wide gates," Callidus replied. "But we have lots of wizards. Why don't we build *lots* of small, point-to-point gates?"

"That's a great idea," said Celéri. "I have ideas like that all the time. I'll claim it as my own."

Of course you will, thought Callidus. Her response reminded him of the pair of communications rings. He removed one from his belt pouch and handed it to Celéri, then made her memorize the phrase she'd need to open it. "Next time you have such an idea, you can let me know directly."

"Thank you," said Celéri. "I promise to use it wisely."

Not likely, thought Callidus. Then he reconsidered. *I didn't have the best judgment myself when I was sixteen.*

"Good," said Callidus aloud. "See that you do. Now finish your tea and biscuit. I have to let Machaera and my lieutenant wizards know there's going to be a change in plans." *This should make Sirénae happy,* thought Callidus. *I hope she stays that way—at least long enough for us to get through the current engagement.*

Chapter 26

Second Evacuation

King Nûd and Bonnie stood to one side of a large cavern watching a dozen long lines of people and wagons cross the interface of the wide gate leading to Three Mountains Valley. Nûd could see the familiar landscape near Rōlin and Peregrína's home on the other side and looked forward to stepping through himself soon. It would be a pleasure to return to the grander scale of the western lands where he'd lived most of his life. Unfortunately, it would be several hours before he could do so. As king, he considered it his duty to ensure the evacuation was complete and everyone in the cave-complex was safe first. Duke Háiddon was already on the other side directing the flow of wagons, handcarts, livestock, pets, and households.

"It's going well, don't you think?" said Bonnie.

"Well enough," said Nûd. "We're lucky that everyone knew the process after our first, even quicker move to the caverns. People are so glad about the prospect of sunlight they're eager to leave."

"It helps that we have less to transport now, too," said Bonnie.

"I know," said Nûd. "We don't have all the food and livestock we had then. I'll have to figure out a way to compensate the farmers who sacrificed their cows so we could eat."

"Could you get Eynon to collect gold to give them?" asked Bonnie. "I loved the story you told about how the two of you extracted gold from the Melyncárreg river."

"I could, but I won't," said Nûd. "If there's suddenly a lot more gold around, it will lose its value."

"Really?" asked Bonnie.

"Yes," said Nûd. "That's what happened to the Roma across the Ocean when huge deposits of gold were found in central Afarika. The four emperors had to close the mines and gild the roofs of half the state buildings in Roma Mater to restore confidence in its worth."

"Did you read that in a book?" asked Bonnie.

"More than one, actually," Nûd replied.

"It seems that the library in Melyncárreg holds a wider range of topics than the one at the Institute in Bhaile Pónaire," said Bonnie.

"Wait until you see it," said Nûd. "You'll be impressed—but be prepared to hold your nose."

"Are there books on unsavory topics?" asked Bonnie.

"No, it's not that," said Nûd. "It's just that the air in Melyncárreg stinks like rotten eggs."

"I'll suffer through the smell for the sake of scholarship," said Bonnie, smiling. She squeezed Nûd's hand and he squeezed back. "With a bit of research, perhaps I can devise a semi-permeable sphere of solidified sound that filters out the sulphur."

"That would be great!" said Nûd. He was particularly uninterested in having his voice return to its former *rusty hinge* timbre and worried returning to Melyncárreg would have that effect. *Would my voice changing make a difference in how Bonnie feels about me?* Nûd wondered. *For that matter, can a king be respected if he sounds like an old barn door opening when he speaks?*

Bonnie broke Nûd's train of thought by tugging on his arm. "Look at that family," she said, pointing at a square cart with large wooden wheels close by. "There must be a dozen children in there, all under ten." A stolid ox pulled the cart at a measured pace, its wheels squeaking with every revolution, while several associated adults tried—mostly successfully— to keep the children from falling out. The children's laughter was even louder than the sound of the cart's wheels and echoed off the cavern's roof before it abruptly cut off as they crossed the barrier.

"Do you want a big family?" asked Nûd.

"What?" asked Bonnie, whose attention had been focused on generating a tendril of solidified sound to ensure a child hanging off the back of the cart actually made it through the interface.

"I asked if you wanted a big family," said Nûd. "It's a natural thing for people planning to marry to talk about."

"I'm not sure," Bonnie replied. "I wasn't convinced I *would* marry— until I met you."

"The same is true for me," said Nûd.

"You know, you never did formally ask me to marry you," Bonnie noted.

"I didn't?" asked Nûd.

"No," said Bonnie. "I think we both just assumed we would—and so did everyone else."

"People keep asking if we've set a date—as if we both didn't have enough to worry about dealing with keeping everyone safe and coping with the invasion," said Nûd.

"By people, you mean your mother?" asked Bonnie.

"Not just her," said Nûd. "Princess Rúth and Doethan have been teasing me and Duke Háiddon keeps hinting that the two of us need to find time to *discuss important matters related to the royal succession.*"

Bonnie laughed. "Your friends have been kind to me, then," she said. "The only one pushing me has been my cousin Uirsé, and I can push back about when she's going to marry Salder. She says they want to wait until after we've dealt with the invasion."

"Duke Háiddon does have a point," said Nûd. "We should probably make things official and get married soon, since trying to figure out who the rightful king of Dâron would be if we don't produce an heir would give royal genealogists fits."

"That's not a good reason to get married," Bonnie began. Then she stopped and reconsidered. "On second thought, it probably *is* a good reason to get married sooner rather than later." The smiled at Nûd. "The things I do for king and kingdom," she teased.

"And it's not even *your* kingdom," Nûd teased back, since Bonnie had been born and raised in Tamloch.

"It will be once we're married," she replied.

"I suppose you're right," said Nûd. "And the practicing will be fun."

"Practicing?" asked Bonnie.

"To produce a dozen children," said Nûd. He managed to keep his face expressionless until Bonnie raised one eyebrow, then the other. After he grinned, she replied.

"Two," said Bonnie firmly. "Maybe three."

"Children?" asked Nûd.

"Days," Bonnie replied. "If we're going to marry, I'd like to get it over with."

"Fercha and Princess Rúth will be disappointed they won't have time to put together a huge production," said Nûd. He looked at Bonnie and saw her nodding. "That's part of your plan, right?"

"The king is wise," said Bonnie.

Nûd shook his head. "That's not a lot of time for a royal wedding."

"You're the king, so by definition it will be a royal wedding no matter if we have it in the palace in Brendinas or by jumping over a sword right here in this cave."

"True," said Nûd. "Though my mother is correct about the banquet hall at the castle in Melyncárreg being a perfect spot for a wedding—if you can filter out the smell of sulphur."

"I'll work on that as soon as we're in Three Mountains Valley," said Bonnie.

"Good," said Nûd. He especially did not want to say his wedding vows in his sulphur-tinged voice.

Bonnie kissed Nûd and several of the nearest families headed through the wide gate turned and smiled. "Kiss him again," said a little girl walking beside her father and holding his hand. When Bonnie complied, the child clapped and waved as she crossed the interface.

"You should assign better land to the farmers who gave up their stock," said Bonnie when she broke their kiss.

"Excuse me?" said Nûd. "I thought we were talking about weddings."

"We *were* talking about how to compensate farmers who sacrificed their stock," said Bonnie. "You got us off on a tangent about libraries, sulphur, and how many children we wanted."

"Two, maybe three," said Nûd.

"Children?" asked Bonnie, seeming pleased that they were both thinking about the same numbers.

"No," said Nûd, grinning again. "I'll have two or three times the land assigned to the farmers who gave up their stock."

"That sounds equitable," said Bonnie.

Nearby, the lines of people and wagons going through the gate were getting shorter. The tens of thousands of people in the cave-complex around them were nearly through and the sounds of conversations, bleating goats, and mooing cows were much softer, making it much easier for Nûd and Bonnie to hear the rapid foot-falls of leather boots on stone as a messenger in sky-blue livery ran toward them from a distant passage.

"Your Majesty, Your Majesty!" the messenger shouted. She wiped sweat from her face and continued. "One of the northern-Dâron refuge caves is flooding. The people there have to get out immediately!"

"Is it an attack?" asked Nûd. He noticed water was dripping from the messenger's boots, supporting the truth of her news.

"No, heavy thunderstorms," said the messenger. "The caves north of the Rhuthro Valley are naturally flooded, with a river running through them. It's just that the rains have been so heavy the water is rising and there's nowhere for the people to go. I came through a gate connecting our caves to here, but it's not big enough to get everyone out in time."

Nûd turned to Bonnie. "Can you help? Fercha's assisted the people in most of the smaller caves already using Eynon's mobile gates and went through to Three Mountains Valley a few hours ago. Eynon himself is on the surface above *these* caverns with Merry, Inthíra and the others tasked to defend us."

"I can certainly help," said Bonnie. "We can use one of Eynon's mobile gates as well. He gave me a pair of rings that generate them. I'd promised to analyze the rings to see if I could improve them."

"That's great," said Nûd.

"Follow me, please, good mage," said the messenger, motioning back the way she had come. "The gate to the northern caves is this way."

Nûd hugged Bonnie. "Be safe," he said. "I'll clear this wide gate so the people arriving from the northern caves can use it. Once you open your gate, these caves will start filling with water as the new people come through. If you can't close your mobile gate, all these caverns will flood as well."

"Stay safe yourself," said Bonnie. She blew Nûd one last kiss over her shoulder as she sped off toward the passage, matching the messenger stride for stride.

Nûd watched her for a few breaths, then set himself to helping the last remaining families and carts make their way through the wide gate. Weeks ago, Fercha had determined how to stabilize wide gates without requiring wizards to anchor each of the corners, so Nûd was on his own. The wizards remaining on this side of the gate—other than Bonnie—were on the surface. Nûd was counting the last dozen people remaining when he recognized Aleña approaching.

"I've checked the side passages for stragglers," Aleña told Nûd. The short young woman from the Isles of Dogs who'd recently married Valentius motioned toward the gate and continued. "Once these last few cross the interface, that should be everyone."

"Thank you," said Nûd. "There will be more coming—they're escaping from one of the northern-Dâron caves. It's flooding and things may get wet here soon."

"I can swim," said Aleña, sharing a shy smile with Nûd. "You were wise to set up gates connecting us with the other caverns."

"I'm glad they proved helpful but was worried those gates might provide a way for the emperor's spies to map out all our sanctuaries once they found one of them," said Nûd.

"Instead, they gave us a way to save lives, not lose them," said Aleña. "Valentius tells me his father says it's not an easy thing to be a leader."

"He's right about that," said Nûd. "I look forward to getting to know your husband better."

"He's told me the same thing about you," said Aleña. She interlocked and released her fingers nervously. "Do you have a way to contact him and the others on the surface? I'm worried about him."

"I can ring Eynon," said Nûd. "He's up there with Merry now. Rocky, my wyvern, is with them too."

"And your wife's owlberron?" asked Aleña.

"We're not married, yet, but yes," said Nûd. He selected the ring Eynon had recently given him and triggered it with a phrase of command. Three chimes sounded and the ring expanded to a yard wide. "Hello, Eynon," said Nûd. "How are things looking up there?"

"Challenging," said Eynon. "We've found imperial forces an hour's march to the north. Including dragons."

"It's a good thing we've nearly completed our evacuation then," said Nûd. He filled Eynon in on the people who would soon be arriving from the flooded northern caves.

"My friends Gruffyd and Nyssia are in those caves," said Eynon.

"Bonnie is using one of your mobile ring-gates to rescue them," said Nûd.

"Then I'm sure she has things well in hand," said Eynon. "That being said, you should be up here. I think things are going to get interesting."

"I have to ensure everyone gets to Three Mountains Valley safely," Nûd protested.

"Go," said Aleña. "I will guide the last group."

"Are you sure?" asked Nûd.

He didn't hear Aleña's answer since Eynon had *ad hoc* gated into the cavern, pulled Nûd onto his flying disk, and transported them both to the surface before Nûd could react.

Chapter 27

Up the Abbenoth

"Keep them moving," Lieutenant General Belisaria told Giérra, the legate in charge of the legion in the vanguard. "The emperor wants us to put these Northern Clan Lands barbarians in their place quickly."

"Of course," Giérra replied. The legate was a tall, well-muscled woman with a scar on her cheek from the mountains of Éberria. "I completely understand and that shouldn't be a problem. The roads are up to imperial standards and the legionnaires are doing better than twenty miles a day."

Belisaria knew that was an exceptional pace, but she wanted to get to the northern mountains even faster—without exhausting her forces. She said as much to Giérra. "I still wish we could speed things up."

"There *is* a way we could make better time," the legate suggested. "If wizards could make us pull-stones."

"You're talking about putting the troops on barges?" asked Belisaria.

"I am," said the legate. "There are plenty of trees along the shore to build them, and elephants to drag the cut logs to the river."

"But will the elephants be willing to board the barges to go up-river themselves?" mused Belisaria.

"They're not afraid of water," said the legate. "From what I've seen, they love it."

"How much time would we lose building the barges, versus continuing to march?" asked Belisaria.

"A day, I expect," said the legate. "But we'd move four times faster. In my experience, pull-stones can move a barge at ten miles an hour, even against the current."

"And perhaps our mages know tricks to make military caliber pull-stones that would be even more efficient," said Belisaria. "The supply barges seem to have no trouble keeping up with our march."

"That's part of what gave me the idea," said the legate.

"How will the legionnaires feel about being cargo on a barge instead of moving on their own?" asked Belisaria.

"If they don't have to march, they'll love it," said Giérra.

"I expect they will," said Belisaria. "I'll give the necessary orders."

* * * * *

Thousands of trees were felled in short order—a much easier process using sharp planes of solidified sound instead of saws and axes. Náegosh, the senior wizard assigned to Belisaria's command, had his battle mages cast the spells most often used to strengthen log stockades for a new purpose. Soon, the cut tree trunks were bound together into hundreds of sturdy rafts. Belisaria was pleased that their new flotilla was finished in half a day, not the full day Giérra had expected. The sun was still a few fingers above the mountains on the western horizon when Giérra and Náegosh found the lieutenant general to inform her that the work was completed.

"Well done," said Belisaria. "I'm quite pleased and will make sure General Machaera and the emperor hear of your efforts."

"Many thanks," said Giérra. The legate turned to Náegosh. "Do you think it's safe for us to travel at night? We could make even better time that way."

"I don't see why not," the wizard replied. "Especially if we scout ahead for obstacles on the river."

"Or forces waiting in ambush on the banks," added Belisaria. "I've been warned that the Northern Clan Landers are experts at such things."

"We're still more than a hundred miles south of their lands," said Giérra. "I'll expect they'll wait until we're closer to try any tricks."

"I hope you're right," said Belisaria.

"We've managed to get excellent results with an experimental pull-stone spell, by the way," said Náegosh. "They'll only last for a month, but the new stones will give us one and a half times the speed of our previous military-grade pull-stones."

Belisaria clapped her hands. "That's excellent," she said.

"There is one problem," said Giérra.

"Only one?" asked Belisaria.

"It's about our supplies," said the legate. "We're using them up faster than we anticipated."

"Why is that?" asked the lieutenant general.

"Because we haven't been finding deer and small game to supplement the rations we carry," said Giérra.

"I find that hard to believe," said Belisaria. "Every legion I've ever commanded has had foragers able to bring back meat for the pot."

"That's true in my experience as well," said Giérra. "But they haven't come back with as much as a brace of coneys—and it will get worse when we're speeding up the river on rafts instead of marching."

"Because the foragers won't be able to keep pace?" asked Náegosh. "Can my wizards help?"

"Only if they can spot deer for us from the air," said Giérra.

"We don't have time for that," said Belisaria. "We'll just have to defeat the Northern Clan Landers and claim their supplies."

Giérra and Náegosh nodded. That was as good a plan as any.

"Now," said Belisaria. "Let's get everyone—and all the elephants—on the rafts and head upriver."

* * * * *

Northern Clan Chief Arminta felt a vibration on her left hand. She removed a gold ring and heard three chimes as it expanded.

"Hello, old friend," said Arminta. "It's always a pleasure to see you, even through a ring's interface."

"Likewise," said Queen Signý of Bifurland. "Unfortunately, I'm not calling with a mutual opportunity for diplomatic larceny this time."

"I didn't expect you to be," Arminta answered. "My guess is that it has something to do with the invaders."

"Correct," said Signý. "There are seven legions sailing up the Abbenoth to attack you."

"And two hundred elephants," Arminta added.

"You always had excellent spies," said Signý.

"Here in the Northern Clan Lands we prefer to call them scouts," said Arminta.

"You can call them expert treasure finders for all I care," said Signý with a smile. "It looks like I don't have anything to share with you, then. You already have the latest news."

"I suspect there's more to your call than informing me about invading Roma troop movements," said Arminta.

"That's a reasonable assumption," said Signý. "Especially since the invaders will be in your territory five days earlier than expected."

"Oh?" said Arminta. "They've switched to rafts and military-grade pull-stones, then?"

"It's a joy to speak with someone who picks things up quickly," said Signý.

"Likewise," said Arminta. "I expect that you have *more* new information to share?"

"That's true," said Signý. "Sírénae and a rapid strike team are in southwestern Dâron, about to raid one of the allies' cave complexes."

"Which will be empty, I assume?" said Arminta.

Queen Signý smiled across the communications ring's interface, then nodded. "Bjarni and I have been asked to attack Nova Eboracum while the emperor is away."

"A diversion to keep her off balance?" asked Arminta.

"Precisely," said Signý. "We're hoping to raid their warehouses and appropriate their stores."

"Clever," said Arminta. "We've been driving all the game away from the legions marching north. There's not a squirrel, deer, or rabbit within five miles of either bank of the Abbenoth."

"How did you manage *that*?" asked Signý.

"I think I'll keep our specific methods to myself," said Arminta. "At least until we've been temporary allies is a bit longer."

"In case you want to do the same thing to *us* some day?" said Signý.

Arminta didn't say anything in reply, which was answer enough.

"Be that way," said Signý. Her brows furrowed for a moment, then she smiled. "I do have one last tidbit to share. It relates to the invaders' elephants." The Bifurland queen told the Northern Clan Lands chief and managed to keep a straight face as she did so.

"Oh my," said Arminta after she'd stopped laughing.

"Amber will deliver a trumpeter later today," said Signý. "Laetícia assured me he knows all the proper signals."

"Very good," said Arminta. "We'll take excellent care of him."

"Thank you," said Signý. "Remember, the goal isn't killing the emperor's forces, it's starving them out, so they'll have to leave."

"I understand," said Arminta. "If we killed their legionnaires, they'd have fewer mouths to feed."

"I knew I wouldn't have to spell it out for you," said Signý. "By the way," she continued. "Given your excellent network of *scouts,* you wouldn't be interested in a dozen dragons to assist them with aerial observations, would you?"

"Sigrun and Rannveigr are pestering you for a more active role against the invaders?" said Arminta.

Signý nodded. "They're more annoying than cats at feeding time," said the queen.

"I have children, too," said Arminta, "though mine are grown. I'll do my best to keep your daughter and her friends safe but can't make any guarantees."

"War is war," said Signý. "At least the emperor isn't sending any of her dragons north with the legions attacking *your* people."

"Dragons are fast on the wing," said Arminta. "And it isn't that long a flight from Nova Eboracum to our mountains. Might we see the huge blue and green dragons from our side of the Ocean I've heard reported?"

"Possibly," said Signý. "But if things go as I expect, Bifurland may be able to assist with a *big* surprise of our own."

"Please keep me posted," said Arminta. "I *love* surprises—for our opponents."

"So do I," said Signý. "So do I."

Chapter 28

Planning a Raid

"That's exactly the information we need," said King Bjarni. "It will make our mission to raid the invaders' warehouses much easier to execute."

"We're glad to help," said Côbb across a communications ring's interface. "Réah and I have learned a lot working as servants in the emperor's palace."

"I'm glad you're there," said Bjarni.

"What I don't hear while working in the stables, Réah learns while serving meals," said Côbb. "The invaders seem to ignore our presence."

"I suppose you don't need to be an illusionist to be invisible," said Bjarni.

"Not if you're wearing servants' livery," said Côbb. "Réah says the kitchens are great places for gossip—and it's fascinating what information cavalry officers will share while waiting for their mounts."

"I don't doubt it," said Bjarni. "Has anyone suspected the two of you are wizards?"

"Not as far as I can tell," said Côbb. "Réah and I have buried our magestones in the big park in the middle of the island, so they won't be detected and give us away."

"What about your communications rings?" asked Bjarni. "Won't those be detected as magical?"

"We put them on wall sconces below wizard lamps," said Côbb. "That way, they look like decorations and the magic in the lamps disguises the rings' wizardry."

"Be careful," said Bjarni. "It wouldn't do to have you or Réah caught ringing us up to share information."

"I don't think we need to worry about that," said Côbb. "I'm ringing from the *cloaca maxima*."

"You're in the sewers?" asked Bjarni.

"I am," said Côbb. "The great sewer beneath Nova Eboracum, or as the emperor wants us to call it, Sírénaeopolis Magna." He angled the communications ring, so it showed the gray stone walls and channel for effluvium behind and below him.

"Given that news, I'm pleased we're not using a pair of Eynon's new rings with interfaces people can step through," said Bjarni. "And I'm especially glad the smell isn't coming through along with your face and words."

"The smell doesn't bother me," said Côbb. "I shovel horse manure most of the day."

"And I have two hundred cows and have done my share of shoveling," said Bjarni. "Cow manure is one thing, and rivers of human waste are quite another, however."

"Judging by the levels in the channel, there's less waste being produced by the people in the city," said Côbb. "Our plans to starve the invaders out seem to be working."

"Unfortunately, those plans do put a crimp in our usual style of raid," said Bjarni.

"Do tell?" said Côbb.

"Well," said Bjarni, running one calloused hand through his long blond beard, "We'd usually dash in and set fire to our opponents' vessels…"

"But you can't do that because the invaders will need those ships to take them away from Orluin when they run out of food," Côbb completed.

"Yes, blast it," said Bjarni. He smacked his fist onto the table in front of him and Côbb watched a dark liquid in a heavy pewter mug slosh dangerously.

"Drink some of your ale before you spill it," said Côbb. "I have an idea for your consideration."

"I'm listening," said Bjarni after he'd swallowed two mouthfuls of dark ale. "Most of my jarls think they're wiser than I am, so I'm used to it."

"At least until Queen Signý bends their ears and proves otherwise," Côbb replied.

Both men laughed.

"This idea is only possible thanks to Eynon's new mobile gates," Côbb continued. "Fercha tells me the moves from the caverns to Three Mountains Valley in the far west are going well and should be completed soon. That will free up lots of the new gates for other uses."

"What? You want us to invade Nova Eboracum in force?" asked Bjarni.

"By no means," said Côbb. "I'm suggesting something more subtle—and even more effective, given our overall plan."

"I think I see," said Bjarni, stroking his beard again. "Those maps you gave to Amber are part of it, if I guess correctly."

"You do," said Côbb. "The maps show the location of every warehouse holding food and drink in the city."

"They're quite a fine piece of work," said Bjarni. "They're exquisitely drawn and precisely detail what's stored where, down to the last barrel. It must have taken you and Réah weeks to draw them."

"I wish we could claim responsibility, but Réah and I didn't draw them," said Côbb. "A young friend of mine named Távi has that honor."

"Please convey my compliments to your friend, then," said Bjarni.

"I will," said Côbb. "The maps will allow Amber to *ad hoc* gate into each warehouse with one of a pair of mobile gates."

"Then my warriors can remove all the stores through the gates, leaving the warehouses empty," said Bjarni.

"And the invaders even closer to starving," said Côbb.

"Without a battle," said Bjarni. "Unless there are guards at the warehouses."

"My sources say the warehouses *are* guarded," said Côbb. "But they're on the *outside,* not the inside."

"I see," said Bjarni. "Won't there be people inside the warehouses distributing food to the kitchens around the city?"

"In the morning," said Côbb. "But not after noon. Deliveries are only made once a day."

"Interesting," said Bjarni. He looked like a waterwheel was turning gears and a millstone inside his head.

"You see the possibilities?" asked Côbb.

"I do," said Bjarni. "Is Sírénae in the city? She has a quick mind, I've heard."

"She's in southwestern Dâron, about to raid a cave complex," said Côbb.

"An *empty* cave complex?" asked Bjarni.

"That's my understanding," said Côbb.

"Who commands in the city then?" asked Bjarni.

"Admiral Pixo, if what Réah overheard is accurate," said Côbb.

Bjarni's fist pounded the table again, but this time the lower level of ale in his mug didn't attempt to escape. "The sailor who was so confused he attacked the emperor's ships in Nova Eboracum harbor? That's perfect."

"I thought you'd be pleased," said Côbb.

"Oh yes," said Bjarni. "Pixo has experience fighting Nordlanders across the Ocean and will expect Bifurlanders to be much the same in our tactics. That will make the outcome all the more surprising."

"If everything goes the way we expect," said Côbb.

"True enough," said Bjarni. "Thank you for the reminder to stay wary."

"I can guarantee you good intelligence about the warehouses," said Côbb. "My friend Távi will see to that."

"Will you and Réah be leaving Nova Eboracum after the raid?" asked Bjarni.

"I can't see how anyone would be able to tie us to the attack, so we'll stay as long as it seems prudent," said Côbb. "I hope I'll have a chance to share the invaders' reaction to losing most of their food."

"You and your wife are brave," said Bjarni.

"We're old," said Côbb. "It feels good to do something useful that *doesn't* involve wizardry for a change."

"I'll make arrangements to have the food we commandeer sent west to help the refugees manage until their own crops come in," said Bjarni.

"That would be very helpful," said Côbb. "You're lucky the invaders haven't bothered you in the north."

"If we let them establish a foothold in Orluin, it would only be a matter of time until they attack us," said Bjarni. "We want them gone as much as you do."

"I hear you will be assisting the Northern Clan Landers as well," said Côbb.

"We'll do our part," said Bjarni.

"I'm glad you're on our side now," said Côbb.

"So am I," said Bjarni. "This way we get access to wide gates and the products of Eynon's impressive imagination."

"The apprentice becomes the master," Côbb whispered to himself.

"What?" asked Bjarni.

"Nothing important," said Côbb.

"Keep me posted on any further developments," said Bjarni. "I have a diversion to plan so that Pixo won't have time to worry about the warehouses."

"I'm looking forward to it," said Côbb.

"So am I," said Bjarni. He drained his mug and enthusiastically slammed it back down on the table in front of him.

Côbb canceled his ring's connection and resolved to keep his distance from the waterfront for the foreseeable future.

Chapter 29

Wet Feet for the Emperor

"It's impolite to kidnap your king," said Nûd as he turned his head to speak to Eynon. It was difficult for Nûd to move because the young wizard had him in a bear hug. "You don't have to hold me so tight, either," Nûd added,

"Look down, Your Majesty," said Eynon, trying hard to keep a note of teasing from his tone.

Nûd did as his friend instructed and realized they were floating more than a thousand feet in the air above the mountains of southwestern Dâron. From that height, the sun was easy to see as it was beginning its journey up from the eastern horizon. "That changes things," said Nûd. "I now support you holding me, at least long enough for me to shift around behind you, so you can see where you're flying."

"My king is wise," said Eynon, teasing even more broadly. "I'll make you some distance-seeing lenses to improve your vision. I'm disguising our presence with a solidified sound illusion, but if you focus on that ridge to the north, you'll see why I brought you here." Nûd turned his head in the indicated direction and Eynon continued. "By the way, Your Majesty, I didn't kidnap you," he said. "I transported you expediently so I could appraise you of our tactical position."

"I suppose I should further demonstrate my wisdom and say, 'Thank you,'" Nûd replied. After a few more seconds gazing north, Nûd shook his head and sighed.

"What is it?" asked Eynon.

"Dragons," said Nûd. "They're not in the air, they're on the ground in various openings in the forest on the side of the mountain beyond that ridge. Soldiers would never see them from ground level, but they're easy to spot from above."

"They must be here to protect the emperor," said Eynon. "They're too big to be useful inside the caverns."

"I expect they'll be assigned to burn any of our people trying to leave the cave complex," said Nûd. "It's a good thing we've got your amazing new mobile gates, so we don't need to use the main exit."

"I'm glad my discovery has proved so useful," said Eynon. "Has Bonnie had a chance to start analyzing the magic powering the mobile gates yet?"

"Unfortunately, no," said Nûd. "She's too busy trying to get your friends and their colleagues out of the flooded northern caves at the moment."

"That's what you'd said," Eynon confirmed. "It makes me wonder if we can't use all those flood waters to arrange a special welcome for Sírénae and her forces."

"Great minds think alike," said Nûd. "If you have a few extra mobile gates, perhaps we can even increase the flow."

"You'll have to ask Fercha about them," said Eynon. "She has most of the ones I've made."

"There's probably not time for that," said Nûd. "We can hope one gate's worth of water will be enough." He rubbed the muscle behind his left ear that always got tight when he thought about talking to his mother.

"It's not like we want to drown any invading legionnaires," said Eynon.

"But it would be a pleasure to get the emperor's feet wet, at least," said Nûd.

"Maybe she'll catch a cold," said Eynon.

"She'd probably drink a healing potion as soon as she had a sniffle or a tickle in her throat," said Nûd.

"I'd bet she drinks one every day no matter how she feels, in case someone tries to poison her," said Eynon.

"Especially now that she has Gwýnnett as an adviser in residence," said Nûd.

"That's an excellent point," said Eynon. "Do you think Gwýnnett will try to kill Sírénae?"

"Unfortunately, no," said Nûd. "Gwýnnett is smart enough to realize her position depends on Sírénae's authority." Nûd paused and pressed his lips together before speaking again. "My guess is

Gwýnnett will attempt to give the emperor drugs or herbs to make her more suggestible."

"Like she did with Túathal?" asked Eynon.

"Yes," said Nûd. "And her husband, Prince Dâri."

"I'm glad *I* don't have to be around Gwýnnett," said Eynon. "She makes the skin between my shoulder blades feel like bugs are crawling on it."

"My cousin Dârio says the same thing, and she's his mother," said Nûd.

"Ugh," said Eynon. "Just talking about it makes me want a bath."

"Let's wait for that until we're in Three Mountains Valley or Melyncárreg," said Nûd. "I'll feel better with more than a thousand miles between us and the emperor—and her advisers." He felt Eynon shudder as he stood on the flying disk in front of him. "Be strong," said Nûd. "Be wise. You're my new Master Mage and I'll need your skill and wisdom to counter the foul plans that people like Gwýnnett and Túathal and Hibblig come up with."

"Yes, Your Majesty," said Eynon.

Nûd watched the young wizard stand straighter and heard him take a deep, centering breath. "Good," said Nûd after a moment. "The dragons change things," he continued.

"What do you mean?" asked Eynon.

"We'd hoped to slow the advance of the imperial forces with illusions," said Nûd. "But dragonfire negates any illusion it touches."

"As we'd learned outside Riyas," said Eynon. "But wasn't the whole idea of slowing the imperial advance buying more time to evacuate the caverns?"

"True enough," said Nûd. "The evacuation is nearly complete, so we need to change our tactics. Now we want to draw our opponents into the caverns—and get their feet wet." Nûd stared down at the green mountains below him, taking in the large black shapes occupying the biggest meadows to the north. "We also want to draw their dragons away from the emperor and keep them away from Nova Eboracum and the Northern Clan Landers."

"Ah," said Eynon. "I see what you mean. We need dragon bait."

"What do you suggest to serve that purpose?" asked Nûd.

"Dragons, of course," said Eynon. Nûd could hear Eynon's smile in his tone.

"Do you intend to request aid from Viridáxés and Zûrafiérix, then?" Nûd inquired.

"No," said Eynon. "They should remain hidden until they can be used with maximum effect. I was thinking that Inthíra and Merry and I could each manage to generate two dragon illusions each and fly them off even farther south and west."

"I like that idea," said Nûd. "The imperial dragons would be compelled to give chase." Nûd put a hand on Eynon's shoulder and spoke. "You wouldn't make your dragon illusions as big as Viridáxés and Zûrafiérix, though, would you?"

"I was thinking we'd make our dragon illusions just a little bigger than the emperor's dragons," said Eynon. "Big enough to seem a threat, but not so large as to presage the true size of *our* great dragons."

"I'm impressed," said Nûd. "I knew you were clever and creative, but I didn't know you were sneaky."

"My sister and I were quite good at pulling tricks on each other when we were younger," said Eynon. "I learned how to be sneaky in self-defense."

"That explains it," said Nûd. "I wish I had a younger sister. How is Braith, by the way?"

"She was giving singing lessons to children in the caverns to help them pass the time, last I'd checked on her," said Eynon. "I expect she's in Three Mountains Valley with my parents now."

"I'm glad she's doing well," said Nûd. "What do you suggest our soldiers who've been guarding our retreat do while you and Merry and Inthíra are luring away the emperor's black dragons?"

"Gate through to Three Mountains Valley?" Eynon suggested.

"I suppose you're right," said Nûd with a nod. "But Quintillius and Valentius will be disappointed not to cross swords with Sírénae's legionnaires."

"They'll get over it," said Eynon.

Nûd poked Eynon in the ribs with a finger and the young wizard jumped, causing his flying disk to tilt and Nûd to hold Eynon more tightly. "Make it so," Nûd commanded.

Eynon continued to mask their presence from the emperor's forces and performed a short jump with an *ad hoc* gate to appear at the camp near the entrance to the refuge caverns where the allied defenders waited. He sought out Merry and Inthíra while Nûd explained the revised plan to Quin and Valentius. The two generals grumbled but saw the wisdom of avoiding a direct confrontation. While Nûd was talking, Bonnie flew up from the mouth of the cavern to land beside him.

"Is everyone out?" asked Nûd.

"Yes, but the water level is rising quickly," said Bonnie. "It was lucky I arrived when I did to help everyone get out of the flooded northern cavern safely."

"Thank you for your timely rescue," said Nûd. He kissed Bonnie's cheek and gave her the same sort of smitten smile he'd often seen Eynon give Merry.

"Béryl and Rocky are in Three Mountains Valley with Rōlin and Peregrína," said Bonnie, answering the question that Nûd had planned to ask next. She leaned close and whispered in his ear. "I made a wall of solidified sound to hold back the flood waters so their outflow wouldn't reveal the entrance to the caverns," said Bonnie.

Nûd smiled. Bonnie sensed what he was thinking and smiled back, laughter dancing in her eyes.

Eynon, Merry, and Inthíra finished their conversation and joined Nûd, Bonnie, and the others. "There's a slight change in plans," said Eynon.

"Oh?" asked Nûd.

"Inthíra's not coming with us," said Eynon.

"I'm not fast enough," said Inthíra. "I'm afraid the emperor's dragons will catch up to me."

"I can move quickly using line-of-sight gating," added Merry. "And Eynon can *ad hoc* gate himself—or both of us, for that matter—if the dragons get too close."

"Will you still be able to generate six dragons?" asked Nûd.

"That won't be a problem," said Inthíra. "Eynon and Merry tried generating tiny models and they can each create four dragons at a time."

Nûd laughed. "Dragon's with small scales, or small-scale dragons?" he teased.

Bonnie delivered a light slap to Nûd's near shoulder with the back of her hand and made a face at Nûd.

"Size doesn't matter," said Inthíra. "Once you've built a model it's straightforward to make it larger."

Nûd grinned. "I hope that frees you up for another assignment?"

"How may I serve Your Majesty?" asked Inthíra.

"I want to observe what happens when Sírénae's forces invade the caverns," said Nûd. "Could you keep Bonnie and me hidden with your illusions while we watch from high above?"

"I'd be pleased to," said Inthíra.

"On one condition," said Quintillius.

"What is it?" asked Inthíra.

"You take one of Eynon's mobile-gate rings with you so you can pop out in a hurry if you're spotted," said Quintillius. "Before she left, Laetícia made me promise that I'd ensure Nûd considered his own safety."

"Understood," said Nûd. "And give Laetícia my thanks, wherever she's off to."

"Here," said Bonnie, holding out a gold ring to Quintillius. "Take this one through to Three Mountains Valley. I'll hang on to the other one I used to rescue people from the flooding caves."

"It sounds like we're ready," said Nûd "Everyone gate out except for Eynon, Merry, Inthíra, Bonnie, and me."

"See you soon," said Bonnie to the departing leaders.

"Fly swiftly," added Valentius, speaking to Eynon and Merry. "Not that you'll need that much incentive if you're being pursued by six or seven dragons."

Valentius, Quintillius, and the others didn't tarry. They promptly stepped through a mobile gate to Three Mountains Valley. Their departure was timely, because seven black dragons rose into the sky to the north a moment later. Their obsidian-colored hides caught the sunlight as they wheeled and turned above the emperor's forces. The attack on the cavern was beginning.

"Time for us to cause a distraction," said Eynon.

"Be careful not to let your illusions be struck by dragonfire," said Merry.

Eynon gave Merry a you-don't-have-to-remind-me look, then he and Merry disappeared from sight and eight dragons, four green, four blue, launched themselves skyward from the rocks near the entrance to the cavern. Nûd judged the illusionary dragons to be only a bit larger than the emperor's.

"Time for us to disappear like Eynon and Merry?" Bonnie asked Inthíra.

"We're already hidden," Inthíra replied. "Shall we ascend to give His Majesty a better view of the battle?"

"Of course," said Bonnie, motioning Nûd to stand behind her on her flying disk.

"I don't know about His Majesty, but I'd appreciate a higher vantage point," Nûd teased.

"Is it a battle if only one side is present?" asked Inthíra. "I'm not familiar with fine distinctions in military terminology."

"I should have asked Quintillius to stay with us so he could explain the various troop movements," said Nûd. "Yet another example of my lack of wisdom."

Bonnie elbowed Nûd in the ribs, none too gently, and the king of Dâron let out an undignified, "Uff!" He started to tickle Bonnie until another elbow to the ribs convinced him that was also unwise.

"The emperor's dragons have spotted Eynon and Merry's illusions," said Inthíra.

All three of the observers smiled as they watched seven dragons chase eight dragons rapidly winging their way southwest. The eight were maintaining the gap between them and the seven.

"I would have never been able to keep up," said Inthíra. "Eynon and Merry are moving a lot faster than I can fly."

"Look, in the sky," said Bonnie. "Wizards on flying disks."

"Scouts *and* shock troops," said Nûd.

"I'd have thought the black dragons were there for their shock value," said Bonnie.

"They must be puzzled by our lack of opposition," said Inthíra. "I made sure they couldn't see our troops earlier, so they have to be wondering what we're up to."

"I expect they wanted an easy, showy victory to impress the emperor," said Bonnie.

"I think they were more interested in capturing our food," said Nûd. "Killing or enslaving people seeking refuge in the cave complex is just a bonus."

"Here come the legionnaires," said Inthíra, who had generated distance viewing lenses of solidified sound for herself. Nûd was still using the ones Eynon had made for him. Bonnie realized she was the only one at a disadvantage and created a set of her own.

"They're like a purple and gold line," said Bonnie.

"With pointy *pilums* ready to prick their foes," added Inthíra.

"Hah!" said Nûd.

"What?" asked Inthíra.

"Nothing," said Nûd. "I'm just fond of alliteration." He remembered Inthíra's earlier comment about how size didn't matter and decided he'd enlist Bonnie's help—and maybe Laetícia's—to help find a worthy lover for Inthíra, now that Doethan was married to Princess Rúth. He looked behind and slightly above the marching legionnaires and laughed again, more loudly this time.

"Careful," said Inthíra. "I'm hiding us from sight, but if we make too much noise, we may draw attention to ourselves."

"Sorry," said Nûd. "I just spotted Sírénae. She's flying on some sort of sedan chair with an awning, supported by four wizards' disks."

"I see it," said Bonnie. "The awning cover is purple, with gold fringe."

"Is that snow gryffon we've heard about with her?" asked Inthíra.

"I don't think so," said Nûd. "Though it's not easy to tell from this far away, even with distance-viewing lenses."

Over the course of the next thirty minutes, the imperial forces covered the mile or so from their original location to a point near the entrance to the caverns, which was slightly to the west in a bowl-shaped depression in the stone of the mountain. The scout wizards set up a perimeter around the bowl, and some hovered near the entrance itself, which was now only camouflaged by strategically placed plants and shrubs. Three hundred legionnaires made their way up the steep side of the depression, ready to charge inside.

Nûd, Bonnie, and Inthíra watched the emperor's flying sedan chair descend into the bowl behind the first wave of attackers. A woman in polished gold armor wearing a long purple cloak stepped down from the chair to stand in front of it. She raised her right hand above her head, then pointed at the entrance. Nûd wasn't sure—it was too far away for him to hear—but he assumed Sírénae was shouting, *"Impetus!* Attack!"

He put his hand on Bonnie's shoulder as the legionnaires moved to enter the cavern. "Now would be good," he said.

"Yes, my king," said Bonnie.

Nûd squeezed Bonnie's shoulder again to let her know he understood she was teasing him, then he watched with joy as Bonnie dispelled the wall holding back the accumulated water inside the cavern. A wave of turbulent liquid shot out from the cavern's entrance and swept the legionnaires away, filling the bottom of the bowl half a yard deep with muddy-brown water. The emperor was knocked off her feet and was left sitting with only her head and neck above the flood before the wizards guiding her transport could assist Sírénae to her feet and return her to her chair in the air.

A lightning bolt cast from a wizard on the ground flashed by, dangerously close to their location.

"I knew we shouldn't have made so much noise," said Inthíra.

"Time to go," said Nûd.

Bonnie opened the ring for the mobile gate she carried and the three of them left the scene just before five more bolts of lightning intersected at their previous location.

Chapter 30

Warehouse Liberation

"I've heard of dragonships, but that's ridiculous," exclaimed Admiral Pixo as he gazed out at Nova Eboracum harbor from a balcony near the top of a tall tower in the imperial palace. The sun had set a few hours ago and the water was only illuminated by wizard lamps along the shore and the glowing torch of the New Colossus sculpture standing near the harbor's entrance. Gliding along the water were two long, narrow, and oh-so-massive dragon-prowed ships—one green and one blue. Pixo had never seen ships so large. They each seemed as big as castles, as huge as thirty of his most powerful warships laid end-to-end.

Instead of conventional canvas sails, these sea-behemoths carried translucent sails made from what seemed like fish bladders, held aloft by an upright mast that extended far higher than any tree he'd encountered in five decades. He pulled a collapsible metal tube from a leather case at his belt, extended it, and put it to his eye. Pixo's augmented vision could now detect hooded figures in yellow robes standing at the base of each mast. There were no other people visible aboard the vessels, but the giant ships moved gracefully back and forth on the harbor's smooth waters as if a full crew of experienced sailors controlled their courses.

Pixo heard shouts from the waterfront and redirected his distance-viewing tube to see thousands of Roma gathered along the piers and promenades, observing the strange ships. It seemed like half the population of the city was there, staring at the enormous vessels.

"Océllus!" Pixo shouted. The wizard assigned to the admiral joined Pixo on top of the tower from the chamber below where he'd been reading a treatise on magical techniques using Platonic solids.

"Fire and lightning!" Océllus exclaimed when he saw the dragonships. "They're bigger than the biggest warships—they're practically floating islands." The short, wiry, gray-haired Athican wizard shook his head.

"I need to know if they're illusions," said Pixo. "The blasted locals have fooled us too many times with their visual trickery."

"It would be trivial to determine whether or not they're real with dragonfire," answered Océllus.

"If Sírénae had left us any dragons," complained Pixo. "How else can you confirm what our eyes are seeing?"

"Forty conventional fireballs in one spot should do it," said Océllus.

"Then get busy and round up the wizards you need to make that happen," Pixo ordered.

"I would if I could…" said Océllus, his voice trailing off with a tinge of regret.

Pixo sighed. "But all the available wizards are with the emperor or up the Abbenoth, is that it?"

"There are sixty wizards in the city," said Océllus. "Unfortunately, only twenty of them are offensive."

Pixo rolled his eyes and grumbled under his breath.

"You know what I mean," said Océllus. "Twenty-five of the remaining wizards are healers and couldn't throw enough fire to light a candle. The other fifteen are injured from Sírénae's research project to build wide gates."

"What about you?" asked Pixo. "You're a senior battle wizard. Don't your fireballs have enough power to identify illusions all on your own?"

"Perhaps," said Océllus. "But I have a better idea. Send one of your ships close enough to fire a few ballista bolts at one of them. I'll fly above to see if the bolts pass through illusions or hit real hulls."

"That's a good thought," said Pixo. "I'll tell my captains to set the bolts on fire to make them easier to spot."

"Excellent," said Océllus. "How fast can you get one of your ships into position?"

"They're in position now," said Pixo. "The dragonships are close to the city. There's no reason why my warships can't shoot from where they're moored at the docks."

"I'll get moving then," said Océllus. He climbed on his flying disk and launched himself off the balcony. Behind him, he heard Admiral Pixo bellowing orders to subordinates.

* * * * *

"Everyone is in position, Your Imperial Majesty," said Magister Umbrose over a communication ring's link from the chamber of his private office. "The Bifurlanders' distraction has already started, but as we expected, they're going for our warehouses, not our legions."

"The decoy supplies are in place, then?" asked Sírénae from the mountains of southwest Dâron.

"They are," said Umbrose. He noticed that she was no longer wearing her polished gold armor. His spies had told him about Sírénae's recent mishap with the water flowing out of the cave and he did his best to hide any hint of a smile.

The emperor continued speaking. "You told the troops to wear slippers, not boots, as I instructed?"

"I did," said Umbrose. "Their cat-like treads will be soft on the cobblestones."

"Like burglars?" asked Sírénae.

"Like watch-keepers lying in wait to thwart burglars," Umbrose answered.

"Hah!" said Sírénae. "Tell them to muffle their armor as well."

"Of course," said Umbrose. "I'll tell them."

"Remember—we need hostages, not bodies," said Sírénae. "And any associated magical artifacts they might have—particularly anything related to gates."

"I know the plan," said Umbrose. *I ought to,* he thought. *I came up with it, after all.* "How soon can you be back to enjoy our victory, Your Imperial Majesty?"

"Almost immediately," said Sírénae, "if Pixo's niece hasn't wandered off chasing bees, beer, or butterflies again. She can take me back to the capital via an *ad hoc* gate."

"Good," said Umbrose. "I'll keep you posted on our progress." He cleared his throat and looked around his office, even though he knew he was alone, then spoke. "What's your opinion on Celéri?"

"She's easily distracted, but malleable," said Sírénae. "I will see that she is assigned to you, not Callidus, moving forward."

"Splendid," said Umbrose. "I look forward to molding another mage capable of *ad hoc* gating."

"I'm counting on you to ensure her loyalty—to *me*—as well as your efforts to improve her skills," said Sírénae.

"I won't disappoint you," said Umbrose.

"See that you don't," replied Sírénae. She broke the connection.

Umbrose took a mental note of the emperor's constant—and by this time almost unconscious—use of intimidation and resolved to be more sparing in his own application of that tactic. He felt it was more effective as the exception, rather than the rule, in communicating with subordinates. He'd once known a privateer in the Middle Sea who had promised to kill his first mate every morning, just to keep him in line. After a few years of not following through, it became more of a joke than a serious threat. Umbrose knew he wouldn't make that mistake with Celéri.

* * * * *

"Roll those barrels faster, my friends," King Bjarni urged. A dozen feet away, Queen Signý controlled one of Eynon's rings establishing a portable gate.

A dozen men and women sped up their efforts to push supplies through the portable gate from the warehouse in Nova Eboracum to a barn far to the north in Bifurland. Similar teams of Bifurland raiders were in five more warehouses near the waterfront, since the gates no longer meant Bifurlanders needed longships to carry out their informal *supply requisitions.*

"Careful! Not *that* fast," said Queen Signý in an urgent whisper as a pair of barrels careened off course toward the gate and collided, causing their tops to pop off.

"Thunder and lightning," said a woman who'd been pushing one of the barrels. She quickly turned the barrel upright, but not before a third of its liquid contents had sloshed out, soaking her boots. "Hey!" said the woman, making no attempt to stay quiet. "This isn't beer—it's just water!"

"And this one is filled with sand," said the man who'd been pushing the second barrel. The contents of his barrel had spilled out and combined with what was in the first to form a wet slurry, like a small stretch of sandy beach, on the floor of the warehouse. "I don't understand."

"I'm afraid I do," said Queen Signý. "Let's get out of here *now!*"

* * * * *

In the harbor, a dozen flaming ballista bolts were launched from the decks of ships at anchor, following Pixo's command. Océllus, high above, watched them pass through the giant dragonships and extinguish with angry hisses when they struck the water.

Illusions! As I expected, thought Océllus. *It's difficult to believe that ships that large could be real.* A bolt of lightning launched from the deck of the illusory ship flashed past his shoulder, close enough for Océllus to feel some of its energy. *Maybe it's not completely an illusion,* he considered. Océllus used his own modest powers of disguise and headed back to the tower where he'd left Admiral Pixo as fast as his flying disk could carry him.

* * * * *

Queen Signý, King Bjarni, and the dozen Bifurlanders with them didn't move fast enough, unfortunately. Half a hundred of Sírénae's legionnaires suddenly materialized when the illusion cloaking their presence dropped. They surrounded the royals and their subjects.

Umbrose and three of his spy-wizards flew in above the soldiers' heads to stand in front of the gate and bar entrance. Umbrose himself stepped through the interface and returned with the warrior from the far north who'd been controlling the other side of the gate. The gate closed and Umbrose removed the ring from the Bifurlander's hands, then crossed to Queen Signý to take the one she held.

"So kind of you to visit, Your Majesties," said Umbrose.

Legionnaires held spears to their royal necks and the necks of their subjects, so King Bjarni and Queen Signý chose not to fight back.

"Please follow me," Umbrose continued. "The emperor has informed me that you and your people are to be her *guests.*"

"Guests?" Bjarni repeated, almost laughing as he spoke.

"I don't think that word means the same for the emperor as it does for most people," said Queen Signý.

"In that, you are correct," said Umbrose. "Move along."

Chapter 31

Nûd Sorts Things Out

Three Mountains Valley was filled with tens of thousands of people milling about, setting up tents, tending animals, and staring at the unfamiliar snowcapped peaks to the west. Close to Rōlin and Peregrína's solidly built log home, Nûd stood on the back porch and addressed a collection of kingdom nobles, provincial leaders, and village elders.

"There's plenty of grass for dairy and beef cattle east of here," said Nûd, projecting his voice so that everyone gathered could hear him easily. Eynon, Merry, and Bonnie stood to Nûd's right while Rōlin and Peregrína were to his left, near the door to their kitchen. Nûd pointed down the valley and continued. "Wheat farmers should head south and get a crop in the ground as soon as possible. The growing season here is shorter than we're used to."

Most of the people listening to the king nodded, though some seemed eager to ask questions.

"That's right," added Rōlin. "I have seeds that will germinate quickly. We'll also need to plant barley—it's hardy and thrives in this climate."

"Barley means beer!" shouted one of the Dâron nobles who looked like he'd had plenty of beer to drink over the years, even after recent short rations in the caverns.

"Only if we have enough surplus grain to brew it," said Nûd. "If not, barley means porridge to feed hungry mouths."

"We'd best plant lots of it then," said the noble. Others in the crowd laughed and so did Nûd.

"I have seeds for barley as well," offered Rōlin. "Plus seeds and cuttings for beans and sugar beets."

"What are sugar beets?" asked an elder from a village on the Moravon river south of Tyford.

"They're fat roots the size of a baby's head and as sweet as honey, without the need for bees," said Rōlin.

"Except to pollinate them," added Peregrína with a smile. The listeners gathered 'round shared her expression.

"We won't lack for meat in the short term," said Nûd. "There are several large wisent herds close by, and lots of game in the forests."

"I saw deer with strange antlers to the north up the valley," noted a senior Roma administrator from west of the Abbenoth. "They look like they'd be good eating."

"Those are pronghorns," said Nûd. "They're quite tasty, if you can catch them."

"I haven't seen a deer that can outrun an arrow," said a second Dâron noble, the prickly Duchess of Whitrose who had been surprisingly even-tempered and supportive while they were hiding in the caves.

"Good hunting to you," said Nûd. "Just know they're fast and love to leap."

The duchess laughed and loosed an imaginary arrow from an equally imaginary bow to illustrate she understood Nûd's advice. "What about shelter?" she asked. "Where can we stay to be out of the elements? We can't live in tents all year."

"I'll show you how to make cabins from logs," said Rōlin. "Like this one," he continued, waving at his home.

"Though not so large or elaborate," said Peregrína. "At least not initially."

"There are plenty of trees nearby," said Nûd. "Our wizards—and Eynon's mobile *ad hoc* gates will help us cut and transport the logs expeditiously."

Bonnie stepped forward until she was even with Nûd. "I will coordinate that effort," she said. "In the meantime..." she began, looking at Nûd.

"In the meantime, many of you will be able to take shelter at Melyncárreg," Nûd continued. "There's a large empty castle there, but be warned, it smells like rotten eggs in the vicinity."

"So long as it's warm," said another village elder who truly was elderly. "My bones won't like it if I'm outdoors overnight."

"You'll be quite cozy, especially if you sit beside a fire," said Nûd. "There are dozens of fireplaces in the castle."

"Excuse me," said a man who spoke with a voice of authority. Nûd saw that the speaker stood beside the Duchess of Whitrose and recognized him as Baron Nobblig, one of the nobles who had been particularly challenging to manage in the caverns. "What about defending ourselves?" said the baron. "I've heard there are wild gryffons and wyverns and even dragons in western Orluin."

"That's a very good point," said Nûd.

Rocky, perched atop an outcrop of stone off to one side of Rōlin and Peregrína's home, chose that moment to bellow and remind everyone of his presence.

"At least *one* wyvern will be helping to protect us," Nûd noted, waving to Rocky.

"I've dealt with wild gryffons *and* western dragons not far from here," said Eynon. "I can give our wizards tips on how to deal with them. Tell your people to blow on horns if you run into trouble."

Merry put a hand on Eynon's forearm and spoke. "We can hope that the wyverns and dragons won't come too close, with so many people here now."

"I wouldn't count on that," said Nûd. "Beasts in the west aren't afraid of us, and the gryffons in particular are aggressive hunters." He spoke directly to the Duchess of Whitrose and Baron Nobblig. "I'd like the two of you to organize groups of soldiers to guard us as we work. Archers' arrows should discourage gryffons, while swords and spears should suffice for wolves and big cats."

"What about dragons?" asked Baron Nobblig. "Are any of them as big as the ones that attacked Riyas? Should we build ballistas?"

"I wouldn't recommend it," said Rōlin. "Western dragons aren't as large as Viridáxés and Zûrafiérix, but they are big—and quite intelligent."

"It is wiser to parlay with dragons than to fight them," said Peregrína.

"That's good advice," said Nûd.

"I think most of the dragons have flown east, anyway," added Eynon, remembering that Kârkingórēx and his weyr were even now winging their way across the continent toward Nova Eboracum.

"What?" said Merry.

"What?" echoed Nûd.

"Didn't I tell you about that?" said Eynon. Merry made a face at him and Eynon's cheeks turned red.

"We can worry about the local dragons later," said Nûd, sparing Eynon further attention. "We also have to prepare for supplies we expect will be *liberated* from the invaders' warehouses by our Bifurland allies this evening. They're staging everything to Bjarniston, taking some barrels to support the Northern Clan Landers' attacks on the emperors' legions up the Abbenoth, and transferring the rest out here."

"You mean we're stealing them?" asked Duchess Whitrose.

"Liberating is a much better term to use during wartime," said Baron Nobblig.

"For once, I agree with him," Nûd whispered to Bonnie.

"How can we be sure the emperor's scout wizards won't find us here?" asked a familiar voice from the back of the assembled men and women. After a moment's thought, Nûd recognized it as belonging to Glenys, Eynon's mother.

"An excellent question," said Nûd. "The answer, unfortunately, is that we can't. We *are* two thousand miles west of Dâron, Tamloch, and Occidens Province, however. Sírénae's spy wizards don't have gates to take them here directly, and it would take them weeks to fly that distance—if they even knew Three Mountains Valley existed."

"And..." prompted Peregrína.

"And we've got a few surprises planned to keep the emperor and her minions distracted," said Nûd.

Lléwys, Rōlin's squirrel familiar chose that moment to pop out of Rōlin's beard and chitter his excitement. Chee clutched Eynon's hair in surprise and Ace started to bark until Merry put her hand on his head and calmed him.

"More than the raid to *liberate* supplies?" asked Duchess Whitrose.

"A good deal more," said Nûd.

"If everything goes as planned," said Peregrína.

Nûd turned to Peregrína and flashed her a look that made it clear she'd said too much. "Speaking of plans," said Nûd, "we need to plan for even more people arriving in Three Mountains Valley and vicinity soon."

"The Tamlochers?" asked Baron Nobblig.

"And the allied Roma," added Rōlin.

A Roma legionnaire in the assemblage listening to Nûd struck her armored fist against her *lorica segmentata* and made its plates chime. A dozen more legionnaires nearby did likewise.

"The ones who aren't here already," said Rōlin, with a nod to the Roma.

"I've talked to King Dârio, Earl Marshal Jenet, Governor General Quintillius, and Senior Magister Laetícia," said Nûd. He held up his left hand and opened it wide to draw attention to the gold communications rings clearly visible on his fingers. "There's good land for crops and access to trees and water on the other side of the mountains to the west and the Tamlochers will settle there."

"What about us?" asked the legionnaire who'd first pounded her chest.

"You'll have fertile lands to the east," said Nûd. "There are forests and lakes in that direction as well."

The legionnaire and her comrades lifted their right arms and nodded at Nûd, acknowledging and accepting his words. There was a buzz of conversation like a nest of wolf-hornets as everyone listening switched to talking to the people beside them.

"I'll have maps for everyone," said Peregrína. She stepped down from her back porch and began handing out copies of the appropriate maps for the leaders of the Dâron, Tamloch, and Occidens Province contingents.

Nûd was pleased there was enough open land nearby to resettle everyone. He'd spent several hours talking with Rōlin and Peregrína, consulting their maps, and even flying over the lands close to Three Mountains Valley with Rocky to confirm there were adequate resources for all the newcomers. He whispered to Bonnie. "It's strange that I never got to know the territory more than a day's hike from Melyncárreg and Travelers' Rest until I made friends with Rocky and could fly."

"Damon never gave you a tour on his flying disk?" asked Bonnie softly.

Nûd shook his head slightly, just enough to indicate the answer was *no*.

"Where is the old curmudgeon now anyway?" asked Bonnie.

"On a secret mission," whispered Nûd.

Bonnie twisted her torso, causing one edge of the flying disk strapped to her shoulders to catch Nûd in his right shoulder blade.

"Hey!" he said, louder than he'd intended.

"Don't you trust me?" asked Bonnie.

"Of course," said Nûd. "But now isn't the time to tell you."

"Soon," said Bonnie.

Nûd nodded and Bonnie rubbed his back where her flying disk had struck him. He smiled at Bonnie then clapped his hands above his head to get everyone's attention. Rocky decided to reinforce Nûd's action by bellowing, which proved even more effective.

"This won't be easy, I know," said Nûd, once all eyes were focused on him again. "We have to build shelters and plant crops, starting from scratch thousands of miles from our homes."

"It's a lot better than cowering in caves," said Baron Nobblig, his voice carrying.

"Agreed," said Nûd. "It will certainly be good to feel the sun and wind again."

"Too much wind, at that," said Duchess Whitrose, who held her elaborate, wide-brimmed hat tight against her head against a sturdy breeze that was sweeping down the valley.

"Better too much wind than the close air in the caverns," said one of the legionnaires.

The wind chose that moment to shift from the north to the west, bringing with it a mouthwatering scent.

Rōlin moved to stand beside Nûd and addressed the crowd. "Can you smell something good?" he asked.

"Aye!" came shouts from the assembled listeners. The shifting breeze was carrying delicious smells toward the crowd.

"Those are roasting wisents," said Rōlin. "Nûd warned us our new guests would be hungry, so we got them started yesterday."

"Let's eat!" said Nûd.

More cheers came from the listeners, then they dispersed to follow their noses, or more precisely, to follow Rōlin who led the way to the spits. Peregrína climbed the steps to the back porch and waved as she entered her kitchen to ready additional dishes to supplement the savory wisents.

"Nicely done," said Bonnie. She leaned up and kissed Nûd on the cheek.

"Good job," said Merry. "My father couldn't have done better."

"From what I've heard about Derry, that's high praise," said Nûd.

"You reassured everyone that everything is under control," said Eynon. "You're a good leader."

"It's nice to know that reading history helps me preserve the illusion I know what I'm doing," said Nûd with a smile.

Eynon projected an illusion of a marble statue of Nûd holding an outstretched sword and striking a noble pose on Rocky's back. Everyone laughed.

"Now I've got to learn how to use a sword," said Nûd. "I have to live up to that statue."

"Later," said Bonnie. "We need to get in line for roast wisent."

Chapter 32

A Delayed Birthday

Eynon, Merry, and their familiars were leaning against the boulder beside Rōlin and Peregrína's cabin where Rocky was perched. The wyvern was still gnawing on a haunch of unroasted wisent above them, so Eynon and Merry made sure they were under one of Rocky's sides to avoid dripping juices. That location was doubly wise, since Rocky's hindquarters as well as his mouth offered challenges of different sorts for anyone below them. Eynon swallowed the last bite of his roast wisent wrapped in flatbread, savoring the sauce Peregrína had made from ground mustard seeds, vinegar, and grated horseradish.

Merry stretched and yawned, then bent down to rub Ace's head, a process made easier because her familiar was in his dog form. Chee looked up and imitated Merry's stretch, then waved to Eynon. He noticed the raconette's motion and stroked his hand along the fur of Chee's silky back. A vibration a lot like a purr transmitted itself to Eynon's hand and up his arm.

"Well," said Eynon. "It looks like we're safe..."

"For now," said Merry. "We have to make sure Sírénae and her spies can't find us here."

"I'm hoping they'll run out of food and leave Orluin before her scouts can make it this far west," said Eynon. He lifted his arms above his head and yawned, mimicking Merry and Chee. Then he completed a maneuver that had been a classic thousands of years earlier and put his arm around Merry's shoulders when he lowered it.

Merry leaned against Eynon and sighed. "We've got *so* much to do in the next few days."

"Helping the rest of the refugees come west, cutting down trees for shelters, assisting the Bifurlanders and Northern Clan Landers with their expected confrontation..." Eynon began.

"Crafting more mobile *ad hoc* gates as well," Merry continued. "We'll need additional pairs of rings to link the Tamloch and Occidens Province settlements to Three Mountains Valley."

"Right," said Eynon. "I wonder if anyone else can learn how to make them?"

"I expect Fercha and Doethan could do it," said Merry. "Verro, too. And some of the allied Roma wizards, I expect."

"Probably," said Eynon, squeezing Merry's shoulder. "Are you comfortable enough with the process to teach others how to make them?"

"I think so," said Merry. "Peregrína has documented all the steps and written them down, in case you're not here and I have any questions."

"Do you think that's a good idea?" asked Eynon.

"Writing down how to build mobile gates?" said Merry.

"Yes," said Eynon. "What if one of Sírénae's agents steals the instructions?"

"To do that, they'd have to be in Three Mountains Valley, and that means we'd have much larger problems to deal with," Merry responded.

"I won't worry then—at least not *too* much," said Eynon. "But you know it's only a matter of time before lots of wizards know how to craft mobile gates."

"Lots of wizards on *our* side, I hope," said Merry. She took a deep breath and watched Rocky gnaw the last of the meat off a wisent's hind leg bone before she spoke again. "You do have a good point, though," she said at last. "I'm pleased you included an unlocking phrase for the mobile-gate rings, like the ones we have for communications rings. That will make it harder for them to be used against us if any are lost or captured."

"It seemed sensible," said Eynon. "I'll be sure to keep using passwords in the next batch I make—probably tonight in Rōlin and Peregrína's kitchen."

"If it's cleaned up from all the food she made to feed everyone," said Merry.

"There are plenty of people around to help with tidying her kitchen," said Eynon. "Young people, in particular, could be enlisted to assist. I could ask Braith and her friends..."

At that moment, Eynon's sister appeared around one side of Rocky's boulder holding something on a plate in front of her. Eynon and Merry were surprised and stepped apart. Ace yipped and Chee chittered happily, recognizing Braith.

"There you are!" said Eynon's sister. Her face was covered in freckles and her mouth was turned up in a smile. "I should have known you'd be close to Rocky."

"We weren't hiding," said Eynon. "Is anything wrong? How can I help?"

"You're not the one I was looking for big brother," said Braith. "I brought something for Merry." She held out the plate, which turned out to be supporting a cake the size of half a head of cabbage.

Eynon eyed the cake warily. It was a golden-brown hemisphere drizzled with honey.

"Don't be that way," said Braith. "I didn't bake it, Mother did."

"Oh, that's better then," said Eynon. He leaned in to inhale the cake's delightful aroma.

"It's not for you," said Braith. "It's for Merry."

"Me?" asked Merry. "Why would Glenys bake a cake for *me*?"

"She said you never got a special meal to celebrate turning sixteen, so she decided to make you a cake as a belated present," said Braith. "When was your birthday?" she asked. Braith offered the cake to Merry and Merry somewhat awkwardly accepted it.

"A month after the spring equinox," said Merry after ensuring the cake wouldn't slip off the plate. "With everything that's happened, I completely lost track of it." She smiled at Eynon.

"You started your wander year a bit early," said Eynon, smiling back.

"When a polite young man wandered onto my family's estate and my father invited him to dinner," said Merry.

"After I burned down one of his oak trees," said Eynon. He pulled Chee back from an attempt to stick a paw in Merry's cake.

"You burned down what?" asked Braith.

"When he found Fercha's lost artifact at a crossroads," said Merry.

"Fercha lost her artifact?" asked Braith. "How does she work magic?"

"She made a new one," said Merry.

"Please don't say anything about it," said Eynon. "The fact that I have *two* artifacts is a secret."

"I'll keep quiet," said Braith. "If I can have a slice of cake."

"That can be arranged," said Merry. She led Braith and Eynon over to Rōlin and Peregrína's back porch where the three of them sat on the steps and Chee and Ace accompanied them and watched with interest.

"You can use my knife," said Eynon as he handed his blade to Merry. She cut a quarter of the cake into four wedges, giving Eynon and Braith each a full slice and tossing Chee and Ace half a wedge each. Rocky was too focused on his wisent haunch to notice the distribution.

"This is really good," said Merry after she'd chewed and swallowed her first bite. "Why is it round on top, not flat like the cakes *my* mother bakes?"

"It's made in a pot, not a pan," said Braith. "The pot rests in hot coals and is covered by more of them so it turns into a small oven."

"That's fascinating," said Merry. "When you turn the cake out onto a plate, the rounded part is on top. It's quite pretty."

"I think so, too," said Braith. "When I try to bake cakes, they end up as gooey messes or burnt."

Eynon turned away so Braith couldn't see his expression.

Merry had another bite of cake. "I can taste the Applegarth honey," she said, "but there's something else Glenys must have added to the batter."

Eynon licked his lips and gazed toward the western mountains for a moment as if considering his answer. "It's tincture of birch bark," he said. "Mother would always ask me to gather new birch shoots in the spring and strip their bark. She'd steep the bark in hot water, then boil it down to strengthen it."

"It goes well with honey," said Braith. "Mother never made *us* cakes flavored with birch bark."

"She did, but the flavor was too subtle for your child-like palate," said Eynon solemnly.

Braith made a face at Eynon—the same one she'd been making for years.

"I'm glad that a small portion of the coracle-full of honey we collected is being put to good use," said Merry, offering a distraction. She reached down to rub Ace's head and noticed the rockhound was acting strangely. His nose was pointing to the northwest and he began to transform into his flying form. Chee became agitated as well. A faint sound came from the mountains. Braith cupped her hand around an ear and Eynon and Merry cast spells to augment their hearing. An insistent horn was blowing in the distance.

"That sounds like trouble," said Eynon. He swallowed the last bit of his wedge of cake and licked his fingers. Then he pulled his flying disk from his shoulders, mounted it, collected Chee, and rose into the air. Merry joined him only seconds later on her own flying disk. Ace was already flying northwest.

"Take me with you!" shouted Braith.

"Save the rest of the cake," said Merry. "I'll want another slice when I get back."

"I will," said Braith, pitching her voice to carry. When Eynon and Merry were too far away to hear she added, "I don't get to have *any* fun." Then she saw Eynon's knife still resting on the plate and laughed. "Well!" she said. "If they're going to leave me behind, the least I can do is have another slice of cake!"

Chapter 33

Kobs and Gobs

Eynon and Merry could still hear shouts and screams ahead of them to the northwest, but now they also heard the sound of massive, leathery wings beating behind them. Eynon looked over his shoulder and saw Nûd aboard Rocky just a few wyvern-lengths behind them. "Thanks for joining us," said Eynon, magically amplifying his voice so Nûd could catch his words.

Seconds later Nûd and Rocky were alongside the two young mages. "I had to come," said Nûd. "A king defends his people."

"I expect that Eynon and I can deal with any threat," said Merry. "But it's good to have you here."

"I also wanted to get away from Baron Nobblig," said Nûd. "The man's voice makes my back teeth hurt."

"I remember my father saying something similar," said Merry.

"Look!" said Eynon, pointing ahead and below them. "That's where the screams are coming from."

Ace left his position keeping pace with Merry and dove toward the herd of cattle milling about on flat scrublands. Men and women were clustered around individual cows and fending off attacks from small, strange-looking humanoid creatures using any improvised weapons they could find. They shouted to discourage the creatures and screamed when claws or teeth meant for cows struck a human instead. Every time they dislodged one creature, two more popped out of the ground to take its place.

Ace decided to do his part. He grabbed one of the furred attackers in his jaw and threw it to one side, then went back to find another one and repeat the process.

"Blast!" said Nûd. "The kobs and gobs are stirred up again."

"Kobs and gobs?" asked Merry.

"Kobolds and goblins," Nûd replied.

"Oh them," said Merry, smiling at Nûd as if her friend was joking.

"I thought those were just scary monsters from stories designed to frighten children," said Eynon.

"Maybe that's all they are back east," said Nûd, "but out here, they're real troublemakers."

"I can see that," said Merry as she observed dozens of hard to identify creatures try to pull over one of the cows. She used solidified-sound lenses to enhance her distance vision and immediately saw the attackers more clearly. The creatures were somewhat human in shape and furry, like woodchucks back in the Rhuthro valley. They had heads like shovels and huge front teeth like beavers. When she took in their prominent dark eyes, she sensed they suggested more than an animal intelligence. The creatures' shoulders were broad, and their forearms were massive, seemly designed for moving earth, like badgers. Their hands or paws had long claws, like sloths, probably to assist with digging as well, Merry assumed. Their hind legs were short, and their feet were wide, reminding Merry of spatulas.

Merry heard more people shouting and moos of distress from a cow. She saw that the attackers came in multiple types—smaller, brown-furred ones a few inches under two feet tall, and larger gold-furred ones three feet tall. The smaller ones were surrounding the cow's legs while the larger ones were on the cow's back, tearing at the frantic bovine's hide with their claws and teeth.

"They're ugly, and beautiful, at the same time," said Merry.

"I agree," said Nûd. "The small ones are the kobs. They dig tunnel complexes and collect nuggets of whatever metal they find during their excavations. They leave piles of gold outside the gates of the castle at Melyncárreg and Damon gives them glass beads and lumps of salt in return."

"What about the big ones?" asked Eynon.

"Those are the gobs," said Nûd. "I don't know if the goblins are a different species or just a larger variety of kobold, but they dig tunnels, too. They're more aggressive and leave piles of bones as offerings, not gold. Both kobs and gobs like to eat wisents whose legs get stuck in the holes to their tunnels."

"It seems like there's no shortage of holes," said Eynon. "The ground below is riddled with them."

"It's sort of an obstacle course for wisents," said Nûd. "Once there are too many holes, the herds take other migration routes and the kobs and gobs have to move or shift to smaller game. It's just our bad luck they took our cattle for wisents."

"How do we fight them?" asked Eynon. "There are so many!"

"Are they smart?" asked Merry. "Are they beasts or more like people?"

"Somewhere in between, I think," said Nûd. "They remind me of small, chaotic children."

"Most small children are the embodiment of chaos," said Merry.

"Kobs and gobs are more so," said Nûd.

"I believe you," said Merry.

"I'll ask again," said Eynon. "How do we fight them? If I throw fireballs or lightning at them, I'll kill the cows and the people defending them, not just kobs and gobs."

"We can try getting their attention, then scare them off," said Nûd.

"What do you recommend?" asked Eynon.

Nûd thought for a moment then spoke. "Merry, why don't you throw a fireball overhead."

"I can do it," said Eynon.

Merry laughed.

"We want to get their attention, not knock everyone down and melt the snow off the tops of the mountains," said Nûd.

Eynon nodded. "Point taken, my king," he said with a grin. "Sometimes I don't know my own magical strength."

"Sometimes?" teased Merry. "Let me show you how it's done." She leaned her head back, drew on the power of the congruency in her sapphire-and-silver artifact, and launched a fireball only as big as her outstretched arms a hundred feet overhead. It exploded with a not-insignificant *boom* and a fountain of red, orange, gold, and blue-white flames.

Everyone below paused and looked up—even the poor cows being attacked. The kobs and gobs chattered at each other and Chee began to mimic them, repeating the sounds in Eynon's ear.

"Now what?" Merry asked Nûd.

"Let *me* try something," said Eynon. He smiled at Merry, put his hand on his magestone, and concentrated. Seconds later, a thirty-foot red-furred cross between a kobold and a goblin appeared on a bare patch of ground nearby. It drew and held the attention of all the attackers by spreading its arms wide and bringing its hands together like a thunderclap, giving the defenders time to extricate the cows from the holes they'd stepped in. The giant illusion began to dance from side to side, grunting rhythmically. The kobs and gobs mirrored its movements and grunted along. After several minutes of this, the illusion stopped moving and bellowed, "Go home!" in a voice so deep and loud it made the earth tremble.

Merry suppressed a smile over Eynon's tendency to overdo things. She glanced over and saw Nûd was doing the same.

"Go home!" the kobs and gobs repeated.

Eynon turned to Nûd. "You didn't tell me they could understand what we say."

"I don't know for sure that they can," Nûd answered.

"It seems like Eynon got his message across," said Merry.

The kobs and gobs were streaming back into their holes and disappearing from the surface. Soon only one brown-furred kob with bits of shiny metal braided into the fur under its chin and one golden-furred gob wearing a bone necklace remained. They spread their arms wide, then brought them together and clapped, much as Eynon's illusion had earlier.

"I have an idea," said Eynon.

Merry shrugged her shoulders.

"Help fight?" said the giant illusion.

"Help fight!" said the remaining kob and gob in distorted but recognizable words.

"Good!" said the illusion. "Now go home!"

The last two creatures clapped their hands again, then dove into nearby holes.

"That was strange," said Merry.

"Very strange," said Eynon. He canceled the illusion and the giant kob-gob disappeared. "Do you think they understood what I said?"

"Maybe," said Nûd. "Damon used to talk to them when he saw them bringing offerings to Melyncárreg, but I could never tell if they knew what he meant."

"We may find out later," said Eynon. "I have some ideas about how to use the kobs and gobs against the invading Roma, if they're willing. I think I can recruit them to serve as an early warning system if any invaders make it this far west."

"They can see in the dark and sense body heat, if that helps," said Nûd. "That could make them very effective at spotting any of Sírénae's wizards scouting for us at night."

"Sounds good, so long as you're not depending on the kobs and gobs as your sole defense," said Merry. "I don't see any harm in it, and I'd rather have the kobs and gobs as friends than enemies."

"I agree," replied Nûd and Eynon at the same time.

The three humans descended and spoke to the people herding the cows. They turned out to be from a village east of Tyford and were quite pleased their cows had been saved. Nûd advised them to head east to a spot a few miles away where the ground was harder to dig but where new grass was plentiful. He made a note to tell Duke Háiddon to keep people away from this area.

"You two should head back and get busy making more mobile gates," said Nûd, standing next to Rocky.

Chee was crouched beside a kobold that was trying to recover from being grabbed and tossed a dozen yards by Merry's familiar. Ace was standing beside Merry on her flying disk in his dog form where she could discourage him from making a meal out of the kob. When Chee stroked the kobold's head, the startled creature jumped up and ran down into the nearest hole. Chee rejoined Eynon and sat on his shoulder, hoping for attention.

Eynon stroked Chee's fur, enjoying its softness. "Where will *you* be?" he asked Nûd.

"Rocky and I are going to collect a couple of wisents for your new friends," Nûd replied. "It's the least we can do for our new allies."

Nûd and Rocky flew off, leaving Eynon and Merry and their familiars hovering a few feet above the hole-pocked plain. Merry stared at Eynon until he felt her gaze and turned to face her.

"What?" asked Eynon.

"You have a way of turning every sort of creature into your friend," said Merry. "I don't understand it."

"Not every sort of creature," said Eynon sheepishly. "Just most of them, sort of."

Merry gave Eynon a mock grimace and wagged her finger at him. "I'm fine with you making friends with the kobs and gobs," she said. "And I was *very* pleased to hear about you making friends with the western dragons."

"Kârkingórēx is a nice enough sort," said Eynon, trying to hold off Merry's inevitable *but.*

"But I'm going to draw the line at basilisks," she said at last, turning her frown into a wide smile.

Eynon grinned back. "I'd *never* risk being friends with a basilisk," he replied. Then he stroked his chin. "Though I reserve the right to use them against our enemies."

"That's fine," said Merry. "From what I hear, the emperor could probably stare one down, though."

"You're probably right," said Eynon. "Gate back, or fly back?"

"Gate back," said Merry. "We've got a lot of work to do."

"And there are still ways we can celebrate your belated birthday," teased Eynon.

"Perhaps tonight?" asked Merry.

"Perhaps?" Eynon responded.

"Tonight," said Merry.

Chapter 34

Guests of the Emperor

King Bjarni was not surprised and far from pleased that Emperor Sírénae's notion of hospitality included heavy manacles on his wrists and ankles. He could feel that he had a bag of some sort of thick black fabric over his head that blocked his sight, and from testing the limits of his bonds he seemed to be chained, spread-eagled, to a wall. The links holding his hands and feet gave him less than six inches of motion. The room was damp and clammy, so he assumed he was being held in a dungeon below the governor-general's palace. *No,* he thought. *The imperial palace. At least that's what it is for now.*

"Is anyone there?" he asked, trying and succeeding to keep any sense of panic from his voice.

His words echoed off stone walls, but he received no reply.

"Hello?" he said, speaking louder than before. "HELLO?"

His ears, made sharper by the silence, heard only the scrabble of what he assumed must be the rats who considered the dungeon their home. He wondered if the rodents resented his presence disturbing their routine, then realized they probably considered him a new potential source of food. Suddenly, Bjarni was glad his captors hadn't removed his boots. He wondered if he could remove them himself, along with the manacles around his ankles, but promptly discovered the metal was pressing too tightly into the leather for that to be feasible.

After minutes, or perhaps hours of silence, Bjarni heard the tromp of footsteps, then the squeal of hinges. He could feel cooler air on his exposed hands and waited for what he knew was to come. While he couldn't *see* it, he could sense there must be a wizard lamp glowing in the room.

"I trust you're comfortable," said Magister Umbrose. His tone suggested a sneer. "The emperor has instructed me to provide you with better accommodations if you'll tell us how the mobile gates are made."

Bjarni laughed underneath his hood. Umbrose or one of his subordinates slapped Bjarni's head, knocking it to one side until it almost touched Bjarni's shoulder.

"Or, failing that, since you aren't a wizard," Umbrose continued. "I need you to tell me everything you know about where the rebels are hiding now—and what the Northern Clan Landers have planned as well. Intelligence of that sort should not be beyond you."

"You don't know much about Bifurlanders, do you?" said Bjarni, enunciating carefully so his words could be made out clearly through the fabric.

"I know the customs of the Nordlanders across the Ocean," said Umbrose. "How different could Bifurlanders be?"

Bjarni laughed again.

"Remove the hood," barked Umbrose.

Bjarni felt the bag being ripped from his head in one savage tug, taking a handful of his hair with it in the process. As his eyes grew accustomed to the dim light in the room, he saw a short, ferret-faced wizard in gray robes looking entirely too pleased with herself.

Umbrose nodded at the wizard, then glared at Bjarni.

Bjarni met his gaze and lifted one eyebrow.

"You find this amusing?" said Umbrose.

"I do," said Bjarni. "Remind me to tell you about Bifurland coming-of-age customs someday."

"Let me guess," said Umbrose. "You have to wrestle a walrus and shove one of its tusks up..."

"Not a walrus," said Bjarni. "An arctic dire wolf. We have to bring back a pelt."

"What's an arctic dire wolf?" asked Umbrose. "I haven't heard of them from the Nordlanders."

"That's because there aren't any of them on the other side of the Ocean," said Bjarni. "Arctic dire wolves have white fur and are as much bigger than a standard wolf as a great cave bear is bigger than an average brown bear."

"You're saying I can't intimidate you?" asked Umbrose.

Bjarni smiled.

"I look forward to proving you wrong," said the spymaster. "But that will have to wait until the emperor arrives. She's interrogating your mate at the moment. Is her name Signý? All the screaming I heard makes it hard to remember."

Bjarni continued to smile. Signý would never scream. She'd brought back her own arctic dire wolf skin. For good measure, his smile seemed to disconcert Umbrose. Behind his expression, Bjarni wasn't optimistic about his prospects for survival. Amber had no idea where he was being held. He wasn't even sure Bifurland's master mage knew he and Signý and their companions had been captured, though the odds of that were high, since the supplies they were supposed to gate through to Bjarniston hadn't arrived and the man controlling the other end of the mobile gate was missing.

"Did my wife frustrate Sírénae to the point of screaming, then?" Bjarni asked Umbrose. "She pushes me close to that extreme at times, and I know I provoke her as well. I worry more when she speaks softly than when she raises her voice, though."

"I'm not concerned about your marital squabbles, barbarian," said Umbrose. "I want to know where the rebels have gone. They weren't in the caverns when we arrived."

"There are a great many caverns in Orluin," said Bjarni. "Perhaps they found new ones."

"And perhaps I haven't provided you with sufficient incentive to talk," said Umbrose. "You may reconsider when rats start tearing the flesh from your feet."

Bjarni began to worry. It seemed that leaving him with his boots was *not* an oversight but an opportunity for further torment. He remained stoic as the ferret-faced wizard removed one manacle and one boot at a time, refastening each bond in turn.

Umbrose stepped closer and removed Bjarni's woolen socks with two impatient jerks. The magister pulled a slim dagger from somewhere in his robes. Four quick slashes left lines of blood oozing from the upper surface of each of Bjarni's feet. "I *may* be back in an hour or two," said the spymaster. "The emperor will look forward to you being more tractable." He turned to his associate and waved her toward the door. "Don't replace the hood," said Umbrose. "And leave a wizard lamp. I want him to *see* the rats when they appear."

The spymaster followed his subordinate out the door and pulled it shut with a heavy metallic thunk.

Bjarni took a deep breath and flexed his ankles, held fast by the manacles. He could feel rivulets of blood sliding between his toes from the cuts Umbrose had inflicted. For several minutes he listened for any indication of rats scrabbling in the walls and heard nothing except a soft scraping. Then a block of stone near his calves slid out of the wall and fell to the floor with a thud. A child of ten or twelve emerged from the hole and brushed dust from mid-length hair.

"I thought he'd never leave," said the child.

"Umbrose can be rather tiresome," said Bjarni. He smiled at the new arrival. "And who might *you* be?"

"Távi," said the child. "Côbb and Doethan and the lady Roma wizard told me to keep an eye on the dungeons to see who the invaders might capture."

"You mean Laetícia?" asked Bjarni.

"I think that's what she goes by," said Távi. "I worry more about the metal of her coins than her name, though as spymasters go, she's a far sight better than Umbrose. He'd torture you as soon as talk to you."

"So I've noticed," said Bjarni, staring down at his feet streaked with blood.

"Let me free you," said Távi. The youth pulled a key from a cloth pouch and used it to release Bjarni's hands and feet. "They use the same key for all their manacles," Távi noted. "We've had copies for years."

"I thought the invaders were only here for a few months," said Bjarni as he rubbed feeling back into his wrists and ankles.

"True enough," said Távi. "But the newcomers used the restraints forged by the Roma before them. The lady wizard spymaster is a kinder sort than Umbrose, but she's still a spymaster."

"I... see..." said Bjarni.

"Well, be about it then," said Távi.

"Be about what?" asked Bjarni.

"Putting your boots back on," said Távi. "Signý thanked me for rescuing her and your warriors. She told me to be quick about seeing to your release. I wouldn't want to disappoint the Queen of the Bifurlanders, and she promised me a dozen gold coins if I hurried."

"That sounds like Signý," said Bjarni. He wiped the blood from his feet with the hem of his tunic and slid thick wool socks on before stuffing his feet into his boots. "Now what?" Bjarni asked.

"Follow me," said Távi. The youth crawled back into the wall through the hole made by the missing block of stone.

Bjarni noticed two iron handles fastened to the inside of the stone block so he wasn't surprised by Távi's next instruction.

"Be sure to pull the block back in place when you leave."

Chapter 35

Sword Lessons

Nûd was standing on a level patch of ground a few hundred yards from Rōlin and Peregrína's cabin. He was tentatively swinging a long sword with a dragon's head pommel and a hilt wrapped with sky-blue leather. It wasn't the royal Dâron sword of state, just a serviceable blade for everyday use by Dâron kings and princes, but Nûd swung it with all the confidence of a novice rider trying to break in a wild stallion.

Bonnie was on her flying disk a few feet beyond the blade's maximum reach, floating a few inches above the ground and ready to retreat skyward if Nûd lost focus. She was also watching a circle of gold—a mobile gate—perpendicular to the ground not far away. It glowed with magical energy.

Opposite the gate, Valentius and his new wife Aleña were watching Nûd experiment with his blade from a safe distance and offering words of encouragement.

"Don't hold it so tightly," said Valentius. "Use your legs and hips to power your blows—your arms and wrists are just to guide your weapon."

"Easier said than done," said Nûd when he had almost dropped his sword. He held the blade in front of his face, contemplated the wavy pattern in the steel for a moment, then awkwardly returned it to its scabbard. "I'm not used to holding a steel sword, just practice blades. Real swords are heavier—and more dangerous—to me and anyone around me."

"I know," said Bonnie. "That's why I'm glad Béryl and Rocky are off hunting. They might injure themselves laughing."

"No need to rub it in," said Nûd.

Nyssia, Merry and Eynon's friend, was also observing. She stood behind Bonnie and had one hand on a wheeled wooden rack holding swords of various lengths, widths, and styles, including a Roma *gladius,* a knight's broadsword, and one of the man-tall great two-handed blades favored by the Northern Clan Landers. Next to Nyssia was a thin man with a long, blond mustache and a small pointed beard wearing a narrow blade with a bell guard. He resembled Nyssia so completely that he had to be her father. The man watched Nûd intently, as if he'd been analyzing Nûd's every motion.

"Don't give up," said Nyssia. "It takes time."

"I won't, but..." Nûd began. He stopped in mid-sentence when two familiar figures emerged through the nearby mobile gate. Dârio and Jenet had just come through from the northern caves where a large percentage of the people of Tamloch had sought refuge.

"That's it," said Dârio. "Everyone's through."

"The caves are empty," added Jenet. "We're the last to cross. I've got the ring supplying the other end of the gate with me."

"Let me help you close it down," said Bonnie. She slid her flying disk until she was next to Jenet and helped the two rings controlling the gate shrink down and click together into a united double-width ring.

"Welcome, Cousin," said Nûd, glad to have a respite from sword practice. He grasped forearms with Dârio.

"It's good to be back in fresh air," Dârio replied. "Thank you for reserving good land for my people."

"Rōlin and Peregrína are excellent advisers on such matters," said Nûd. "Quintillius and Laetícia came through not long ago with a contingent of Roma from Nova Eboracum and went off toward the east to find their stakes. Your Tamlochers are already heading due west. The gate you need is over there is beyond the cabin."

"Excellent," said Jenet.

Nûd extended his right arm to greet her the same way he had Dârio, but Jenet had other ideas. She took his arm and used it as a lever to pull Nûd's head down close enough for her to put her arms around his neck and hug him. When Jenet released Nûd she kissed each of his cheeks in turn, delighting in how her kisses made Nûd's face turn red. Bonnie, not to be outdone, stood on her flying disk and floated up high enough to hug and kiss Dârio the same way Jenet had greeted Nûd. The only difference was that Dârio's face expanded into a broad grin as he stepped back from Bonnie and spun her around on her disk until Nûd had to stop her rotation before she got too dizzy.

"Did you encourage Jenet to do that?" Nûd asked Dârio.

"For us, advice tends to go in the other direction," said Dârio. "Though I may have mentioned that you didn't grow up receiving a lot of affection."

"My apologies for embarrassing you, Nûd," said Jenet. "I just wanted to welcome you to the family. You look so much alike you feel more as if you're a brother to Dârio, not a first cousin."

"No harm done—quite the opposite," said Nûd. "And I did appreciate the warmer than expected greeting."

Jenet smiled and nodded, glad that Nûd wasn't displeased.

"It was fun going for a spin with you," said Bonnie, addressing Dârio.

Dârio grinned at her and reached down to hold Jenet's hand. "How is my great-grandmother faring?" he asked. "All this moving around and living underground must have been hard on her."

"She's living with Rōlin and Peregrína in their home, cousin," Nûd replied. "She seems in good spirits and even promised to make currant cakes on a soapstone griddle once things are less hectic."

"That's wonderful news," said Dârio. "I'll have to give her a kiss before we leave."

Bonnie tugged on Nûd's shoulder and whispered in his ear. "I thought she was *your* great-grandmother?"

"She's a great-grandmother to us both," replied Nûd. "By love and birth."

Dârio paused for a moment and looked around, taking in what had been in progress. "Now that our familial arrival rituals are out of the way," he said, "it seems like our presence has interrupted something." Dârio smiled and acknowledged the others. "It's good to see you Valentius. You, too, Aleña." More hugs were exchanged.

"Quintillius and Laetícia encouraged me to get to know you all better," said Valentius. "They seem to think a new sort of sensibility is being created here in the west that combines the best of Orluin's Roma, Bifurland, Tamloch, and Dâron. I agree with them and want to learn more."

"An excellent idea," said Dârio. "Imagine what we could accomplish if we weren't fighting each other."

"Or Sírénae!" said Aleña.

Bonnie clapped, seconding Aleña's sentiment.

Nûd said, "May it be so. Soon."

There was a brief pause in the conversation and Dârio turned to the man with the long blond mustache and pointed beard. "Master Cléthyd, if *you're* here, I'll bet I'm interrupting a lesson in swordsmanship. And Nyssia—I hear you're married now. It seems like a decade since the two of us fenced with willow switches."

"Only eight years, *O Mighty King of Tamloch,*" Nyssia replied with more than a touch of laughter in her voice. "I still remember the welts I put on your arms—though you gave as good as you got."

"If you've been studying with your father all these years, I'm sure we'd still be well-matched," Dârio replied. "I remember what the captain of my royal guard told me about your test for membership, back when I was still king of Dâron. You managed to impress him, and that's not easy."

"You talk as if that was years ago instead of mere months, my love," said Jenet. "The more important question is whether we're staying to assist in training Nûd in the art of the sword, or if we're leaving immediately to help our people get settled down south."

"You're free to either stay or go," said Nûd. "I just want to learn how to stay alive and not embarrass myself with a blade."

"Oh, that's easy," said Dârio. "Just don't grab the pointy end."

"Thank you for that, cousin," said Nûd. "Perhaps you can help me avoid such errors."

"Unfortunately, Jenet's right. We really can't stay," said Dârio. "I'll just offer a few words of advice."

Nûd gestured for Dârio to continue.

"You'll never become a master swordsman in a season," said Dârio. "Anyone who has trained with a blade for more than a few years will be able to defeat you."

"That's not reassuring," said Nûd.

"But it is realistic," said Nyssia.

"So how do I show I'm a fit king?" asked Nûd. "Being good with a blade seems to be a prerequisite."

"You've been reading too many stories," said Jenet. "Being a king is a matter of putting your people's welfare before your own."

"And you can always find a war leader or champion to swing a sword," said Dârio. "Duke Háiddon or Swordmaster Cléthyd would be good candidates for such roles."

"Don't be disheartened because you can't gain Dârio's level of skill overnight," said Swordmaster Cléthyd, speaking for the first time. His voice was a crisp tenor that would cut through the chaos of a battlefield. "Your best course for now would be to do what's not expected. Most of the people skilled in the art of the sword are trained in one of a small number of standard forms. There are rules and expectations that are followed. If you surprise your opponent and use your sheathed blade as a quarterstaff, for example..."

"My opponent might start laughing, which would give me time to smack him in the head with my pommel," offered Nûd.

"Something like that," said Swordmaster Cléthyd. He moved a hand to twirl the end of his mustache, then shifted it down to stroke his pointed beard. "Nyssia, attack your king. Half-speed."

"Yes, father," said Nyssia. She removed a slim blade from the scabbard at her hip and advanced on Nûd, the tip of her point rotating hypnotically close to eye level.

Nûd backed away and tried to pull his broadsword from its sheath, nearly tripping himself in the process. Nyssia closed, preparing to mock skewer Nûd through the throat, so Nûd allowed himself to fall over the end of his sheathed sword and land on the ground in front of Nyssia. Taking advantage of the motion that had already started, he began to roll into her ankles and tried to knock her off her feet. Nyssia, however, was too fast for him. She backed away with the grace of a dancer to avoid Nûd's rotating body.

With the advantage of his much longer reach, Nûd's arm shot out and tried to grab one of Nyssia's legs but was unsuccessful. The young woman deftly avoided Nûd's arm but overlooked the scabbarded sword at Nûd's hip. Using his other arm, he gripped its pommel from his place on the ground and flipped the sword around on his belt so one covered edge hit Nyssia behind her knees, knocking her onto her buttocks. Nûd then rolled in the other direction, away from Nyssia. After a moment, he stood and put a dozen paces between himself and Swordmaster Cléthyd's daughter.

Nyssia didn't get up. At first Nûd thought she may have had the wind knocked out of her, then he realized she was laughing. So were Dârio, Jenet, Valentius, and Aleña. Bonnie, in a show of support, refrained.

"That was nicely done," said Valentius. He slapped Nûd on the back. "I'm quite rusty after my imprisonment. Perhaps I'll be a better sparring partner for you than Nyssia. I could show you a few tricks I learned in Alexandria, and you could help me regain my previous form."

"I'd like that," said Nûd.

Swordmaster Cléthyd extended an arm to Nyssia and helped her to his feet. He frowned at her and she stopped laughing but kept smiling.

"How many times have I warned you not to underestimate an opponent?" he asked his daughter.

"At least ten times a day since I stopped crawling and started walking," said Nyssia. "I expected Nûd would try to grab me but didn't think he would use his sheathed sword to knock me over."

"Why not?" asked Swordmaster Cléthyd. "It knocked *him* over, after all. That should have made you alert to the possibility."

Nyssia bowed to her father. "You are correct, as always, Swordmaster," she said in a tone that children have used with fathers since the times before the First Ships. "I will do better next time."

"I know you will," said Cléthyd. "Now Nûd—I was impressed. You did the right thing."

"By tripping over my sword?" asked Nûd.

"No," said Swordmaster Cléthyd. "By running away instead of trying to grapple with Nyssia or incapacitate her. Once you were within reach of her blade, she would have sliced into your heart."

"Good to know," said Nûd.

"This way, you live to fight another day," said Swordmaster Cléthyd.

"Isn't it cowardly to run away?" asked Nûd.

"Not when your opponent is skilled with a sword and all you have is a blade that might as well be a stick—at least in your hands," said Cléthyd. "The kingdom needs a king, not the confusion of a disputed succession after your death."

"When you put it that way," said Nûd, shaking his head.

Bonnie gave Nûd a hug and he smiled.

"We need to leave," said Jenet. "Say good-bye, Dârio."

"Good-bye, Dârio," answered the new king of Tamloch.

Together, holding hands, Dârio and Jenet walked off toward the site of the mobile gate to the Tamloch territory in the west.

"Daughter," said Swordmaster Cléthyd, "find a sword for Valentius, if you please. And ones for Bonnie and Aleña as well. They'd certainly benefit from instruction."

"With pleasure," said Nyssia as she moved toward a rack where spare blades were kept.

Swordmaster Cléthyd nodded to Valentius. "We can start with you showing me some of those new techniques from Alexandria."

Chapter 36

Offloading Barges

The expedition heading north to subjugate the Northern Clan Landers and claim their food was going well, at least in Giérra's opinion. They hadn't been attacked yet, and that was a good thing. The barges had just pulled past the place where a large river entered the Abbenoth from the west, several days' *pull* above Nova Eboracum, or Sírénaeopolis Magna, as the emperor now insisted it be called.

You can't really call being carried upstream by pull-stones sailing, thought Giérra. *Sails had nothing to do with their progress.*

Unfortunately, the legate's prediction had been right about the seven legions running short on rations, especially since their food supply couldn't be supplemented by hunting. Even the two hundred elephants on the barges toward the back weren't happy about the lack of food, since they weren't allowed to get off and graze. At least there was plenty of water. It had been raining for several days and the legionnaires and their beasts would be happy to see the sun when it next appeared. Lieutenant General Belisaria found Giérra before the clouds broke, however.

"We're going to disembark in an hour or so," said Belisaria. "On the western bank. My maps say it's a day's march to where we'll have to turn west to get to the mountains where the barbarians live and I want the legions to be on land and in good order, not strung out along the river."

"Good," said Giérra. "What should we do with the gilded treasure barge?"

"We don't need it now since the Northern Clan Landers have decided to give battle on an open field," said Belisaria. "Send it back downriver."

"Under guard?" asked Giérra.

"There's no need," said Belisaria. "It's a fake—the chests aboard it are filled with lead and scrap iron."

"I should have guessed," said Giérra. "That's the emperor's style."

"True enough," said Belisaria. "How are our extra-large-sized shock troops faring?"

"The elephants will definitely appreciate getting off the river," said Giérra. "I expect they want a chance to eat fresh leaves and grass. Their tempers are getting short, according to their handlers."

"We don't want them too full, though," said Belisaria. "Short-tempered elephants will be more of a threat to our opponents."

And to us, thought Giérra. "Yes, Lieutenant General," she said.

"Pass the word," said Belisaria. "We'll get off at the first suitable spot we find and can use the logs from the barges to build a protective stockade for our supplies."

Such as they are, thought Giérra. *I hope our foragers can find game in the vicinity. I'm tired of lentils.* "I'll see to it," said Giérra. "Just let me know when the forward scout wizards have identified a likely landing area."

Giérra had no sooner conveyed Belisaria's instructions than she received word that a suitable landing spot had been found. It was a flat section of ground just north of a small stream before the Abbenoth grew wider and shallower.

A good thing, too, thought Giérra. *It wouldn't do to have our barges run aground.*

She informed the legions' leadership and supervised the complex process of getting every legionnaire, every horse, every elephant, and every modius of wheat onto dry land without more than the usual grumbling—or trumpeting, in the case of the elephants. There was a bit of a problem when several elephants on barges toward the rear of the expedition decided to jump in the river and walk to shore, but since the river wasn't deep at this point, none of the huge beasts seemed inconvenienced.

Giérra watched several of the elephants extend their trunks above the surface to breathe while their feet were on the mud of the river bottom. *Just like I used a reed to get air and surprise my brothers when we swam in the pond back on our family's farm,* she thought. *I wonder what my brothers would think of me now, as a legate commanding seven legions?*

she considered. *They'd probably continue to think she was odd for wanting to be a soldier, not a farmer,* she reflected.

It would have been faster and easier if the elephants could have hauled the barges to the top of a nearby rise where the stockade was to be assembled, but the beasts had other ideas and were happily munching on fresh grass and new leaves, ignoring all instructions from their handlers to do otherwise.

I can't blame them, thought Giérra. She had a few barges unbound into their constituent logs and set legionnaires to muscling barges uphill, using the logs as rollers. Work went faster when one of her subordinates asked if pull-stones could help speed the process. A bit of experimentation proved that using pull-stones was quite effective and Giérra instructed one of her clerks to make a note in the young man's record. Giérra would keep him in mind for the next round of promotions—always a high probability after a battle.

Wizards used magic to bind the barges, set upright, into a solid fortress large enough to hold their supplies, plus the senior commanders and wizards. Giérra had her legions set up their encampments around the stockade, with due attention spent on defense. The elephants, once they'd eaten, would bugle their alarm if strangers approached, alerting the camp, but alarms were no substitute for soldiers' vigilance.

The foragers were reporting back empty handed, unfortunately. They'd found a few onions along the banks of the stream, so they'd be a little more flavor in tonight's lentil pottage, but no meat. *I'd give an aureus for a haunch of venison,* she considered. *And I wouldn't insist it be cooked first. For that matter, I'd be happy with half a hare.* She decided to speak to one of the foragers to find out why they couldn't find any game, since she was sure Belisaria would ask why there wasn't meat for the officers' stewpot. She summoned one of them to her tent, which had been erected inside the stockade.

"It's like this, legate," said a woman with a nose that had been broken more than once. The forager wasn't wearing her lorica—clanking plates scared away game—but she did carry a longbow and a quiver of arrows over her shoulder. "We can't find any animal larger than those tiny striped brown squirrels and they're up a tree before we can catch or shoot them," the forager continued. "It's like someone beat the bushes and frightened every beast away from the river. Even the rabbits are gone, it takes a lot of work to scare all them such off."

"Did you see any signs of people about?" asked Giérra. "Barbarians? Or Occidens Province Roma?"

"Plenty of signs," said the forager. "These lands are farmed, or usually left undisturbed for game, but every barn and farmhouse we visit is empty and stripped clean of food."

"That's unfortunate," said Giérra.

"What's unfortunate are the traps we encounter," said the forager. "They've left us pit traps and snares and heavy tree trunks that come crashing down on us if we misstep. Me and my friends have had to ask for a dozen healing potions, and one of us was killed when a pair of hidden logs hanging from ropes crashed together and crushed her skull."

"It sounds like the way the hill tribes fought us in northern Éberria," said Giérra.

"The very same," said the forager. "But the hill tribes didn't frighten off all the game."

"They probably didn't think of it," said Giérra.

"Could be," said the forager. "At least we got some onions for the pot."

"That's small consolation," said Giérra. "But better than nothing."

"One of those elephants would be a feast for us all," said the forager.

"Should I tell the lieutenant general that's your suggestion?" asked Giérra.

"No need to credit me, good legate," the forager replied. "Feel free to put it forth as your own idea."

"I'll take the notion under advisement," said Giérra with a smile.

The forager smiled back and understanding she'd been dismissed, departed.

Belisaria won't like my news, thought Giérra. *But she's a realist, not an optimist. War doesn't always work the way we want it.*

Giérra left her tent and walked outside the stockade, then circumnavigated the walls until she was standing in the fortification's northwest corner. Looking out, she could see the forested slopes of the mountains where the Northern Clan Landers were supposed to live. Turning west, she saw that the clouds were mostly gone, and the sun was turning the horizon bright red-orange as it descended.

Red sky at night, soldiers delight, thought Giérra. *I'll be glad to be done with rain for a few days. It's easier for a battle to be fought without rain or fog confusing us.* Giérra shrugged her shoulders and felt the familiar weight of her lorica settle on her body. *You could have been a farmer,* she mused, not for the first time.

"I'd best report to Belisaria," she said to herself. "She'll want the news, good and bad—not that there's much good." *And I'll have to remember to tell her about the traps.*

Chapter 37

Sírénae and Umbrose

Sírénae was far from pleased when Admiral Pixo's niece, Celéri, transported her from the entrance to the caverns in southwestern Dâron to her throne room in Sírénaeopolis Magna using an *ad hoc* gate. Thraxa wasn't waiting for her, which was a disappointment. Seeing her bloodthirsty pet always calmed her when she was angry or frustrated.

Thraxa must be off being groomed, thought the emperor. *It's amusing watching her handlers try to smooth her feathers using soft brushes on long poles from well outside the snow-gryffon's cage.*

She nodded at Celéri to acknowledge her help in getting her back quickly, then dismissed the promising young mage with a wave of her hand. "Stay close by," said the emperor. "I may need you to take me north to the legions up the Abbenoth soon."

"I've never *been* up the Abbenoth," Celéri reply. "I can't gate you where I've never been."

"Find Callidus, then," barked Sírénae. "Perhaps he's been there and can take you."

"He hasn't been there, either," said Celéri in a sweet, sing-song voice Sírénae recognized the young used to mock their elders.

"We'll have to wait until my dragons return from southwestern Dâron, then, and have one of them fly us north," said the emperor.

"I could fly you myself," offered Celéri.

"Dragonback is more comfortable for long flights," said Sírénae. "The ride will give us time to get better acquainted."

"I look forward to it, Your Imperial Highness," said the young mage.

"In the meantime, spend time with Magister Callidus and learn what he knows about magic. It shouldn't take long," said Sírénae.

Celéri inclined her head and was about to gate out when someone knocked on the throne room's side door.

"Enter!" Sírénae ordered.

A servant in imperial livery entered and whispered to Sírénae. Celéri watched the emperor's expression grow even more angry than usual. The servant, dismissed, left as if she couldn't put distance between herself and the emperor fast enough.

"Find Umbrose and tell him I need to see him. *Now!*" said Sírénae.

Celéri could practically see thunderbolts flashing over Sírénae's head.

"As you command, Your Imperial Majesty," said Celéri.

A small pop of air filling the space where she'd been provided punctuation for the young wizard's rapid exit.

* * * * *

Umbrose tapped on the side door to the throne room but didn't wait for an invitation before walking in and bowing before Sírénae, who was seated on her raised throne, glowering down at him. He knew what was coming and had been through this sort of treatment from the emperor many times before.

"You *lost* them!" Sírénae shouted. "How could you *lose* such valuable captives as the king and queen of Bifurland?"

"And a dozen of their northern minions," Umbrose added. Distracting Sírénae with irrelevant details was often a successful strategy for reducing her wrath.

"Burn and blast their minions," said Sírénae. "How did Bjarni and Signý escape?"

"I don't know—yet," said Umbrose.

"You don't *know?*" said Sírénae.

"Not with complete confidence," said Umbrose. "But I do have theories."

"I'm listening," said Sírénae. "Impatiently."

"Of course, Your Imperial..." said Umbrose.

"Get on with it," Sírénae ordered. "Tell me these *theories.*"

"First, Laetícia may know secret ways into and out of cells in the dungeons below the palace," said Umbrose, holding up one finger.

"A distinct possibility," said Sírénae. "Or they may predate Laetícia and be something built by a previous governor-general or spymaster."

"True," said Umbrose, while raising another finger. "Second, a wizard who can *ad hoc* gate and is familiar with the palace dungeons rescued them."

"Like Laetícia..." said Sírénae.

"Or that young prodigy from Dâron we've heard about," said Umbrose.

"Earnon," said Sírénae.

"Eynon," whispered Umbrose.

"Whatever," said Sírénae. "Do you have more theories?"

Umbrose raised a third finger. "One of the guards could have been bribed to release them, though I consider that possibility unlikely."

"Because they fear the consequences should you discover their treachery?" asked Sírénae.

"No," said Umbrose. "Because they fear *you* might do so. Your Imperial Majesty has a certain reputation concerning such things."

"And Thraxa is always hungry," said Sírénae. She made a sound somewhere between a chuckle and an evil laugh and Umbrose had to struggle to retain his composure and keep his expression neutral.

The emperor held up four fingers and wiggled them at Umbrose, who thought they reminded him of the worms that gnawed at corpses.

"The fourth possibility is one that must always be remembered," said the spymaster. "Some unknown actor or actors using unknown methods or magic to remove King Bjarni, Queen Signý and the other Bifurlanders."

"Pah!" spat Sírénae. "I hate not knowing how their escape was accomplished." She bit her lower lip and spoke quietly. "Have we considered that they're still in their cells but have been hidden by illusions?" she asked.

"One of the first things I tested," said Umbrose.

"What about secret passages?" asked Sírénae.

"That's a promising line of inquiry," Umbrose replied. "I have wizards tapping the walls, checking for hollow spaces and loose stones. I'll alert you as soon as we identify possibilities—or eliminate them."

"Are there builders' plans for the dungeons available?" asked Sírénae.

"I believe there *were,* but they've been removed," said Umbrose. "That's why I suspect Laetícia may have a hand in this. She's often allied with the Bifurlanders against Tamloch and Dâron."

"That was before their blasted alliance," said Sírénae. She pressed her fingertips together and stared down at her spymaster from her high throne. "Tell me, Umbrose. Was I foolish to invade Orluin?"

Umbrose was shocked by Sírénae's candor but didn't let his surprise show on his face. "Perhaps," he answered after a long pause. "If Quintillius and Laetícia had joined our side—if Occidens Province and the three kingdoms on this side of the Ocean had not allied—if they'd stood and fought instead of trying to starve us, I'd have given high odds for our complete victory." Umbrose watched Sírénae's face and saw an expression that mirrored his own. "However," he continued. "As things stand now, it might be a wiser course to withdraw to the Isles of Dogs and take *their* stores, so our troops can be fed and have time to regroup before returning to complete your conquest."

"We may not have a choice in the matter if we can't capture supplies from the Northern Clan Landers," said Sírénae. "In that case, a temporary strategic withdrawal may be our only option."

"We could slaughter the elephants to buy us some time," Umbrose suggested.

"Or send scouts west to find one of those wisent herds that disrupted Tamloch's invasion of Dâron," said Sírénae.

"You could send Pixo's niece on that errand," said Umbrose. "She could gate back immediately if she found the beasts."

"I've changed my mind about Celéri," said Sírénae. "Once she learns what she can from Callidus, I still want you to work with her, but most of the time I want her by my side. I have *plans* for her."

"Plans to use her to replace *me?*" asked Umbrose.

"Don't be a fool," said Sírénae. "It would take her a decade to match your deviousness—but she can *ad hoc* gate and doesn't think the same way most of my wizards do—yours, *or* those reporting to Callidus. I'm hoping she can be a counterbalance to the allied cowards' young wizard Earnon."

"Eynon," said Umbrose.

"Whatever," Sírénae repeated. "She's an unknown quantity, and she's on *our* side. Agents of chaos have their advantages."

"I see your point," said Umbrose. "Under your tutelage, and my own, Celéri can be a sharp spear-tip pointed at our enemies."

"Though she *did* bring me honey," said Sírénae. "It would almost be a shame to turn a sweet young wizard into a well-honed weapon."

"But not so much so that we're not going to do it," said Umbrose.

"Precisely," said Sírénae. "And one more thing…"

"Yes?" asked Umbrose.

"See who stole the roast the cooks promised me for dinner. It seems to have gone missing. I've raised a hue and cry in the kitchens, but no one knows where it is."

"I'll put my best people on it," said Umbrose. "They'll slice to the heart of the mystery."

"Funny man," said Sírénae, her voice expressionless. "When we find the thief, I'll slice *him!*"

First honey, now a roast, thought Umbrose as he left the throne room. *What's next?*

Chapter 38

Callidus and Celéri

Callidus had gated back from the debacle in southwestern Dâron earlier and was now trying to straighten out the new deployments of wizards who'd been part of the failed attack. Three secretaries were seated at a long table writing down notes as Callidus dictated instructions. It took a lot of paperwork to manage wizards—at least the way the Roma did it. Callidus and his transcribing assistants all looked up with a start when the door to the office slammed open and Celéri stomped in.

"Callidus, we need to talk," said the young wizard in a peremptory tone.

"Make an appointment," said the magister, turning his head away.

"Now!" said Celéri. "Emperor's orders."

"Indeed," said Callidus. He was about to wave the secretaries out of the room, but Celéri interrupted.

"Not here," she said. "Come with me."

Celéri leaned forward, put her hand on the magister's shoulder, and popped out via *ad hoc* gate, leaving the secretaries retrieving scraps of paper blown about by the in-rushing air.

* * * * *

"Where *are* we?" asked Callidus.

The specifics of their location were easy to determine. They were standing on top of a tall, slim tower in the midst of a veritable forest of similar towers built into both sides of a narrow gorge. A clear, swift-running stream ran through the gorge's center, sounding almost musical as it flowed over its rocky bed.

"Where do you *think* we are, old man?" asked Celéri.

The younger wizard, her hand still on the magister's shoulder, began tapping her toe.

"This looks like the Valley of Towers, Dâron's center for academic wizards," said Callidus. "I've never been here, but it matches what I've heard."

"What? A valley full of towers?" asked Celéri. "You can't get more obvious than that."

"Only if it's a valley full of *wizards'* towers," said Callidus. "Which," he noted after another glance around, "this seems to be."

Celéri pulled her hand back and struck both of hers together in a slow clap. "The man *can* find his hat if it's on top of his head," she said.

"What's gotten into you?" asked Callidus. "And *why* are we here?"

"Ambition," said Celéri. "And I wanted to have a private place for a serious conversation. I flew here shortly after we arrived in Nova Eboracum to see if there were any books left in the wizards' libraries."

"Were there?" asked Callidus.

"No," said Celéri, sounding not particularly happy about her answer.

"We could have just cast a privacy sphere," said Callidus.

"Insufficient," said Celéri.

She doesn't know how to cast one, Callidus realized. "At least this place seems deserted," he said.

"It is," said Celéri. "And there's a low-level aversion spell in place to discourage people from wandering into the valley by accident."

"How did you manage to find your way in?" asked Callidus.

"The spell only works at ground level, not on wizards using flying disks," said Celéri.

"That makes sense," said Callidus. "What's so important you need this level of privacy for our conversation?"

"I need your help," said Celéri. "I'm planning to replace Sírénae— and you're going to help me do it."

Callidus didn't reply. He didn't meet Celéri's gaze, though he knew the young woman was staring at him, waiting to see how he'd respond. "I don't understand," he said at last. "Do you want my job? I expect Sírénae will be grooming you for it soon, if she hasn't already started."

"Not *your* job," said Celéri. "Hers."

"You want to be *emperor?*" Callidus exclaimed. "How could you? Wizards don't rule. That's one of the oldest customs of our civilization."

"Come now," said Celéri. "How many powerful wizards have commanded various quarters of the Empire using weak emperors as their pawns?"

"Many," said Callidus. "But Sírénae would never be your puppet."

"She might be, if Gwýnnett's potions work as promised," said Celéri.

"Gwýnnett was unsuccessful the last two times she tried that approach," said Callidus. "At least according to what her traveling companion Kennig told me."

"You'd believe an illusionist?" said Celéri. "They lie with every breath. He's probably not nearly as handsome without a seeming of solidified sound cast around him, too. And he has atrocious taste."

"Oh?" offered Callidus, who had found Kennig to be at least an *honest* rogue.

"Yes," said Celéri. "He wouldn't sleep with me and I practically threw myself at him."

"I see," said Callidus. *Celéri was going to be a problem. She had all of* Sírénae's questionable, self-serving ethics and very little of the emperor's wisdom, guile, and experience. "Do you think the legions will follow you?" he asked.

"They will when I feed them," said Celéri. "When their bellies are empty, they'll hail any Caesar who promises them a meal."

"And how do you propose to do so?" asked Callidus. "Sacrifice the elephants?"

"Of course not," Celéri answered. "We'll commandeer the locals' food."

"And how will *you* find the cowardly natives when all the emperor's forces have not?" asked Callidus.

"I have my ways," said Celéri.

The smile she gave Callidus reminded him far too much of Sírénae for comfort. *What had happened to Pixo's niece? She'd seemed both guileless and somewhat scatterbrained, but now she was talking like a budding Umbrose or worse.*

"How can I help you overturn thousands of years of tradition and take control of Sírénae's forces?" asked Callidus. "I'm not exactly the emperor's favorite person, even though I am her senior magister."

"Yes, but I need you and your wizards to organize the hundreds of gates we'll need to move legions to the allies' refuge and defeat them," said Celéri. "Remember, I told you about that approach."

"You did," said Callidus. "But we'll need wizards at both ends to build those gates. How do you propose to get them to the distant location?"

"I have my…" began Celéri.

"…ways, right," said Callidus. "Are you going to steal the mobile-gate rings Umbrose captured from the king and queen of Bifurland?"

"Steal is such a harsh term," said Celéri, "even though it would be accurate. Let's say *requisition for a higher purpose* instead. I'll need the mobile gate to send the wizards through so they can build the far ends of all the traditional gates. I can't carry them all by myself."

"I'm glad to know you don't want me solely for my *ad hoc* gating ability," said Callidus.

"That's much less of an issue now that I can *ad hoc* gate myself," said Celéri. "However, I would appreciate your assistance in recruiting Xaxidiánus to our side. I'll need his speed to reach the allies' refuges."

"And to cover for you with Sírénae, I expect," said Callidus. "Xaxidiánus would be missed—especially if he's gone for any length of time. How long do you think it will take to find where the allied locals have gone?"

"I don't know," said Celéri. "It depends on how far they've traveled. It could be days, perhaps even a week."

"So you want me to make excuses to Sírénae about the absence of her most powerful dragon and a promising young wizard for a week?" asked Callidus.

"While having your wizards build one end of lots of small gates, yes," said Celéri. "It will be a lot easier if we can get the emperor to eat or drink something dosed with one of Gwýnnett's potions," she added.

"That's true," said Callidus. "Unfortunately, the wizards who test Sírénae's meals for unusual substances work for Umbrose."

"The spymaster will be somewhat distracted soon," said Celéri. "Sírénae wants me to study with him—and with her."

"I suspect you can be quite distracting when you want to," said Callidus. "You plan to make Umbrose more suggestible first, then shift to Sírénae?"

"That seems like the best order," said Celéri. "Despite Kennig's lack of interest in my body, he did agree to use his illusions to make it seem like Xaxidiánus is still in Celériopolis Magna."

Callidus shook his head. "I'll pretend I didn't hear that. When did you become so calculating? You always seemed naive to me."

"I've found it's better to be underestimated," said Celéri. "Just like when I put those Dâron mages Eynon and Merry off balance by immediately admitting I was a spy."

"You were a Roma from the Western Empire," said Callidus. "What else would they think you were?" He sighed and shook his head. "This whole plan is mad, you know."

"Mad? Or bold?" she answered.

"You're so young," said Callidus.

"So was Alexander. And Caesar."

"Gaius Julius was fifty-one," said Callidus.

"I was talking about Augustus," said Celéri.

"He was thirty-six when he became emperor," said Callidus. "You're what? Seventeen?"

"Sixteen," said Celéri. "But I'm a powerful wizard. I can *ad hoc* gate—and throw huge fireballs. Would you like to see me destroy one of those towers?" She pointed to a collection of spires nearby.

"No need for that," said Callidus. "I've seen your big balls in combat wizards' martial drills."

"You think I'm a fool and a child, don't you?" said Celéri.

"I think anything that removes Sírénae from power and replaces her with someone more amenable to reason is a good thing," said Callidus. "Where do we start?"

Chapter 39

Northern Clan Lands

Signý, Bjarni, Amber, and Clan Chief Arminta of the Northern Clan Lands stood together on a high ledge overlooking a broad green valley and a large blue lake to the east. A mix of pine and hardwood trees was at their backs, the latter showing their new spring leaves.

"Congratulations on your escape from Sírénae's clutches," said the clan chief.

"It wasn't through any foresight or work on our part," said Signý.

"We were saved by a gang of street urchins from Nova Eboracum who know every hiding hole and hidden passageway in the city," said Bjarni. "They were recruited to support us by Laetícia's coin and acts of kindness by Doethan, as I understand it."

"My sense of things is that Sírénae makes enemies by breathing," said Arminta. "I'm not surprised you found unexpected allies."

"I'm sorry I was unable to rescue you myself," added Amber.

"You were busy working with Arminta, preparing for the battle with the Roma heading up the Abbenoth," said Signý. "And you'd never been in the dungeons below the governor-general's palace, so you couldn't have gated in to retrieve us."

"Still..." said Amber.

"We understand..." said Bjarni. "I'm glad we escaped without harm."

"You're wincing as you walk when no one is looking," Amber replied.

"A minor annoyance," said Bjarni. "I've had worse injuries playing with Sigrun's gold dragon."

"I hope you were wearing armor when you were wrestling with that beast," said Signý.

"Well..." said Bjarni.

Amber jumped in and changed the subject. "Why do you want to meet the invaders down in the valley instead of here in the mountains? I thought your usual strategy was to allow your opponents to enter your domain and reduce their numbers with traps and ambushes, not meet them head on."

"For one primary reason," said Arminta. "This time we *don't* want to kill Roma. You've told us the more mouths these Roma have to feed, the sooner they'll leave Orluin. We want them to leave quickly, not stay and cause us ongoing problems." She adjusted the bow and quiver over her shoulder until it was more comfortable, then pushed back the hood on her green-patterned cloak and smoothed down her muted green, brown, and black kilt. "Our local Roma are a different matter. They're not strong enough to take us. But confidentially, if Sírénae sends *all* her legions against us at once, even we Northern Clan Landers might have problems."

"While only seven legions shouldn't be a challenge?" teased Signý.

"Certainly not," said Arminta. "They'll be even less trouble with assistance from Bifurland."

"Thank you for saying so," said Bjarni. "We'll do what we can."

"I'm sure you'll be a *big* help," said Arminta. "Considering that this enterprise is a *mammoth* undertaking."

The Bifurlanders laughed and gazed east.

"Have you selected the site for the upcoming engagement?" asked Signý.

"Yes," said Arminta. "It's between the lake and the river. There are hills where we can dig in and set up non-lethal traps."

"I look forward to seeing what you consider fits in that category," said Bjarni.

"Arminta has shown me a good place to erect a wide gate north of the battlefield," said Amber. "It will be good practice for our wizards to build and maintain one."

"We have small boats on the lake and a wooden bridge across its narrow north end, where the river it feeds is located," said Arminta. "My Clan Landers can retreat that way, and once we take the boats and burn the bridge it will be difficult for the invaders to follow us."

"If everything goes according to plan," said Signý.

"Which it seldom does," added Bjarni.

"Confusion to the enemy and not to us," said Arminta. "Did you bring any of that famous Bifurland mead with you?"

"I just might have a bottle with me," said Signý. She shifted her backpack so she could reach it and removed a jug the size of one of the orange gourds that had been discovered growing wild here in Orluin. "Pull the cork and have a drink," said the queen. "Then pass it around. We can share this one and I'll have four more delivered to you for your senior people."

"That would be lovely," said Arminta. She deftly removed the cork using fingers strong enough to crack walnuts, took a deep draught, and passed the jug to Signý, who did likewise. Bjarni drank next and handed the jug to Amber, who waved it off.

"No thank you," said the wizard. "I'm gating."

"And wouldn't like to end up in the throne room of Sírénae's palace, then?" teased Arminta.

"I'm more fond of unhybridized eagles and cats than the two of them in combination," said Amber. "And I like the emperor even less than her pet."

"I'll drink to that," said Bjarni, taking another swig.

Signý claimed the jug back and drank, then Arminta had another turn.

"I want to talk with you later about recruiting some of your mead makers to help with our non-lethal traps," said Arminta to Signý after the clan chief had swallowed.

"From one queen on behalf of many others, I'm sure something can be arranged," said Signý.

No one spoke for a few minutes as they shared more of the mead and stared eastward beyond the lake at the beautiful valley far in the distance. The Abbenoth wasn't visible, but the low hills between that river and the lake could be seen, shrouded in a thin white mist the sun was already burning away.

"How well is your program of driving off game, large and small, in the lands along the Abbenoth proceeding?" Amber asked Arminta.

"Far better than I'd expected," said the clan chief. "I assigned experienced hunters to work with a few of our most resourceful young mages and they came up with several clever ideas to drive animals away from both shores of the river."

"Such as?" asked Amber, showing professional interest.

Arminta took a deep breath, then spoke. "I suppose I can share a few of our secrets," she said.

"Thank you," said Signý. "We're eager to appreciate your creativity."

Arminta smiled. "One option is using selectively permeable walls of solidified sound that push animals, put not plants, ahead of them," she said. "Another is setting up smoke generators that make creatures think the forests are on fire."

"Could those be used to help disguise forces before battles?" asked Bjarni.

"Quite possibly," said Arminta. "We can discuss that later. One of the wizards took the roar of a mountain lion and made it a hundred times louder. Even the bears didn't like that one. We made the mage only use it twenty miles north of the invading legions. She was quite proud of herself."

"Rightfully so," said Amber. "Our observers with listening spells learned new Roma idioms when the foragers reported back to their superiors." The Bifurland wizard paused to consider, then asked, "Does anyone know what a dung beetle might be? One of my scouts said the lead forager told a centurion he couldn't even find food fit for one of them."

"I would think, given the name, that their function and diet would be self-explanatory," said Signý.

Bjarni chuckled softly, then covered his mouth to hide his grin. "The only thing they have to eat on the invaders' barges is boiled beans," he said.

"They call them lentils, dear," said Signý.

"Whatever," said Bjarni. "I expect the barges echo with the sound of *trumpets*."

"Is that what you call them?" asked Arminta. She was smiling, too. "Speaking of trumpets, Laetícia gated one of her trumpeters over to us yesterday. He says he knows all the right notes to play."

"Good," said Signý.

"Just don't feed him beans," said Bjarni.

"Sometimes you act younger than Sigrun," said Signý.

"Sometimes?" said Amber.

"Not you, too," protested Bjarni.

"At times like these, I'm glad my children are grown," said Arminta. "Not that keeping my sub-chiefs in line isn't like running a nursery most of the time."

"Would you like to visit the prospective battlefield and see the terrain firsthand?" asked Amber, refocusing the conversation once again.

"Yes," said Bjarni and Signý in unison.

"Aye," answered Arminta. "It can't hurt to see it again."

"Crowd in tight on my flying disk, then," said the Bifurland wizard.

A large *pop* woke a sleeping owl in a nearby tree, but it didn't ask the obvious question.

* * * * *

When they emerged at the center of the planned site of the upcoming battle after Amber's *ad hoc* gate transported them, Bjarni looked around and stomped his foot in approval. He winced at the pain from the cuts he'd been given and endured one of *those* looks from Signý. His entirely accurate translation of the look was *after you've examined the battlefield, you're drinking a healing potion, or else.*

"This is marvelous," said Bjarni, pointing to the east at fortifications built long ago by Occidens Province engineers. "The low walls on the hillsides will provide us with a strong defensive position, and the stone keep on the highest hill will be an excellent place for our wizards to work, right Amber?"

"As you say, Bjarni, though many of us will be busy off to the north creating and maintaining a wide gate."

"Legionnaires built those low walls," Signý reminded her husband. "The engineers just designed them and supervised." She turned to Amber. "Remember to make your gate tall as well as wide."

"I'll try to keep that in mind, old friend," Amber answered. "Is something bothering you? You're focusing on irrelevant details, and that's not like you."

"Spending time in Sírénae's dungeons would upset anyone," said Signý. "I'm worried about the outcome of this battle. If we're defeated, it could cost us the entire continent."

"I doubt that," said Bjarni. "Quin and Dârio and Nûd won't surrender. And this new man, the son of the southern emperor, seems like a stalwart leader as well—for a Roma."

"Valentius," said Amber. "His wife is Aleña. He made sure we saved his ship filled with obsidian magestones. We'll be using some of the smaller ones, turned to powder, to build our wide and *tall* gate."

"Good, then," said Signý. "I'll make sure my spear is sharp and my shield is in good repair."

"You've got thralls for that," said Bjarni.

"Soldiers who allow others to prepare their arms and armor are fools," said Arminta.

"*Ealdamon's Epigrams,*" said Signý. "I know, and I'll handle the final inspection and adjustments myself." She assumed a fighting stance, holding an imaginary spear and shield.

"You're my favorite warrior," Bjarni told Signý.

"And you're mine," Signý replied. "We'll both make it clear to our soldiers that this battle is critically important, not just another raid."

"Strong, beautiful, *and* wise," said Bjarni.

Signý smiled and mimed throwing her imaginary spear at her husband. Amber created an illusion that it was a real spear and made it seem to strike Bjarni in the sternum and emerge from his back.

Bjarni pretended to stagger. "I'm gravely wounded," he cried.

"I thought you said you were going to treat this battle seriously?" said Arminta. "My soldiers know that every battle with the Roma is serious and a defeat could mean we lose our lands and our freedom."

"My apologies, good clan chief," said Bjarni. "You're right. I expect my capture has affected *me* more than expected as well."

The four of them stood uncomfortably, turning their eyes toward the south and east. It was easy to see the Abbenoth from here.

"How far away are the invaders now?" asked Signý.

"They've left their barges and set up fortifications a day's march south," said Amber.

"What about Roma scout wizards? If they're only a day's march south of us, should we worry about encountering them," asked Bjarni.

"I doubt they'd be here this early, but we should be on our guard," said Arminta.

"I will augment my hearing," said Amber.

"How will we draw the seven legions north?" asked Bjarni.

"Some of my clansfolk are showing themselves and shouting insults," said Arminta.

"Do they paint themselves blue?" asked Signý.

"You're thinking of the *Southern* Clan Landers," said Arminta. "We paint ourselves a dozen shades of green, so we can blend back into the forest. We also wear armor to fight. We're not stupid."

"Clearly not," said Signý.

"The most effective things they shout to draw the Roma north appear to be food-related," Arminta continued. "They're getting great results by describing the sumptuous feasts we eat every night."

"You mean you don't have feasts every night?" asked Bjarni.

"Just a few times a year," said Arminta. "The rest of the time it's acorn-flour flatbread and skewered squirrel."

"Beans aren't sounding that bad now," muttered Bjarni.

"I'd say I was stretching your leg, but you're tall enough already," said Arminta. "We eat the same thing most people eat—whatever we've stored or is in season. We'll be having roast venison tonight, if you'd all like to join us."

"We'll come after we've spoken with our own thains and warriors," said Bjarni. "No need to save us venison, but we'll bring more mead."

"Not too much," said Arminta. "We'll need clear heads in the morning."

"Understood," said Signý.

Twigs snapped behind them, sounding like cracks of lightning in the morning quiet. A pair of fireballs flew toward Arminta and the Bifurlanders. They were large enough to incinerate them all, but Amber's shields were faster. The wizard threw up a sphere of solidified sound in less than an eye blink and the fireballs splashed around it like water falling over a cliff striking a boulder at the bottom.

"Down!" shouted Amber.

None of the other three fell to the ground. Arminta went to her knees and nocked an arrow. Bjarni pulled his massive double-bladed axe off his back and weaved his way toward the direction of the as-yet-unseen wizards who'd thrown the fireballs, and long knives appeared in Signý's hands as she circled toward their attackers from the side opposite Bjarni's advance. Amber rose above the field, throwing balls of solidified sound near the spot where the wizards must have been when they'd launched their flaming missiles.

Both an arrow and a throwing knife struck flesh and the illusion spell around the spy-wizards vanished like a drop of dew caught in the noonday sun. Both wizards were young. Arminta's arrow took the man in the shoulder and the hilt of Signý's knife was protruding from the front of the woman wizard's right hip. Both were in shock, all the more so when they saw Bjarni and his axe steps away from them.

"Don't kill us," they shouted. "We surrender."

"Give me your magestones," Bjarni commanded.

The pair of young wizards obeyed without delay. The woman handed her magestone—a silver pendant with a stone of polished obsidian—to Bjarni. The man took off his magestone, an amethyst on a leather wrist band, and did the same. Both wizards had copper squares engraved with *XIII* around their necks.

"Here," said Bjarni, tossing the confiscated magestones to Amber. "Take them to the healers in Bjarniston." He helped the injured wizards onto Amber's flying disk and helped hang their disks on Amber's back. The Master Mage of Bifurland and her cargo gated away.

"We still make a good team," said Signý.

"Always have, always will," said Bjarni.

"I hope I get my arrow back," said Arminta.

"Nice shooting, nice throw," said Bjarni.

Signý nodded.

"Thank you," said Arminta.

"Are you sure you want Sigrun and her friends flying reconnaissance over the battlefield?" asked Bjarni.

"I think we'd find it hard to stop them," said Signý.

"Fine," said Bjarni. "Unless the emperor's dragons show up."

"Unless that," said Signý.

Bjarni turned to Arminta. "So, Clan Chief. Show me where you want the gate to go."

The three of them walked across the still-wet grass toward the north.

Chapter 40

Réah and Callidus

Réah the kitchen drudge tapped her knuckles on the outer door to the suite assigned to Magister Callidus. "You requested mulled wine, good wizard?" she asked through the door, pitching her voice to carry through the thick wood.

"Enter," said Callidus, who had been working late to make up for the time he'd spent with Celéri. He unlocked the door and pushed it open with constructs of solidified sound. "Put it on the table," he said when he saw the servant with a tray.

Réah saw the indicated table between the chair Callidus occupied and a similar one that was obviously for visitors. She tiptoed over and set the tray with the wine, a goblet, and a small plate of cheese and flatbread down beside the magister. She could see from the way he was lacing and unlacing his fingers that his mind was not at ease. "Is something bothering you, magister?" she asked.

"What? Oh?" Callidus responded, seeming to notice her as a person rather than a servant for the first time. Something about Réah's eyes caught and held his attention. "Yes," Callidus replied. "I have a lot on my mind—and now have much more than I'd first expected."

"I've been told I'm a good listener," said Réah. "Sometimes talking about your troubles with someone not caught up in them can help."

"Unfortunately," said Callidus, "one lamentable dimension of my dilemma is not being able to discuss it with *anyone*." He stopped making baskets with his fingers and put his hands together under this chin instead. "What about you?" he asked. "Do you have anything disturbing *your* mind? Perhaps focusing on your problems can provide me with perspective on my own."

"What would a cook's problems matter to a king, Your Wizardness?" said Réah. "You wouldn't care about not having enough hard cheese for the imperial staff's dinner table and nothing but beans to eat instead of meat."

"You'd be wrong about that," said Callidus. "And I'm no king, though I understand your meaning. Finding enough food for us is one of my biggest concerns."

"Now that's a surprise," said Réah. "I would think all your time would be spent on doing the wizardly things the emperor asks of you."

"I spend a lot of my days just making sure all the wizards under my command are assigned to duties that fit their skills," said Callidus.

"Like flyin' and spyin' and shootin' bolts of lightning from their fingers?" asked Réah.

"Scout wizards—spies, that is—are Magister Umbrose's concern," said Callidus. "And at present, my smartest wizards are trying to figure out how to make wide gates like our foes do."

"Wide gates?" asked Réah. "Like the kind you'd need for cattle instead of goats?"

"Not quite," said Callidus. "Do you know *anything* about wizards' gates?"

"I know a wizard can walk in *here* and come out *there,* good magister, but that's the limit of my small brain," said Réah

"You seem a perfectly sensible woman with a brain that's far from small," said Callidus. "A standard wizard gate is the size of the door to this room. One, maybe two, can walk through it abreast."

"Yes, Your Wizardness," said Réah.

"Please stop calling me that," said Callidus. "One never addresses a wizard that way." He looked at Réah more closely. "You didn't come over from the Western Empire, did you?"

"No, good wizard," said Réah.

"Call me Callidus," said the magister. "At least in private, or *magister* if anyone is around."

"Yes, *Callidus,*" said Réah, reluctantly.

"There's no need to be afraid of me," said the wizard. "Do *you* have a name?"

"Yes," said Réah.

Callidus rolled his eyes and Réah put her hand over her mouth to hide a smile. "You were teasing me?" asked the magister.

"Yes, Callidus," came the reply, this time with a grin. "Call me Réah."

"That's a nice name," said Callidus. "Where are you from?"

"Dâron," said Réah. "I worked in the kitchens in the royal palace in Brendinas, but we hid instead of leaving with everyone else. There wasn't any food left when we finally came out, so we made our way to Nova Eboracum because kings and emperors always find ways to eat, and we're not afraid of hard work."

"We?" asked Callidus.

"My husband Côbb and I," said Réah. "He works in the stables shoveling manure."

"I see," said Callidus, feeling surprisingly disappointed by that news. The *last* thing he needed was any sort of relationship. His life was complicated enough as it was, but there was something particularly attractive about Réah. Callidus couldn't put a marker on exactly what it was, but the woman had depths to her he wanted to plumb. *Stop that,* he told himself. *You're in deep enough with Sirénae and Celéri. Keep thoughts of plumbing the depths of someone who already had a partner to yourself. And besides, Réah was older than he was by a decade. Not that age matters when you're past half a century.*

"Is something the matter?" asked Réah after the conversation came to a halt and Callidus appeared adrift in thought.

"What? Uh, no," said the wizard after he pulled himself back into the moment. *I've got it,* he realized. *My mind is casting about for anything to distract itself from the intractable problems before it.* "I'm. Perfectly. Fine."

"I don't think so," said Réah. "You seem to be trying to play twenty games of *shah-mat* in your head while juggling a dozen sharpened axes and avoiding a pair of angry bulls."

"That's more true than you know," said Callidus. "Though instead of two bulls, substitute a snow-gryffon and an arrogant young she-panther."

"Sirénae and Celéri, then," said Réah. "You'll have to do a better job of dissembling if you want to hide their identities."

"Really?" asked Callidus. "I'll give you that the snow-gryffon is self-evidently obvious, but I'd think there would be no shortage of young she-cats."

"It's the *arrogant* part that made it easy," said Réah. "Celéri acts like an immature scatterbrain at times, but I've seen through her act. She thinks she's better than all of us."

"That's sophisticated reasoning for a kitchen servant," said Callidus.

"Thank you, Senior Magister Callidus," said Réah.

"What happened to a simple *Callidus* without any titles?"

"My apologies, Callidus," said Réah. "Is this room warded, by the way?"

"I beg your pardon," said the mage. "What do *you* know about wards?"

"I know enough to watch my tongue if we can be overheard," observed Réah.

"Wise *and* sophisticated," said Callidus. He lifted his arms over his head and brought them down to his sides, generating an opaque double-walled hemisphere of solidified sound around himself and Réah.

Réah smiled.

"Who *are* you?" asked Callidus.

"A friend, if you'll have me," said Réah.

"You feel like a wizard, but I can't sense your magestone," Callidus continued, setting aside her answer.

"We have something in common," said Réah. "We're both wise, or at least somewhat so."

"You're not carrying your magestone," noted Callidus. "How can you stand being away from it?"

"The wizard makes the artifact, the artifact does *not* make the wizard," said Réah.

"You've read *Ealdamon's Epigrams?*" asked Callidus.

Réah allowed one corner of her mouth to turn up and raised an eyebrow.

"Asked and answered," said Callidus. "So much for any pretense of me being wise."

"Would you like some wine, Callidus?" asked Réah. She moved to pour some into the goblet on the table.

"Do you think *that* advisable?" asked the wizard.

"You might benefit from wine before this conversation continues much further," said Réah. She filled the goblet and held it out.

Callidus motioned for Réah to sit beside him, inside the bounds of the privacy sphere, and indicated she should drink first. "After you," he said. Callidus waited until she'd had a swallow and passed the goblet to him before drinking himself.

"Thinking of Princess Gwýnnett's potions?" asked Réah.

"Trying to regain some wisdom, and exercise caution with a stranger," said Callidus.

"You could get to know a new friend instead," said Réah. "Laetícia told me you have concerns about Sírénae. She was surprised you stayed in the emperor's service, actually. I hope that Celéri proves less of a problem than Sírénae, though the two of them do seem to be carved from the same stone."

"I should have guessed Laetícia sent you," said Callidus. "She always did think three steps ahead."

"Laetícia *didn't* send me," said Réah. "I'm here on my own to do what I can to head off a disaster."

"Just one disaster?" asked Callidus. "You weren't wrong about juggling a dozen sharpened axes. Dropping any of them could be disastrous."

"Then let me help," said Réah. "If you need to get word to Laetícia or the kings of Dâron or Tamloch or Bifurland, I can assist you."

"I can see the value in such a service," said Callidus. "Were you responsible for freeing Bjarni and Signý and their people?"

"Only indirectly," said Réah. "Many of the great and small are allied against Sírénae."

"I'll take comfort in that," said Callidus. "I once believed in her leadership, but now the only reason I remain is to reduce the damage she's bound to do—if I live."

"Which you won't if you're found out," said Réah. "At least inside this sphere they'll think you intend to dally, not ally." Réah gave Callidus a smile that was so quick he wasn't sure he'd seen it. "Do you want a communications ring so you can reach me?" asked Réah.

"It's probably too dangerous," said Callidus. He rubbed his chin then returned to lacing and unlacing his fingers. "On second thought, I believe I will. Contacting you in other ways would be even more risky and every action I take is dangerous these days."

"Here, then," said Réah. She placed a plain gold band in the magister's hand. "If you wear it with all your others, no one will notice."

"I can hope," said Callidus. He put the ring on the table and took Réah's hand in his, squeezing it gently before releasing it.

Réah nodded, acknowledging the power of touch and human connection. She knew Callidus didn't have many friends, though kitchen gossip had mentioned something about his strong bond with one of the emperor's dragons.

"I do have something important to share with you *now*," he said after a few heartbeats. "Celéri told me she knows how to find one of the allies' current hiding places."

"Really?" said Réah. "I'll be sure to pass that information along." She picked up the goblet and had another sip of wine. "I can see why you have to mull it. It's a very poor vintage."

"We're down to the amphoras of our worst," said Callidus. "Even for nobles. Soon we'll be drinking vinegar, and this isn't far from it." He rubbed his lips. "Your strategy's working. We're running low on food as well."

"Good," said Réah. "You'll have to leave if you want to eat."

"But where can we go?" asked Callidus. "The Isles of Dogs are far away, and Valens will have them well defended."

"I have friends who have made mapmaking their life's work," said Réah. "Did you know there's an island south of here that's larger than the Green Isle? They say you can harvest three crops a year there."

"You have my attention," said Callidus. "Tell me more."

Chapter 41

Distractions and Talismans

"I'm *tired* of making pairs of mobile-gate rings," grumbled Eynon. "I must have made a hundred of them by now, all with unique pass phrases." He stood up from the stool he occupied at a tall table in the same room in the castle at Melyncárreg where he'd crafted his artifact. There were still flecks of gold on the ceiling remaining as evidence of apprentice-level mistakes in that process. He put the new mobile-gate ring-pair he'd just finished at one end of the table next to the nineteen others he and Merry had made that day.

Merry wrapped a slip of paper with the pass phrase for the latest ring around Eynon's most-recent creation. "I'm tired of *helping* you make them, but we need them so our settlements here in the west can stay connected," she said. Merry slid down off her stool and squeezed Eynon's hand for a moment.

"And we can move our forces where we need them quickly if we have to fight Sírénae's legions, I know," said Eynon. "It's just tiresome."

"I'm not pleased to be spending so much time in Melyncárreg, either," said Merry. "You seem to have gotten used to the sulphur smell, but my nose is still telling me the place stinks."

"And the water..." Eynon made a face that looked like he'd just bitten a *very* sour green apple. "It's easier to stand the smell if you rub mint oil on your upper lip."

"Did you learn that from Damon?" asked Merry.

"No, from Fercha," said Eynon.

"That makes sense," said Merry. "I'll try it. What mint are you using?"

"Ummm... teaberry," said Eynon. "It grows wild in the Coombe and I always liked its scent. Every time I rub in a drop, it reminds me of home."

"I'm glad I asked," said Merry. "Otherwise, I would have gone with wintergreen and the two scents would clash when we kiss."

"Speaking of kissing..." said Eynon.

Merry grinned at Eynon and ignored his leading comment. "Where *is* Fercha these days, do you know?" she asked. "And Verro, too, for that matter."

"Last I heard they were working with Laetícia and Mafuta on wide gates across the Ocean," Eynon answered. "Something about contacting the Southern Empire."

"That would be impressive," said Merry. "Maybe we could visit there once Sírénae is defeated?"

"And see the Sphinx and the Great Pyramids?" asked Eynon. "And the Rose City of the Nabateans? And the Colossus of Rhodes?"

"It's clear you really love Robin Goodfellow's *Peregrinations*," said Merry. "So do I, for that matter. We'll have to visit the Lighthouse of Alexandria, too. It's on the way."

"And see the skull of the Cyclops, Polyphemus, on the Isles of Winds, near Sicily," said Eynon.

"Doethan said it belonged to a pygmy elephant, not a giant," said Merry.

"Don't spoil it for me," said Eynon. "There are so many things I want to see!" Merry watched Eynon's expression change from a comedy mask to a tragic one in the space of a single breath. "But I can't see them," said Eynon sadly. "I'm the Master Mage of Dâron and I have responsibilities."

"Have you forgotten you can *ad hoc* gate?" asked Merry. "And you have communications rings? If Nûd needs you it would be simple for you to pop back. You're not a prisoner of your position."

"Do you really think I'd be able to *ad hoc* gate across the Ocean?" asked Eynon. "I'd have to take a fixed gate there first—or a ship."

"I don't see why not," said Merry. "You don't seem to have any problem with *ad hoc* gates between Melyncárreg and Dâron."

"But that's over land," said Eynon. "The Ocean is water, and incredibly wide. I'd have to account for a large amount of spherical curvature."

Merry grabbed Eynon's arm and pulled his upper body down far enough so she could kiss the center of his forehead. "I don't think it matters," she said, after giving Eynon a look that reminded him of Braith's expression when she met a new puppy.

"What do you mean?" asked Eynon.

"Let me think," said Merry. She pressed her lips together and stared at a spot on the wall—a splatter of gold, it turned out— while Eynon waited. He was tempted to put a drop of teaberry oil on her upper lip but didn't want to distract her. Finally, she replied. "I can't *ad hoc* gate the way you do, but from what I can tell, gates bring *here* and *there* together with nothing in between," Merry began. She pinched two sides of her left sleeve together to illustrate.

"I'm following you so far," said Eynon.

"So if there's no distance between here and there when you gate, the Ocean shouldn't matter," said Merry. "Distance shouldn't matter, either."

"But folding water isn't the same as folding fabric," said Eynon. "Water doesn't fold."

"Of course it does," said Merry. "You can *ad hoc* gate from one side to the other of the steaming lake south of us, right?"

"I don't think I've tried, but I think so," said Eynon. "We can test that later."

"You can gate from Nova Eboracum to Brendinas and that goes over an arm of the Ocean," said Merry. "And the Bifurlanders' fleet of long-ships gated from the Brenavon to Nova Eboracum harbor, too."

"True enough," said Eynon. "But that means Laetícia should be able to *ad hoc* gate back to the Southern Empire directly, so why would she and Mafuta and the others need to build a gate to get there?"

"I think they're building a *wide* gate," said Merry. "And maybe Laetícia doesn't know she can *ad hoc* gate home, because she hasn't tried?"

"Maybe she knows a reason why it isn't a good idea," said Eynon. "There are so many adjustments to make."

"Fercha is helping Laetícia with the wide gate to the Southern Empire," said Merry. "I'm sure they'll figure it out between the two of them."

"Mafuta's working on it too," added Eynon. "But I don't think I'm ready to consider an *ad hoc* jump across the Ocean even after I've sailed or gated to the other side."

"Why are you being so pessimistic?" asked Merry. "It's not like you."

"I'm sorry," said Eynon. "I can't explain it well. There's something in my head that automatically adjusts my *ad hoc* gates for various characteristics of the starting and ending locations, like where the sun is in the sky, the altitude, the earth's rotation, and so on. Fixed and wide gates establish the necessary congruencies before they function. When I *ad hoc* gate some part of my brain does it for me without thinking. Crossing the Ocean is a *very* long way to travel."

"It makes more sense now that you've explained it," said Merry. "Maybe my brain hasn't figured that part out yet and it's trying to protect me by only allowing me to make line-of-sight gates."

"Interesting," said Eynon. "That could be. Right now, I'm worried that I won't be able to *ad hoc* gate at all, since next time I'll be worried about *how* I do it, rather than just trusting my instincts."

"I could just kiss you and make you forget to be worried," Merry teased.

"Would you like a drop of teaberry oil on your upper lip first?" asked Eynon.

"I could just inhale yours," said Merry. She proceeded to distract Eynon with kisses and be similarly distracted by him in turn.

"Now that we've had fun standing up, I have to report that this work room isn't the best place for having fun horizontally," said Eynon.

"We could walk upstairs to our bedroom," said Merry.

"Or I could just *ad hoc* gate us there," said Eynon.

"If you're confident your brain knows how," said Merry, fully prepared to kiss Eynon again.

"I think so," said Eynon. "But don't blame me if we end up in Farnam's cabin on the Rhuthro by accident."

"I could think of worse places to be," said Merry. "Just don't gate to Sírénae's throne room."

"Yes, dear lady," said Eynon.

"Afterward, we could gate down to Three Mountains Valley for dinner," Merry suggested. "The air and water are delightful there, unlike our present environs."

"Rōlin and Peregrína's home is chaotic, unfortunately," said Eynon. "All their guest rooms are occupied and there must be a thousand people camped around it."

"Only a thousand?" said Merry. "The resettlement process must be going well."

"That's what I hear," said Eynon. "Bringing everyone west has turned out to be an excellent idea." He gave Merry another kiss. "Ready to gate upstairs?"

Before Merry could answer there were three loud raps on the workroom door.

"Who's there?" asked Merry. Quite a few people from Dâron, Tamloch, and Occidens Province had been sent to the castle at Melyncárreg, so it wasn't *surprising* to hear a knock, just startling.

"It's Bonnie," came a familiar voice from the other side of the door. "Let me in."

"I'll do it," said Eynon, opening the work room door with a construct of solidified sound.

Bonnie practically fell into the room in her eagerness to enter. She seemed to hover, without falling over, and levered herself back upright fast enough to fully vertical by the time she reached Eynon and Merry. "I'm glad I found you," she said. "Doethan wanted me to get word to you."

"About what?" asked Merry. "And if it was so important, why didn't he ring us? Eynon and I both share communications rings with him now."

"I don't think he wanted to disturb you if you were in the middle of making more mobile gates," said Bonnie. "Goodness knows, that's critical. We need them." She noticed the pile of twenty mobile-gate ring-pairs on the table. "Could you show *me* how to make them?" Bonnie asked. "I want to analyze what's essential to the process and what's not. Does the ornamentation on both rings have to be the same, for example?"

"I'd be glad to show you how I make them," said Eynon. "If you have any aptitude for it, I'd be glad to have you take over responsibility for making them in the future as well."

"Actually *making* rings is secondary, once I've learned how the process works," said Bonnie. "The theoretical binding of matched congruencies is..."

"Did you have an important message for us from Doethan?" asked Merry, interrupting Bonnie before she went into full-academic mode.

"It's not really from Doethan," said Bonnie. "It's from one of our spies in Nova Eboracum."

"I wonder if it's Távi?" said Merry.

"Who?" asked Eynon.

"Doethan didn't say," Bonnie continued. "It was just news from someone he trusted."

"What's the news?" said Merry.

"Celéri, a young invading Roma wizard..." said Bonnie.

"We know who she is," said Eynon.

"You do? Good then." Bonnie took a breath. "Celéri told someone she knew how to find the allies' new location. Since you're the only ones who've met her, Doethan thought you should be informed."

"Gruffyd and Nyssia met Celéri too," said Merry.

"They're not wizards," said Bonnie.

"Right," said Eynon. "Not that their magical status should matter. Did the trusted source provide any hints as to *how* she would find us?"

"No," said Bonnie. "Just that Celéri was confident she could."

"What would she use to determine our location?" Eynon asked, not speaking to anyone in particular.

"A talisman is the usual method," said Bonnie. "With the right talisman, a person can be tracked across a continent."

"I've *got* to learn more about wizardry," Eynon muttered. "Damon never said *anything* about such things."

Merry was more pragmatic. "How can we identify a talisman?" she asked.

"You build a construct of solidified sound like *this*," said Bonnie, crafting a transparent ball the size of a large apple.

Eynon and Merry examined it until they felt confident they could reproduce the sphere and its contents.

"Then you make lenses like *this*," Bonnie continued, generating eye coverings much the same as those used for seeing things at a distance or at night. "You have to make the lenses sensitive to colors beyond violet. These lenses also making looking at flowers *much* more interesting."

"We can look at flowers later," said Merry. "Do you understand how to make the lenses too, Eynon?"

"I've got it," Eynon replied. "The three of us can sweep the castle, Three Mountains valley, and all the new settlements."

"It's easier than that," said Bonnie. "Watch and listen." Bonnie squeezed the sphere of solidified sound and it generated a wave of light all of them could see using their new lenses. Two loud *pings* like striking steel with a forge hammer immediately echoed in the room.

"What?" said Eynon.

"I saw something," said Merry. "Squeeze the sphere again."

Bonnie did so and the two *pings* rang out, even louder this time.

"I see them," said Bonnie.

"Them?" asked Merry.

"Two pings," said Eynon.

"One came from each of you," said Bonnie.

"Celéri's presents," said Merry, removing the cloisonne and amethyst sprig-of-lavender pin from her robes.

"It looks like we were the ones played for fools, not Celéri," said Eynon, taking off his pin as well. "What should we do?" he asked Bonnie.

"My advice would be to take them far from here," Bonnie replied.

"I know the perfect place," said Eynon. He held his hand out to Merry and she gave him her pin. A few seconds later Eynon was hovering on his flying disk and *popped* out, only to return a few minutes later.

"Where did you go?" asked Bonnie.

"A cave overlooking the great harbor at the Tempest Isles in the middle of the Ocean," said Eynon. "I flew down to a beach, found a sea turtle, and glued both talismans to its shell with a little magic. Celéri is welcome to try to find them there."

"Well done," said Merry. "It's good to know your ability to *ad hoc* gate hasn't been compromised by overthinking."

"Thanks to your wholehearted assistance," said Eynon.

"I think I'm missing something," said Bonnie. "Now," she said, dispelling the sphere and the lenses. "Can you show me how to make a pair of mobile-gate rings?"

Chapter 42

Celéri Searches

"There's nothing east of us except the Ocean," said Admiral Pixo when Celéri consulted him before beginning her search for the hidden Orluin allies.

"But my tracking sphere lights up to the east," Celéri replied, holding the globe of solidified sound up for Pixo's inspection.

"It's pointing southeast, not east," said her uncle. "That's the direction we came from to get here."

"I thought we sailed due west from the entrance to the Middle Sea?" said Celéri.

"You're forgetting the storm that blew us off course," said Pixo. "Wizards may fly straight courses, but sailing ships go where the winds blow them."

"Unless wizards make the winds," said Celéri.

"Even then, wizards can't out blow a storm," said Pixo.

"I'll bet I could," said Celéri.

"Remember the ancient Athicans' warnings about *hubris,* dear niece," said Pixo. "I've found it wiser to let my actions..."

"Speak louder than my words, I know," Celéri interrupted. "But it's not bragging if you can actually *do* what you say."

"That may be so," said Pixo. "I would also note that it isn't smart to give the emperor any indication you might be a threat to her rule."

"I'm not worried about Sírénae," said Celéri. "My magic makes me stronger than she is, especially now that I can *ad hoc* gate."

"I think every Roma in service to the emperor has been informed of your new talent," teased Pixo. "Does your tracking sphere give you any indication of how far away the items it's tracking might be?"

"More than five hundred miles and less than a thousand, as far as I can tell," said Celéri. "It isn't easy to read the indicators precisely for talismans more than a hundred miles distant."

"Has your sphere pointed consistently in that direction?" asked Pixo.

"I'm not sure," said Celéri. "When I'm inside and can't see the sun I'm not sure which direction is which. I thought it was pointing west for a while, but I may have been wrong."

"Sailors know their orientation at all times," said Pixo. "Didn't your father teach you anything about that?"

"He died when I was five, as you well know," said Celéri.

"Oh, yes, well—you're right," said Pixo. "Forgive an old man if he wants to forget a sad time." He lowered his eyes for a moment then looked back up. "Did your mother or your wizard tutors teach you to read the stars, at least?"

"I read books on wizardry, not the night sky," said Celéri. "I can recognize the Legionnaire with his three-star sword belt and the Big and Little Plows, but not much more than that."

"Your education is sorely lacking then," said Pixo. "Have Xaxidiánus name more stars and patterns for you on your flight. That old dragon knows them all—probably better than I do at this point."

"I'm glad Callidus was willing to enlist the dragon's aid on my behalf," said Celéri. She smiled, knowing that she had effectively blackmailed Callidus into requiring Xaxidiánus to transport her. Neither of them had bothered to ask for the emperor's approval. Imperial forgiveness, if needed, would be gladly granted once Celéri reported in with the allies' new location.

"If you do find the allies—and more importantly, their supplies," said Pixo. "Don't allow yourself to be seen. They might move again."

"Yes, Uncle," said Celéri, using a tone only used by the young when addressing older relatives.

Pixo paused before replying, then decided to speak. "You might be able to save time by having Magister Callidus *ad hoc* gate you to the Tempest Isles. They're almost eight hundred miles southeast of here. You could take a reading on your tracking sphere and see which direction your talismans are from there."

"I don't need Callidus," said Celéri. "I've been to the Isles myself."

"But you didn't know how to *ad hoc* gate when you were there," said Pixo. "Can you just remember a place where you've been before you developed your new ability?"

"Let me check," said Celéri. She gated out and almost immediately reappeared again. "I can," she said. "I went to a cabin by a river in western Dâron and back again. I didn't know how to *ad hoc* gate when I was there initially."

"Did you surprise anyone?" asked Pixo. "Is the river navigable?"

"No, and I don't know—and don't care," Celéri answered. "Navigating rivers is your department. I just fly across them."

"Understood," said Pixo. "One last word of caution," he added.

"What now?" said Celéri.

"Speak circumspectly," said Admiral Pixo. "Sírénae has ears everywhere, and so does Umbrose. If you say it, they'll know it."

"I'm not worried about Sírénae—*or* Umbrose," said Celéri. "They should be worried about *me.*"

"That's what I mean," said Pixo. "I'd rather sleep with a cobra than be heard speaking ill of the emperor or her spymaster."

"I'm not you, Uncle," said Celéri.

"True enough," said Pixo.

"I'm going on dragonback anyway. They may be hiding farther east. Ring me if anything important happens while I'm gone," said Celéri.

"Of course," said Pixo. "Safe travels."

"Don't attack any more of our own ships," said Celéri. She waved a hand to indicate her imminent departure and gated away without a further word.

* * * * *

Celéri rode on the back of Xaxidiánus as the dragon carried her through a cerulean sky above the dark green waves of the Ocean. The sun was halfway up to noon and his obsidian-colored scales shimmered and reflected a myriad of shades in its light as his measured wing beats drove them onward.

"Oh great and powerful one," said Celéri. "Might it be possible to increase our rate of travel? I'm sure Your Magnificence is capable of more."

Xaxidiánus snorted. "I have no need for flattery—I know my own measure. Say what you mean and say it plainly."

"Uh," said Celéri.

"Let me try," said Xaxidiánus. "I suspect you wanted to say, 'Come on, you big lizard. Can't you go any faster?'" He turned his head around so he could see Celéri's face. "Was that right?"

"Close enough," said Celéri. "I'll speak directly in the future."

"Good," said Xaxidiánus. "You probably read about dragons loving compliments in stories."

"What human child hasn't?" said Celéri.

"There's something to those tales," said Xaxidiánus. "I must be an exception, since I don't trust them. Compliments only come my way when someone wants something from me." The dragon turned his head back to face forward, allowing his clear nictitating membranes to slide down and protect his eyes again. "Callidus always tells me what he thinks without embellishments, and I've grown to appreciate it."

"Well then, lummox, can you?" asked Celéri.

"Can I what?" replied Xaxidiánus.

"Go faster," said Celéri. "The sooner I can confirm the location of the allies and their food supply, the sooner I'll be an imperial hero."

"You're on this quest for fame, not fortune or duty?" asked Xaxidiánus.

"I'm interested in fame as a steppingstone to greater power," said Celéri. "If the legions know that *I* am the one who found them bread and wine, I'll win them to me."

"Grab their bellies and their brains will follow?" asked Xaxidiánus.

"Something like that," said Celéri. "Armies truly do march on their stomachs."

"Dragons fight for the emperor and the legions for more pragmatic reasons," said Xaxidiánus.

"Do tell," said Celéri.

"It's true," said Xaxidiánus. "We can hunt for ourselves—or fish if it comes to that. But without the emperor's protection, we are wild dragons, and thus targets of heroes across the four empires and Roma Mater province."

"And Orluin," said Celéri.

"Well, yes, Orluin as well. As soldiers in the emperor's skies we can wreak havoc with thousands of spears on our side. Wild dragons have those same spears aimed *at* them," Xaxidiánus continued.

"So you serve out of fear?" said Celéri.

"I fear nothing," said Xaxidiánus. Angry puffs of black smoke rose from his nostrils.

"It sounds like you fear living free," said Celéri. "You'd rather serve the emperor and prey upon her enemies than be prey for would-be heroes yourselves."

Xaxidiánus flew on for several wing beats before speaking. "Perhaps that is one valid way of looking at it," he said at last. "It's a matter of our innate draconic nature versus what every dragon raised for the legions is taught in military creches from the day we first emerge from our eggs."

"Dragons serve the Imperium?" asked Celéri.

"We serve our emperors and their designated commanders," said Xaxidiánus. "Our power is greater than any single soldier, so our sense of duty must be stronger still."

"Would you serve me?" asked Celéri.

"If ordered by the emperor," said Xaxidiánus.

"Or asked by a friend like Magister Callidus?" asked Celéri.

"Yes," said Xaxidiánus. "I'm here, aren't I? Friendships can be stronger than formal commands."

"May I be your friend?" asked Celéri.

"Time will tell about that," said Xaxidiánus. "I've just met you and you're very young."

"I'm old enough to have ambitions," said Celéri. "My friendship could be valuable to you in the years ahead."

Xaxidiánus snorted again. Two more puffs of smoke rose from his snout—white ones this time.

"I'm not just ambitious, I'm powerful," said Celéri. She heard a rumbling from the dragon's throat. "Are you laughing at me?"

"Yes," said Xaxidiánus. "You speak of being powerful—to a dragon."

"I can cast lightning bolts and throw fireballs," said Celéri.

"I can breathe fire and lightning, too," said Xaxidiánus. "And frigid blasts as well."

"But you can't make *ad hoc* gates," said Celéri.

"And you don't have wings," said Xaxidiánus. "Wizards aren't dragons and dragons aren't wizards. We each are what we are. I can't cast illusions, but my fire can dispel them. You can make constructs of solidified sound and I cannot. Power is relative."

"Speaking of relative power," said Celéri. "Could you please fly faster, O Great and Powerful Xaxidiánus?"

The rumbling from the dragon's throat intensified.

"I could," said Xaxidiánus, "but I won't. It's hundreds of miles to reach the Tempest Isles. I flew almost that distance bearing Magister Callidus to Nova Eboracum not that long ago. If I fly faster now, I'd have to stop and feed on the way, catching a small whale or a dozen large fish, and then take time to digest my meal. As the old Athican saying goes, 'Slow and steady wins the race.'"

"That story was about a tortoise, not a dragon," said Celéri.

"And I'm flying a great deal faster than a tortoise can walk," said Xaxidiánus. "I've planned out this trip to get you to the Tempest Isles in the shortest time I can manage. I'll feed while you're looking for your talismans."

"You could have just said that to begin with," said Celéri.

"You brought up your search for fame," said Xaxidiánus. "I wanted to understand you better. Perhaps that's the beginning of a friendship."

"Perhaps, indeed," said Celéri.

"If you can *ad hoc* gate, why don't you jump to the Tempest Isles and see if your talismans are there?" asked Xaxidiánus.

It was Celéri's turn to pause. "Because my uncle suggested it," she said softly, knowing dragons have excellent hearing.

"Ah," said Xaxidiánus. "So if a new *friend* made the same suggestion…?"

"Keep flying," said Celéri as she unstrapped herself from her harnesses and stepped onto her flying disk. "I'll be back."

Xaxidiánus heard one *pop,* followed half an hour later by another. Celéri had returned. "Any news?" he asked.

"Here," said Celéri, dangling a large green sea turtle in front of the dragon's snout on a tendril of solidified sound. "I brought you a snack."

"Thank you," said Xaxidiánus as he crunched the shell and swallowed. "I sense this creature had a special significance."

"The talismans were attached to its shell," said Celéri. "I was lucky it was sunning itself on a beach near the great harbor instead of out at sea."

Xaxidiánus didn't laugh. "Are we turning around now?" he asked.

"You are," said Celéri. "I'm gating back to the palace." *Pop!*

Xaxidiánus laughed loud enough to sound like an approaching thunderstorm and draw the attention of a pod of dolphins cavorting on the surface below. "And to think," he said, "this could have been the beginning of a beautiful friendship."

* * * * *

Umbrose obeyed an imperial summons and appeared in the emperor's private study.

"We may have a problem," said Sírénae.

"What *sort* of problem?" asked the spymaster.

"The listening device I have in that fancy saddle I gave to Xaxidiánus has captured—and sent me—a fascinating conversation," said the emperor. "Listen."

Some minutes later, Umbrose and Sírénae were smiling at each other.

"Does she remind you of anyone?" asked Sírénae.

"Both of us," said Umbrose. "But without an *iota* of discretion."

"We've got our work cut out for us to turn Celéri into a useful tool," said Sírénae.

"Instead of a liability," said Umbrose. He extended one hand and then the other. "Carrot or stick?" he asked.

"Yes," said Sírénae. "The only real question is which approach to use first."

Chapter 43

With the Seven Legions

The sun was two hours from setting over the Roma encampment on the west bank of the Abbenoth. Somewhere wood was being chopped and a hammer was pounding out dents in a shield, making a musical counterpoint to orders being shouted and soldiers responding with their usual grumbled protests. A sweet smell rose up from hickory logs on a fire.

Giérra, the legate with responsibility for the legions deployed against the Northern Clan Landers, climbed the hill to the stockade, glad that her own tent was inside it, not far from her commander's. She cleared her throat outside Belisaria's tent and announced herself. "Giérra reporting, Lieutenant General."

"Come in, come in," said Belisaria. "The quartermaster saved me an entire cup of third-rate Caledonian wine and I'll share it with you."

"Grapes grow in Caledonia?" asked Giérra.

"Not many," said Belisaria. "After you have a taste of the wine, you'll appreciate that's not a bad thing."

Neither woman moved to reach for the cup of wine resting on a wooden folding table between Belisaria's camp desk and her cot.

"As you say," said Giérra. "I'm *so* glad to be off the river. I like to have stable ground under my feet, not water."

"If you'd wanted to be a sailor you would have joined the imperial navy, eh?" teased Belisaria. "We can leave sea battles—and river battles—to Admiral Pixo and *his* forces." Belisaria stretched and returned her hands to her hips, with one resting lightly on the hilt of her gladius.

Giérra stretched as well, mirroring Belisaria's motions and not quite successfully stifling a yawn.

"Stop that," said Belisaria, covering her mouth to hide her own reflexive yawn. "I still have reports to write for the emperor before I can sleep. Has everyone been fed? Are the camps in order? The latrines dug? What about the elephants?"

"Yes, yes, yes, and they're grazing," said Giérra. "I think the big beasts are as glad to be back on land as we are." She thumped her right fist on her chest and made her *lorica* jingle to indicate she was giving at least a somewhat formal update. "The troops have been fed, but it's beans again and not a lot of them. The grumbling for meat is getting louder and our foragers have returned empty-handed. Half our forces are ready to charge up the mountains to find the barbarians' stores and commandeer them immediately."

"If we let them try, we'd lose half of them to the Northern Clan Lander's traps," said Belisaria. "Our advance scouts have been marking the locations of dozens of them so we can avoid them when we march north."

"That's what the foragers told me as well," said Giérra. "We lost one of them to a log-smashing trap and had to waste healing potions on several others for less drastic injuries. What does our senior wizard have to say about *his* scouts?"

"Náegosh was none too pleased to be assigned to lead the wizards on our expedition," said Belisaria. "Once he stopped grumbling, he told me two of his people haven't returned as yet. I'm concerned they may have encountered barbarians hiding in ambush with crossbows."

"Or Northern Clan Lander wizards?" asked Giérra.

"Could be," said Belisaria. "The scout wizards that *did* return say there's an excellent spot for our sort of battle a few hours north of here, east of a big lake. They said they saw warriors in kilts assembled on its western bank."

"You think the barbarians are gathering to fight us on an open field?" asked Giérra. "That makes no sense, at least from what we know of their usual tactics."

"It smells like a garum factory in midsummer," said Belisaria. She sighed. *Even beans were better with garum and we're almost out of it,* she thought. *When we do run out, we'd better find something other than beans for the troops to eat or the legions may mutiny. Maybe it's time to slaughter one of the elephants?*

"I can't figure out the trick to it, can you?" asked Giérra.

"No," said Belisaria, "but I'm worried the two missing scout wizards did and paid a price for it."

"I hope not," said Giérra. "We'll just have to be ready for whatever the barbarians throw our way."

Three familiar chimes sounded in the tent. Both women looked at the rings on their fingers.

"It's mine," said Belisaria. "My connection to Machaera, probably to ask when my reports will be ready." The lieutenant general expanded the relevant ring and saw Machaera's face on the other side of its interface. She didn't look pleased."

"*Ave,* General," said Belisaria.

"*Ave,* Belisaria. Giérra," Machaera answered.

"I'll leave," said the legate.

"No, stay," said Machaera. "You'll want to hear what I have to say, too. I have good news and bad news."

"I suspect more of the latter than the former from your expression," said Belisaria. "What's the good news?"

"You're getting dragons," said Machaera.

"How many?" asked Belisaria.

"Seven," said Machaera.

Giérra winced.

"With that number of dragons, I can guess the bad news," said Belisaria. "Please don't tell me..."

"The emperor is arriving this evening to take overall command of the seven legions," said Machaera. "I'll be flying up with her and apparently so will Magister Umbrose, Magister Callidus, and Magister Celéri."

"Who is Magister Celéri?" asked Belisaria.

"Admiral Pixo has a niece named Celéri," said Giérra. "I *think* she's a wizard, but a fairly junior one. She's barely a woman."

"She's a magister now," said Machaera. "Pixo's niece can *ad hoc* gate, so she gets the title."

"I hope she's as sensible as her uncle," said Belisaria.

Machaera pressed her lips together and shook her head from side to side in small motions.

"I see," said Belisaria.

"Sírénae will be in overall command," said Machaera. "I will be commanding the legions, with the two of you reporting directly to me. It's up to Sírénae in the end, of course, but I expect you'll each have two legions in battle—the flanks most likely—while I take three legions and form the center. Magister Callidus will coordinate the efforts of the dragons with Xaxidiánus and Magister Umbrose will be the link between the emperor and Náegosh."

"Who will be responsible for the elephants?" asked Giérra.

"Who has that role now?" asked Machaera.

"A dwarf from Ostia named Maximus," said Giérra.

"I know the man," said Machaera. "He'll do, if one of his elephants doesn't step on him in the meantime."

"He's lasted this long," said Belisaria.

"And life is short," said Machaera. She laughed and the others did as well, releasing tension.

"This will be perfect," said Belisaria. "Replacing the commanders in the field with new leadership immediately before a battle."

"What could go wrong?" mused Giérra, earning hard looks from Machaera and Belisaria, then shrugs to show they wondered the same thing.

"Will that bird-lion of the emperor's be coming as well?" asked Belisaria.

"I don't think so," said Machaera. "She didn't bring Thraxa when we attacked the caverns in southwestern Dâron."

"Good," said Giérra. "That screeching creature's presence is bad for morale."

Machaera put a finger to her lips and Giérra got the message. What they said might be overheard by the emperor's spies. Every communications ring could potentially be tapped.

"When will you and the emperor be arriving?" asked Belisaria.

"After dark, I expect," said Machaera. "We'll look for your campfires."

"So long as the emperor arrives *after* dinner," said Belisaria. "She wouldn't be happy having only beans and Caledonian wine."

"I'll see that we bring food for her breakfast along," said Machaera, understanding her subordinate's challenges. "We might be dining on haunches of venison and barrels of ale from the Northern Clan Lander's larders by dinner time."

"I like your thinking," said Belisaria. "And it seems that the barbarians *are* going to stand and give battle on an open field."

"Sírénae had heard rumors to that effect," said Machaera. "That's one reason why she's coming to take command."

"Umbrose has ears everywhere," muttered Giérra. "More than half of the wizards on Náegosh's staff are probably paid by the spymaster as well."

"Not that there's anything *wrong* with that," said Belisaria, covering for Giérra's criticism. "Do you know if the Northern Clan Landers have dragons?"

"I haven't heard anything about it if they do," said Machaera. "There are rumors about Orluin dragons as big as castles, but I think that's all they are—rumors."

"So we will have superiority in the air," said Belisaria.

"And greater numbers on the ground as well, I expect," said Giérra. "From what my people tell me, the barbarians don't farm, they just harvest the fruits of the forest. They can't support a large population."

"Their warriors managed to defeat five legions sent against them previously," said Machaera. "Which reminds me. Sírénae wants those legions' standards back. It's a matter of imperial honor."

"She would be happier with food than imperial eagles, I expect," said Giérra.

"The emperor won't be happy until she has both supplies *and* standards," said Machaera.

"Get used to disappointment," muttered Giérra under her breath.

"What?" asked Machaera. "I couldn't hear you."

"It's nothing," said Belisaria. "See you tonight. We'll build a bonfire to guide you in."

"Since I'm sure the barbarians know exactly where to find us already," said Giérra softly.

"Our connection is breaking up," said Machaera. "Stay vigilant."

The interface went black and the communications ring contracted. Belisaria replaced it on her hand. "Why did you say such things?" she asked Giérra.

"I don't like this," said Giérra. "Not the smallest bit. We don't know what tricks the Northern Clan Landers are planning, our troops are hungry and surly from short rations, and the emperor herself is arriving to lead her legions to victory or blame us for defeat."

"At least I don't have to question your competence at strategic analysis," said Belisaria. "I agree with you on every point. I just don't think it's wise to advertise it." She stretched again and returned one hand to the hilt of her gladius. "The emperor was an excellent field commander when she was younger," Belisaria noted. "Then, as she climbed to the purple, she became more and more a political animal and lost sight of what it takes to be victorious against enemies wielding swords, not words."

"It's a matter of keeping the troops' spirits up," said Giérra. "Our soldiers' morale matters more than Sírénae's ego taking credit for a triumph. I'd rather have you or Machaera as my emperor."

"Speak that softly, my friend. Very softly," said Belisaria. "Tent walls are thin."

"I'm not saying anything we both haven't heard from walking the camp," Giérra whispered. "The legions are as hungry for an emperor who inspires them as they are for red meat. It was one thing to follow Sírénae west across the Ocean for glory and fortune and to shove our spears up the anatomy of the other three empires, but fighting an invisible enemy while tightening our belts on short rations wasn't what we volunteered for."

"Again, I agree," Belisaria replied softly. "But the only thing to do about it is give Sírénae her victory, and hope food and a share of booty improves the legions' spirits."

"I suppose you're right," said Giérra. "Perhaps we could do our own part to raise morale before the sun sets?" She pulled her gladius a few inches out of its scabbard.

"Sword practice?" said Belisaria, suddenly smiling. "I need to work out the stress in my neck from preparing reports, and we haven't practiced in at least a week."

"We'll give the troops a good show," said Giérra.

"And maybe teach the newer recruits a thing or two," said Belisaria.

"I'll let you win, of course," said Giérra. "That would be best for morale."

"You'll do no such thing," said Belisaria. "Let's get on with it before we lose the light."

Chapter 44

At the Imperial Palace

Sírénae was in a large common room at the imperial palace shared by four suites she'd assigned to Princess Gwýnnett, Túathal, Hibblig, and his cousin Kennig. The emperor sat on a high-backed well-padded chair across from a divan where Hibblig was crowded far too close to Gwýnnett, at least as Sírénae read the other woman's body language.

Why doesn't Gwýnnett slip Hibblig a potion that reduces libido? Sírénae wondered. Then she had a sudden insight. *Gwýnnett's giving him something to increase his libido for her own pleasure or amusement. Or to control the wizard more easily. Intriguing.* Sírénae leaned back in her chair. *The princess has reminded me of an important lesson,* the emperor considered. *Never attribute to foolishness what can better be explained by guile.* She let a small smile appear on her lips. *It should have been fresh in my mind from Celéri,* she realized.

Kennig was seated on a chair a few feet away, using his illusions to play a game of *shah-mat* with himself where all the pieces were magical creatures, except for the wizards' towers in the four corners. Sírénae used her peripheral vision to observe a white hippogryff move one square forward and one diagonally to defeat a black goblin and take its square. Continued surreptitious glances determined that Kennig was using the game as a distraction so *he* could observe *her.* *His interest is flattering, of course,* she thought, *but lovers wanted her to pay attention to their needs as well. Servants are so much easier. I can just command them to pleasure me exactly the way I prefer or suffer the consequences.*

Túathal was pacing between the grouping of chairs and a leaded-glass window on a wall a dozen feet distant. The window overlooked an interior courtyard filled with spring flowers and their scent wafted up to perfume the common room. Tamloch's deposed mad monarch still wore the gaudy vellum crown covered with gold leaf and painted gemstone images Sírénae had given him.

"Flowers, powers, spiral towers," said Túathal in a soft sing-song voice.

"That's a bit better than before," Sírénae told Gwýnnett. "He's still rhyming, but he's not as loud."

"I'm still making adjustments," said Gwýnnett.

"Why don't you just toss the batty old buzzard into a cell to rot?" asked Hibblig.

"Come now," said Sírénae. "Túathal is a king and must be treated with all due deference. You never know, I might need a puppet on the throne of Tamloch in the future—or a captive monarch to parade through the streets for my triumph."

"Eats, meats, streets," said Túathal.

"Do you have any idea what sets him off?" asked Sírénae.

"It's some internal logic in his scrambled mind," said Gwýnnett.

"Find. Mind. Kind," said Túathal from the window.

"I think he's fighting back against Gwýnnett's potions," said Kennig. "He had an exceptional, if delusional brain, and these rhymes are the only way he has to hide his true intentions and reveal them at the same time."

"Interesting theory," said Sírénae. "How do you interpret *flowers, powers, spiral towers?*"

"It starts with a word based on something he's just seen or heard, like *flowers*," said Kennig.

Sírénae nodded.

"Then *powers* can refer to either your power as the emperor or the power of wizardry," Kennig continued.

"That makes a strange sort of sense," said Sírénae.

"As for *spiral towers,*" said Kennig. "Fercha is reputed to have a tower ornamented with a blue marble spiral somewhere in the Rhuthro valley."

"The Rhuthro is a river, a tributary of the Moravon, west of Tyford," said Hibblig.

"I don't need you telling me where to find rivers in my own domains," barked Sírénae. "I can read a map. Is it upstream or downstream from Rhuthro Keep?"

"Downstream, I think," said Kennig.

"I'll have Umbrose send a scout wizard to search Fercha's tower for clues about how to build wide gates," said Sírénae. "That is Fercha's specialty, isn't it?"

"One of them, I believe," said Kennig.

"What about *Eats. Meats. Streets?*" asked Sírénae.

"Why don't you try," Kennig suggested.

Sírénae ignored his lack of formal address and started. "*Eats* is a commentary on our problems finding food, I expect."

"Good," said Kennig. "And *Meats?*"

"More of the same," said Sírénae. "But I'm not sure where *Streets* fit in, unless Túathal is predicting food riots in Sírénaeopolis Magna."

"That's how I'd read it," said Kennig.

"Túathal is a lunatic," said Hibblig. "Why are you even bothering with this exercise?"

"Because I find it amusing," said Sírénae. She stared at Hibblig and the wizard looked at the floor and shifted a few inches away from Gwýnnett on the divan. "I hope Túathal isn't a prophet," said the emperor. "And I did stop by for a reason."

"How can we be of service, Your Imperial Majesty?" asked Gwýnnett.

"I need something to help me properly develop a new wizard," said Sírénae. "She's powerful, but full of herself. I need something that will make her compliant, without diminishing her magical abilities."

"Would you prefer liquid or powder form?" asked Gwýnnett. "I already have both on hand."

"I assumed you would," said Sírénae. "Both, I think. How often would she need to take it?"

"Once a day should be enough," said Gwýnnett. "Twice a day might affect her magic as well as her will."

"That should be manageable," said Sírénae.

"I'll make the first dose a bit stronger so you can suggest she make drinking her *tonic* part of her waking ritual," suggested Gwýnnett. "Once the habit is formed it becomes self-reinforcing."

The princess stood, walked to her suite, and returned a few moments later with a small bottle of liquid and a vial of gray powder. "Take these," said Gwýnnett, handing the bottle and vial to Sírénae. "A thimbleful of powder in a quart jug should last for several weeks. The potion is more concentrated. Three drops on her tongue will ensure she obeys you. But remember, *you* have to give her the first dose from your own hand. She will connect you with happiness and seek your approval so long as she continues to take the formulation."

"Excellent," said Sírénae. "I knew it was wise to welcome you. Unfortunately, I have to leave for a few days and lead seven legions against the Northern Clan Landers."

"May I join you?" asked Kennig. "I'm tired of palace life."

"I'm content to stay with Gwýnnett," said Hibblig.

Sírénae smiled, wondering what combination of herbs Hibblig ingested daily.

"We'd welcome an illusionist of your skill level," said Sírénae. "We'll be flying north on dragonback in an hour or two, as soon as Xaxidiánus returns from his hunting expedition. Magister Callidus said he had to go far out to sea to find enough fish."

"Thank you, Gracious Emperor," said Kennig. "I'll be ready." On the illusionary shah-mat board a black basilisk vizier was skewered by the horn of the white unicorn queen, then the entire board vanished in a puff of non-being.

"Enjoy your uninterrupted time together," said Sírénae. "I'm off and have a dozen things to do."

"Things, rings, kings," said Túathal in a much louder voice as the emperor left the room.

Chapter 45

Gathering Allies

The kitchen at Rōlin and Peregrína's home in Three Mountains Valley was crowded. Nûd, Bonnie, Dârio, Jenet, Quintillius, Laetícia, Valentius, Inthíra, and Dukes Háiddon and Néillen were tightly packed, sitting around one end of the long trestle table that occupied most of the room. Eynon and Merry were there as well, but they opted to stand and assist their hosts by circulating with trays of the thin currant biscuits the Old Queen had made on a soapstone griddle early that morning. Chee and Ace were sleeping peacefully on the back porch, curled up together.

Everyone had been informed of this meeting by ring and gated in by Eynon, by previously established mobile gates, or by using their own wizardry. Doethan and Princess Rúth were at the opposite end of the table and Doethan tapped his pewter cider mug with hilt of his dagger to get everyone's attention. A dozen conversations abruptly ceased, and all eyes turned to Doethan.

"I'm going to open the connection," Doethan announced. "Bjarni, Signý and Amber are ready, and Arminta, the clan chief of the Northern Clan Lands is with them."

A trio of familiar tones sounded and a ring in Doethan's fingers expanded to a six-foot diameter, not the usual three. Doethan had a special affinity for communications rings and knew how to grow the interface so it would be easier for everyone around the table to see clearly. As expected, Bjarni and Signý were there, seated together, with golden-robed Amber behind them. To Signý's left sat an older woman with short gray hair and a well-lined face that radiated dignity and hard-earned wisdom.

"Thank you for coming together," said Signý. "This is Arminta. I've already briefed her on your identities."

Arminta nodded and so did everyone around the table in Three Mountains Valley, looking like a collection of bobbing ducks in a pond chasing bread crusts. Arminta, to her credit, didn't laugh.

"It appears we'll have a battle tomorrow," said Bjarni. "Bifurland and the Northern Clans will stand together against seven of Sírénae's legions..."

"...but we'd like to ask for aid from Dâron, Tamloch, and Occidens Province as well," said Signý.

"As we'd planned from the start," said Dârio.

"I thought we were going to avoid large battles, so the invaders had more mouths to feed," said Nûd.

"The purpose of *this* battle is to show Sírénae to be a poor general," said Arminta, "not waste warriors' lives on their side or ours."

"That shouldn't be difficult, since she *is* a poor general," said Valentius. "My father told me she was once reasonably competent, but she let becoming emperor of the West go to her head."

"Our spies support that assessment," said Arminta. "The legions are far from happy that the glorious victories Sírénae promised when she was exiled haven't materialized."

"So we can't let this battle *become* such a victory," said Laetícia.

"Our spies say the same thing about the legions' frustrations," said Nûd. "Salder gave a particularly detailed report."

"What forces do you need from us?" asked Quintillius.

"We have plenty of archers and skirmishers among our people," said Arminta.

"And Bifurland will bring its spears and axes," added Signý, "plus *larger* combatants."

"I'm looking forward to *that*," said Eynon.

"However," said Bjarni, "we still need cavalry. Bifurlanders ride sea steeds with keels, not the four-footed variety."

"Heavy cavalry, especially," said Arminta. "We need to entice the legions to attack and armored knights pose a substantial threat that must be countered."

"Both Tamloch and Dâron can supply heavy cavalry, and light cavalry as well," said Dârio, inclining his head to Nûd to confirm his cousin's agreement.

"And foot soldiers," added Jenet, looking to Duke Háiddon.

"From Tamloch *and* Dâron," said the Duke. "Plus more archers if you need them."

"Only if they're skilled enough to harass but not actually hit their targets," said Arminta. "My Clan Landers will be using arrows to herd the invaders rather than perforate them."

"What about the legions of Occidens Province?" asked Quintillius. "We're eager to do battle."

"How could we be sure to tell one legion from another?" asked Princess Rúth.

Bonnie smiled at the princess and nudged Nûd, who opened his arms expansively and spoke. "The good people of Dâron and Tamloch worked together to solve that problem," he said.

Merry, warned in advance, took that as her cue to hold up a tabard she had just retrieved from a sideboard. She shifted position so Bjarni, Signý, Arminta and the others gathered in Three Mountains Valley could see it. The tabard was sewn from three vertical stripes of fabric from left to right, using Tamloch green, Occidens Province red, and Dâron sky blue. A wide gold band of fabric representing Bifurland went from shoulder to shoulder.

People applauded the tabard design on both sides of the ring's interface.

"Well done, Nûd," said Signý "You may have also designed the banner of Allied Orluin."

"Thank you, Your Majesty," said Nûd.

"It certainly is... *colorful*," said Arminta.

"True enough," said Nûd. "I apologize that it doesn't include anything to symbolize the Northern Clan Lands."

"We're not much for colors that don't help us blend into our forests," said Arminta.

"I could add a bit of muted tartan fringe at the bottom?" Nûd offered.

"That's not necessary," said the clan chief. "We're glad to be your allies for now, against the invaders, but once Sírénae's legions are driven off, we'd prefer to be left alone. I'll be busy enough arbitrating the fights our clans have with each other to waste time worrying about you flatlanders."

"Understood," said Nûd. "Here's to future cordial, if distant, relations."

Arminta nodded.

"Do you have enough tabards for a thousand legionnaires?" asked Quintillius.

"Yes, and more besides," said Bonnie. "Princess Rúth organized the effort."

Rúth wagged a finger at Bonnie to gently chastise her for giving away Rúth's role in the process after she'd asked the leading question allowing the tabard to be displayed.

"Sorry," mouthed Bonnie softly.

"A thousand legionnaires from Occidens Province, plus heavy cavalry and infantry contingents from both Dâron and Tamloch," said Signý. "That should do nicely."

"Our spears and axes will deploy to hills on the eastern side of the proposed field of battle," said Bjarni. "There are fortifications built by Occidens Province in years past there already."

"I know the spot," said Quintillius. "There's a big lake just west. The valley in between is where you expect to give battle?"

"Correct," said Arminta. "And that big lake will be very important. The Northern Clan Lands forces will primarily assemble at the northern end of its eastern shore, to draw the much larger invading Roma force onto the valley."

"And they'll be surprised when my legion and the Dâron and Tamloch forces gate in?" asked Quintillius.

"Something like that," said Signý.

"How can *I* help?" asked Eynon. "Do you want me to freeze the lake, like I did the Brenavon? Would you like me to make illusions, like I did at Riyas? I'm glad to do whatever you need."

"Thank you, Eynon," said Nûd. "I'm sure we'll get to that in due time."

Merry turned her back to Eynon to hide a smile, then bit off a morsel of currant biscuit so she wouldn't be tempted again later on when Eynon could see her.

"What about dragons?" asked Duke Néillen.

"Since Sírénae is taking command of all seven legions for the battle, we can expect all seven of her blacks to be there," said Amber.

"No, that was a given," said Duke Néillen. "I meant *our* great dragons."

"What part of *we're trying not to kill Sírénae's legionnaires* didn't you understand?" asked Jenet.

"But Viridáxés and Zûrafiérix are so powerful..." Duke Néillen responded.

"If you haven't heard, Zûrafiérix is guarding her clutch and Viridáxés is guarding *her*," said Nûd. "I found out when Eynon gated me to their island yesterday to check on them."

"There are *nine* eggs," said Eynon. "Each one is too big for me to wrap my arms around."

"How marvelous!" said Inthíra. "There will be new great dragons on this side of the Ocean."

"It will take a hundred years for them to be big enough to be useful in battle," said Nûd. "And in the short term, we won't be able to call upon Viridáxés and Zûrafiérix for assistance."

"It's unfortunate dragon eggs need to incubate for two years before they hatch," added Valentius. "There's no denying Zûrafiérix is a truly remarkable dragon, and I'm sure her offspring will be equally impressive."

"Can't we assign soldiers to guard Zûrafiérix so that Viridáxés can fight for us?" asked Duke Néillen. "He *really* hates the Roma."

Quintillius and Laetícia turned to stare at Néillen.

"I mean the *invading* Roma," the duke corrected.

"The only way that could happen would be if Viridáxés was convinced Sírénae and her invaders were a direct threat to Zûrafiérix," said Nûd.

"Which they certainly are," said Dârio. "The issue is are the invaders an immediate threat or a long-term one?"

"And the answer to that, more broadly, is clearly both," said Jenet. "So we will have to proceed without our largest assets and do the best we can."

"We'll still have *some* large assets," said Signý.

"Indeed we will," said Laetícia. "The trumpet player we've sent you says he's being treated quite well by your people, by the way, Arminta. Thank you."

"Our pleasure," said the clan chief. "It makes me happy to see a man enjoy slow-roasted boar as much as he does."

"So long as he's still able to play his horn when needed," said Laetícia. "You wouldn't be roasting boars just upwind of the invaders' camp, would you?"

"And allowing the lovely smells to waft their way, while they're getting by on only boiled beans for dinner?" asked Arminta. "That would be cruel."

Knowing looks jumped from face to face around the kitchen table.

"Once we regain control of Nova Eboracum and Occidens Province, I think you can be assured *we* won't attack you in the future," said Quintillius.

"That's good to know," Arminta replied. "I hope your successors and their successors have long memories."

"Not much chance of that, eh?" Bjarni interjected.

"That's something for another day," said Signý.

"Where are Fercha and Verro?" asked Merry after finishing her currant biscuit.

"They're still working with Mafuta on making a functioning gate across the Ocean," said Laetícia.

"My father says the entire Imperium stands ready to help us defeat Sírénae," said Valentius. "He apologized for allowing her and her legions to go into exile instead of insisting she do the honorable thing."

"He means kill herself," Merry whispered to Eynon.

"I'd be glad to correct that oversight if some wizard would gate me into her throne room," said Duke Néillen.

"You'd have to get by her snow-gryffon first," said Doethan. "It would be much better if her troops rebelled against her."

"And it sounds like we're making excellent progress toward that end," said Quintillius.

"They'd have to toss out Umbrose, too," said Laetícia. "If he remains spymaster, any new emperor will be caught up in his webs."

"I know how to deal with both Sírénae *and* Umbrose," said Valentius. "Take his magestone and drop them off on a tiny island far from anywhere. The two of them can blame and berate each until they're old and gray."

"A fitting punishment," said Laetícia.

"It would be even better if we could exile Gwýnnett and Túathal along with them," said Jenet.

"They wouldn't last a year with Gwýnnett present," said Dârio. "She'd find some way to poison them all and do it out of spite."

Nûd listened to his cousin's words and realized he greatly preferred a mother who wasn't around very often to one who was actively trying to harm him.

"I know a few islands far to the north, populated only by arctic cave bears that might serve as destinations," said Bjarni.

"We should speak later," said Valentius.

"Aren't you forgetting something?" asked Princess Rúth. "Verro's not here and Eynon's too inexperienced, but Laetícia and Amber should know what I mean."

"You're talking about how we'll deploy our wizards in combat," said Laetícia. "Thanks for the reminder. I've been so focused on gates across the Ocean I'm neglecting my duties."

"I have not," said Amber. "Most of Bifurland's wizards will be focused on one of three tasks: opening mobile gates, guarding mobile gates, and protecting our warriors from enemy magic."

"That sounds wise," said Laetícia. "I'll assign wizards to defend our gates and legions and should have some *qua-qua* teams available to deploy to distract dragons."

"It may take more than *qua-qua* teams this time," said Doethan. "I heard from a little bird that invading wizards have developed special lenses for dragons to reduce their susceptibility to the game's hypnotic patterns."

"I'll send mages skilled in offensive magic instead, then," said Laetícia.

"Fercha and Verro will have to set aside their research to lead Dâron and Tamloch's mages in battle," said Dârio.

"I'll remind them of that fact," said Laetícia.

"It will be a challenge for our wizards to fight dragons *and* the invading battle mages simultaneously," said Inthíra. "Illusions may help against wizards, but dragons can banish them with their fire."

"With luck there will be enough chaos on the ground," said Signý. "It might help if you made an illusion of low clouds to hide the battlefield from the dragons and battle wizards in the air."

"I can do that," said Inthíra.

"You said you'd tell me what I could do to help," said Eynon.

"You've done a great deal to help already," said Nûd. "Your mobile gates—the ones you and Merry have worked so hard on—will be the way we deploy troops rapidly."

"Yes," said Laetícia. "Well done, both of you. We never expected to have so many so soon."

"Thank you," said Merry. "But could you answer Eynon's question, please? Do you need some powerful magic only he can do performed on the battlefield or not?"

"We do," said Signý. "Though the precise form of that magic depends on how Sírénae chooses to deploy her forces. I'll explain..."

Chapter 46

Nûd and Valentius

"Your Majesty," said Valentius as he followed Nûd onto Rōlin and Peregrína's back porch after the meeting was over. "Might I have a few minutes of your time?"

"Of course," Nûd replied. "I'm just heading to that outcrop a bowshot to the west to check on Rocky, my wyvern. We can talk as we walk."

"Thank you, Your Majesty," said Valentius.

"Please call me Nûd unless we're somewhere formal," said Nûd. "Your rank as the son and likely heir of an emperor is higher than mine as the ruler of a kingdom in Orluin."

"On the other side of the Ocean, I'm just a citizen of the Imperium, like millions of others," said Valentius. "I've served as a provincial governor and a general commanding legions, but at present I hold no office or position."

"Formally," said Nûd. "Informally, everyone seems to know your father is grooming you to step into his shoes when he's ready to retire in a few years."

"There's no guarantee the other emperors will accede to my father's wishes," said Valentius. "After the mistake they made by confirming Sírénae as Western Emperor, they're going to be much more careful in their vetting."

"How many votes do you think you'd have if Valens stepped down right now?" asked Nûd.

"Two for sure," said Valentius. "My father has a vote until he's off the throne, and Phraátēs the Lion..."

"Emperor of the East," said Nûd.

"You've studied the Imperium," said Valentius.

"I've spent a lot of time with scrolls and books," said Nûd. "What about Flavia Drusilla?"

"The Emperor of the North is trying to have her candidate elevated to be the new Western Emperor," said Valentius. "She's withholding her approval of my candidacy for the South to ensure my father's support for Gertrude of Mainz, the governor of the Rhineland. She remained loyal when Sírénae rebelled, so Flavia considers that sufficient reason to offer her the purple. That, and the fact that Gertrude and Flavia served together in five different postings after attending the Imperial School of Good Governance and Gertrude always deferred to Flavia. With Gertrude as Emperor of the West and Flavia as Emperor of the North, Flavia would effectively control half the Imperium."

"And you'd rather you did?" asked Nûd. They were approaching Rocky, so he shortened his stride.

"Of course not," said Valentius. "Too much power concentrated in a single person would damage the Imperium. That's why Sírénae was exiled. She wanted to add North Afarika to the West."

"My understanding is that she was also quite difficult for the other emperors to work with," said Nûd.

"They're *all* difficult to work with—at times," said Valentius. "No one is made an emperor in the Imperium because of their sweet disposition."

"Point taken," said Nûd.

"Sírénae, however, was difficult *all* the time," said Valentius. "If the sun was shining, my father would remark on that fact to Sírénae and she'd claim it was just a wizard's fireball hanging in the sky or the product of a skilled illusionist."

"I can see how that would be annoying," said Nûd.

"The other emperors would have tolerated that as a not-so-amusing quirk if she hadn't tried taking Mauretania, my father's northwest Afarikan province," said Valentius. "Sírénae had just put down a rebellion in the mountains of northern Éberria and moved her army into Southern Empire territory without warning. It took us months to reclaim our land. Taking Mauretania was the last bag of grain on the donkey as far as the other three emperors were concerned. Add to that her attempt on my father's life with poison and having me taken prisoner and she's become truly *persona non grata* across the Imperium."

"I'm surprised so many of her legions went into exile with her," said Nûd.

"She'd convinced them that they'd all be executed as traitors if they didn't join her expedition to Orluin," said Valentius. "Given a choice between death and the prospect of glory, riches, and land, most legionnaires opted to follow her across the Ocean."

"I see," said Nûd. "So with no glory or riches, and land not yet distributed..."

"...because Sírénae has to keep her forces together until the allies are defeated..." said Valentius.

"...support for Sírénae is waning," said Nûd.

"Exactly," said Valentius. "It was wise to take all your people and food and hide. Whoever came up with that idea is a brilliant strategist."

Nûd didn't reply. Instead he waved to Rocky, who was only a hundred steps distant, gnawing on what looked like the carcass of a particularly large wisent.

"It was your idea, wasn't it?" asked Valentius. "Well done."

"Thank you," said Nûd quietly. His next words were louder, as if he was eager to change the subject. "Tell me. How does the First Citizen stand on your candidacy to replace your father?"

"Horatius Apenninus is currently straddling the dragon's back on the matter," said Valentius. "He won't come down on either side until he senses whose faction is stronger."

"If you don't mind my play on words," said Nûd, "What will it take to *tip the scales*?"

"A prominent role for myself in defeating Sírénae wouldn't hurt," said Valentius. "Mafuta and Laetícia are sending reports back to the Imperium and they're followed quite eagerly by Flavia, Phraátes, and Horatius as well as my father."

"I'll keep that in mind as our situation develops," said Nûd. "I see Rocky has finished eating his wisent. Would you like to go for a ride?"

"Very much so!" answered Valentius.

After rubbing the bony ridges behind Rocky's ears, Nûd showed Valentius the best places to put his feet to climb onto the wyvern's back. Once Valentius was in his saddle, Nûd helped him fasten the straps that would hold him in place if

Rocky decided to execute acrobatic maneuvers in the air. Nûd strapped himself in and directed Rocky to take flight.

"Where would you like to fly?" asked Nûd.

"Up!" said Valentius. "I want to get a sense of this land from above and see where everyone has been settled."

Nûd spoke to Rocky and the wyvern flew higher. The two men could sense the wyvern's muscles move beneath them and feel the blasts of wind from each powerful wingbeat. Soon they were at a point where the air was thin and much colder.

"Is that high enough for you?" asked Nûd.

"Yes," said Valentius. "Perhaps even a bit *too* high."

"Rocky was demonstrating his flying ability and showing off, weren't you, my friend," said Nûd, rubbing Rocky's neck.

They descended until the temperature increased and the air was richer. Even at their reduced altitude, they could see a slight curve in the horizon in the cloudless sky.

"The view is magnificent," said Valentius. "Is that Melyncárreg to the north where the smoke is rising? I can see a large castle."

"Yes," said Nûd. "I was brought up there, mostly by my grandfather."

"Your grandsire was named Damon, also known as Ealdamon, author of *Ealdamon's Epigrams*?" asked Valentius.

"The very same," said Nûd.

"How long has he been dead?" asked Valentius.

"He's *not* dead as far as I know," said Nûd.

"Then why isn't he here helping the allies?" asked Valentius. "Isn't he Dâron's Master Mage?"

"My grandfather handed *that* title off to Eynon," said Nûd. "I didn't think it was fair of him. Eynon is still too trusting and innocent for the role, but I wasn't consulted."

"So where did Ealdamon go?" asked Valentius.

"To the Great Falls to spend time with my grandmother, Seren, now that they've reconciled," said Nûd. "Last I heard."

"Your grandmother is Princess Seren? The one from the stories who disappeared? Isn't there a statue of her in Brendinas?" said Valentius, tossing out questions faster than Nûd could answer them.

"Yes to all of them," said Nûd. "Seren's daughter Fercha is my mother."

"And Verro is your father?" asked Valentius. "I thought I'd heard that and it's easy to see you're related."

"Also correct," said Nûd. "Dârio is my first cousin."

"Because Dârio's father is King Túathal of Tamloch and he and Verro are brothers," said Valentius. "Laetícia explained it to me and if not for my years of experience dealing with family trees that look like knotted squid's tentacles back in the Imperium I would have been completely lost."

"Humans do like to make things complicated, don't we?" said Nûd. Rocky bellowed and Nûd patted his neck.

"Wyverns prefer to keep their relationships simpler, then?" Nûd asked his mount. A low rumble from Rocky's throat served as confirmation.

"Was that your wyvern laughing?" asked Valentius.

"It was, as far as I can tell," said Nûd. He asked Rocky to circle and pointed out the places each group from the cavern refuges to the east had been resettled. Instead of being divided into Dâron, Tamloch, and Occidens Province communities, the people had sorted themselves out based on the caverns where they had been earlier. He pointed out this observation to Valentius. "I think we're building something new here," he said. "Like the four colors on the tabard I held up at our meeting, the disparate allies are beginning to sew themselves together."

"That's what I wanted to talk to you about," said Valentius.

"I wondered," said Nûd. "You didn't want to be interrogated about politics in the Imperium and your odds of becoming the next emperor of the South."

"I enjoyed our conversation on that topic," said Valentius. "And it illustrates the matter I wanted to discuss."

"You want my support in ensuring you have the credit for defeating Sírénae?" asked Nûd.

"Yes, though not if I haven't earned it," said Valentius. "But that's not why I wanted to talk. I wanted to give you some advice, one leader to another, and friend to friend if you think we've reached or will soon have that status."

"I'm *glad* to have you as a friend," said Nûd. "I like having some-one around who's also interested in discussing Imperial politics—and knows more about the subject than I do. I've been fascinated by such things from reading Roma history books in the library in Melyncárreg and hearing Rōlin and Peregrína tell stories of their travels in the Imperium."

"There, you're proving it again," said Valentius.

"Proving what?" asked Nûd.

"Proving that you're a good king," said Valentius.

"I know I'm king," said Nûd. "Technically, at least. Though I wasn't raised as a prince, like Dârio, and taught to be a knight and a monarch. I never had king lessons."

"Are you sure?" asked Valentius.

"What do you mean?" asked Nûd. "I spent my time in Melyncárreg cutting wood, repairing trails, cooking meals, and reading."

"You learned to serve others, the value of hard work, and the world's collected wisdom distilled in books and scrolls," said Valentius. "That sounds like fine preparation for kingship."

"But I only learned the crossbow and quarterstaff, not the sword," Nûd protested.

"Kingship is not the same as mastery of the sword," said Valentius. "I'm not one of the best with a blade, but I've honed my strategic mind to a razor-sharp point so I can direct legions under my command with confidence—and so my legions can have confidence in me."

"But you were raised as a prince, or an emperor's heir, which is even more important," said Nûd.

"So were you," said Valentius. He tugged on Nûd's shoulder so Nûd would turn and face him. "Was your grandfather a stupid man?" Valentius asked.

"Far from it," said Nûd.

"Did he know you were the rightful heir of Dâron?" Valentius continued.

"Of course he did," said Nûd.

"Then what makes you think he wouldn't have ensured you received an appropriate education?" asked Valentius.

"Wait, what?" asked Nûd. "He never told *me* I was heir to a throne."

"But *he* knew, and I'm sure the man who wrote *Ealdamon's Epigrams* would have taught you well, or even better, put you in circumstances where you could teach yourself."

Nûd turned back to face in their direction of travel. For a few minutes the only sound was the wind rushing past them as Rocky circled.

"Damon didn't want me to get a melon head," said Nûd after a long pause. "He treated me like a servant because that's what a good king is."

"A servant to his people," said Valentius. "Any other insights?"

"A sword is an offensive weapon," said Nûd. "A quarterstaff is better for defense. If I came to the throne, he wanted me to think first of defending Dâron, not attacking our neighbors."

"Good," said Valentius. "You're figuring it out. It will probably take you another week or two before you'll put everything in place. I expect that you'll want to strangle your grandfather at first..."

"I'm already there," said Nûd.

"But by the time you're done thinking, you'll want to hug him."

"Maybe," said Nûd. "Thank you for providing a valuable perspective. I couldn't see it."

"I'm glad to help," said Valentius. He leaned forward and spoke louder so his voice would be sure to reach Nûd's ears. "I have a few more bits of advice," he said. "Call them king lessons, if you will."

"I'm listening," said Nûd.

"Stand up straight—kings don't slouch. Stop apologizing for your inadequacies—your people want to be inspired, not depressed because their monarch has self-doubts. All kings have them, they just don't show them, except to their closest confidants."

"Is that everything?" asked Nûd.

"No," said Valentius. "There's one more. Get it through your thick skull that you're already a good king, not a poor shadow of one. You're three times the strategist your cousin is—maybe twice as good as Jenet—and Dâron, all of Orluin for that matter, is lucky to have you."

Rocky trumpeted his agreement. Nûd patted the wyvern's neck in appreciation, then laughed when Rocky shifted to deep rumbling in his throat.

Chapter 47

Bonnie and Jenet

Bonnie, Jenet, and Eynon were cleaning and reorganizing the table in Rōlin and Peregrína's kitchen after the recent meeting. Jenet could see that Bonnie wanted to talk to her alone because the wizard kept trying to say something but stopped short of actually doing so.

"Eynon," asked Jenet. "Where's Merry?"

"In the Map Room, I think," Eynon answered. "She wants to see the drawing Peregrína made of the site of the battlefield."

"You should be familiar with the site as well," said Jenet. "Why don't you head over to the Map Room and examine the drawing with her."

"That's a good idea," said Eynon. "Are you sure you don't need my help?"

"Not until tomorrow," said Jenet. "Then you'll really be needed."

"Take a currant biscuit to Merry," said Bonnie. "She might appreciate a snack later tonight."

"Better yet, take two," said Jenet, "You'll both need to keep your strength up." She wrapped two biscuits in a clean square of linen and handed them to Eynon. He smiled at Jenet and Bonnie, bowed, and *ad hoc* gated away, presumably to the Map Room.

"Oh, it's that way, is it," said Jenet. "Show off."

"Gating down the hall?" asked Bonnie. "He's just eager to see Merry and exercising his talents."

"I winked at him before he disappeared and he winked back," said Jenet.

"But all you said was *you'll both need to keep your strength up...*" said Bonnie. She stopped and thought for a moment, then started to blush and turned away so Jenet couldn't see her face. When Bonnie turned back, her cheeks were no longer red. "It's not fair," she said. "I'm just past twenty and a small bit of teasing about lovemaking can affect me like that."

Jenet gave Bonnie a gentle smile. "I take it you and Nûd have recently become lovers?"

"Is it that obvious?" asked Bonnie. She watched Jenet's expression and held up her hand. "No, don't tell me. I know the answer."

Closing the three steps between them, Jenet gave Bonnie a hug and continued to hold her until Bonnie released her.

"Thank you," said Bonnie. "I didn't realize that was what I needed until you started."

"You're always welcome to ask for a hug whenever you want one," said Jenet. "I grew up in a family that hugged a lot. You should ask my father for one. He can make you feel safe from anything for a few minutes."

"Nûd makes me feel that way when *he* hugs me," said Bonnie.

"I'm so glad," said Jenet. "It took Dârio months to understand that someone could offer him a hug without wanting something. Of course, his horrid mother used to *demand* them, so his initial reluctance when he spent time on my family's estates makes a certain degree of sense."

"Scholars at the Institute in Bhaile Pónaire didn't hug," said Bonnie. "Not even after delivering a particularly excellent lecture."

"Their loss," said Jenet.

"I used to hug my cousin Uirsé when we were students together," said Bonnie. "She's going to marry Merry's brother soon."

"I know," said Jenet. "And you can stop stalling. What did you want to talk about?"

"Being a queen," said Bonnie. "I've told Nûd I'm fine with it, but inside my brain the prospect is terrifying. I don't want to disappoint Nûd *or* the kingdom."

"What makes you think I have any special knowledge about being a queen?" asked Jenet. "I'm quite new in that role myself and have been much more focused on learning what it takes to be Tamloch's Earl Marshal than Dârio's future partner on the throne."

"Yes, but you're a Duke's daughter and grew up in court," said Bonnie. "You know things. I was off at the Institute surrounded by elderly scholar-wizards studying Congruencies and non-Euclidean Geometry."

"I know less of court than you think," said Jenet. "I spent most of my life on our estates—big farms, mostly. My father brought my sister Linette and me to live in Brendinas only after *that woman* insisted Dârio spend most of his time there. I think she sensed we were a good influence on him, and she wanted him away from us and wrapped like a spiral ring around her finger."

"You're talking about Gwýnnett?" asked Bonnie.

"Yes. She's a poisonous woman," said Jenet. "I'm sorry it turns out she's *not* dead. And Túathal, too."

"Túathal wasn't a good king," said Bonnie. "Too many people in Tamloch were afraid of him. Some of my instructors were concerned Túathal might ask them for some magical device or another and they'd be killed if they couldn't produce it fast enough."

"I'm amazed that someone as good and noble as Dârio could have *that woman* and *that man* as parents," said Jenet. She started pacing along the length of the kitchen, shoving chairs and benches underneath the table.

"Put them on top instead," said Bonnie. "I'll sweep underneath. Nûd and I have that in common. We both know how to clean."

"Of course," said Jenet. She took a deep breath and held it, then squared her shoulders and began putting chairs and benches on top of the table.

Bonnie found a broom near the back door and started sweeping. Instead of bending down to reach what dust, dirt, and food morsels were under the middle of the table, Bonnie controlled the broom with constructs of solidified sound.

"That's clever," said Jenet when she'd finished with the chairs and benches. "Did Merry tell you about the magically animated broom in Fercha's tower? I think a small congruency followed it around on the floor to gate what the broom swept up far away."

"How delightful," said Bonnie. "And what a good idea." She focused on her artifact and generated a congruency the size of a saucer under the table, then pushed everything she'd gathered up into it.

Jenet clapped. "Nicely done!" she said.

"Fercha and I haven't had much time to get to know each other," said Bonnie. "Nûd isn't particularly comfortable around his mother and that's a sore spot I don't want to press on. Maybe methods for animating brooms will provide a good excuse to start a conversation?"

"At least you'll have a better future mother-in-law than I will," said Jenet.

"True," said Bonnie. She leaned the broom against the side of the table, walked to Jenet, and gave the younger woman a hug.

Jenet held the hug as long as Bonnie had earlier, then smiled at Bonnie when it ended. "You came to me to talk about the challenges of being a queen and we've ended up talking about my problems more than yours," said Jenet.

"I don't mind," said Bonnie. "Hearing your challenges makes me feel better, like I'm not alone."

"We future queens need to stick together," said Jenet.

"Agreed," said Bonnie. They clasped four hands in the space between them.

"If you really want to know what it takes to be a queen, I know who you should talk to," said Jenet.

"Queen Signý?" asked Bonnie.

"No, Queen Carys," said Jenet. "Her room is just down the hall and we can tell her how much everyone enjoyed her currant biscuits."

Chapter 48

Queen Carys

"Come in, come in," said dowager queen Carys, wife of the late monarch of Dâron, King Dârioth XXIV. She was seated in an overstuffed chair beside a bed, with a small table to one side and a sewing basket at her feet. Carys motioned for her guests to sit on the bed, the only place available for them to sit. "It's so kind of you both to visit a lonely old woman," she said.

Jenet laughed and Bonnie looked bewildered.

"I don't see a lonely old woman here," said Jenet. "Perhaps a wise and crafty spider in her lair, waiting to sense touches on her webs..."

"Jenet!" said Bonnie. "Don't be rude."

"Accurate descriptions are seldom held to be rude by those they describe," said Carys. "For that matter, there are a good many *less* complimentary words she could have used, though I might wish for a better metaphorical creature to stand for me than a spider."

"I couldn't think of one," said Jenet.

"Nor can I," said Queen Carys, "and I've been considering the question for many years longer than you have."

"More than a century?" asked Jenet.

"Now you *are* being rude, so I'll call you *child* to punish you for your impertinence," said Carys.

"My apologies, Aged Ancestor," said Jenet.

"A distant ancestor, through your mother's family," said Carys.

"Very distant," teased Jenet. "Tell us, what was it like to come across the Ocean on the First Ships?"

Carys stuck her tongue out at Jenet and turned her attention to Bonnie. "Perhaps you are more polite than the Earl Marshal of Tamloch and the future mother of my great-great-grandchildren," said the old queen. "Especially since you'll soon have the same status, at least regarding babies."

"Just not *that* soon, please," said Bonnie.

"Well, don't dawdle for *too* long about it," said Carys. "I won't live forever. My bones ache, despite the weekly healing potions they give me. Those potions should be saved for wounded soldiers."

"You're worth it," said Jenet. "Over the years, your wisdom has helped many soldiers avoid the necessity of drinking healing potions."

Carys nodded in appreciation and smiled at Jenet. "That's better," she said.

"What makes you think you won't live forever?" Jenet asked. "When you're close to death, we can bury you in the magestone quarry south of Brendinas where Zûrafiérix was sleeping. A thousand years from now some future adventurers can find you, dig you up, and benefit from your greatly enhanced wisdom."

"If sleeping with magestones works on humans the way it does on dragons, I'd also be taller than Fercha's tower by then," said Carys. "My giant might as well as my mind could then be put to good use in Dâron's service."

"If there *is* a Dâron in a thousand years," said Bonnie.

"Why wouldn't there be?" asked the old queen.

"Because your great-grandsons of heart and blood, along with other far-sighted leaders from Occidens Province and Bifurland are forging something new on this side of the Ocean," Bonnie answered. "In a thousand years, Dâron may just be a distant memory—the name of an ancient region in the nation of United Orluin."

"United Orluin," said Queen Carys. "I suppose Orluin would be simpler, but *United* Orluin would remind everyone of the importance of standing together."

"Have you seen Nûd's new tabards for our Roma?" asked Jenet.

"Green, red, sky-blue, and gold?" asked Carys. "That's at least one color too many, but I suppose three colors won't do for four allies. I helped sew a few before my fingers got stiff. The tabards are easy to identify, at least." She reached into her sewing basket and handed Bonnie a bundle of folded cloth. "Open it out," said old queen.

Working together, Bonnie and Jenet unfolded the cloth and found it was a rectangle four feet high and eight feet long that almost went from one wall to the other on the narrow dimension of the queen's bedroom.

It was a flag large enough to be seen across a battlefield. The three vertical stripes on the tabards were changed to horizontal stripes on the banner, with sky-blue at the top, green at the bottom, and red in the middle. The gold stripe for Bifurland ran parallel to where a flagpole would be attached.

"This is marvelous," said Bonnie.

"It will be a true asset on the field," added Jenet.

"It must have been a lot of work to sew it quickly," said Bonnie.

"It was, but not for me," said Queen Carys. "I had to stop sewing after two tabards. Princess Rúth and Doethan organized it, using men and women from Dâron, Tamloch, Bifurland, and Occidens Province in its making."

"You understand the power of symbols," said Jenet.

"So do you, *child*, and you learned that lesson much earlier than I did," said Carys. She waved toward the flag, saying, "Fold that back up and put it to good use tomorrow."

"We will," said Jenet.

"What shall we call it?" asked Bonnie.

"The flag?" asked Jenet. "Does it need a name?"

"I think it does," said Bonnie. "It takes too long to say *Go out and fight for the Green-Red-Blue-and-Gold.*"

"She has a point," said Carys.

"The Rainbow Banner?" suggested Jenet.

"Not enough colors for that," said Carys.

"And we don't want to add imperial purple to the flag," said Bonnie. "That would remind people of Sírénae."

"Granted," said Jenet. "Besides, adding *more* colors would get complicated."

"What about the Four Color?" asked Bonnie. "Fight for the Four?"

"That will do," said Queen Carys. "And after we win tomorrow it will have a new name..."

"What's that?" asked Jenet.

"Old Victory," the queen replied.

That observation made them all smile. Bonnie and Jenet folded the new battle flag into a tight square and Jenet tucked it into the hood of Bonnie's wizards' robes. Jenet noted with some pleasure that Bonnie was now wearing robes that were half Tamloch green and half Dâron blue. Somehow it had seemed so natural Jenet hadn't even been aware of the change. Clearly, Bonnie also understood the importance of symbols.

"I hope you're right about us being victorious," said Jenet. "We've fought Roma legions from Occidens Province for centuries, though not so much in recent years since Quintillius and Laetícia assumed leadership there. We don't know if fighting legions commanded by Sírénae will be different."

"Which kingdom do you mean when you say *we*, Jenet?" asked Bonnie.

"Why..." Jenet began, then stopped, resuming after a moment's pause. "I was about to say, 'Why Dâron, of course, because I'm the daughter of a Dâron duke and spent most of my life there, but now I'm responsible for Tamloch's forces, though I work closely with my father who's Earl Marshal of Dâron." Jenet shrugged and threw up her hands. "I guess I mean both," she said.

Carys beamed. "I'm so glad to hear that," said the old queen. "Twenty-four and I tried our best to bring the two kingdoms closer during our reign, but in the end our efforts failed."

"Thanks to Túathal's machinations?" asked Jenet.

"And Gwýnnett's malign influences," said Carys. "Though now with the kings being first cousins, the odds of long-lasting peace between Dâron and Tamloch are higher than they've ever been."

"If we can get rid of Sírénae," said Jenet.

"Who's *Twenty-four*?" asked Bonnie.

"That's right, you're not from Dâron," said Carys. "My husband, the Old King, as he was known once his hair turned gray, was Dârioth, the Twenty-fourth of that Name, King of Dâron and High Lord of the Southern Reaches. I used to call him Twenty-four as a joke when we were alone."

"Pillow talk is a delight," said Jenet.

"I miss it," said Carys. "Even though the king's mind had gone a decade before his body, it was still a joy to whisper together."

"I thought the Southern Reaches were part of Dâron, not something separate," said Bonnie.

"They are *now*," said Carys. "But that wasn't true several centuries ago."

"You were there, though, weren't you?" asked Jenet. "Can you give us an eyewitness account? Had the lava that once covered the surface of the earth cooled by then?"

Carys sniffed and shook her head. "Bonnie, you and I will have a lovely time conversing together," said the old queen. "We can completely ignore this *ill-mannered child* who has seduced my great-grandson Dârio into her bed. Tell me, what did *you* come here to talk about?"

"Uh..." said Bonnie.

"I apologize, Your Majesty," interrupted Jenet. "Please forgive my poor choice of words."

"Of course," said Carys.

"I know you were but a babe-in-arms all those centuries ago and would therefore have no memory of what transpired," said Jenet. Before Carys could wave a stern, admonishing finger in her direction, Jenet spoke again. "What Bonnie's trying to say, though her tongue is tied like the string of a kite caught in a tree on a windy day, is that she'd like your advice on being a good queen. She's told Nûd she'll marry him, but she's worried she won't properly measure up as his queen."

Carys gave Bonnie her full attention. "Do Jenet's words capture what you wanted to say?" asked the old queen.

"Yes," said Bonnie. "I've led the sheltered life of a scholar-wizard and don't know the first thing about being a queen."

"Knowing what you don't know is the beginning of wisdom," said Carys. "It took me ten years to go from a shy girl who was happier with her head in a book to a confident woman and the king's valued partner."

"I don't know if I have ten years to learn," said Bonnie. "Nûd's new at being king, I have no conception of what a queen should do, and the kingdom is topsy-turvy trying to defeat Sírénae and settle in out here in the west temporarily."

"That summary shows far more self-knowledge and analytical skill that I had when I was your age," said Carys. "I think you'll do fine. Just use your own judgment and seek out advice from people who know more than you do about individual matters."

"Like who?" asked Bonnie.

"Princess Rúth would be a good place to start, though she's not as familiar with protocols specific to Dâron," said Carys. "You can start with Inthíra for that or consult with my daughter when she returns."

"Princess Seren?" asked Bonnie.

"She goes by Astrí now," said Carys. "And other names."

"That's good advice, thank you," said Bonnie.

"And be sure to know who *not* to ask for advice under any circumstances," said Jenet.

"Gwýnnett!" said Bonnie and the old queen simultaneously.

The three women laughed together, and it was clear that Bonnie was reassured about the burden of a queen's crown. They hugged and Bonnie and Jenet stepped to the door.

"One last thing," said Jenet.

"We wanted to tell you everyone loved your currant biscuits!" said Bonnie.

"I'm so glad," said Carys. "I'll give you both the recipe."

Chapter 49

Celéri's Plan

Celéri *ad hoc* gated from the back of Xaxidiánus to her room in the palace at Sírénaeopolis Magna in an eye blink. *If I can't be a hero to the legions and show up Sírénae by finding the cowardly allies, I can at least ensure we defeat the Northern Clan Landers and capture their food,* she thought. *Everyone will hail me if I don't just win a victory, but victuals as well.*

After a brief conversation with a friend occupying the room beside hers to hear the most recent rumors, another *ad hoc* jump took Celéri to the office of Magister Callidus. The two of his secretaries present when she appeared took one look at the young wizard and hurried out the door without waiting to be asked, closing it firmly behind them.

"I need you to get the mobile gate rings from Umbrose," Celéri announced.

"Nice to see you, too," said Callidus. "I take it your mysterious way to locate the allied locals was not successful."

"What a brilliant deduction," said Celéri. "I'd given Eynon and Merry locating talismans and found them attached to a sea turtle on the beach at the Grand Harbor on the Tempest Isles."

"So Xaxidiánus informed me when I checked in with him by communications ring," said Callidus.

"Dragons can use communications rings?" asked Celéri. "How do you make one big enough to fit one a dragon's claw?"

"You don't," said Callidus. "Xaxidiánus hangs his on a blackened steel chain around his neck. If you don't know where to look for the glint of gold, you'd never spot his ring."

"Oh," said Celéri.

"You'd know this if you'd ever served as a dragonrider," said Callidus. "As you would have in a year or two in the normal progression of your career. Riding Xaxidiánus to the Tempest Isles on a whim, after black-mailing me into asking him to carry you doesn't count as proper training."

"Whatever you say, old man," said Celéri.

Callidus sighed, then spoke. "You need the mobile gate from Umbrose to move a hundred or more wizards north to the seven legions?" he asked.

"Yes," said Celéri. "A hundred wizards should be enough to construct the northern end of the narrow fixed gates. You get the mobile gate and collect the wizards I'll need, while I fly to the legions so I can *ad hoc* gate to and from their current encampment and coordinate the wizards' rapid transit."

"I think our assignments are out of balance," said Callidus. "All you have to do is fly quickly, while you've left me with the twin challenges of acquiring the mobile gate rings from Umbrose *and* getting enough wizards that I'll have to ask our esteemed spymaster for a loan of his personnel in order to make up the necessary numbers."

"Those tasks shouldn't *be* a challenge for a seasoned senior magister such as yourself," said Celéri.

"If you're so clever, how would *you* recommend I get what you've asked for?" asked Callidus.

"It's simple," said Celéri. "Tell Sírénae what we're doing."

Callidus raised an eyebrow. "I thought *you* wanted all the credit," he said.

"I do, and I'll get it," said Celéri. "Eventually. We need Sírénae's backing to have another seven legions ready to gate from Sírénaeopolis Magna to the northern battlefield, anyway. Machaera would never allow me to simply commandeer legions without Sírénae's approval."

"I understand the individual words you just used and the order you put them in, but your meaning escapes me," said Callidus. "I don't see how filling Sírénae in on your plan would lead to anything other than *her* claiming credit for the victory and the Northern Clan Landers' food as spoils of war."

"Please don't connect *food* and *spoils* when you talk to Sírénae," said Celéri. "It's unappetizing. We're claiming their food and drink by right of conquest."

"Are you trying to avoid answering my original question?" asked Callidus.

"Not at all," said Celéri. "Sírénae can try to take credit, but I will be the one with the northern legions coordinating the preparations. Everyone there will see that *I* am the one doing the work, while Sírénae comes sailing in on dragonback in the morning to muck up the order of battle and make unreasonable demands. The legionnaires and their commanders will see through her bluster and know *I'm* the one who made their victory possible."

Callidus was less optimistic. He'd seen Sírénae fall into a metaphorical latrine before and come out smelling like a field of lavender flowers from east of Nárbo.

"Perhaps," he said. "What if Sírénae decides to take one of the gates created by the double-century of wizards you want me to collect? Then *she* would be with the northern legions talking about how the battle strategy for tomorrow was all *her* idea."

"I don't think so," said Celéri. "You've worked with Sírénae for decades. You should know she won't be able to resist flying in with a wing of seven dragons at sunrise. She knows what that would do for her legionnaires' morale."

"You have me there," said Callidus. "That's exactly what the emperor would do—and will do, I expect."

"If Sírénae does go north tonight," said Celéri, "I'll send *you* north and I'll work with the southern seven legions, explaining the strategy to them and demonstrating how to use the new approach to fixed gates I've invented."

"A new approach?" asked Callidus. "What have you come up with now?"

Celéri explained, then pulled a piece of parchment from a stack on the magister's desk, turned it over, and sketched out her invention.

"Have you tested this?" asked Callidus.

"It will work," said Celéri. *I'll build one as soon as I get to the northern legions,* she resolved. *There's no reason why it shouldn't work.*

"We'll need lumber now, too," said Callidus.

"We needed wood for the traditional fixed gates," said Celéri. "Now we'll just need more of it. There are plenty of trees where the northern legions are camped."

"But what about here in Nova Eboracum, I mean Sírénaeopolis Magna?" asked the magister.

"Cut down trees in that big park in the center of the island," said Celéri. "They're not particularly useful."

Callidus hid his reaction from Celéri the same way he would have from Sírénae. He couldn't expect a sixteen-year-old to respect two-hundred-year-old trees. "I'll figure something out," he said. "At least we have plenty of magestone dust, even if it's dust from blue stones, not obsidian."

"Where does it come from?" asked Celéri.

"A huge quarry south of Brendinas on the Brenavon," said Callidus. "A lot of the rocks there were already pulverized. You can collect the blue dust with shovels."

"Good," said Celéri. "Get squads of slaves or legionnaires lined up to start shoveling and be ready to send several wagonloads of dust north through the mobile gate once I *ad hoc* gate back to establish it." She tilted her head and tugged on a strand of hair by her ear. "That reminds me," said Celéri. "We're going to need the wheels from every wagon you can find."

"I'd realized that the minute I saw your drawing," said Callidus. "My list of assignments is growing."

"You're up to it," said Celéri.

"I'm glad to know you think so highly of me," said Callidus.

"Lose the sarcastic tone and we'll have a better working relationship," said Celéri.

"I will if you will," Callidus replied.

"If we were dueling with swords instead of words..." said Celéri.

"I'd have drawn blood," said Callidus. He nodded at Celéri. "But you would get your own cuts in."

"Thanks to my youthful energy," said Celéri.

"Youth and energy count for less than experience and guile," said Callidus. "At least with swords."

"If you say so," said Celéri. "Just use your experience and guile to check off the items on your list and remember, it is better to ask for forgiveness than permission."

"You clearly don't know Sírénae well if you think that approach will work with her," said Callidus, shaking his head. "Shouldn't you be going?" he asked after a short pause.

"I should," said Celéri. "It's easier to fix an *ad hoc* gate location in your head by sunlight, not torchlight. Have you found that to be the case as well?"

"I use wizard lamps at night," said Callidus. "That way I can adjust the brightness."

"How illuminating," said Celéri. "Ring me if you run into problems."

The young wizard pushed open the pair of windows in the magister's study, stepped onto her flying disk, and flew off without a backward glance.

Well, thought Callidus. *At least one of my problems is going away, temporarily. I need to review my rosters and see how many wizards I'll need to request from Umbrose. Once I know that, I'll schedule a conference with Sírénae. Won't that be a pleasure...*

* * * * *

Celéri guided her flying disk north along the Abbenoth, speeding upriver as fast as she would if all the dragons on both sides of the Ocean pursued her. After feeling the wind sting her eyes and slow her progress, she independently replicated the trick Eynon had used to increase his velocity by creating a teardrop-shaped wrapper of solidified sound around herself and her flying disk. Her pace nearly doubled and as an added benefit she no longer needed lenses of solidified sound to protect her eyes.

Improving on Eynon's technique, she moved higher, where the air was thinner, and went incrementally faster still. Celéri found a way to breathe comfortably inside her teardrop, even when several miles above ground, by opening a congruency inside her wrapper that linked to thicker air far below.

I'll be at the legions' encampment soon, she thought. *The Northern Clan Landers will be in for quite a surprise, and so will Sírénae.*

Chapter 50

Eynon and Merry

"I suppose I should familiarize myself with the battlefield," Eynon told Merry as the two of them sat on Rōlin and Peregrína's back porch. Chee and Ace curled up like a pair of pill bugs between them.

"That would be wise," said Merry. "How close have you ever been to that area?"

"Not very," said Eynon. "Nova Eboracum is probably the closest."

"I hope you can *ad hoc* gate somewhere other than Laetícia's tower," said Merry. "I expect Sírénae's unsavory spymaster has taken up residence there."

"I doubt it," said Eynon. "He seems like someone who'd be more at home underground in the shadows."

"Maybe down in the cisterns?" asked Merry.

"I was thinking more like the sewers," said Eynon.

Merry shook her head. "Wherever Umbrose has made his lair, there will probably still be guards in Laetícia's tower—if Sírénae hasn't chosen to live there herself."

"Then we're lucky I know several places for *ad hoc* gating around the city," said Eynon. "You're coming with me, I assume?"

Merry gave Eynon a how-could-you-even-ask-such-a-question look. "I have to come along to keep you out of trouble," she said.

"I certainly seem to need *that* service more often than not," said Eynon. He reached over their sleeping familiars and held Merry's hand.

"To start with, I can focus on keeping us hidden with illusions, so the Roma archers don't spot us in the air and decide to use us for target practice," said Merry.

"Good idea," said Eynon. "Arrows in any part of my anatomy would be distracting."

"Or potentially fatal," teased Merry. "If you can't get your shields up fast enough."

"Speaking of getting something up…" said Eynon.

"We can do that after we're back," said Merry. "It will probably help us both get to sleep more easily on the eve of battle." She squeezed Eynon's hand.

"That's a rationale for lovemaking I hadn't heard before, not that reasons of any sort beyond mutual desire are required," said Eynon.

"I *desire* to complete this scouting trip sooner, rather than later," said Merry. "Remember, the sun is higher farther to the east."

"That's right," said Eynon. He stood, still holding Merry's hand until the two of them had to use both hands to remove their flying disks from their backs and stand on them.

"Come along, sleepyheads," said Merry to Ace and Chee. "We're going exploring."

"Chee!" said Chee as he jumped from the porch floor to Eynon's shoulder.

Ace was in his small dog form. He tilted his head as he considered Merry, then stepped onto her flying disk like it was his personal chariot.

"No barking," Merry told Ace. "This is a secret scouting mission."

Ace sat on his haunches and waited for them to depart. Chee saw Eynon put a finger to his lips and mirrored the movement. "Chee…" he whispered softly.

"I think we're ready," said Eynon. "Hold my hand again."

"Do we need to hold hands for you to *ad hoc* gate both of us?" asked Merry.

"No," said Eynon. "I just *like* holding your hand."

Merry smiled and slid the edge of her flying disk over Eynon's so she could give him a hug. "I like holding yours, too. Where will you gate?"

"Remember that theatre where the treaty of alliance was signed?" asked Eynon. "I've got *that* location etched into my brain."

"But…" said Merry.

Before her sentence was finished, she found herself standing with Eynon on a familiar stage in Nova Eboracum. Their unexpected arrival completely surprised a troop of actors and musicians in the middle of rehearsing a production. Several of the actors wore lion skins over their shoulders and elaborate wigs that looked like manes. Another had a mask with tusks like a boar and yet another had a face elaborately painted a bluish white with a red nose and a yellow beard. Musicians sounding horns, blowing flutes, and beating drums stopped when the strangers appeared.

Thinking quickly, Eynon generated a burst of light as intense as a lightning bolt but without a bolt's crackling power. Chee clutched Eynon's neck and Ace started to shift to his flying form but stopped when he realized it wasn't necessary. Merry wrapped them all in an illusion that made them look like a tree with a broad crown of new spring leaves growing at stage center. As everyone's vision cleared, one of the drummers upstage allowed her hand to fall and her drum gave a deep-throated *basso* note of punctuation. *Boom!*

"Take us up," whispered Merry. "Get us out of here. I'll make us look like a cloud."

"Here we go," said Eynon softly. "Exit stage skyward."

Instead of shooting into the air like a crossbow bolt, Merry changed the nature of her illusion and the two young wizards gently wafted above the theatre in the guise of fluffy white cloud-stuff. Eynon, and the prevailing winds, carried them slowly out of sight of the thespians. They heard horns, flutes, and tentative drumbeats resume behind them as they departed.

"I was going to warn you that might happen," said Merry. "Theatres are often in use, for rehearsals if not for performances. The Roma love theatre. That looked like a dress rehearsal."

"Are there plays where the actors *aren't* dressed?" asked Eynon.

"Only erotic farces," said Merry. "I've only heard about them—I've never seen one. My father said he wouldn't take me until after my wander year."

"He wanted to make sure you were mature enough to understand it?" asked Eynon.

"No," said Merry. "A baron's estate includes many farms. I grew up around animals and was well aware of the mechanics. I think he was just embarrassed for me to see his reaction to erotic farces. One of the pictures I saw in a book of plays featured a man with a member as long as he was tall. It had to be tied to his shoulders with cords."

"That sounds like fun," said Eynon, "I've never seen a play of any sort performed, though I have read a few Athican comedies in a book one of my uncles loaned me."

"You'd like watching them," said Merry. "I've seen a few at Tyford in Taffaern's inn yard. Traveling players stop there from time to time and my father took me. He claimed it was part of my education."

"I'd like to improve *my* education," said Eynon. "Maybe *you* can take *me* to see a play after Sírénae is defeated."

"It would be my pleasure," said Merry. "Perhaps you can even see a play performed *in Athica* once we solve the challenges of gating across the Ocean."

"That would be wonderful, if all our *ifs* come true," said Eynon. "Did you recognize what they were performing? I certainly didn't."

"I didn't either," said Merry, "but it seemed Afarikan, which puzzles me."

"Why so?" asked Eynon.

"Theatrical troops tend to produce works that praise local nobles," Merry replied. "These players came over with Sírénae and should be expected to put on works set in the Western Empire, yet that play was set in Afarika, which is Southern Empire territory."

"I don't understand," said Eynon as he configured a protective teardrop of solidified sound around Merry and their familiars.

"I read a book that said actors often use their plays to criticize rulers," said Merry. "They become the voice of the people."

"I don't understand," said Eynon. "You said earlier that theatrical troops stroke nobles' egos. Now you say they puncture them. Which is it?"

"I suppose it's a delicate balance," said Merry. "Keeping their patrons happy enough to continue supporting them, while speaking greater truths hidden in playwrights' lines."

"Like a jester telling a queen *she's* the fool?" asked Eynon.

"On a larger scale, yes," said Merry.

"You're reading a lot into actors wearing lion skins," said Eynon. He squeezed Merry's hand as he accelerated.

"Maybe, maybe not," said Merry. "I'll see what Laetícia thinks when I tell her. I think actors performing Afarikan-themed plays might mean something."

"Brace yourself," said Eynon. "I'm going to go even faster."

"Instead of doing that, please go higher," said Merry. "I want to try something."

Eynon angled sharply upward and soon the air was so thin the two of them could barely breathe.

"That's high enough," said Eynon. "I'm feeling light-headed. I wish we could get richer air."

"So do I," said Merry. She seemed to have a sudden inspiration and nudged Eynon's ribs with an elbow. "Tell me, O Magnificent Master Mage of Dâron. How do you breathe when you're underwater?"

"Hah!" said Eynon. "I'm a fool. Let me open a congruency." A few seconds later there was plenty of air in the teardrop. "What did you want to try?" he asked Merry.

"This," she said, leaping the four of them through space dozens of miles ahead in an extended line-of-sight gate.

"Wow!" said Eynon. "That's faster than flying. Do it again!"

Merry obliged, and soon they were far up the Abbenoth. "I wouldn't have been able to jump us such a distance without far-seeing lenses," said Merry. She pointed ahead and to the left, west of the river. "I think I see the camp of the invading Roma legions."

"I see them too. The elephants look like big gray rocks," said Eynon. "Are you still maintaining our cloud illusion?"

"Yes, but I'll renew it," said Merry. "It's gotten a bit tattered and they may have scout wizards patrolling."

"Not *this* high, surely," said Eynon.

"Probably not," said Merry.

As her words left her mouth, a teardrop-shaped construct of solidified sound zoomed by fast enough that the wind from its passage buffeted Eynon, Merry, and their familiars.

"CHEEE!" cried Chee.

Ace growled and prepared to change forms to give chase, but Merry stopped him.

"What was *that?*" asked Eynon after he covered Chee's mouth with one hand.

"I'm not sure, but I think it was Celéri," said Merry. "She had short black hair and her wizards' robes were deep purple—not the shade used by Laetícia and her wizards. I couldn't tell if her robes were embroidered like Celéri's since she went by too fast."

"You saw more details than I did," said Eynon.

"I had on my far-seeing lenses," said Merry.

"Can you still see her?" asked Eynon.

"Yes," said Merry. "She landed inside the stockade on the hill."

"She was probably delivering a message from Sírénae to the general in charge," said Eynon. "I wonder if she gained the emperor's favor for bringing back a boatload of honey?"

"I don't give a pip if she earned the emperor's favor or not," said Merry, "though it must have been an important message for her to be moving that fast. I didn't know Roma mages knew that solidified sound trick."

"There's a lot we don't know about *these* Roma," said Eynon. "I guess we should continue north to meet Bjarni and Signý in the mountains at that rocky ledge they gave as a landmark."

"And Arminta, the clan chief of the Northern Clan Landers," said Merry. "Remember to treat her with respect."

"So long as she and her people aren't as barbaric as the *Southern* Clan Landers," said Eynon.

"She didn't seem that way on our kitchen table conference," said Merry. "Just treat her like one of the village elders in the Coombe."

"I'll try," said Eynon, "but village elders from the Coombe didn't try to kill me and launch a sneak attack at the battle of the Brenavon."

"You brought half a mountain down on their heads, so I'd say you and the Southern Clan Landers are even at this point," said Merry.

"I don't think *they* see it that way," said Eynon.

"You're probably right," said Merry. "Look ahead—there's the lake!"

"I see it," said Eynon. "That means tomorrow's battlefield is that broad expanse of grass between the lake and that line of low hills along the river."

"Will it work, do you think?" asked Merry.

"The geometry's perfect," said Eynon. "I just have to determine the depth of the lake. I'm going to need a *lot* of water!"

Chapter 51

Kennig and Callidus

Magister Callidus heard a knock at the door to his office and rose from his desk to answer it himself, since both his secretaries were off confirming the availability of various mages. "Who's there?" he asked as he neared the door.

"It's Kennig," came the answer. "Can you spare a moment?"

Callidus opened the door, waved Kennig in, and closed the ornately carved and painted portal behind them. He was pleased that *this* visitor hadn't *ad hoc* gated directly into his office as Celéri had done earlier and now understood why Umbrose had never allowed Callidus to visit him in *his* office. He remembered the illusionist from when Sírénae had introduced Gwýnnett's companions earlier and wondered then how Kennig was connected to the princess, the deposed mad king, and Gwýnnett's blustering wizard lover.

"I don't really have a moment to spare, but I'll make one," said Callidus. "I'm busier than a cat in a granary rounding up enough wizards for a special project."

"That's one reason why I'm here," said Kennig. "I want to offer my services. I'm bored, and if I have to spend another hour listening to Gwýnnett's petty prattling and Túathal's insane rhymes, I think I'll go mad myself."

"There's a lot of that going around," said Callidus. He decided to offer Kennig a seat, despite all the work that remained. They took the chairs on either side of the table where Callidus and Réah had shared a goblet of mulled wine earlier. "Sense seems to be in short supply."

"Nearly everything is in short supply these days," said Kennig. "I needed to talk to someone more connected to the real world, and you were the only person I could think of. Gwýnnett is so caught up in believing her own lies that I have to watch my tongue to make sure I don't contradict her latest delusion. I expect you face the same challenge with Sírénae."

Callidus didn't respond immediately. Instead, he crafted a translucent hemispherical privacy dome around them.

"My apologies," said Kennig. "I should have requested privacy before mentioning the emperor."

"That would have been wise," said Callidus. "We don't know each other well, and your presence here could be part of a plot by Gwýnnett or Sírénae to catch me speaking against them."

"I'm only here *because* I know you're against them," said Kennig. "I was talking to an old groom in the stables—I think his name was Côbb—and he said you'd be a sympathetic ear and may have something for me to *do* instead of remaining in Gwýnnett's suite with my self-important cousin."

"That would be Hibblig?" asked Callidus.

"Yes," said Kennig. "The man was an insufferable blowhard when we were young, and he grew worse every year. Now Gwýnnett has him twisted around her little finger in a spiral tighter than a pig's tail."

"I wondered what connected you to Gwýnnett's party," said Callidus. "You'd been an illusionist in the court of Dârioth the Twenty-fourth?"

"Yes, and then I exiled myself for killing a man before the king could do it," said Kennig. "My rival and I both wanted the same woman and I let my temper get the better of me and blasted him with a lightning bolt."

"That does sound like an extreme reaction to a rather common provocation," said Callidus.

"It was," said Kennig. "Not that he didn't deserve it. He'd beaten her when she wouldn't negate the charm that suppressed her fertility."

"I see," said Callidus. "I might have killed him too under similar circumstances."

"It wasn't my responsibility to take the villain's life," said Kennig. "That right belonged to the king and I knew it, but I couldn't let him walk around with that smirk on his face."

"Was there anything left of the man?" asked Callidus.

"Just cinders," said Kennig.

"Good," said Callidus. "Did the woman press charges in the king's court?"

"I have no idea," said Kennig. "I flew off toward the Southern Clan Lands as soon as I could pack a bag and leave."

"Another instance of the impetuousness of youth?" asked Callidus.

"Indeed it was," said Kennig. "I'd like to think I'm older and wiser now."

"One doesn't guarantee the other," said Callidus.

"Gwýnnett proves that," said Kennig. "I hate not being able to eat anything in her presence, not that there's much to eat."

"Doesn't Sírénae provide you with full rations?" asked Callidus.

"She did," said Kennig. "But now there's hardly anything on our plates and what we're given is more beans than bread. We've had no meat at all for over a week."

Callidus inspected Kennig. The illusionist was slim, and his cheekbones were well-defined, but he didn't seem to be starving. "You seem surprisingly robust for a man who won't eat in Gwýnnett's presence," he said. "Not that I disagree with your caution."

"I don't miss meals," said Kennig. "I disguise my appearance and have my beans with the senior officers. It seemed better than inadvertently consuming something that would make me Gwýnnett's lapdog, like Hibblig." He smiled at Callidus. "Sometimes I blend in and make myself invisible so I can prowl the kitchens and appropriate a special something meant for the emperor's table."

"So *you're* the reason Sírénae was ranting to Umbrose about a missing roast," said Callidus. "How marvelous. I'd like to shake your hand. Come to think of it, I'd like to confirm you're flesh and blood and not a projection of solidified sound." He extended his hand and the two men shook.

"Not to give away too many tricks of the illusionist's trade," said Kennig, "but I *could* have made a simulation of myself with warm hands that feel like they belong to a living person. It takes a lot of concentration, and I'd have to be hidden within sight of you to handle all the various nuances, but I could do it. When I was young, I helped Queen Carys when the Old King was ill."

"You simulated Dâron's ruler?" asked Callidus.

"Only briefly, and at the request of the queen," said Kennig. "She was the true monarch for a decade after the Old King's mind began to fail. When I went into exile, I heard that a talented young woman—also a powerful illusionist—took over and helped Queen Carys keep up appearances. I wish I could have met her. There are so few illusionists, we seldom have a chance to meet and discuss techniques."

"That might explain the giant kraken that attacked our ships coming into the harbor at Nova Eboracum," said Callidus. "One of her illusions, perhaps?" He remembered the illusionist aboard the *Cloud Dancer* when Valentius had been rescued and assumed it was the same woman Kennig referenced.

"I missed that one," said Kennig, "but it sounds quite clever. I'm pleased to hear she's still around."

"I trust you'll have a chance to reconnect at some point," said Callidus. He hoped Kennig didn't end up meeting her on the opposing side in tomorrow's battle. "You said you wanted something to do?" asked the magister.

"Just name it," said Kennig. "How can I assist? Preferably by doing something that doesn't involve interacting with Sírénae, Umbrose, or Gwýnnett."

"Have you ever made a standard gate connecting two places?" asked Callidus.

"Certainly," said Kennig. "More than a dozen. They're easy if you have a frame, magestone dust, and glue."

"Excellent," said Callidus. "Have you ever used solidified sound to turn logs into lumber?"

"To make gate frames?" asked Kennig. He thought for a moment. "You're making a *lot* of gate frames. Give me the plans and I'll turn birch and beech trees into beams and boards before you can say *Robin Goodfellow*. I served as a one-man sawmill for a month in the Southern Clan Lands just using solidified sound to win a bet with a clan chief."

"That's good news indeed," said Callidus. "With your help, we'll make Celéri's absurd timetable work after all."

"Celéri?" said Kennig. "There's a strange one. I'd thought she was older, but the more she spoke, the more it was clear she was far too young for me—not that she didn't try her best to seduce me. She was asking Gwýnnett for potions to make people suggestible."

"Was she?" asked Callidus. "I'm not surprised. She's another challenge. Gwýnnett doesn't have any mischief that can work on contact or be aerosolized, does she?"

"I wouldn't put either of those options past her," said Kennig. "That's a big reason why I don't want to be in her suite any longer. I don't want to turn into Hibblig." He pushed back an unruly shock of hair. "How far away are the trees you want me to cut?"

"Only a few miles," said Callidus.

"Don't you have any farther away?" teased Kennig.

"Out of sight, out of mind?" asked Callidus.

"I'll be out of Gwýnnett's sight and Túathal is out of his mind," said Kennig.

"Is he?" asked the magister. "Do you really think so? If he wasn't consuming the potions Gwýnnett gives him, perhaps he'd be more sane."

"You're welcome to try drying him out for a few weeks to see," said Kennig. "If I were you, I'd lock him in a dungeon cell when you do. There's something not right about that man."

"That's why he and Gwýnnett are so well matched, I expect," said Callidus.

"You haven't seen them interact as much as I have," said Kennig. "The only person of significance to Túathal is Túathal. The rest of us might as well be mere simulacrums, like the illusions I make of actors on a stage." He put his fist below his chin for a few seconds to think. "Then again, perhaps Gwýnnett *is* the same. The only person Gwýnnett cares about is Gwýnnett."

"I could say the same about Sírénae," said Callidus. "There are vanishingly few of us who put what's good for the Imperium above ourselves."

"I can't say I'm as high-minded as you are in that regard," said Kennig. "I've been out for myself for the past score of years, though I'll admit I've been bothered by an irritating strain of nobility of late. Perhaps it's a reaction to spending time with Gwýnnett and Túathal? I have to do *something* to balance the scales."

"Is it your intent then to strike back against the empire?" asked Callidus.

"That's hard to say," said Kennig. "I'd have no trouble at all striking back against the *emperor*. She's bad news for us all. I'm surprised you still serve her."

"Someone has to advise her when she acts unwisely," said Callidus.

"And that's a full-time job, I'm sure," said Kennig, smiling.

"It keeps me busy," said Callidus. "Not that she listens to my advice that often any longer."

"It's not easy to serve someone you don't respect," said Kennig. "The Southern Clan Landers taught me that lesson. If they don't like the current clan chief they move farther away and build a cabin on the other side of a mountain. If enough of them don't like the current clan chief, there's soon a new chief."

"That sounds like the history of emperors across the Imperium," said Callidus. "At least until the Imperial School of Good Governance was established."

"Sírénae must have slept through her lessons, then," said Kennig. "And Umbrose, her shadow..."

"Is confident he can keep her alive," said Callidus. "He keeps a tight rein on his tongue, but I wonder just how many of Sírénae's words are Umbrose's, spoken by her lips?"

"Does it matter if they say the same thing?" asked Kennig. "The more I think about it, the more my head hurts."

"Let me distract you, then," said Callidus. "Are you a wheelwright, along with being a sawmill, a gate builder, and a theatrical producer?"

"What do you need?" asked Kennig.

Callidus explained, showing him Celéri's drawing.

"That's no problem at all," said Kennig. "Just find me a really big tree and I'll slice off and round all the wheels you want."

Chapter 52

Giérra and Belisaria

"Do we send in legions or elephants first?" Giérra asked Belisaria as they looked out over the early-morning mist rising from the fields to the north.

"That's up to Sírénae and Machaera," the lieutenant general answered.

"I'd rather march ahead of elephants than behind them," said Giérra with more feeling than Belisaria expected.

"Why so?" Belisaria asked. Then she figured it out. "Oh," she said. "Even worse than marching behind horse cavalry."

"Exactly," said Giérra. "I'd put the elephants on our right flank, on the side with the old walls and fort on the ridge above the river. Their bulk can screen us from enemy archers."

"You think the Northern Clan Landers have archers already in place then?" asked Belisaria.

"I do," said Giérra. "You're the one who told me those barbarians specialize in tricks and traps. I expect the main battlefield to be riddled with camouflaged pits filled with spikes—and worse."

"I'll have Náegosh send scout-wizards ahead to mark the traps they can identify," said Belisaria.

"Good," said Giérra. "I'll pass the word to the individual commanders. Their legionnaires will appreciate anything we can do to protect them from ignominious death."

"Be sure to tell them I'm concerned about saving them from death of any sort," said Belisaria. "In battle the goal is not to die for the glory of the Imperium, but to give your opponents that honor."

"They know," said Giérra. "And they appreciate that you won't waste their lives on foolish martial gestures." The senior legate spat at a tuft of grass a few feet away. "It's just that they aren't convinced the emperor shares your concern for their welfare."

"Machaera does," said Belisaria.

"That won't help us if Sírénae won't listen to her advisers," said Giérra.

"What have you heard?" asked Belisaria, knowing that Giérra, as a long-time officer who'd worked her way up through the ranks, had a better network of informers than she did.

"Scuttlebutt from the palace says that the emperor is only listening to two people these days," Giérra answered.

"Umbrose and...?" asked Belisaria.

"A local princess from Dâron named Gwýnnett," said Giérra. "She's said to have a devious mind and be better with potions than a hedge wizard."

"Why would Sírénae care about a princess from Dâron?" asked Belisaria.

"My sources say Sírénae needs Gwýnnett's potions and Gwýnnett needs Sírénae's patronage," said Giérra. "Their minds also work so much alike they're drawn to each other."

"That's disconcerting," said Belisaria. "What about Magister Callidus? He gives good advice."

"Callidus is tolerated, but not trusted," said Giérra. "Sírénae needs him to lead her wizards—the ones Umbrose doesn't control—but she doesn't trust him because he has the audacity to tell her *no* from time to time."

"How *dare* he," said Belisaria in a tired voice.

"The only reason Callidus is still senior magister is that being able to *ad hoc* gate is something of a requirement for the position," said Giérra.

"Thunder and lightning," said Belisaria, suddenly louder. "Does that mean that dark-haired child-wizard who talks too much will be the next senior magister? That would be unfortunate. Callidus has held that position for years."

"I don't know," said Giérra. "Though Celéri does keep going on and on about being able to *ad hoc* gate and the emperor would likely prefer someone who will hop like a rabbit on command."

"That girl is no rabbit," said Belisaria. "Did you see the way she ordered our wizards around? Náegosh was nearly kissing the hem of her robes in his eagerness to do her bidding."

"You're right about that," said Giérra. "And if those strange wheeled contraptions she designed work as promised..."

"They should guarantee our victory," said Belisaria.

"I never think *anything* is guaranteed," said Giérra, "especially when it comes to battles. There are too many things that can go wrong."

"Thank you for that correction," said Belisaria.

"Speaking of things going wrong, when do you expect the emperor to arrive?" asked Giérra.

"Soon," said Belisaria. "Look for seven dragons flying up the river. She'll be riding Xaxidiánus, with Machaera, Umbrose, and Callidus following along on the others."

"Not Celéri as well?" asked Giérra.

"I wouldn't risk a dice throw on it," said Belisaria. "She'll *ad hoc* gate here soon."

"Correction," said Celéri from a few steps behind them. "I used an *ad hoc* gate a few minutes ago."

"How long have you been listening?" asked Giérra.

"How long have you been talking?" asked Celéri. She smiled, showing teeth.

"My apologies, good wizard," said Belisaria. "We didn't hear you arrive. Wet grass doesn't make much sound when you walk on it."

"Look down," said Celéri. "I wasn't walking."

Giérra and Belisaria laughed, nervously, when they realized Celéri was still on her flying disk, skimming an inch above the ground.

"That's a clever trick," said Belisaria.

"I'm a clever *girl,*" Celéri replied. "Or perhaps a clever *child-wizard,* though I do thank you for your compliment on my leadership skills. It almost counterbalances your critique about me talking too much."

"Our apologies," said Giérra. "We meant no disrespect."

"Really?" said Celéri. "There's no need to lie to me—and I'm quite interested in learning more about your web of informants in the palace, good legate."

"Is there something particular you'd like to know?" asked Giérra.

"What does your network say about the legions' level of support for Sírénae?" asked Celéri. "Is it still as strong as ever?"

"This is in confidence?" asked Giérra.

"I won't tell the emperor if you won't," said Celéri.

"What do *you* think the legions' sentiments to be?" asked Giérra, using the traditional approach of responding to one uncomfortable question with another.

"I think they're losing confidence in Sírénae," said Celéri. "They're hungry and frustrated because there's no one here to fight. They want a victory, then a feast, then farms allotted to each legionnaire so they can get on with their lives."

"You have an excellent grasp of the feelings in the ranks," said Giérra.

"My sources aren't as extensive as the legate's," said Belisaria, "but they report much the same sentiments."

"I'm glad to have that confirmation," said Celéri. She rose a few inches on her flying disk until her eyes were level with the older women's. "And when my *contraptions* deliver our victory, I also need your help."

"How could *we* help *you,* good wizard?" asked Belisaria.

"By making sure every soldier and auxiliary in camp knows that our success in battle was *my* doing, not Sírénae's," said Celéri. "Sírénae will claim the wheeled frames were her idea, but you can spread the truth that they were *mine.*"

"I have no problem with sharing something true," said Giérra.

"I don't either," said Belisaria. "We've all had more than enough of the emperor's lies."

"Remember these words and share them," said the young wizard. "Celéri brought us victory!"

Giérra moved a few steps away and found a wooden board about two feet by three lying in the grass. It was left over from constructing floors for the nearby officers' tents. "Can you use your magic to put your words on this wood?" asked the legate.

"Of course," said Celéri. "Just watch!" A congruency-powered flame appeared at the end of her finger and she wrote the message in large, fiery letters.

Belisaria took the board, held it over her head and said, "In this sign, conquer!"

Giérra thumped her right fist on her lorica making the metal plates ring.

"Keep it hidden when Sírénae arrives," said Celéri. "You'll know the right time to raise it."

"Of course," said Giérra. "We're not fools."

"You let me sneak up behind you and hear your private conversation," said Celéri.

"Perhaps we're fools after all," said Belisaria.

Giérra smiled and nodded.

"You're also wise for choosing the victorious side," said Celéri. "And if fools you be, at least you're *my* fools."

"May we serve you in any other way?" asked Belisaria, hoping that the answer would be *no*.

"Yes," said Celéri. "But give me a minute. I have to think."

The older women watched as the young wizard rose until she was a dozen feet above their heads and had rotated twice, observing the encampment and the expected battlefield to the north. Some of the dew had vanished from the grass when Celéri descended.

"If Sírénae and Machaera never arrive to take charge of our forces, would the two of you follow *my* commands?" asked Celéri.

Giérra pointed at the sign and nodded.

Belisaria said, "You just told us the emperor sent you and you spoke with her voice."

"Yes. Yes I did. That's a very good way to spin it," said Celéri. "It protects you and still gives me the credit."

"Would you like us to show you our proposed disposition of forces?" asked Giérra.

"I would, but make it quick," said Celéri. "I need to distract a dragon."

Chapter 53

Before Battle

Duke Háiddon stood near King Nûd on Rōlin and Peregrína's back porch in Three Mountains Valley, sharing a quiet conversation. King Dârio, Earl Marshal Jenet, Duke Néillen, Governor General Quintillius and Valentius—the war leaders of the allied forces—were with them. Everyone was waiting for the signal to gate east to the battlefield. Here in the west, it was well before dawn and still quite dark except for scattered wizard lamps provided by Doethan, Inthíra, and dozens of other mages from across Orluin.

In the broad fields behind the porch, both Dâron and Tamloch had contingents of heavy cavalry literally chomping at the bit to move forward. Archers from both kingdoms had already been sent through gates to add their numbers to the Bifurlanders dug in on the hills to the east of the battlefield. Occidens Province had a thousand legionnaires in tight ranks wearing the new four-color tabards Nûd had designed. The soldiers of Dâron and Tamloch wore four-colored ribbons on each shoulder and the knights of each kingdom had similarly hued crests on their helms. Near the war leaders, a bannerman with a Dâron father and a Tamloch mother rode a tall horse and carried the battle flag Queen Carys had commissioned.

"It's not that impressive in the dark, is it?" asked Nûd, waving a hand toward the host.

"It will be in daylight, to be sure," said Duke Háiddon. "Inthíra has promised some illusions to make our arrival at the battlefield spectacular."

"So long as she keeps herself safe while doing so," said Nûd.

"There's no such thing as safe on a battlefield," said Duke Néillen. "Death can strike from any direction."

Duke Háiddon gently jabbed a gauntleted hand into the small of Duke Néillen's back to warn Néillen to change the subject. *Anyone could see that Nûd was nervous, like many before battle,* thought Duke Háiddon. *He doesn't need to be reminded about the capriciousness of death.*

Duke Néillen, Túathal's former Earl Marshal, was still on probation of a sort. He had been given a chance to prove himself in the upcoming engagement by commanding Tamloch's heavy cavalry, since Jenet was a horse archer, not a knight. Duke Néillen wisely chose not to add to his words and Duke Háiddon gave him credit for at least a small measure of wisdom thereby.

Nûd cares about every man, woman, and beast on that field, mused Duke Háiddon. *While Dârio wants to win with little loss of life. I think Nûd would be happier if the battle could be avoided altogether. I'm not sure which king is wiser.*

Jenet clapped her hands to get everyone's attention. "One more time," she said. "Our object is *not* to engage the enemy. We're bait to entice the invading legions into positions we've prepared for them."

"The first one of my legionnaires who trades sword blows with an invader will be cleaning latrines and shoveling manure until retirement," said Quintillius.

"Tamloch's forces know the plan, Earl Marshal," said Dârio. "I think they'd rather face *my* wrath than yours if they let battle lust get the better of them."

Jenet gave Dârio a smile, then her face became serious again. "What says Dâron?" she asked Nûd.

"Dâron will do its part," said Nûd. "They know the importance of this engagement."

Valentius caught Nûd's attention and stood upright, with his shoulders back. Nûd did the same, looking more like a king in the process.

"Good," said Jenet. "Queen Signý reports all our archers are in the ditches on the eastern hills with plenty of shafts at the ready. They've set stakes to repel foot soldiers if any invaders decide to head east to dislodge them."

"Why are we even *using* archers if we don't want to kill the invading legionnaires?" asked Duke Néillen.

"If you'd been listening instead of talking when I explained that, *Your Grace,* you would know that the archers' primary role is encouraging our foes to move in the right direction for our purposes," said Jenet. "A few thousand goose-quilled shafts work even better at herding soldiers than sheepdogs do at herding sheep."

"Baaaa..." Duke Néillen bleeted.

Duke Háiddon poked Néillen in the back again and Duke Néillen clasped his hands and bowed to Jenet.

"My apologies, Earl Marshal," said Duke Néillen.

Jenet waved a dismissive hand in the duke's direction and continued. "Signý says Bifurland's axe-wielders are on the slopes of the eastern hills near the old Roma fort," said Jenet. "They're ready to defend the archers and provide a more substantial incentive for the invading legions to stick to the left and center of the field."

"As we expected," said Nûd. "What about their elephants?"

"They're arrayed in two squares of a hundred each, according to Signý," said Jenet.

"Left, right, or center?" asked Valentius.

"Right," said Jenet. "You called it."

"They want the elephants to screen their legions from our archers," said Valentius. "It's an old trick in the Southern Empire, right Quin?"

"Indeed," said Quintillius. "I hope our trumpeter is close enough for the big beasts to hear his calls."

"Signý assures me he is," said Jenet. "And the Bifurlanders' big surprise is ready to gate through when called for."

"What's the current disposition of the invaders' forces?" asked Duke Háiddon.

"There are four legions in a broad front between the lake and the elephants," said Jenet. "Three understrength legions are in the gaps behind and between them."

"Understrength?" asked Quintillius. "Why so? Does Signý have details?"

"She said more than five hundred legionnaires are in the rear, pushing some odd sort of carts," Jenet answered.

"I don't like the sound of that," said Nûd. "Sírénae must have something tricky of her own planned."

"Arminta told Signý that her spies report the carts aren't Sírénae's doing," said Jenet. "They're a brainstorm of a young mage named Celéri."

"The dark-haired spy-wizard Eynon and Merry met on the Rhuthro while collecting honey?" asked Nûd.

"I expect so," said Jenet.

"Are there reports of Sírénae's arrival?" asked Quintillius. "Our plan depends on her impulsiveness and arrogance as a commander."

"That's right," said Valentius. "You served under her in Nárbo."

"My least-favorite assignment," said Quintillius. "I wonder if General Machaera or Belisaria, her lieutenant, is in charge? Did Arminta mention who's senior legate?"

"Someone named Giérra," said Jenet. "If I'm remembering the name correctly."

"Giérra's good, and that's bad—for us," said Quintillius. "She will have her legions ready for anything, and Belisaria is green enough to listen to her advice."

"So we're hoping Machaera commands?" asked Dârio.

"No," said Quintillius. "Machaera's competent, too, if not brilliant. She's responsible for turning Sírénae's overconfident *charge at everything* approach into sensible strategies. We want Sírénae in overall command."

"Can we still win if she's not?" asked Nûd.

"Probably," said Quintillius. "They still think we're outnumbered by five to one."

"Because they can only see the Bifurlanders, the archers, and the thousand foot soldiers from Dâron and Tamloch we sent through last night?" asked Dârio. He looked to Jenet for confirmation.

Jenet nodded. "They know we're not outnumbered by that large a margin," she said. "The invading legions came up the river to take the Northern Clan Landers' stores, so they must be aware the Clan Landers are close at hand."

"And probably worried because their scouts can't spot them," said Dârio. "I know I would be. Fighting Clan Landers, North or South, is like battling sharp-pointed smoke."

"They're gone before you feel their spear tips pierce your breastplates," said Quintillius. "I'm glad Arminta and her clans are on our side this time."

"Signý says the shipment from Bifurland Arminta requested arrived yesterday," said Jenet. "Everything is in place and didn't interfere with Eynon's work."

"Speaking of Eynon," said Nûd. "Is he confident his constructs will do what's necessary?"

"Merry said it was a bit of a morass at first," said Jenet. She paused while everyone laughed. "But she's pleased to report that the lake *was* deep enough."

"Good," said Duke Háiddon. He turned to Quintillius. "Where are Laetícia and Mafuta?" he asked.

"And where are Fercha and Verro, for that matter?" asked Duke Néillen.

"You must have been asleep when I told everyone after dinner last night," said Jenet. "Were you sleeping with your eyes open again?"

"Maybe," said Duke Néillen. "It's a skill every soldier masters."

"I expected a question like that from *him*," said Jenet, pointing a finger at Néillen, "but you, *father,* should know better than to be distracted during a briefing."

"The Earl Marshal of Dâron does not need to be censured by the Earl Marshal of Tamloch," said Duke Háiddon with a grin. "I must have had too much roast wisent and barley bread and dozed off after dinner."

"At least *his* eyes were closed," said Dârio. "I'm surprised you missed that."

"You and I can talk about that later, my *king*," said Jenet, grinning. "And a grown daughter can censure her father whenever he deserves it, Papa. That's standard in most families."

"So long as you remember that cuts in both directions," said Duke Háiddon. He reached past Dârio to give Jenet a hug, then released her and said, "Well?"

"Well what?" asked Jenet.

"Where are Laetícia, Mafuta, Fercha and Verro, of course," said Duke Háiddon. "Wasn't the Earl Marshal of Tamloch keeping up with the conversation?"

"My apologies, honored sire," said Jenet. "I lost the thread of our discussion after being needled."

Nûd and Dârio clapped to recognize Jenet's wordplay.

She bowed and deigned to answer the original questions. "All four aforementioned wizards are busy working on wide gates that will work across the Ocean," said Jenet. "They will be available to assist us in battle if necessary but believe perfecting such gates could end the threat from Sírénae in a few hours."

"While making Orluin a satellite of Roma's Imperium," Dârio whispered to Nûd.

"One problem at a time," Nûd replied softly.

"Sign.ý says Fercha and Mafuta are complaining about corrections for the curvature of the Earth, or something like that," said Jenet. "Apparently making gates between two points within an eighth of the rotation of the planet of each other is simple. Longer than that is increasingly difficult the farther the distance between origin and destination."

"What about points north and south of each other?" asked Nûd. "Are they difficult to bridge?"

"I don't know," said Jenet. "You'll have to ask your mother."

"Or Mafuta," said Quintillius, knowing that Nûd and Fercha had a difficult relationship. "Laetícia confirms all the mobile gates are in position, by the way."

"Thank you," said Jenet. "I assume we would have been informed if they weren't." She took a few steps left and right on the porch, making boards squeak and working off nervous energy. Then she stretched and spoke. "Arminta asked for the use of a mobile gate so her clan folk could attack the invaders' baggage train and take what little food they have left," said Jenet. "I authorized giving her one of our spare gates for that purpose since it helps our cause of starving the invaders out. Any objections?"

No one replied.

"We may regret that later," Quintillius whispered to Valentius.

"Later is later," said Valentius. "Live today, regret tomorrow."

"I hope Sírénae is the one with regrets after our battle," said Quintillius.

"Does anyone have concerns we should discuss before we gate east?" asked Jenet.

"I have three," said Duke Háiddon.

"And I have one more besides," said Duke Néillen.

"How do you know your concern isn't one of the ones I'll be mentioning?" asked Duke Háiddon,

"Our minds work in very different ways," said Duke Néillen.

"You have me there," said Duke Háiddon. He held up a finger. "First, who commands the invaders--Sírénae, or one of her generals?"

Everyone signaled they agreed that concern was valid.

Háiddon raised another finger. "Second," he said, "what are those strange wheeled carts the legionnaires detached from their legions are pulling?"

"Who knows?" said Dârio.

Most of the others simply shrugged.

The duke put up a third finger. "Third," he asked, "how does their strange young wizard figure into any of this?"

"Celéri," said Nûd. "She worries me. What if she's as precocious and powerful as Eynon?"

"Then we'll set Eynon and Merry against her," said Jenet. "Problem solved."

"I wish I had your confidence," said Nûd,

"You'll get there," Duke Háiddon reassured him. Háiddon turned to Duke Néillen. "Did you have a different concern?"

"Yes," said Duke Néillen. "Once we convince Sírénae's legions to leave, where should they go? Assuming we'd have any influence in the matter..."

Rōlin spoke up from inside the kitchen where he and his wife had been listening through an open window. "We can help you with that," he said. "Peregrína and I have a few ideas..."

Chapter 54

Distracting Dragons

Celéri *ad hoc* gated back to Sírénaeopolis Magna hoping to find Sírénae and her dragons still in the palace courtyard. Instead of gating to her room, she decided to appear above the imperial palace in airspace usually reserved for wizards' combat practice. Celéri was relieved to find all seven dragons were still crowded into the courtyard, so she used her limited powers of illusion to render herself invisible and descended to float within earshot of the dragons and assembled humans.

I should look up Kennig again, thought Celéri. *Even if he won't sleep with me—not that I won't give that another try—perhaps I can pay him to teach me how to improve my skills at crafting illusions? For now, simple invisibility is good enough.*

It was easy to spot the emperor, since she was wearing her golden armor. Her servants had cleaned and polished it after the debacle in southwestern Dâron. Celéri smiled. As usual, Sírénae was angry. Celéri augmented her hearing to catch the emperor's every word.

"What do you mean, you won't carry me, you overgrown crocodile," Sírénae shouted at Xaxidiánus. "I *order* you to fly me up the Abbenoth."

"Give all the orders you want," said Xaxidiánus. "But I will be transporting Callidus, my usual rider. Mégàrotáxus will carry you."

"I insist on *you,*" said Sírénae. "You're clearly the largest and most impressive dragon I have."

"And that is precisely why I won't carry you, Emperor," said Xaxidiánus. "Our foes will expect you to be on my back and will send their strongest attacks against *me*. If you ride Mégàrotáxus, who is almost as large as I am and gives a smoother ride, you won't be as much of a target for our opponents' wizards and archers."

Sírénae paused and her expression changed from anger to calculation. "I can see the wisdom in that," she said. "Very well. You and Callidus can draw the enemy's fire while I follow on Mégàrotáxus." She turned to General Machaera. "You take that dragon, and Umbrose can ride his usual mount."

"You just told Machaera to ride my usual mount, Your Imperial Majesty," said Magister Umbrose.

"Once I'm aboard Mégàrotáxus, I don't care who rides which dragon," said Sírénae. "We just need to get on with it since we're late already."

"They won't start the battle without you," offered Callidus. He was waiting to mount Xaxidiánus until Sírénae had mounted first.

"I should say not," said Sírénae. She slapped the obsidian-colored hide of Mégàrotáxus to get the dragon to kneel for boarding and scrambled up to the saddle in front of his wings. "Especially after I authorized another seven legions for that scheme of Celéri's." She fastened her safety harness and waved. "Hurry," Sírénae shouted. "Battle awaits!"

Machaera and Callidus exchanged glances that spoke volumes then mounted their dragons. Umbrose chose to *ad hoc* gate directly above his dragon's saddle instead of climbing her scaly side. Callidus preferred to stretch his muscles whenever he boarded Xaxidiánus. Too much record keeping often kept him from regular exercise. He was glad to be riding his friend and happier still *not* to be riding with Sírénae.

"Ready?" Callidus asked Sírénae.

"More than ready," the emperor answered. "Let's get moving."

Celéri watched all seven dragons, in order of seniority, launch themselves up from the courtyard in a flurry of powerful wing beats and saw them set course north up the Abbenoth. She zoomed ahead and hovered, invisible, above Mégàrotáxus, then considered the best way to prevent or delay the dragon's arrival at the battlefield.

My illusions aren't good enough for a convincing distraction, thought Celéri. *Yet, anyway. Fireballs and lightning bolts would be insufficiently subtle.* Several more minutes of pondering various options didn't come up with a solution until a metaphorical wizard lamp appeared above her head. *I could just ad hoc gate Sírénae somewhere far away, she realized. Then she thought bigger. Why stop with just the emperor? Maybe I can ad hoc gate an entire dragon! What's the worst that can happen?*

"Callidus could probably give me a list of dire consequences, each one worse than the one before," she muttered to herself. "I don't want his words of caution, so I'll only tell him about my plan if I succeed."

Celéri considered grabbing the long, black tail of Sírénae's dragon and gating him away with that level of contact, but she changed her mind and opted for a physical link with Mégàrotáxus close to his center of mass, right behind the saddle Sírénae currently occupied. She found a spot with no spinal ridges, transferred her flying disk to her shoulders, and sat.

"Who's there?" exclaimed Sírénae. "I can hear you breathing!"

I've got to improve my skulking skills, thought Celéri. *Or at least learn to inhale and exhale more softly.*

A roar came from nearby. Mégàrotáxus had sensed Celéri's arrival. "Somebody is *touching* me!" complained the dragon.

Celéri could tell that Mégàrotáxus would soon start twitching and bucking, which would be a distraction of sorts, but would only slow Sírénae's arrival at the battlefield, not prevent it.

Time to give ad hoc gating a dragon a try, she determined. Squeezing her legs around the dragon's back, Celéri extended her senses to encompass Mégàrotáxus from snout to tail, remembering at the last second to add Sírénae. After taking a deep breath, Celéri tightened all the muscles in her face, pressed her tongue against her teeth, and *ad hoc* gated far to the west. The dragon and two humans emerged in the skies above the steading on the Rhuthro where Celéri had collected honey with Eynon, Merry, Gruffyd, and Nyssia a few days earlier.

Mégàrotáxus did *not* react to the jump the way Celéri had expected. Every time *she* gated, her mental frame of reference quickly snapped in place to match her new surroundings. The dragon was in obvious pain, bellowing and trumpeting as if hot pokers were being inserted under his scales. Mégàrotáxus bucked and spun, as if trying to reestablish the link between the internal compass in his brain and the new coordinates where Celéri's *ad hoc* gate had instantaneously transported him.

Without benefit of saddle straps, Celéri was tossed off in a random direction. She lost quite a bit of altitude before she could shift around to board her flying disk and regain her own equilibrium. Mégàrotáxus was still struggling, however. He thrashed the air above the Rhuthro, looking like a giant fish fighting an anglers' hook, before losing altitude and flopping on his chest into a marsh on the eastern bank.

Celéri saw the dragon was dazed but still twitching. She refreshed her invisibility illusion and skimmed lower to check on Sírénae. When Celéri was immediately above Mégàrotáxus she could see Sírénae thumping the dragon's neck with both fists, demanding that he get up and fly her to the battlefield. After a few minutes of futile fist-banging, Celéri watched Sírénae unfasten her harness straps and slide down the side of Mégàrotáxus, who was no longer twitching but still breathing.

It was difficult not to laugh when Celéri saw Sírénae's booted feet touch the marshy ground and begin to sink. For continued amusement, with every step the emperor took away from Mégàrotáxus, she sank deeper into the mud until she was stuck waist deep.

That should provide sufficient delay, thought Celéri.

The emperor's demands for assistance echoed from the marsh across the river to the western bank, but after Celéri *ad hoc* gated away there was no one except an unconscious dragon to hear her.

Celéri popped out in the sky where she'd been before she'd transported the emperor. She'd expected to see that the other six dragons had continued to fly north but instead saw they were circling a spot close to Celéri's position.

"I'll say it again," Machaera was shouting to the other dragon riders. "I've *never* heard a *pop* that loud before."

"And a dragon hasn't disappeared from the sky like that before," said Callidus.

"Neither has an emperor," said Umbrose, clear in his own priorities.

"Where is Mégàrotáxus!" bellowed Xaxidiánus.

"We're still trying to figure that out, old friend," said Callidus. "Stay calm. We'll find him."

"It sounded like the *pop* you wizards make when *ad hoc* gating," said Machaera. "Who or what could do that to a *dragon*?"

Celéri saw Umbrose and Callidus exchange a glance and guessed they both were thinking *she* might be responsible. It was time to delay the spymaster. Celéri made physical contact with *his* dragon and *ad hoc* gated to a few feet above the beach on the Tempest Isles' great harbor where she'd found the sea turtle with her lavender talismans.

Prepared this time, she leapt from the dragon's back and rode her flying disk up for a spectacular view of the dragon hitting the water and throwing up spray like a pod of toothed whales breaching. She didn't bother to check on Umbrose as the dragon submerged, sending tall waves against the sandy shore from its struggles. He was a powerful wizard and could rescue himself.

It won't take Umbrose long to ad hoc *gate back to Sírénaeopolis Magna,* thought Celéri. *But unless he has a locating talisman on the emperor, which I doubt she'd permit, it will take him a long time to find her. One more to go!*

Celéri jumped back to the sky north of the city again and grabbed Machaera's dragon this time. She transported the general and her mount to the pool outside the caverns in southwestern Dâron where Sírénae had ignominiously met with a wall of water earlier. She stayed long enough to ensure the dragon's head was out of the water and watched as Machaera disentangled herself from her harness and reached dry ground before she gated back to Callidus and Xaxidiánus. Celéri hovered a few feet in front of the magister and dropped her illusion of invisibility.

Callidus saw her, shook his head slowly, and clapped three times. "That was impressive," he said.

"Where are my wing mates?" roared Xaxidiánus. *"What have you done with them?"*

"They're fine," said Celéri. "Or they will be in a few hours when they're less disoriented. I left them in three different places, but they'll be back in a few days, I'm sure."

"Should I roast her?" Xaxidiánus asked Callidus.

"I wouldn't advise it," said Callidus. "You might find yourself *ad hoc* gated with your own sense of place scrambled."

"What sort of a wizard would do that to a dragon?" asked Xaxidiánus.

"A young and talented one who hasn't served with a wing of dragons as yet," said Callidus.

Celéri bowed. "Delicately put, magister," she said. "Now let's head north. We have my victory to win."

"Hop aboard, then," said Callidus, pointing to the saddle behind him.

"She's not riding on *my* back!" grumbled Xaxidiánus.

"Just hurry up," said Celéri. "I'll meet you there."

Chapter 55

The Battle Begins

"Sírénae hasn't arrived yet," remarked King Bjarni from his position atop one of the remaining walls of an Occidens Province fortification on the hills east of the broad green plain where the battle would soon begin. From his elevated vantage point, he could see the blue waters of the lake to the west as well.

"She could have had her spymaster gate her in," said Queen Signý.

"You said the emperor would swoop down at dawn on dragon-back to boost her legions' morale," said Arminta. "I haven't seen any dragons."

"I don't understand it," Signý replied.

"Their commander, whoever she or he might be, is moving elephants and legions forward nonetheless," said Bjarni.

"We can only hope the person giving orders is as overconfident as the emperor," said Signý. The queen of Bifurland opened a communications ring connecting her to Merry. "Tell Eynon to wait until all seven legions are on the battlefield before dispelling his constructs of solidified sound," Signý ordered.

"We know the plan," said Merry. "Eynon's having no trouble holding his constructs in place."

"Even against all that hydraulic pressure?" asked Bjarni.

"It doesn't appear to be a strain," said Merry. "I'm the one keeping our position hidden with a cloud illusion. We're about five hundred feet above the leading legion."

"I see you," said Arminta. "You look like a little lost sky sheep." The Clan Chief turned and spoke to the wizard beside her. "Thank you for the distance-viewing lenses, Amber. They make it much easier to see what's happening."

"My pleasure," said Bifurland's master mage. "I'm glad my wizards were able to deliver all those *presents* for our *visitors*."

"We will soon see how much they're appreciated," said Arminta.

"I've ordered our Northern Clan Lands skirmishers to pound their spears on their shields to entice the elephants to move forward."

"When they're opposite our position, we'll signal the trumpeter," said Signý.

"I love a good animal show," said Bjarni. "What do you hear from Sigrun and Rannveigr?"

"They say our *big surprise* is ready to go in the forest just north of the battlefield," said Signý.

"Their small gold dragons will help keep our big surprise in good order," said Amber.

"Is it time to give the word to Nûd, Dârio, and Quintillius?" asked Bjarni.

"Yes," said Signý. "We want Sírénae's legions to advance farther. It's time for our forces to gate through and draw them out. I'll pass the word."

* * * * *

"I'm sending the elephants forward on the right," Belisaria informed Celéri as they observed the field from a platform on top of a hastily assembled wooden observation tower.

"And our legions will begin to advance on the left and center," added Giérra from her position beside Belisaria.

"But there's hardly anyone to fight," said Celéri. "I only see a few thousand soldiers in a thin line near the trees half a mile north of us."

"Look closer," said Giérra. "There are many more Northern Clan Landers waiting for us to take the field. They're experts at camouflage."

"And I'm sure there are still more opponents present we *can't* see," said Belisaria.

"Why don't we blast them with fireballs to flush them out?" asked Celéri.

"Because they have wizards ready to generate shields to negate them," said Giérra. "Náegosh and his wizards have tried that already."

"We'll just have to overwhelm them then," declared Celéri.

"Thanks to your *contraptions,* good wizard," said Belisaria.

"Have the wizards working for Náegosh also scanned the battlefield for traps?" asked Celéri. "I don't want to lose legionnaires to barbarian trickery."

"We were pleasantly surprised," said Giérra. "The scout-wizards report that the ground on the field of battle is firm except close to the lake where it's marshy."

"You were wise to suggest keeping the elephants on our right then," said Celéri. "It wouldn't be good for them to get bogged down. I'm surprised there weren't pit traps, though."

"Náegosh said his people didn't find any," said Giérra. "There are archers dug in on the hills to the east and a contingent of Bifurlander heavy infantry with axes near the old fortifications, but they're less than two thousand as best his scout-wizards could determine."

"So long as our wizards' shields can protect us from enemy arrows, our legions can deal with a few bearded blond barbarians," said Belisaria.

"You must have been waiting for an excuse to say that," teased Giérra.

"Forgive me. I'm fond of alliteration," said Belisaria.

"You know their women wield axes, too," observed Giérra.

"They're savage northerners," Belisaria replied. "I stand by my words."

"If you two are finished disparaging our opponents, perhaps you can enlighten me on something," said Celéri.

"Sorry, good wizard," said Belisaria. "What would you like to know?"

"Why are we here?" asked Celéri.

"For questions like that," said Belisaria, "you're better off consulting with Athican philosophers."

"No, my good fool of a general," said Celéri in a tone that suggested amusement more than anger. "I mean why are we about to engage with a foe that prefers forest ambushes on an open field?"

"My apologies," said Belisaria. "Giérra and I were discussing that very point yesterday."

"Did you reach any conclusions?" asked Celéri.

"Two," said Belisaria. "Either they want to engage us *before* we reach their mountain home..."

"...or they have some especially unpleasant surprises in store for us that will work best on this sort of terrain," Giérra completed.

"Or both," said Celéri. "Given that we haven't yet identified any unpleasant surprises yet..."

"We're likely to discover them at the least opportune time..." said Belisaria.

"When they'll hurt us the most," said Giérra.

"Then again, we have some surprises of our own," said Celéri.

"Beyond your contraptions?" asked Belisaria.

"Oh yes," said Celéri. "We have *me*."

* * * * *

Jenet received word from Queen Signý and waved her arm to give the signal for all three columns to advance. To Jenet's right, Nûd convinced Rocky to crawl through the wide gate in front of him on his belly scales. With his wings tightly furled, the wyvern just made it under the gate's horizontal crossbar. Bonnie was beside Nûd as Dâron's heavy cavalry, light cavalry, and infantry entered the wide gate behind them.

On Jenet's left, Quintillius and Valentius were in the vanguard and led their legionnaires—wearing new tabards—through their wide gate's interface. Once the first Occidens Province legionnaires had disappeared, Dârio pulled his sword from its scabbard and pointed toward the middle gate. "Orluin!" he shouted, knowing the cry would not cross the congruency and be heard on the other side.

"Orluin!" exclaimed the men and women of Tamloch behind him. The battle cry echoed up and down the field behind Rōlin and Peregrína's home in Three Mountains Valley as the army of the west advanced. Even the spectators who had gathered to see the soldiers off shouted. The echoes were loud enough to bounce back and forth across the valley and startle a herd of pronghorns into hasty flight.

"I hope our enemies act like those pronghorns," said Peregrína from her position next to her husband on their back porch.

"I'm definitely with you on that," said Rōlin. "But I've just thought of something else to worry about."

"What's that?" asked Peregrína.

"Those wide gates work both ways," said Rōlin. "What if our enemies use them to come *here?*"

* * * * *

Rocky stood and moved quickly away from the wide gate as soon as he was through the interface. Like an iridescent black butterfly emerging from a chrysalis, the wyvern spread and stretched his wings before moving to a small mound that marked the boundary between the battlefield proper and a stream carrying water northward from the lake. The stream's outflow was barely a trickle, despite the contributions to the lake's level from generous spring rains.

Nûd and Bonnie climbed a dozen steps up the mound to join Rocky and survey the scene. A few minutes later Duke Háiddon did the same.

"Ready for battle, my king?" asked the duke.

"What do *you* think?" asked Nûd. "I've read books on battles. They never play out the way the generals expect. I don't want to see my people hurt—or Sírénae's people either, for that matter."

"Admirable sentiments, sire," said Duke Háiddon, reinforcing Nûd's royal titles as much as possible.

"Admiral?" said Bonnie. "Is Admiral Sónnel joining us? I thought we were too far inland for our navy to participate in this conflict."

"You know perfectly well what he said," noted Nûd. "I know you're trying to lighten the mood, but you don't need to. I'm fine— just keep as many people safe as you can."

"Starting with you, my king," teased Bonnie.

"Not you too," said Nûd. "It's bad enough Duke Háiddon keeps repeating my title—you're quite obvious about it, Your Grace. I *do* know I'm the king."

"My apologies... Nûd," said Duke Háiddon.

Rocky twisted his neck to see them, snorted, and returned to observing the battlefield.

"Even Rocky has had enough of it," said Nûd.

"I don't appreciate criticism from your dragon," said Duke Háiddon.

"He's a wyvern," said Nûd.

"Count his legs," said Bonnie.

"Nûd has two, clearly," said Duke Háiddon. "And I still think we should have painted him blue."

"Excuse me?" said Nûd.

"Not you, Nûd. Your dragon," said Duke Háiddon.

"We've talked about this and you know my answer," said Nûd. "But thank you."

"For what?" said Duke Háiddon.

"For distracting me," said Nûd. "It's working."

"Rocky's a wyvern," whispered Bonnie. Numbers were important to her.

Nûd reached out and took her hand, giving it a reassuring squeeze. "Thank you, as well."

"For what?" asked Bonnie.

"For being here with me, guarding my back, and getting to know my great-grandmother," said Nûd.

"How did you...?" said Bonnie, starting to form a question.

Nûd squeezed her hand again. "I have eyes and ears everywhere," he said.

"Not the last time we made love you didn't," said Bonnie.

Duke Háiddon smiled and whistled a dozen notes off key to delay further conversation. "Your Majesty," he said, after Nûd's face was less crimson.

Nûd glared at him.

"Nûd, then," Duke Háiddon added. "I see our troops have almost finished crossing through. Why don't you climb aboard your *wyvern* and draw your sword to impress them?"

"Because too many of them have seem me practicing with blades," said Nûd. "I'll head up to my saddle, but my apologies for not learning your lessons fast enough. I'll be using my crossbow from the air and my quarterstaff if I somehow end up on the ground."

"Just keep your sword on your sword belt," said Duke Háiddon. "Even if it never leaves your scabbard."

"Yes, *Your Grace,*" said Nûd.

He ascended Rocky's back and assisted Bonnie as she settled into the saddle behind him. They both waved at Duke Háiddon as he left the mound and returned to confer with his unit commanders.

* * * * *

"You're really good at this," Dârio told Jenet as the two led Dâron's contingent onto the field.

"Thank you," said Jenet.

"That's it?" asked Dârio. "No quibbling over what I said or how I said it?"

"No," said Jenet. "Because your tone didn't make it sound like you were *surprised* I'm a good Earl Marshal. It was just a simple statement of fact."

"Good," said Dârio. "I've been trying to drop the façade that helped keep me safe from my mother all these years and a perpetual sarcastic tone is hard to lose."

"You're slowly succeeding at it," said Jenet. "I appreciate your efforts."

"Appreciate or *appreciate*?" asked Dârio.

"The one that's not sarcastic," said Jenet. "Or is it ironic?"

"I don't think it matters, since I'm trying to avoid them both," said Dârio. "What's tolerable in a prince is not in a sovereign."

"That's wise," said Jenet. "You should tell Nûd that maxim so he can share it with his grandfather for the next volume of *Ealdamon's Epigrams*."

"Where *is* Damon, anyway?" asked Dârio. "And Seren, for that matter?"

"Doethan knows," said Jenet. "And Princess Rúth and Laetícia, I think," said Jenet. "They aren't sharing details with mere kingdom earl marshals."

"Or kings, apparently," said Dârio. He reined in his horse when his own front ranks from Tamloch were even with Dâron's. Jenet stopped her horse beside his.

"Queen Signý says we should advance five hundred paces south once the Occidens Province legionnaires are safely through," said Jenet.

Dârio turned to his left and watched the disciplined provincial forces commanded by Quintillius form up into a fighting front.

Their ranks filled in the space between Tamloch and the low hills where the archers and Bifurlanders were already in place. Each legionnaire had a tall rectangular *scutum* and carried a *pilum* and *gladius*. In the sunlight, Dârio was pleased to see their shields were painted in the colors of the Orluin alliance. "Was that partly your doing?" he asked Jenet.

"Was what?" she replied.

"Painting *our* Roma's scutums," said Dârio.

"I think Quintillius came up with that on his own," said Jenet. "Though maybe Valentius helped."

"I like him," said Dârio.

"Quin? Or Valentius?" asked Jenet.

"Both," said Dârio. "But I was talking about Valentius. I'm learning a lot just watching him. He's a prince at an entirely different level."

"A potential heir to an empire?" asked Jenet.

"Something like that," said Dârio. "He's been kidnapped, rescued by strangers from across the Ocean, and thrown into what must be very odd circumstances, but he remains gracious. The man does whatever he can to help, without seeming to be higher and mightier than we are."

"Unlike Túathal," said Jenet.

"Please don't say *his* name or *her* name in my presence," said Dârio.

"Yes, Sire," said Jenet with a calculated measure of sarcasm.

"Sorry," said Dârio. "I'd appreciate it if you wouldn't remind me of either of my parents before a battle."

"No, I'm sorry," said Jenet. She smiled up at Dârio by way of apology and consulted the ring she used to connect with Queen Signý. Doethan had shown her how to open an interface that was only a few inches instead of the standard three feet to make it easier to use communications rings on horseback.

"Signý says all our legionnaires are through their wide gate," said Jenet. "I'll signal the bannerman to move up and lead the advance."

The man with the banner took his position in front of Dârio and Jenet, far enough ahead so the front ranks could see him and stepped off five hundred paces. As the forces of the Orluin Alliance moved forward they watched as the legions and elephants opposite them did likewise.

Then the ranks of elephants spread out and moved faster, goaded by their riders, building momentum for a charge.

Chapter 56

Big Surprises

Queen Signý watched the elephants advance across the battlefield and come nearly even with the Bifurlanders' position on the hills. *I hope Laetícia's information is correct about the pachyderms' prior training,* she considered. *We're prepared either way, but the results should be amusing for us and disconcerting for the emperor if the elephants respond as expected.*

Signý waved her hand at the trumpeter from Occidens Province loaned by Laetícia. He was standing nearby a few feet downslope with his instrument at the ready. Bifurland's queen watched as the man lifted his long brass horn to his lips and blew. The horn's bore was wider, and its bell was bigger than the trumpets of the Roma she'd seen before at the ceremony where the treaty of alliance was signed. This horn didn't sound like their sharp, high voices or the calls of Bifurland's rams' horns. Instead, it was mellow and deep, like the trumpeting of the elephants themselves.

The man played a simple five-note pattern and Signý smiled to see the elephants stop moving forward and begin forming circles of perhaps a dozen beasts each, trunk to tail. Thanks to the distance-viewing lenses Amber had generated for her, Signý could see the elephants' handlers' obvious frustration as they tried to get the big beasts to follow their orders instead of what had been reinforced by years of constant training. The trumpeter played a different pattern and most of the handlers slid off their beasts when the elephants shifted from simple circling to putting their front legs on the rump of the animal ahead of them.

Archers and axe wielding Bifurlanders laughed when the trumpeter played yet another preset call and the elephants dropped back onto four legs and began dancing in intricate pachyderm patterns. The movements resolved and the laughter grew louder when the observers on the hillsides realized the elephants had formed letters spelling ROMA and S.P.Q.R. Between the elephants and the lake, the advancing legions had stopped to watch the great beasts' odd motions.

At that moment, Amber *ad hoc* gated in beside Signý. "Eynon's not going to like that," said the wizard. "He's going to have to hold his constructs in place longer until the invading legions have moved forward far enough."

"He's young and strong," said Signý. "He'll manage. What about our big surprise?"

"Just give the word," said Amber. "They're ready to go."

"Excellent," said Signý.

Below, the letters the elephants had formed exploded into a chaos of large gray dots as wizards flying up from the invaders' lines began tossing small fireballs and hurling tiny sparking bolts at the big beasts' massive feet. Working together, the wizards got the elephants moving again, north toward the allied forces and the woods along the far end of the eastern hills.

"It was fun while it lasted," said Signý. "Tell Fercha and Verro to open the *very* wide gate."

"And tall," teased Amber. "Very wide *and* tall."

"Just get it open," said Signý. "And keep it open."

"Yes, my queen," said Amber before gating out with a *pop*.

* * * * *

"What's going on?" Celéri demanded. "Did someone feed our elephants moldy hay?"

"I don't know, good wizard," said Belisaria. "I've never fought with elephants before and am not familiar with their care and fodder."

"You're useless," said Celéri. "Where did *these* elephants come from?"

"The Southern Emperor was sending them to Roma Mater for a fête in the Flavian Ampitheatre," said Giérra. "We intercepted their transports on our way through the Pillars."

"I... see..." said Celéri. "Did anyone consider *why* they were being sent to the Ampitheatre? Those elephants aren't trained for battle—they're performers."

"Apparently so, good wizard," said Giérra. "At least we don't have any reason not to eat them now."

"Maybe so," said Celéri, "but I'd like to get *some* use out of them today besides serving as the main course at my victory feast. Tell Náegosh to send a few of his wizards up to *encourage* the beasts to charge the enemy."

"Yes, good wizard," said Giérra. The legate instructed a nearby adjutant who rapidly descended the command tower to pass the message.

"Now we'll see some action," said Celéri.

A hand of minutes later Belisaria waved for the others' attention. "Look!" said the lieutenant general. "The wizards are herding the elephants."

"And not harming them in the process," said Celéri. "Náegosh seems to be a competent magister with at least half a brain."

"Even though they keep sticking him with the Thirteenth Corps of Wizards," said Giérra.

"All the more impressive," said Celéri. "Perhaps I'll credit him with three-quarters of a brain and promote him once we win."

"I'm sure he'd be grateful and prove his worth," said Giérra.

"Are you related to the man?" asked Celéri.

"No, but we've served together before," said Giérra.

"I'll take the matter of his promotion under advisement," said Celéri.

"A statement worthy of a graduate of the Imperial School of Good Governance," said Belisaria.

"I didn't attend," said Celéri.

"With your wisdom, they could use you as an instructor," said Belisaria.

"When I want portions of my posterior kissed, I'll inform you, lieutenant general," said Celéri. "In the meantime, your fawning isn't working."

"Right," said Belisaria.

"Better," said Celéri. "What the...?"

While Belisaria and Giérra watched, Celéri threw herself off the command tower and twisted her body to put her feet on her flying disk. She soared a hundred yards higher and stared and what seemed to be a brown river of *something* flowing across the battlefield toward *her* elephants. Celéri snapped a construct of distance-viewing lenses in place and the brown river resolved into hundreds of mammoths from the steppes of Bifurland, their shaggy hair waving from the wind generated by their own motion. The mammoths were half again as massive as the elephants and their curved tusks were bent into arcs of ivory to sweep away their enemies.

When the mammoths met the elephants, they didn't fight. Instead, Celéri heard both sorts of beasts trumpet at each other— the mammoths sounding deep basso notes making the elephants bugling seem like tenors in comparison. Celéri couldn't believe her eyes when *her* elephants formed lines to head north with their new hirsute friends. Before Celéri could react, the first elephants were disappearing with the mammoths into the woods near the eastern hills.

"No no no no *no!*" screamed Celéri. "Come back!" She started to fly across the battlefield to stop them but calculated the angles and number of beasts and realized she'd arrive too late.

On top of the command tower, well below Celéri's high vantage point, Giérra whispered to Belisaria. "So much for our victory feast."

"At least roast elephant is no longer on the menu," Belisaria replied.

The pair closed their mouths when Celéri returned to join them. "Tell the legions already on the field to advance," said Celéri. "And have all my *contraptions* wheeled over to where the elephants were previously. We can fill in our right flank quickly."

"Yes, good wizard," said Belisaria.

More orders were conveyed down the tower and the three at the top soon saw the results of Celéri's commands. To the left, the legions moved farther forward until they had crossed nearly half the field between them and their opponents. The heavy cavalry and other Orluin troops did not advance to meet them, however. On the right, two hundred wheeled carts, each carrying what looked like an empty door frame, were moved into position at the back of the field the elephants had recently occupied. Congruent interfaces— fixed gates—shimmered in place in each frame and thousands of legionnaires began streaming through them, jumping off the backs of the carts and striding off with clinking lorica plates to form their units.

The legionnaires already on the field pounded their shields with the hilts of their swords and cheered. ROM-A! ROM-A! ROM-A!

Belisaria, Giérra, and Celéri exchanged quick glances, pleased to note the legionnaires were *not* shouting *Sír-é-nae!*

"When we wipe our foes off the field, they'll be cheering Cel-é-ri," said Celéri. "Remember what I told you to say?"

"Celéri brought us victory!" said the two older women in unison.

"Good," said Celéri. "Do all the legions know who came up with the wheeled gates?"

"As you suggested, we're calling them Celéri's Chariots," said Giérra.

"The name is sticking," said Belisaria. "Though sometimes we have to explain who you are. Once we describe you, however, many legionnaires recall you."

Then again, thought Giérra, *most of their recollections weren't complimentary. Not that I'll ever tell this self-important child anything of the sort.*

"How long until all ten new legions are reformed?" asked Celéri.

"Not much longer, good wizard," said Giérra. "You can see five legions have ridden *Celéri's Chariots* to the field already."

"I *do* like the sound of that," said Celéri. "Say it again."

"Celéri's Chariots," said Giérra.

"Celéri's Chariots, Celéri's Chariots!" said Belisaria enthusiastically, thereby earning a raised eyebrow from Celéri.

Giérra reminded herself to caution Belisaria about thinking before speaking, as senior legates had been tutoring lieutenant generals since before the first Caesars.

"Tell the legions already in place to advance," said Celéri. "By the time they've claimed half the field, the new legions will be ready to join them."

"Yes, good wizard," said Giérra. She gave the order and was pleased to see it promptly obeyed. The seven legions on the left, only slightly depleted by legionnaires assigned to position Celéri's Chariots, resumed their march northward.

"Our enemies are just standing there waiting for us in front of the trees. Why aren't they advancing?" asked Celéri.

"Perhaps they're waiting for something," suggested Belisaria, thereby earning another *look* from Celéri.

"I could guess that, fool," said Celéri. "The question is waiting for *what*?"

Shouts of panic rose up from the seven legions on the left near the lake. The legions movements were no longer disciplined. Something unexpected was happening.

"I think we're about to find out," said Giérra. "And we're *not* going to like it."

Chapter 57

Bogged Down

"I've got good news," Merry told Eynon. "Signý says you can release your constructs. The invading legions are perfectly positioned."

"I thought so," Eynon replied. "I've gotten reasonably good at doing magic under high pressure..."

"...but this is a bit too much?" Merry completed.

"Not really," said Eynon. "I could lock the pipes of solidified sound into place, so they weren't hard to hold, keeping the surface of the field solid."

"I'm glad it hasn't been too much of a strain," said Merry. "I'm interested in seeing the results when most of the waters of the lake are transferred under the battlefield."

"We were lucky the lake is a dozen feet higher than the field," said Eynon.

"Not really," said Merry. "It's a plus, but not a requirement. If need be, several of us could have made broad plates of solidified sound and pushed down on the lake's surface."

"I'm glad you didn't have to and could guard my back," said Eynon. "We make a good team."

Merry put her hand on Eynon's forearm to show that she appreciated his comment. She could feel the tension in his body as he held his constructs.

"Here goes," said Eynon.

Merry sensed Eynon's tension suddenly drain away. They both looked at the battlefield below. As planned, the waters of the lake were flowing out from the subsurface pipes of solidified sound Eynon had generated. In seconds, the soil was supersaturated and had turned into deep mud. Armored legionnaires with heavy shields soon found themselves mired thigh deep in a viscous black ooze. Officers on horseback had to deal with their mounts thrashing beneath them as their horses sank into an unstable matrix of grass, topsoil, clay, and water.

The legionnaires' shouts of dismay and frustration were enough to wake Chee and Ace, who'd been sleeping curled up together on Merry's flying disk.

"Chee?" asked the raconette, opening one eye. Ace looked up at Merry.

"Go back to sleep," Merry instructed.

"I'd enjoy some sleep, too," said Eynon.

"If I was with you, we wouldn't be sleeping," teased Merry.

"But sleeping with you helps me sleep," Eynon teased back. "If you follow my meaning."

"It's not hard to follow," said Merry with a smile.

"It will be," said Eynon.

"I don't doubt it, but that's enough," said Merry. "We can both rest and relax when the battle is won. The good news is that our plan worked. Seven legions are out of action without loss of life. Queen Signý told me to congratulate you." Merry pulled Eynon's face down for a kiss, now that she could distract him without risking their trap triggering early.

"That was nice," said Eynon. "What else can I do to earn such a reward?"

"Laugh at my illusions," said Merry. "Watch!"

In the muddy space to the north of the invading legions, Merry generated patterns of sharks' fins circling. The small number of legionnaires in the invaders' vanguard who had available attention to notice the fins cried out in horror and devoted more energy to extricating themselves from the soupy soil.

Eynon laughed and kissed Merry. "Well done, my love," he said. "Add a few kraken arms, why don't you?"

"That's Inthíra's illusion," said Merry. "I don't want to copy her."

"Understandable," said Eynon. "What can we do to slow down all those new legions that have gated onto the field? I wish we had the kobs and gobs around to dig holes."

"Unfortunately, we don't, but I think the Bifurlanders have an answer," said Merry. "I'll see what Signý has in mind. That was clever of Sírénae's wizards to use traditional fixed gates on carts as a brute force way to duplicate the function of our wide gates."

"I'll say," said Eynon. "I'm surprised no one thought of the idea before."

Merry spoke softly with Signý for a few minutes, then turned to Eynon. "You'll never guess what the invaders are calling those gate carts," she said.

Eynon shrugged. "Do tell," he said.

"Celéri's Chariots," said Merry. "Named for your would-be paramour, I'm sure."

"*Our* would-be bed partner, dear lady," said Eynon. "She was clear about that."

"True enough," said Merry. "I'm impressed that Celéri has a creative mind and is more than the naive would-be spy personae she showed us gathering honey."

"She was pretty naive, wasn't she?" said Eynon.

"Yes," said Merry. "She reminds me of another naive creative person of my acquaintance."

"Do I know this person?" asked Eynon.

"Intimately," said Merry. She kissed Eynon again, delighted by the confused look on his face. "Signý asked if there was enough water in the lake to bog down more legions."

"See for yourself," said Eynon, waving to the west. "I only left enough to ensure the fish don't drown and the frog's homes don't dry up."

"I'll tell her we'll have to figure out something else then," said Merry. She paused and tilted her head in thought. "Could we use water from the Rhuthro river to feed pipes under the new legions?" Merry asked.

"Maybe," said Eynon. "If I had hours to build the pipes. It took me half the night to get everything in place for the part of the field closet to the lake."

"I don't think we need to use finesse now," said Merry. "If we could empty the waters of the Great Falls on top of the newly arrived legions, I'm sure Queen Signý would approve."

"I've never been to the Great Falls," said Eynon.

"Never mind," said Merry. "I'll think of something else. Maybe illusions."

"It's a good thing Sírénae's dragons aren't here then," said Eynon. "Their fire could dispel illusions."

"I wish you wouldn't have mentioned Sírénae's dragons," said Merry, pointing to the south. "Here they come."

"Why are there only four?" asked Eynon.

* * * * *

"...we're *not* going to like it," said Giérra.

"You're right about that," said Belisaria. "I don't like it, certainly. How dare they turn a perfectly good battlefield into a bog?"

"My first thoughts are for the legionnaires, not the terrain," said Giérra.

"How could they do that?" asked Celéri. "I thought you checked for traps on the field ahead of time."

"We did, good wizard," said Giérra. "Náegosh assured me..."

"Náegosh was *wrong,* fool of a legate!" shouted Celéri. "Now it's up to *me* to fix things and turn the ground solid again. I'll put my cold anger to good use." She made ready to fly to the legions aid.

"Wait!" said Giérra. "Not *that* way..." Unfortunately, Giérra spoke to empty air. Celéri was already aloft and moving fast.

* * * * *

"A wizard is heading toward us," said Eynon.

"Or the struggling legions," said Merry. "We're just a stray cloud."

"That isn't moving with the wind," said Eynon.

"Fine," said Merry. "I'll make us invisible, let this illusion blow away to the east, and bring in a new cloud illusion from the west. Satisfied."

"I am," said Eynon. "But I hope the incoming wizard is as well."

"It's Celéri," said Merry. "She's focused on the legions, not on us."

"So it is," said Eynon. "She doesn't look happy."

"Would you be if we removed elephants and legions from your *shah-mat* board?" asked Merry.

"Probably not," said Eynon. "Celéri's opening a congruency—a big one."

"What is she trying to do?" asked Merry. "Oh! No! She's..."

"...blasting the muddy field with freezing cold," said Eynon.

He started laughing, but Merry nudged him to stop since it wouldn't be wise to draw Celéri's attention.

"The legionnaires went from thrashing around in the mud to being frozen in place," said Merry.

"It will take them hours to thaw out and get free," said Eynon. "I haven't seen anything that funny since my cousin fell into..."

"We don't have time to talk about your cousin's misadventures," said Merry. "We have new legions and Sírénae's dragons to deal with."

"Yes," said Eynon. "And the new legions have formed up and have started advancing."

"Any other good news?" asked Merry.

"Not really," said Eynon. "We should probably move, though. It's getting cold here."

"Ch-ch-ch-chee!" confirmed Chee as he snuggled into Eynon's shoulder.

"Let's fly north to the allied army," Merry suggested.

"An excellent suggestion," said Eynon. "But let's be subtle about it so Celéri doesn't see us."

"When am I anything other than subtle?" asked Merry before guiding them and their cloud illusion north.

* * * * *

"What do you think?" Callidus asked Xaxidiánus as they flew up the Abbenoth. "Do we stick with Sírénae, switch our support to Celéri, or ask Laetícia to intercede for us and join allied Orluin?"

"Are those our only options?" asked Xaxidiánus as he and the three remaining dragons in his wing flew north. "I could fly us across the Ocean so you could retire to that tower in the hills of Éberria you always wanted."

"Dream on," said Callidus. "It's more likely I could learn how to *ad hoc* gate dragons across the Ocean than either one of us would be permitted to retire."

"At least I'm more likely to keep my head," said Xaxidiánus. "Dragons are in short supply—though so are mages who can *ad hoc* gate."

"Let's consider the possibilities one by one," said Callidus. "I did pledge Sírénae my service..."

"So did I," said Xaxidiánus. "Though I had less choice about it, being raised to serve the Imperium since I emerged from my shell."

"Granted," said Callidus. "But we don't know if Sírénae even remains alive after Celéri took her."

"If Celéri has harmed Mégàrotáxus I'll flame her to cinders," said Xaxidiánus.

"Fine," said Callidus. "For now, we'll assume both the emperor and your wing mate are alive. We know that following Sírénae won't end well."

"That's been obvious since before she was exiled," said Xaxidiánus. "The question is who else can we follow? Not the precocious child-wizard?"

"Celéri is powerful, but naive and overconfident," said Callidus. "I could be a positive influence on her and offer her good counsel."

"She won't listen to anyone other than herself," said Xaxidiánus. "Celéri is a lot like the emperor that way."

"Very true," said Callidus. "Switching from one to the other would be like jumping out of the brazier into the furnace."

"You're inclined to the third option, then?" asked the dragon.

"Laetícia and Quintillius would be glad to have us, I expect," said Callidus. "She indicated as much when Valentius was rescued."

"We still wouldn't be trusted," said Xaxidiánus.

"We might earn their trust in time," said Callidus. "Sírénae and Celéri will *never* trust us—they'll just use us."

"And with that Gwýnnett woman plotting in the background, you might lose your will if you eat or drink the wrong thing," said Xaxidiánus.

"You too, old friend," said Callidus. "You'd just need a larger dose of one of her potions."

"We've reached a conclusion?" asked Xaxidiánus. "We turn traitor to Sírénae and shift our allegiance to Occidens Province?"

"I wouldn't put it that way," said Callidus. "Say rather that we are reaffirming our loyalty to the Imperium."

"I like your words better," said the dragon. "When the time comes, I'm confident my wing mates will trust my judgment and *reaffirm* as well."

Xaxidiánus looked over his shoulder to confirm the other three dragons, without riders, were in formation behind him. They were.

"Good," said Callidus. "We'll have to determine the best way about it once we reach the battlefield. Flying over enemy lines could be misinterpreted. I'd use the ring Réah gave me to reach out, but I doubt a kitchen servant would be anywhere near a battlefield."

"Wise words," said Xaxidiánus. "I was going to dive at the allied commanders to get their attention before I informed them of my loyalty to their side."

"Of course you were," said Callidus. "We also have Celéri to worry about if she's at the battlefield. She said she'd meet us there."

"I'm less worried about *her*," said Xaxidiánus. "Celéri wouldn't harm us. You're like a father to the young woman."

"If I could reach your scaly head I'd check to see if you have a fever," said Callidus, holding back a laugh. "You're delusional."

"I'm not the one who decided to betray an emperor with a hungry snow-gryffon or a young wizard who could probably *ad hoc* gate us to the Moon," said Xaxidiánus.

"Fine, I accept complete responsibility for rejoining the Imperium," said Callidus after thumping the dragon's neck with an affectionate fist. "Let's get the lay of the land before we make any specific plans about how to do it. When will we get there?"

"Since I don't know the exact location I can't say precisely," noted Xaxidiánus. "I think we'll recognize the place without any problem when we arrive. There should be a battle in progress."

"Now who's wise?" said Callidus. "Fly on, my friend. Fly on!"

Chapter 58

Bees and Loyalties

Celéri swooped down to the top of the command tower and resumed her previous position beside Giérra and Belisaria. "That's how it's done," she said to the senior legate and lieutenant general.

"But you…" began Belisaria.

"…rescued those legionnaires so skillfully," inserted Giérra quickly before Belisaria could say anything to upset the capricious young wizard. "How did you come up with the brilliant idea of freezing the mud?"

"Natural talent, I suppose," said Celéri. "I've always thought faster than anyone else."

"A true gift, good wizard," said Belisaria.

Giérra nodded at the lieutenant general, pleased her superior was finally learning better ways to stroke Celéri's oversized ego.

"How long will it take the legions on our left flank to dig out of the frozen mud?" asked Celéri.

"Several hours, at least," said Giérra. "Perhaps a bit less if the temperature rises."

"Hours?" complained Celéri. "Can't they start digging themselves out immediately?"

"Frozen ground is difficult to excavate," said Belisaria.

"And there's only one shovel for each ten legionnaires," said Giérra.

"That's nonsense," said Celéri. "Every legionnaire should have a shovel. What if they need to dig an earthen wall in a hurry?"

"One digs, nine carry," said Giérra. "It's the tested way."

"I still think it's absurd," said Celéri. "See that every legionnaire has a shovel by nightfall."

"Yes, good wizard," said Belisaria. "It shall be as you wish. The senior legate will see to it, won't you Giérra?"

"Of course, lieutenant general," said Giérra. *Fire and lightning! Why is it my lot to deal with a foolish young wizard* and *a foolish young senior officer?* she wondered.

"Would the legionnaires be able to dig out faster if I blasted the frozen ground with fireballs?" asked Celéri.

"That's doubtful," said Giérra. "Being frozen in place they'd have trouble getting out of the way of fireballs."

"I suppose you're right," said Celéri. "At least the ten new legions are available for action. Tell them to advance."

"I will, good wizard," said Belisaria.

"As soon as I order them to pass all their shovels to the legions who are frozen in place," said Giérra.

"Splendid," said Celéri. "The ten legions won't need to build walls. They're attacking."

"I'm glad you approve, good wizard," said Giérra. "You'll see the ten legions are spreading out to cover the entire width of the battlefield," said the senior legate. "The rightmost legion will defend its flank against the archers and Bifurlanders on the hillsides."

"Would you like me to blast those hillsides with fireballs, senior legate?" asked Celéri.

"I don't think that would be wise," said Belisaria.

"I asked the senior legate," said Celéri.

"Belisaria is correct for once, good wizard," said Giérra.

"I beg your pardon..." Belisaria began, then she closed her mouth when she saw Celéri and Giérra's expressions.

"They will certainly have shields of solidified sound protecting them," said Giérra. "Wizards on Náegosh's staff tested their shields before you arrived."

"I... see..." said Celéri.

"A Roma shield wall reinforced with pikes and spears can hold off and defeat barbarians with axes," said Giérra. "We've been doing it for centuries."

"Carry on then," said Celéri.

Together, the three women watched the ten legions move forward. Soon the front ranks of legionnaires had progressed until they were nearly even with the old Roma fortification where the Bifurlanders and archers were dug in.

Celéri was focused on a small, suspicious cloud that had been stationary above the center of the battlefield and was now mysteriously drifting north.

"What are those raised boxes along the bottom of the hillsides?" Belisaria asked Giérra.

"Where exactly?" Giérra replied.

"All along the edge of the hills before they start sloping up, right where our legions will be marching," said Belisaria, pointing northeast.

"Blast and double-blast!" said Giérra. "I'll have Náegosh and his wizards flayed. They said they'd checked that area for traps."

"I don't think the boxes were there earlier," said Belisaria. "Adjust your distance-viewing lenses and look farther down the line. Kilted Northern Clan Landers in camouflage are setting more of the boxes on raised wooden platforms."

"I still can't make them out," said Giérra.

"My younger eyes have no such problem," said Belisaria.

"Neither do mine," said Celéri. "Burnt honey cakes!" she shouted before realizing the inappropriateness of her childlike exclamation and repeating Giérra's expression. "I know what they are," said Celéri.

"Tell us," said Belisaria. "What strange Northern Clan Lands magic are they?"

"They're not magic," said Celéri. "At least not of the sort wizards perform."

Northern Clan Landers had started knocking the boxes nearest the legionnaires off their platforms—and running away as fast as their bare legs could carry them. Screams were already coming from the proximate legionnaires and their tight formations were dissolving into chaos when Celéri told Belisaria and Giérra.

"They're beehives," she said.

* * * * *

"We've been spotted," said Callidus to Xaxidiánus as they reached the battlefield.

Legionnaires on the left flank, strangely stuck in place, began shouting, "Dragons! Dragons!"

"Something odd is happening to the legions on the right flank, too," noted Xaxidiánus. "If the left flank is frozen, the right flank appears to be *dancing*."

"Ergot in their bread rations?" joked Callidus with a rare display of wry humor.

"Only if they have bread left, which I doubt," said Xaxidiánus. "Look out! Here comes Celéri."

The young wizard zoomed up to fly alongside Callidus and Xaxidiánus.

"Great timing," said Celéri. "I'm glad you're here, Xaxidiánus. You and your wing mates have excellent control over your flame blasts, I'm told."

"You were informed correctly," said Xaxidiánus.

"Good," said Celéri. "I want the four of you to fly low along the edge of the hills and destroy every box of bees you see."

"I hear and obey, good wizard," said Xaxidiánus.

"Callidus," said Celéri. "You can shield the dragons from enemy spells and arrows."

"That's an excellent plan," said Callidus. He waved goodbye to Celéri and Xaxidiánus tipped her a wing as he and his three draconic companions headed northeast while Celéri returned to the command tower.

"Are we actually going to burn the beehives?" Xaxidiánus asked Callidus as soon as he was confident the young wizard could no longer overhear them.

"No," said Callidus. "But the closer we can get to Quintillius and the Occidens Province legions in the north—I can recognize them even with those odd tabards they're wearing—the less likely Celéri can intercept us."

"I'll inform my wing mates," said Xaxidiánus. He trumpeted out updates to the dragons behind him and received confirmation that they'd heard and understood.

The senior magister and four magnificent dragons the color of sparkling obsidian sailed low above the rightmost flank of the legions.

Callidus found himself busier fending off stray bees than arrows as the archers decided angering dragons was not a sensible course of action.

Callidus climbed aboard his flying disk and flew ahead of Xaxidiánus. He held his open arms wide and descended in front of Quintillius and Valentius at the head of the provincial legions, saying, "I'm here to join you. So are the dragons."

"Laetícia told me to expect you," said Quintillius.

"We're glad you've come to your senses," said Valentius.

"I hope I'm still glad when the battle is over," said Callidus. He waved to Xaxidiánus and his large scaled friend landed close at hand with his wing mates but far enough away not to startle the officers' horses.

"So do we," said Quintillius. "We still have eight legions to deal with."

"And I have a lot to tell you," said Callidus. "Can you gather your leaders together? I'd only like to share my news once."

"Gladly," said Quintillius. "Follow me, I'll pass the word for us to meet at the center of our line near our standard bearer."

"Be sure to talk fast," said Valentius as he escorted Callidus. "Sírénae's legions won't defeat themselves."

"It's not Sírénae you have to worry about," Callidus replied.

Chapter 59

Celéri Gets Angry

"What in Roma's Seven Hills just happened?" asked Celéri.

"Xaxidiánus and the other dragons didn't flame the beehives and flew to enemy lines with Senior Magister Callidus," said Belisaria.

Celéri glared at the lieutenant general and knocked her to the floor of the platform atop the command tower with a punch from a sphere of solidified sound. "You should stay down there until you learn to recognize a rhetorical question, fool," said the dark-haired young wizard. "Next time you say something stupid I'll toss you *off* this tower."

Belisaria stayed flat on the platform and read the warning in Giérra's eyes to say nothing further.

"How do you plan to retaliate, good wizard," asked Giérra after a few rapid heartbeats.

"Have the closest of the new legions help dig out the men and women frozen in mud," said Celéri. Her voice was quiet, but intense.

Giérra could see the fury in the young wizard's eyes and knew she had more instructions.

"Have our mages spray those blasted bees with water from distant congruencies," Celéri continued. "Hedge wizards can help legionnaires who've been stung and pass out curative cordials."

"As you command, good wizard," said Giérra. The curative cordials were military medical tinctures used to help soldiers cope with minor wounds and injuries. They were much easier to make than healing potions and proportionately less effective, but simple hedge wizards serving with the legions could provide them. Giérra summoned a messenger from one level down in the command tower and passed along the appropriate orders.

Giérra saw Celéri staring north at the enemy army. It seemed to the senior legate that the power of Celéri's gaze could blast her opponents' bones from their bodies if only she gave it leave.

"What next?" asked Giérra.

Celéri didn't turn to face Giérra, but spoke slowly and deliberately, so Giérra heard every word. "Gather every man and woman who can hold a sword," said the young wizard. "Summon all the remaining legions from Nova Eboracum through my Chariots, on my authority and form them up for battle."

Giérra nodded. "Yes, good wizard," she said.

"Try again," said Celéri, her jaw tight.

"Yes… Your Imperial Majesty," Giérra responded.

"Much better," said Celéri. "I want every wizard in the capital—every novice and experienced magister—here on the field within the hour. All of the wizards Náegosh can provide as well, and Umbrose's wizards too, for that matter. Tell them I'm our spymaster now."

"Yes, Your Imperial Majesty," said Giérra, recognizing her cue.

"Any wizard or legionnaire who isn't here to fight for me will face my certain wrath," said Celéri. She spoke louder, but still hadn't looked at the senior legate. "I don't care how many of them die so long as they win me my victory."

Giérra knew Celéri's words would carry to the messengers waiting one level below. Soon the young mage's true feelings would spread across the legions faster than a wizard could gate. The senior legate knew it was time to ensure *her* name was not linked to Celéri's intentions.

"Surely, every legionnaire's life has value," said Giérra. "You wouldn't risk them needlessly."

"I would and shall," said Celéri. "We outnumber our enemies by ten to one and I would see us not decimated but lose nine out of ten to crush our foes."

So be it, thought Giérra. *The legions won't follow such a commander.* "Those orders you must give directly," said the senior legate.

"Just send the troops forward," said Celéri. "I'll lead the advance."

"Yes, Your Imperial Majesty," said Giérra, who now wished she was on the floor of the platform along with Belisaria.

"Follow me if you're able," said Celéri. She stepped on her flying disk and swooped down from the command tower.

"Get up," Giérra told Belisaria. "She's gone but keep your hand on your blade. I plan to as well."

"That girl is infuriating," said the lieutenant general as she rose and wiped off the armored leather skirt of her lorica. "It would be a pleasure to give her a taste of the legions' justice."

"Justice of that sort works better against non-wizards," said Giérra. "Swords don't match up well against fireballs."

"I suppose that depends on which way the wizard is looking," said Belisaria.

"I'll summon two of Náegosh's wizards to fly us to the vanguard," said Giérra. "We can't try to stop Celéri making a bigger mess of things from here."

"On the other hand," said Belisaria. "We *do* substantially out-number our enemies. Imagine the size of Celéri's ego if we win."

"It would be an inflated fish bladder large enough to displace the waters of the Ocean," said Giérra.

Belisaria patted the hilt of her sword. "And I've got just the thing to pop it."

* * * * *

The allied commanders were gathered behind the bannerman. Callidus had finished his update and Nûd, Dârio, Quintillius and the others were all dismayed by the number of legionnaires that continued to flow through the gates on wheels.

"We planned for seven legions," said Jenet.

"And could have handled ten," added Duke Iálddon.

"No plan of battle survives confrontation with the enemy," added Duke Néillen.

"When I want unhelpful epigrams, I'll ask my grandfather," Nûd replied.

Bonnie put a hand on Nûd's shoulder and the king of Dâron relaxed his clenched fists and took a deep breath.

"Do *you* have any good ideas, Eynon? Merry?" Nûd asked.

"We could always return through our wide gates, close them, and leave the invading legions with no one to fight," said Merry.

"That's always an option," said Jenet. "Let me ring Signý and Bjarni so they can contribute."

Everyone waited for the connection to be made.

"Signý says we could send the mammoths and elephants back to disrupt the legions," said Jenet.

"That would lead to a lot of dead beasts and feasts tonight, no matter who wins," said Quintillius.

"And that's *not* a good idea if we still want the invaders to starve," said Dârio.

"What about Celéri?" asked Eynon. "If she can *ad hoc* gate dragons, she's as powerful as a dozen legions herself."

"So are you," said Duke Háiddon. "And Merry's not far behind you in skill."

Inthíra stepped forward. "I could make illusions, like fifty legions from the Southern Empire joining us. Since the invaders' dragons have come over to our side, we don't have to worry about dragon-fire dispelling them."

"At this point, I doubt such illusions would be believed," said Valentius. "And there's scarcely room left on the field to *put* another ten legions, let alone fifty."

"There's another option," said Dârio. "We could fight them."

"If you want to throw your life away and die gloriously, I won't stop you," said Jenet. "Though I wouldn't want to go through the challenges of finding a new husband candidate."

"Who wouldn't be a king," teased Dârio.

"Nûd and Bonnie might have me," said Jenet.

"The more the merrier," said Bonnie, teasing Dârio back.

"Wait. What?" said Nûd.

"Just smile and nod, my love," said Bonnie.

"Getting back to serious options," said Jenet. "We'd best prepare to gate back west and shut our gates behind us. The invading legions are charging."

"My wing mates and I can flame them," offered Xaxidiánus.

"No killing," said Jenet.

"No killing," Xaxidiánus repeated.

Shouts rose up from the Dâron troops on the right side of the allied lines.

"A flank attack?" asked Duke Háiddon.

"No, listen," said Nûd.

The assembled leaders could now make out the shouted cries.

"The dragons are coming! The dragons are coming!"

Chapter 60

Parlay

Giérra and Belisaria found Celéri berating forty wizards gathered in a clump in front of the foremost legion at the center of the battlefield. Only half a thousand yards separated them from a similar grouping of war leaders and wizards opposite them behind a bannerman carrying an odd four-color banner none of the wizards Celéri was upbraiding admitted to recognizing. When the senior legate and lieutenant general landed and stepped off their transport mages' flying disks, Celéri vented at them as well.

"It's about time you two fools got here," said the young wizard. "Do either of *you* know what that banner stands for? None of these useless hedge wizards have any idea."

Belisaria seemed about to speak but closed her mouth when Giérra stopped her with a raised hand.

"Do I *know,* Your Imperial Majesty?" said Giérra. The senior legate watched the reaction of the gathered wizards and nearby legionnaires to her use of an imperial title for Celéri. "I can't know for certain, but it's clear from where it's flying that this is the new flag of the Orluin Alliance. Green is for Tamloch, blue is for Dâron, and the red stripe is..."

"For Occidens Province. Of course. That makes sense," said Celéri. "What about the gold stripe at the hoist?"

"Bifurland," said Giérra. "The kingdom in the far north."

"Named for beavers?" asked Celéri.

"Apparently so," said Giérra.

"Why couldn't any of *you* figured that out?" Celéri asked the two score of wizards. She stomped her boot on the turf and kicked a small rock in the direction of the enemy. "It doesn't matter if Orluin's realms are divided or united anyway," Celéri ranted. "We'll crush them one by one or all together."

"Yes, Your Imperial Majesty," said Giérra.

Celéri stared at the assemblage behind the bannerman. "I think I see Eynon and Merry with the barbarian kings," she told Belisaria and Giérra. "They've got their strange familiars with them."

"Who are Eynon and Merry?" asked the lieutenant general.

"Two novice wizards I met while collecting honey for Sírénae," said Celéri.

"I think Eynon is the name of the wizard who defeated Tamloch's army with a herd of wisents at the Battle of the Brenavon," said Giérra. "I heard from Náegosh who got it from one of Umbrose's spy-wizards that Eynon is Dâron's new master mage."

"Is that like a senior magister?" asked Belisaria.

"Those lying, manipulative..." Celéri began, winding up to express her thoughts on Eynon and Merry.

"Your Imperial Majesty," said Giérra, interrupting.

"What?" said Celéri, ready to lash out with a punch of solidified sound.

"Look west," said Giérra. "I don't think those are birds."

* * * * *

The western dragons circled five hundred feet above the empty ground between the two opposing forces. Without a word to Merry or the allied leaders, Eynon flew up to the dragons' level and looked for Kârkingórēx. The great rust-colored dragon spotted him first and hovered, his snout a few feet from Eynon's flying disk.

"It's good to see you," Eynon told the dragon.

"Corvi the raven told us where to find you," said Kârkingórēx. Puffs of steam rose from the western dragon's nostrils. "He learned the location of this battlefield from the cartographers." Kârkingórēx turned his head to cough and a small jet of fire escaped his mouth before he turned back and continued speaking. "We flew twice as fast as the wind to get here, thanks to your magestone dust and megapede venom."

"I'm glad they worked," said Eynon. "Your timing is excellent and your help against the invading Roma would be most welcome."

"I can see that," said Kârkingórēx. "My weyr and I would be glad to fry all the invading Roma and send the smoke of their pyres wafting east across the Ocean."

"That's quite a poetic image, but it really would be better if you didn't," said Eynon. "We're trying to starve the invaders into leaving Orluin. Killing legions would mean they'd have fewer mouths to feed and their food would stretch farther."

"What if we killed *all* of them?" asked Kârkingórēx.

"Their wizards would retaliate and try to kill you and all of your weyr," said Eynon.

"Not if we fry them first," said Kârkingórēx.

"Zûrafiérix wouldn't like that," said Eynon.

"Oh," said Kârkingórēx. "In that case, I suppose we could be content to just bash legionnaires around a bit." The rust-colored dragon's huge eyes caught Eynon's human ones. "You said my timing was excellent, but am I too late?"

"Too late for... Oh!" said Eynon. "I'm afraid you are. Zûrafiérix is sitting on her first clutch of eggs, by Viridáxés. But perhaps you can father her second clutch if she finds that agreeable."

"I'd like that very much," said Kârkingórēx.

"Before you pay court, I should warn you that Zûrafiérix is five times larger than you are," said Eynon.

"Is she now?" said Kârkingórēx.

"She slept for two thousand years in a magestone quarry," said Eynon. "But don't worry too much. Everyone says that size isn't everything."

"I don't think that phrase was intended to be applied to dragons," said Kârkingórēx. "For that matter, if she's just clutched, it will be two years before she's interested in new suitors. Maybe *I* can sleep in a magestone quarry for most of that time."

"That's not a bad idea," said Eynon. "After you and your weyr help us now."

"Of course," said Kârkingórēx.

Another dragon chose that moment to join them—a familiar brown. "Hello Brünedíxés," said Eynon. "All healed up now?"

"Yes," said Brünedíxés. "Thank you for asking." The brown dragon turned to Kârkingórēx. "The rest of the weyr wants to know what to do next, Boss. Can we start eating Roma?"

"Absolutely not," said Kârkingórēx. "Zûrafiérix wouldn't approve."

"If you wouldn't mind," said Eynon, "I'd appreciate it if you'd land in the empty space between the opposing armies and do what you can—which is quite a lot—to intimidate the invading Roma legions."

"An excellent plan," said Kârkingórēx.

"What about food?" asked Brünedíxés.

"Once the battle is over, there are tens of thousands of whales in the Ocean not far to the east," said Eynon. "And plenty of big fish there, too."

"That sounds better than eating legionnaires," said Brünedíxés. "I'd have to eat a lot of them to get as much meat as a whale, at least from what the cartographers have told us."

"Rōlin and Peregrína speak true," said Eynon. "Some whales are nearly as big as dragons."

"Remember," said Kârkingórēx. "Tell the weyr *no* eating. I'll flame the first drake who tries."

"I'll tell them," said Brünedíxés.

"Thank you both," said Eynon. "As an added benefit, hungry dragons are even more intimidating than ones with full bellies. With you and your weyr pacing in front of the invading Roma, I'm confident we can convince their leaders to parley."

* * * * *

"No," said Magister Callidus. "Absolutely not. You definitely don't want *me* asking Belisaria, Giérra, and especially Celéri to discuss reaching some sort of negotiated agreement. They think I'm a traitor."

"Who else could go and hope to be effective?" asked Jenet.

No one spoke, then Valentius stepped forward. "I could," he said. "And I will. Is there a wizard here who would fly me?"

"I will," said Inthíra. "My illusions should make our hasty escape—if necessary—more successful."

"Giérra is more respected than Belisaria," Quintillius advised. "Address the lieutenant general but speak to the senior legate."

"Why should this army be any different," Valentius replied with a smile.

"Don't worry about either of them," said Callidus. "The challenge will be getting Celéri to agree to parlay. Giérra and Belisaria would support any option that delays their legions fighting more than a hundred dragons as large or larger than Xaxidiánus."

"Wish us luck then," said Valentius. He bowed to Inthíra. "I think it best if we approach without any illusions around us," said Valentius. "Save those skills for a strategic retreat, good wizard. Shall we go?"

* * * * *

"I know who you are," said Celéri when Valentius presented himself in front of her. "You're the likely heir to the Southern Empire. Sírénae kidnapped you, but you escaped."

"You're well informed, good wizard," said Valentius.

"You will refer to me as Your Imperial Majesty," said Celéri.

Valentius remained silent.

"Be that way, son of Valens," said Celéri. "Give me one good reason why we should parlay."

"I can give you over a hundred," said Valens, waving a hand to indicate the wild western dragons facing Celéri's legions.

Giérra looked left and right and saw legionnaires nodding. They were impressed by Valentius as the son of an emperor and a possible future emperor. They also had little interest in fighting dragons.

"What harm could it do to listen to what they have to say, Your Imperial Highness?" asked Belisaria.

Giérra moved closer to Celéri so she could whisper to her. "The legions are watching you, Majesty," said the senior legate. "You may lose their loyalty if they think you're willing to throw them at the dragons instead of hearing what our foes have to say."

Celéri paced ten steps in one direction, ten steps back. Her eyes were narrowed and Giérra imagined a small storm cloud floated above her head, cracking with lightning. When she returned to her original spot, she augmented her voice and spoke so everyone for several hundred yards could hear.

"For the good of the legions, I will agree to parlay and listen to what you have to say," said Celéri. She canceled her amplification and spoke quietly, just to Valentius. "Withdraw your dragons to the eastern hillsides and we can meet in between our two lines in a quarter hour. Be warned that I will blast anyone who violates the standard terms of parlay."

"That's fair on all counts," said Valentius. "In a quarter hour then."

"So long as the dragons withdraw," said Celéri.

"They will," said Valentius.

Inthíra flew them both north without illusions.

* * * * *

The Orluin allies were represented by Nûd, Dârio, Quintillius, and Valentius. Celéri allowed only Belisaria and Giérra to accompany her. Privately, Giérra thought Celéri's ego big enough for three people, so in some ways their delegation outnumbered their opponents' negotiators by five to four. Arminta and Bifurland's leaders agreed not to join this stage of the delicate process, for quite different reasons. The chief of the Northern Clan Lands didn't want to remind the legions of her clans' participation in the battle and Bjarni and Sign‎ý didn't want to increase the size of the allies' delegation, believing smaller numbers could find agreement faster. They were also busy getting over a hundred dragons settled in on the hills around them.

Each of the allied leaders had swords at their belts, though Nûd also held a quarterstaff and leaned on it as he waited for the meeting to begin. The rules of parlay did not include participants going unarmed, just strictures against *using* weapons, and Giérra and Belisaria each had a Roma gladius sheathed at their waist. Celéri was armed only with wizardry and was the only mage among the seven.

After introductions were made, Celéri spoke. "We're here," she said. "What words do you have for us before we annihilate you?"

"Those are strong words for a parlay," said Valentius. He extended his left hand toward the dragons on the hills. "Especially when it would more likely be a mutual annihilation."

"I don't need to be lectured to by the son of a cowherd," said Celéri. "And I won't moderate my speech to avoid offending you."

"That's your choice to make," said Valentius, "and my father has tens of thousands of cows on his estates with little time these days to herd them."

"We have a proposal for you," said Nûd.

"One that should resolve our conflict without bloodshed," said Quintillius.

"But I must have my victory," said Celéri. "That will likely turn the ground red."

"Not necessarily," said Dârio. "Hear us out."

"I'm listening," said Celéri. "But don't strain my patience."

"We won't," said Valentius. He noted the tight muscles of Celéri's jaw and hoped he was correct. Using command voice, he made sure the closest legions could hear the allies' offer. "Our proposal is thus: We will help your legions relocate to an island in a sea south of here. It's larger than Sicily and the Green Isle combined and warm enough to plant and reap three crops a year. We will also provide you with red meat and other food to help you through until your first crops are harvested. We'll even return your two hundred elephants so they can be put to good use hauling stones and building roads. On top of that, we'll provide every legionnaire with a gold *solidus* to fund their farms."

There had been a lot of discussion among the allied commanders about offering payments in gold to the legionnaires, even though Eynon could extract more from rivers in the west. Nûd argued about so much precious metal in circulation raising prices while Jenet pointed out that the invading Roma would be the ones to worry about that on their new island home, not the kingdoms on the mainland of Orluin. In the end, it was decided that offering the gold would help convince the legions to back the idea and apply pressure on Celéri if she balked.

"Those are generous terms," whispered Giérra to Celéri. "Accepting them could *be* your victory. The legions would *love* you."

"Give me a moment, legate," said Celéri. "I need to think." She told Valentius the same and stepped a dozen feet away from the other delegates, pacing and stroking her chin.

Giérra risked smiling at Valentius and received a brief smile in return. Almost everyone avoided looking at Celéri, giving the young wizard privacy for her personal deliberations.

Belisaria's battle-lust was still high, no matter how much Giérra had tried to calm her earlier. The frustrating reversals on the battlefield and the peace proposal from the Orluin allies made her angry. Like Celéri, she wanted her victory. That's why the young lieutenant general wasn't wise enough to look away as Celéri considered the allies' offer. She followed Celéri's every footstep. That meant *she* was the one to shout in alarm when Magister Umbrose *ad hoc* gated behind Celéri, ripped her magestone choker from her neck, wrapped his arms around her torso, and gated them both away with a doubly loud *pop!*

"*Treachery!*" cried the lieutenant general. "This was all a plot to kidnap Celéri. You've violated parlay!"

Belisaria drew her *gladius* and advanced toward the allied Orluin commanders. Dârio was the first to draw his own sword and met Belisaria's first blow with his own steel. The two were well-matched—both long-armed and athletic in style—and the center of the field echoed like ringing chimes as their blades crossed, disengaged, and crossed again.

Legionnaires in the south began cheering for Belisaria. Tamloch troops directly north started up a chant of *Dâr-i-o!* Valentius and Giérra's smiles changed to looks of horror.

"Stop!" shouted Nûd. Risking his own life, he stepped between Belisaria and Dârio and separated their whirling blades with a powerful upward motion of his quarterstaff. Once the two stood apart, Nûd twisted his quarterstaff so it would enforce a minimum distance between Dârio and the lieutenant general. "It wasn't *our* treachery," Nûd announced. "I saw it too. Magister Umbrose took Celéri, not one of our wizards."

Belisaria and Dârio eyed each other, their blades still raised. Giérra thought Belisaria was now less interested in why she was fighting than the act of fighting itself. The lieutenant general finally felt like she was *doing* something after being shunted aside by Celéri.

"Sheathe your sword," said Giérra. "King Nûd is right. *Umbrose* took Celéri."

Nûd nodded to Dârio and his counsin slid his sword into its scabbard in a practiced motion.

"I told you a king doesn't need to be a swordsman," Dârio whispered.

Nûd returned his quarterstaff to a vertical position and held it ready to use again if necessary. "Maybe not…" he replied.

Giérra pointed over Nûd's shoulder at a disturbance in the allied lines. A few minutes later an old man and old woman in shabby clothes came forward to join the delegation. They were leading three people in manacles: a high-born woman, a man with a wild-eyed look, and an overly muscled wizard. A second wizard walked nearby, keeping his distance from the others. Magister Callidus and Inthíra came forward with them.

"Damon! Astrí!" Nûd exclaimed. "It's good to see you, grandmother. You too, Damon. I see you've brought us Gwýnnett, Túathal, and Hibblig."

"I'm not with them," said Kennig. "I'm here on my own."

"We thought it best to secretly extract these *creatures* from the imperial palace and bring them to the battlefield, so they couldn't cause further problems in Nova Eboracum," said Astrí. "Ealdamon *ad hoc* gated us all here."

"I thought your name was Réah," said Callidus.

"It was," said Astrí.

Kennig noticed Inthíra, who had taken up a position behind Valentius, and stared at her. Something about the woman was familiar.

"Close your mouth, Kennig," said Astrí. "I'll introduce you to her shortly. Two such powerful illusionists should have a lot to talk about."

"Now what?" asked Belisaria.

"I don't know about you, but I want to hear more about that big island and the gold they're offering," said Giérra.

"At this point, I think the legions would more interested in the red meat," said Belisaria.

The front ranks of the legion directly south of the delegates pounded their sword hilts on their shields in affirmation.

Chapter 61

In a Dungeon Cell

Umbrose snapped iron manacles around Celéri's wrists and left her dangling, her toes barely touching the stone floor, in a dank cell below the imperial palace in what was, at least for now, still Sírénaeopolis Magna. In the glow of a single wizard lamp in a sconce by the cell door, Celéri could see the spymaster dangle the silver choker holding her obsidian magestone just inches in front of her eyes.

"You'll only get this back after you've sampled one of Gwýnnett's potions," Umbrose told Celéri. "We'll have the poisonous princess mix up something like the concoction she feeds to Hibblig to keep him pliant and suggestible. We know you can't be trusted to remain loyal to the emperor without such assistance."

"I'll never serve Sírénae again," spat Celéri.

"When you're thirsty enough you'll drink, and then it won't matter," said Umbrose.

"You'll never find the emperor," said Celéri. "I've hidden her well."

"Sírénae is already in her throne room, grooming Thraxa's fur and feathers," said Umbrose.

"What? How did you find her so quickly?" asked Celéri as she shifted her weigh from one foot to the other.

"It was simple, really," said Umbrose. "You'd taken me as far to the east as I thought you could manage, so I guessed you'd take Sírénae in the opposite direction. I remembered you'd gone off to find honey along the Rhuthro—while falsely claiming to be one of my spies—so I took a gate I'd found in Fercha's quarters west to her tower on the river and searched until I found Mégàrotáxus half-sunk in a marsh. Sírénae was nearby, naked, and sunning herself on a rock by the side of the Rhuthro, waiting for her clothes to dry."

"How was Mégàrotáxus?" asked Celéri.

"Recovering, if slowly," said Umbrose. "Though you took quite a risk. Disorientation sickness can be fatal for dragons."

"I didn't know," said Celéri.

Umbrose gave a low laugh that cut Celéri's ego like a sharp knife. "There's quite a lot you don't know, *child*. Sírénae and I will just have to teach you, though it's a shame your power will be blunted by Gwýnnett's potions."

"Do your worst," said Celéri.

"Young wizard, you don't know what you're asking," said Umbrose. "If I did my worst—or perhaps my best—you'd never live to see tomorrow's dawn."

"If I get my magestone back, you won't see the dawn either," said Celéri.

"Then I'll have to see you don't get it," said Umbrose. He waved Celéri's choker in front of her again and Celéri lifted her feet and pushed against the wall, trying to get closer to the spymaster.

"Why are you still loyal to Sírénae?" asked Celéri. "Why not take imperial power for yourself?"

"Why *should* I step out of the shadows?" asked Umbrose. "Sírénae and I make an excellent team."

"You and I could make a great team as well," said Celéri. "There would be certain extra *benefits* to *our* partnership."

Umbrose laughed louder. Celéri felt it like a slap in her face. "You really are naive," said the spymaster.

"Sírénae won't sleep with you then?" asked Celéri.

"She prefers more pliable bedfellows," said Umbrose. "Ones who are better at following her orders, which you might be soon."

"I'd rather sleep with Thraxa," said Celéri.

"That could be arranged as well, if you prove intractable," said Umbrose. "Sírénae did say to bring you up for an audience after you've had time to enjoy the ambiance of your current accommodations. Sorry for the foul stench down here, by the way."

"It will smell a lot better when you leave," said Celéri.

"I like your spirit," said Umbrose. "There may still be something of your personality left after a few doses of Gwýnnett's potions.

Maybe you'll retain most of your magical strength even without your will. That will make your training much more interesting."

Celéri stared at Umbrose until the spymaster looked away.

"Time to go," said Umbrose. He walked to the cell door, extinguished the wizard lamp, and left Celéri alone in the dark with the rats and her thoughts.

* * * * *

"Shall we set her free?" the street urchin behind the dungeon cell's wall asked Távi.

"No," said the leader of the urchin's pack. "Or at least not yet. I want to hear what Sírénae has to say to Celéri."

"Maybe I'll learn some new words," said the urchin.

"I expect that's quite likely," said Távi. "Maybe we both will."

Chapter 62

New Leadership

More people, and a few dragons, crowded into the space on the battlefield between the invading legions and the allied forces of Orluin. Jenet, Bonnie, and both Dukes were there now, as were King Bjarni, Queen Signý, and Arminta—plus a few more kilted Northern Clan Landers of some unknown importance. Eynon and Merry stood near Nûd and Dârio, while Amber, as usual, stayed close to Bifurland's royals. Laetícia, Mafuta, Fercha, and Verro were all missing, however.

A dozen legates for individual legions, plus Náegosh and several of his wizards milled about near Belisaria and Giérra, while Kârkingórēx, Brünedíxés, and Xaxidiánus were in an open spot large enough to hold them. They were wingtip to wingtip talking about why it now made sense that the two groups of dragons should be friends instead of enemies. It was a struggle for Kârkingórēx, since he'd been raised from a hatchling to hate the Roma and had passed that antipathy on to his weyr mates. Discussions relating to the best locations offshore to find tasty whales were going a long way to bridge the long-held but now unnecessary animosity between the western and Roma dragons.

On the edge of the collected individuals meeting mid-battlefield, Giérra and Quintillius were holding a quiet, serious conversation. The two had served together when both were younger, and Quin had been temporarily assigned to Sírénae's command in the Western Empire.

"I can't lead the legions to that island you're offering," said Giérra. "I'm a senior legate, but I've never been a general. We need someone truly skilled in inspirational leadership to make our move successful." Giérra motioned toward Belisaria. "She's not up to the job, that's for sure," said the senior legate. "It would be like getting a thick-headed ox to pull a racing chariot."

"Agreed," said Quintillius. "I take it you have someone better in mind?"

"Not Sírénae—she's lost the legion's support—and definitely not Celéri," said Giérra. "She's a laughingstock, insisting on having me call her Your Imperial Majesty. The troops would toss me in the Abbenoth if I even suggested the possibility."

"Machaera, then?" asked Quintillius.

"She's a competent enough general, but about as inspiring as two-day-old fish," said Giérra. "I have someone else in mind."

"I don't need three guesses to know your top candidate," said Quintillius.

"You'll do it yourself, then?" said Giérra.

Quin's expression rapidly changed to show surprise, then horror.

"Me?" he said. "Never in ten thousand years. I *like* it here in Orluin. It's now my home."

"I know," said Giérra. "I just wanted to see the look on your face when you thought I was serious."

"Thank goodness for that," said Quintillius. "I'll speak to him now and see what he says."

"I hope he agrees," said Giérra. "There's no one better for it on this side of the Ocean.

"And few on the other side as well," said Quintillius. "Belisaria won't give us trouble, will she?"

"I can guarantee she won't," said Giérra. "Who knows... with the right mentors she might mature into a competent commander."

"What about Machaera?" asked Quintillius. "Callidus says Celéri *ad hoc* gated her and her dragon to an unspecified destination."

"If Celéri didn't kill Machaera, the general will make her way back to us if she has to walk all the way from the Great Falls," said Giérra. "For all that she's not inspiring, Machaera *is* persistent."

"So she won't object?" asked Quintillius.

"If she's not here, it doesn't matter if she doesn't approve the change in leadership," said Giérra. "By the time she returns, it will already be accomplished. Machaera is a wise enough old soldier to accept that and make herself useful to the new command structure."

"That was my sense of Machaera too, though I'm glad for your confirmation," said Quintillius. "I wish Laetícia was here. She's much more persuasive."

"I don't expect the idea will be too hard to sell," said Giérra.

"Maybe you're right," said Quintillius. He straightened his shoulders and used the advantage of his seven-foot height to scan the varied knots of people around him. Spotting the individual under discussion, Quintillius slapped Giérra on the back and said, "No time like the present."

* * * * *

"I can help you with the projections," Kennig told Inthíra. "There are enough legionnaires on the field that we'll need a dozen projections at intervals across the battlefield to ensure everyone sees and hears the announcement."

"I'd love your assistance," said Inthíra. "I've been trying to figure out how to maximize sight lines without calling on Merry. She and Eynon are having too much fun talking to Rōlin and Peregrína about where to go to find lots of gold to pay the legions."

"The Southern Clan Landers know about gold dust in rivers far to the south, almost where the eastern mountains end," said Kennig.

"That sounds closer than where Rōlin mentioned, dozens of days of flying west of here, on a river that empties into the Western Ocean," said Inthíra.

"There's a *western* Ocean?" exclaimed Kennig.

"So I'm told," said Inthíra. "Peregrína showed me a painting of a beautiful bay there."

"Would you like to visit it with me?" asked Kennig.

"Only once a gate is open between here and there," said Inthíra. "I don't think I'm interested in flying all that way."

"But we could fly together," said Kennig. "Spend nights in a tent together, or out under the stars..."

"Where gryffons could carry us off or basilisks could turn us to stone while we slept? No thank you," said Inthíra.

"We could visit the Great Falls instead," Kennig suggested. "I've heard about a comfortable inn there."

"I'll take it under advisement," said Inthíra.

"I hope that doesn't mean *no*," said Kennig.

"It means *I'll think about it*," teased Inthíra. "Ask me after the announcement—we can see how well we work together."

"You certainly know how to give a man incentive to do his best," said Kennig. "I'm pleased you're willing to give someone exiled from Dâron a chance."

"What?" said Inthíra. "Why do you think you are exiled from Dâron?"

"I killed a man when we fought over a woman we both loved," said Kennig. "I left for the Southern Clan Lands to exile myself before the king's sheriffs could arrest and execute me."

"I know about that," said Inthíra. "That's the reason I had to cut short my training and had to help Queen Carys keep up the charade that King Dârioth the Twenty-fourth was still of sound mind. I don't know whether to kiss you or kick you."

"I'd much prefer the former, but why would you want to do either?" asked Kennig.

"It was wonderful working with the Old Queen, simulating the Old King for public appearances," said Inthíra. "If you hadn't suddenly disappeared, I never would have had the opportunity."

"That makes sense for the kissing part," said Kennig. "Where does the kicking part come in?"

"When you ran off, I was dragged away from my training before I was ready," said Inthíra. "I had to work twice as hard to hone my skills as an illusionist and needed to perfect my illusions twice as fast."

"I'm sorry," said Kennig.

"You should be," said Inthíra. "Did you ever think to check back and see how the king's justice dealt with your case?"

"No," said Kennig. "I killed a rival with a lightning bolt. I realized the consequences before the afterimages of the stroke cleared from my eyes."

"Had you checked you would have learned the Crown Courts ruled the death a justifiable homicide," said Inthíra. "The man you blasted had not only beaten the woman you loved because she wouldn't cancel her fertility prevention charm, he'd done the same to three other women and one of *them* had died since he kept her from receiving a healing potion. You did the kingdom a favor and you're not a wanted man in Dâron. No one on the jury voted to convict you."

"Hibblig should have told me," said Kennig. "That changes everything."

"Hibblig cares only for Hibblig, and now only for Gwýnnett," said Inthíra.

"True enough," said Kennig. "Thank you for telling me about the verdict. You've released me from a prison I've built in my own mind."

"Enjoy your freedom then," said Inthíra.

"Oh I will!" said Kennig. "I feel like I want to soar, and take you north to the Great Falls and a featherbed and a roaring fire and..."

"That sounds delightful," said Inthíra. "But I want bring one important matter to your attention before any talk of sharing feather-beds." Inthíra gave Kennig a tentative smile. "I am who I am," she said. "I don't use my illusions to change my appearance day-to-day. This is what I look like." She moved her hands from her head to her hips. "What about you?"

Kennig grinned and slapped his cheeks with his palms, turning his skin red. "Unfortunately, I've been stuck with these roguish good looks since I came of age," he said. "They've gotten me into more trouble over the years than I care to mention."

"Good," said Inthíra. "I didn't want to try looking under your illusions if you weren't generating any. I'm also glad you're not put off by a woman who is more plain than beautiful."

"Plain? Nonsense!" said Kennig. "Who more than an illusionist to know that physical beauty is only on the surface. I love your curly brown hair and prefer women like you—comfortable in who you are—to all the primped and painted princesses in all the palaces in Orluin."

"Considering the only princesses that fit that description are Rúth, who's happily married; Gwýnnett, who's too dangerous to be near; and Sigrun, who's twelve, that's not saying much," said Inthíra.

"Fine, quibble with my feeble attempt at a poetic speech," said Kennig. "We can talk more on the balcony of our room overlooking the Great Falls."

"Work first, pleasure afterward," said Inthíra. "Remember to amplify sound as well as repeat images. I was thinking we'll need sixteen projections, twelve for the invaders and four for our forces. If you can cover eight..."

* * * * *

Engineers from the invading Roma legions had erected a raised platform so the person addressing the gathered crowd could be seen by more of those present. It was much the same as the command tower in the south, but was only twelve feet high, not twenty. When the speaker reached the top, he stood facing more than thirty-five legions. Giant images of his head and shoulders immediately materialized in the air above the soldiers ranks and columns as soon as he signaled Kennig and Inthíra.

"Friends, Roma, compatriots," Valentius began. "I am Valentius, son of Valens, Emperor of the Southern Empire, and I bring good news!"

The crowd cheered, since everyone could not only see and hear Valentius, they approved of his words. Good news would be welcome after the past dreary months and rumors of a warm island and gold were already spreading through the ranks.

"Sírénae is missing, unwilling or unable to join you on the battlefield," said Valentius.

Jeers and boos rose up from some legionnaires. Others waiting to hear more.

"Yet you abandoned the Imperium at her command as she abandoned you," said Valentius.

All eyes were on him, all ears listened.

"Who among you would like your rebellion erased? Who wants to be restored as a citizen of the Imperium?" Valentius asked.

"I do," a single legionnaire's voice rang out. His words were repeated and chanted by the rest of the legionnaires on the field until they sounded like rolling peals of thunder.

"Follow *me* and I promise to intercede with my father and the other emperors," said Valentius. "Follow me and be citizens once more!"

The shouts from the legions grew even louder until Valentius moved his arms and calmed them.

"You followed Sírénae west for glory, land, and riches," said Valentius when he sensed they were ready for more. "But what did you find with Sírénae in command?" He paused for a beat. "You found *nothing.*" Valentius waited again before reciting a list of failures. "No glory. No farms. No gold. And no red meat."

More legionnaires booed now. Their protests swept like Ocean waves across the ranks.

"What did Sírénae give you to eat?" asked Valentius. He cupped his hand to his ears then lowered and raised his arms, summoning an answer.

"Beans," said a few legionnaires.

Valentius lowered and raised his arms again, asking for more.

"Beans!" came the response, much louder now.

Valentius lowered and raised his arms yet again.

"BEANS!" shouted every legionnaire.

"That's right. She gave you beans," said Valentius. "Follow me and you'll eat red meat. Follow me and you'll have a warm, fertile land of your own, where seeds grow without tilling or weeding and fish abound in the surrounding seas."

"Va-len-ti-us!" one legion cheered.

"Follow me and everyone who pledges their service will receive forty acres of land and a gold solidus to help start your farms," said Valentius.

"Va-LEN-ti-us!" cried legionnaires from a dozen more legions.

"If you will follow me to our new island home, beat your sword's hilt against your shield," said Valentius. He clapped his hands together in a steady rhythm and soon thirty-five legions were matching his beat with the sound of metal on wood.

"My legions," said Valentius. "I promise to serve you with all my mind and will and strength. Now keep your columns open and prepare for me to keep my first promise—red meat! Please note I didn't say you wouldn't have to catch and roast it yourselves..."

Using a prearranged signal to Eynon and Merry, hundreds of wisents from the western plains were released to charge through strategically placed wide gates on the allied side. The wisents were divided and herded through the gaps between the legions with walls of solidified sound. Soon each legion had captured several wisents. Shortly thereafter, wagonloads of wood would arrive from the west so the wisent roasting could begin.

Cheers grew so loud they drowned out the wisents' hoof beats. They rose in volume as Valentius took a bow before joining Magister Callidus on his flying disk and floating down from the raised platform to continued shouts of acclamation.

* * * * *

Nûd and Dârio stood close at hand, watching and listening to the stirring speech Valentius has just delivered.

"That, good cousin," said Nûd, "is a *king*."

"No," said Dârio. "*That* is an emperor."

Chapter 63

Feast and Fellowship

Valentius took Magister Callidus aside after they came down from the raised platform and guided the wizard far enough away from the others so they wouldn't be overheard.

"That went very well," said Callidus. "I had no idea you were such a skilled public speaker."

"When your father is an emperor, you hear a lot of speeches," said Valentius. "I worry that I aimed my words at their emotions—and their stomachs—rather than their minds, but I'm a Roma commander, not an Athican philosopher."

"And hungry men want to be fed," said Callidus. "Your speech fed more than their bellies. You gave them hope."

"Now I have to deliver what I've promised," said Valentius.

"Best of luck with that," said Callidus. "If anyone can do it, you can."

"I was thinking *we* could," said Valentius. "Our new province needs a senior magister."

"I was hoping to take time off and study at the Valley of Towers in Dâron or Tamloch's Institute in Bhaile Pónaire," said Callidus.

"Come with me and you can start your own magical institute," said Valentius. "I need you, Callidus. You're not Sírénae's man and you have good judgment."

"Well..." said Callidus, temporizing.

"If you don't take the job, I'll have to ask Celéri," teased Valentius.

"In that case," said Callidus, "I'll do it. Celéri shouldn't be your problem."

"Thank you," said Valentius. "I think we'll work well together."

"So do I," said Callidus. "I do have a favor to ask in return for accepting the job, however."

"Name it," said Valentius.

"You won't like it," said Callidus.

"That doesn't matter," said Valentius. "Having you as my senior magister will be worth it."

"I need you to accept something graciously," said Callidus.

"I'll do my best," said Valentius.

"You know that Rōlin and Peregrína call our new home *Shark Island,* because it looks like a great shark on their maps?" said Callidus.

"Yes, of course," said Valentius.

"Giérra and Belisaria and Náegosh don't like the name," said Callidus. "Neither do the legionnaires they've talked to."

"Really?" asked Valentius. "What's wrong with Shark Island?"

"It's just that we all have a much better name in mind," said Callidus. "We want you to gracefully accept us using it."

"Tell me," said Valentius. "I can see that a name like Shark Island Province leaves room for improvement. What do the legionnaires want to call it?"

"Valentia," said Callidus.

* * * * *

The allied Orluin armies returned west through their wide gates to the field behind Rōlin and Peregrína's home where wisents had been roasting for hours. Long trestle tables and benches were set up in the field and more food was brought out from the kitchen to make a sumptuous feast. The leaders of the allies, included Bjarni and Signý, were sharing slices of western wisent and mugs of Bifurland mead.

"That was kind of Valentius to agree to take your mother and father and Hibblig with him," said Nûd.

"Valentius didn't say they'd be *with* him in Valentia Province," said Dârio. "He plans to take Hibblig's magestone and drop the three of them off on a lonely coral island far to the south where they can live on turtles and fruit, if they're willing to work at it. He asked my permission to exile Gwýnnett, Túathal, and Hibblig, can you imagine? They can't be far enough away for my satisfaction."

"I'll second that," said Jenet. "Who wants to bet Hibblig ends up doing all the work?"

"I think that's a foregone conclusion," said Bonnie. "Though who knows what Hibblig will do when Gwýnnett's potions wear off?"

"The same is true for Túathal," said Merry. "Without Gwýnnett's potions he may revert to being crazy, not mad."

"What's the difference?" asked Eynon after feeding Chee an acorn.

"Crafty calculations versus confused couplets?" Merry offered.

"I wouldn't want to be Gwýnnett when Hibblig and Túathal realize what she did to them," said Nûd.

"We'll be busy enough helping the invaders relocate," said Quintillius.

"And getting our own people back to their original lands," said Duke Néillen, "though I think some of them will stay out here. They like the big skies of the west."

"It won't take too long for things to return to some semblance of normality," said Damon.

"I'm glad you brought that up," said Eynon. "It wasn't right for you to stick me with being the Master Mage of Dâron while I'm on my wander year. As soon as I collect enough gold for the legionnaires, I'm giving you the title back and continuing to wander, right Merry?"

"Right," Merry replied. "Don't you dare try to refuse, Ealdamon, you old fraud."

"It's only fair, dear," said Astrí. "Let the young ones have their fun."

"If I must," said Damon. "Where do you two plan to go?"

The table conversation was interrupted by the arrival of Verro, Fercha, Laetícia, Mafuta, and Felix via *ad hoc* gates created by Tamloch and Occidens Province's master mages.

"We've done it!" shouted Laetícia.

"How wonderful," said Quintillius. "Done what?"

"Created a stable gate across the Ocean," beamed Laetícia. "Fercha figured it out, mostly..."

"We figured it out together," said Fercha.

"You made a wide gate from here to Alexandria?" asked Nûd.

"No, just to the city of Tíngis in the west of Mauretania, near the entrance to the Middle Sea," said Mafuta.

"But they did make a stable gate across the Ocean," said Verro.

"A wide gate?" asked Eynon.

"Not exactly," said Fercha.

"It's only two feet wide," said Felix. "You have to turn sideways to go through it. They sent me first. The waters of the Middle Sea are beautiful."

"At least the Imperium won't be gating whole armies here to Orluin through such gates," said Dârio.

"But it will make travel from one side of the Ocean to another easier for individuals," said Eynon. "To answer your question, Damon, once I collect the legions' gold I want to follow the footsteps of Robin Goodfellow and see the world."

"Just be back by the end of your wander year," said Damon.

"Take as long as you like," said Astrí. "I'll keep Ealdamon happy in the meantime."

"Thank you," said Merry. "Eynon and I will stay in touch via ring on our travels."

Eynon squeezed Merry's hand and smiled at his friends gathered around the table. Then he frowned and made a face as if he'd just bitten into a sour persimmon. "Does anyone know what happened to Umbrose, Sírénae, and Celéri?"

Chapter 64

Reckoning

Celéri's body ached. Her leg muscles screamed from trying—and failing—to keep her weight off her arms as she balanced on her toes in the dark dungeon cell. She'd had to kick rats or some other vermin away twice and wondered if Umbrose would ever return to take her to the promised audience with Sírénae. After hours, she dozed, only to wake abruptly when Umbrose slapped her cheek. The light from the wizard lamp in the sconce by the door to the cell showed the spymaster's feral face inches from her own.

"Come along," ordered Umbrose. "We don't want to keep the emperor waiting." He used a key to unlock her manacles and held her body up with thick rods of solidified sound, so she didn't slump to the filthy floor. Umbrose generated sharply pointed constructs to direct Celéri up the stairs and convey her to the entrance to Sírénae's throne room, a place where Celéri had never been before. The doors to the room stood open and Celéri could see this was truly a private audience, with no guards present.

Sírénae sat on a high throne at the far end of the room with her snow-gryffon Thraxa beside her. Celéri had never met Sírénae's pet and didn't look at Thraxa now, using her remaining strength to direct a basilisk-like stare at Sírénae.

When Umbrose finished shoving Celéri forward, he positioned her on her knees before the throne.

Sírénae stared down at the young wizard and sneered. "It's a pleasure to see a proud mage bow before me," said the emperor. "When Umbrose and I have broken your will, you'll help me regain my legions and overcome any temporary setbacks Valentius has to offer."

Celéri centered herself, banished her pain, and held her chin up defiantly. "What's Valentius got to do with anything?" she asked. "I heard the proposal he presented, but thought he was just a messenger from the allied Orluin kingdoms."

"That's right, you don't know the rest of it," said Sírénae. "Umbrose took you before you could hear."

"Hear what?" asked Celéri.

"Valentius plans to take my place and lead my legions, but as their governor general, not their emperor," said Sírénae. "Umbrose's spies heard it all."

Celéri laughed. "It sounds like you've already lost, Sírénae. Time to give up your imperial pretensions."

"Never," Sírénae replied. "Valentius is just a minor obstacle on my path to total victory. Your powerful wizardry, under my command, will end his usurpation before my legions can leave Orluin."

"Why should I defeat Valentius for *your* benefit and not my own?" asked Celéri.

"Because I hold your life in my hands," said Sírénae.

The emperor motioned to Umbrose. The spymaster forced Celéri's head down with a plane of solidified sound until her forehead touched the tiled floor. He pushed harder until Celéri felt her nose about to break. Before it could, Sírénae spoke.

"Enough, for now," said the emperor.

Umbrose dispelled the construct forcing Celéri down.

The young wizard pulled her head up, straightened her back, and squared her shoulders. She looked away from Sírénae and her eyes locked with Thraxa's. Celéri sensed a palpable *snap!* of connection linking her to the snow-gryffon as the bond between wizard and familiar established.

"Yes!" said Celéri triumphantly. "Fetch my magestone!" she commanded.

Thraxa launched herself at Umbrose with enough force to break the chain binding her beside the throne. Still in motion, she knocked Umbrose to the floor and screeched. While the spymaster unsuccessfully tried to escape, the snow-gryffon deftly retrieved the silver choker that held Celéri's magestone, using her hooked beak to snatch it from Umbrose's belt.

"To me!" cried Celéri.

Thraxa flipped the choker toward Celéri with a twist of her head. The young wizard stood, caught it the air, and fastened it around her neck in a single smooth motion. Celéri felt her polished obsidian magestone's power return and reveled in her restored magic.

With a few quick words and a wave of her hand, Celéri told Thraxa what to do with Umbrose. The snow-gryffon pounced on the spymaster's prone body, throwing her full weight atop him. She rolled him over and tore at his robes with her beak and claws, rending fabric and flesh until she found *his* magestone hanging low on his chest on a wrought-iron chain.

A single stroke from her beak cut the chain and Umbrose's magestone clattered to the tiles. He reached for it, but Thraxa slid the chain and magestone across the floor to Celéri with a swipe of a paw. Thraxa then kept Umbrose immobile with the pointed tip of her beak at his throat while her talons pierced the flesh of his shoulders.

Umbrose moaned beneath the snow-gryffon, whimpering in pain and afraid to move.

"Good girl," said Celéri. "Clever girl!" She took a moment to stroke Thraxa's fur and feathers.

Thraxa squawked and arched up against her wizard's touch.

"Now," said Celéri, addressing Sírénae and holding her motionless with bands of solidified sound. "We should talk."

Continued in the sixth book
of the Congruent Mage series:

The Congruent Mage

Please visit

www.CongruentMage.com

for more information about
Eynon, Merry and their friends

MAPS

The Battle of the Abbenoth

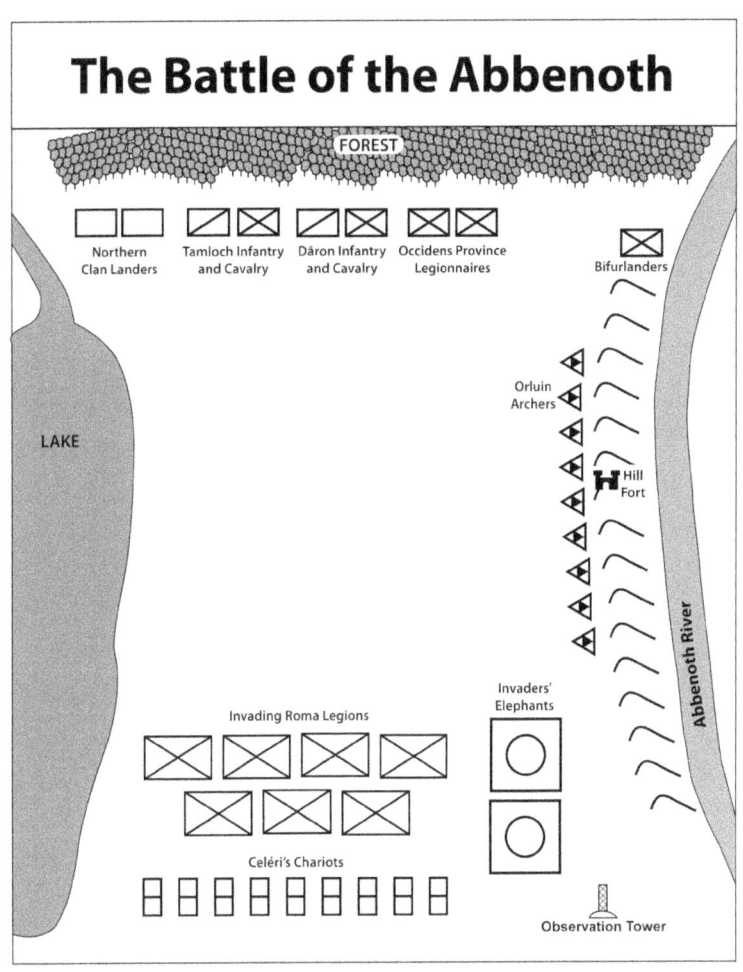

A large color map of the Battle of the Abbenoth
is available at:

CongruentMage.com/maps.html

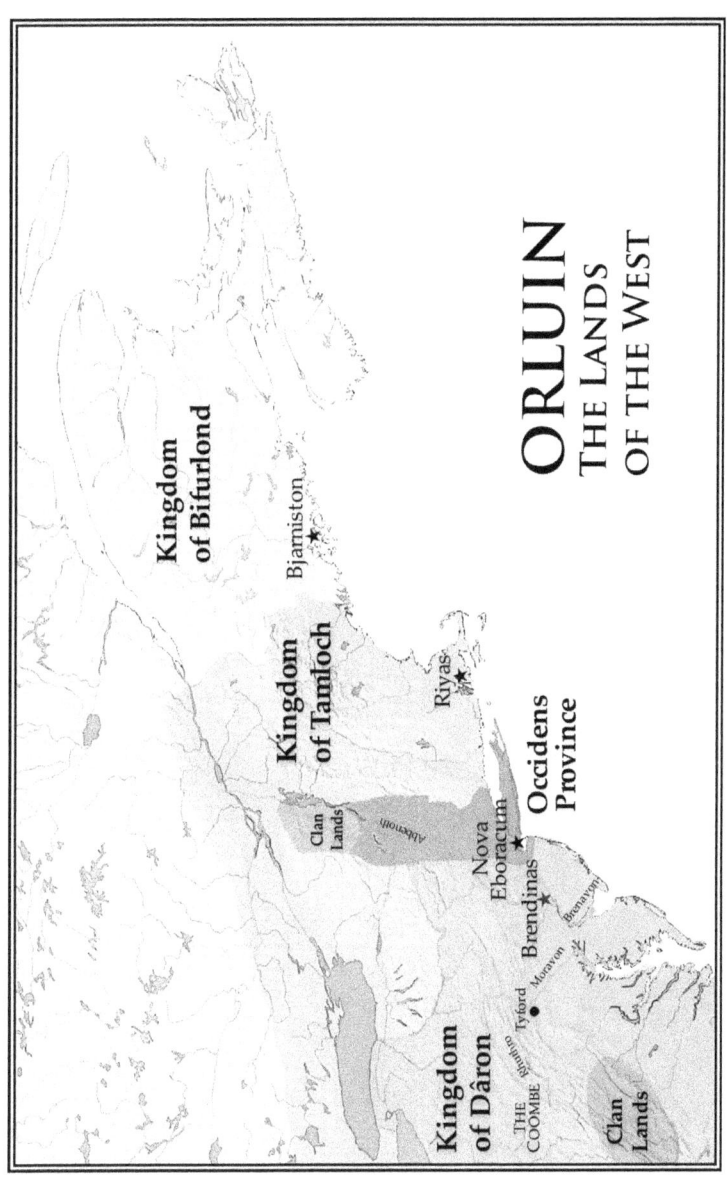

Larger color Orluin and Imperium maps are available at:

CongruentMage.com/maps.html

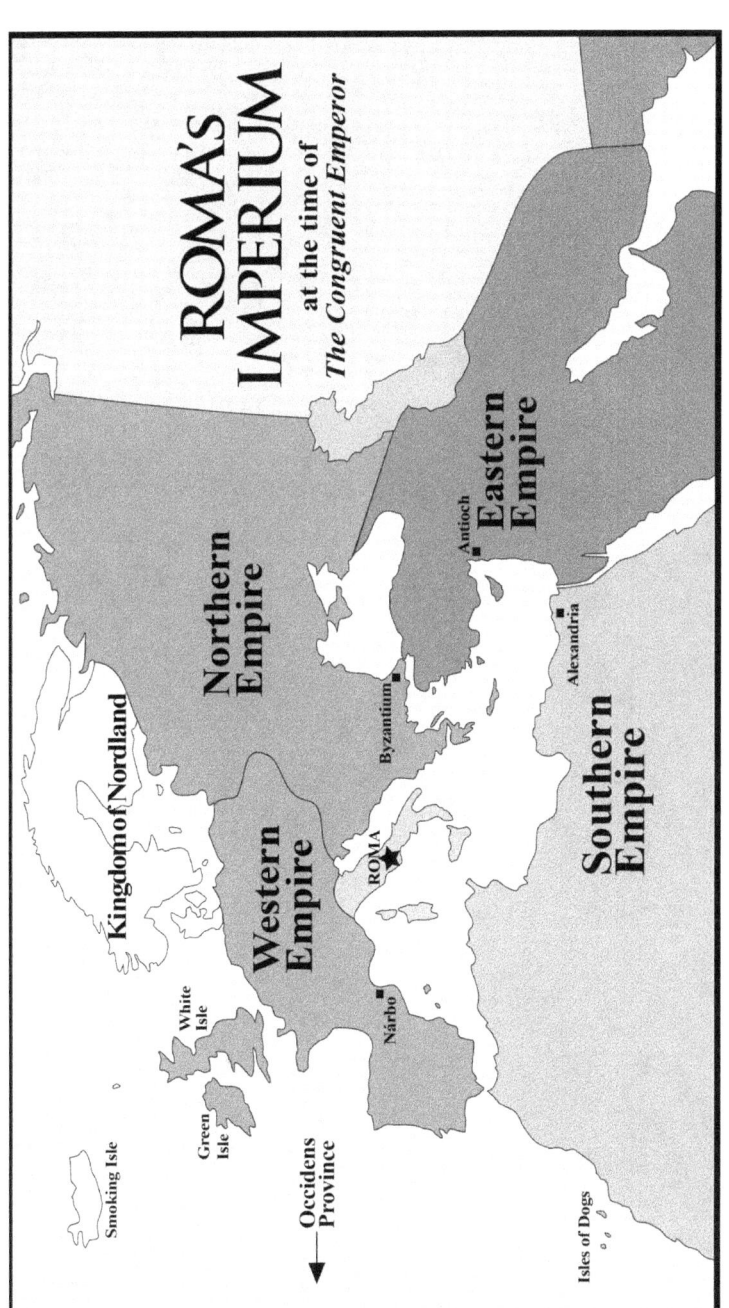

ROMA'S
IMPERIUM
at the time of
The Congruent Emperor

Kingdom of Nordland

Northern
Empire

Eastern
Empire

Antioch

Byzantium

Alexandria

White
Isle

Western
Empire

ROMA

Southern
Empire

Smoking Isle

Green
Isle

Occidens
Province

Nárbo

Isles of Dogs

www.ingramcontent.com/pod-product-compliance
Lightning Source LLC
Chambersburg PA
CBHW070801030726
47504CB00003B/652